J.C. FIELDS

A
CLOAK OF
DECEIT

VINCI BOOKS

By J.C. Fields

The Michael Wolfe Saga

A Lone Wolf

The Last Insurgent

A Matter of Payback

A Cloak of Deceit

For my wife, Connie.

Vinci Books

vinci-books.com

Published by Vinci Books Ltd in 2026

1

A CIP catalogue record for this book is available from the British Library.

Paperback ISBN: 9781036709747

The EU GPSR authorised representative is Logos Europe, 9 rue Nicolas Poussion, 17000 La Rochelle, France

contact@logoseurope.eu

Prologue

On the Azerbaijan side of the Iranian Border
May 19, 2024

The sniper waited patiently, his hide, this high in the mountains of southern Azerbaijan, invisible to any prying eyes due to darkness and fog. He kept his attention trained to the left of his location. Time meant little to him as he lay prone overlooking a valley below.

A voice in his earbud said, "Tango has departed."

Verbally replying to his partner, miles to the north, would be unnecessary. He pressed transmit once to inform his spotter the message had been received. Silence returned to his world as he searched the sky with infrared binoculars. He heard the helicopter before he spotted it.

Returning the optical device to a pocket on his utility pants, he steadied himself behind the suppressed Barrett M82A1 50 caliber rifle and peered through the thermal rifle scope. The heat from the Bell 212 helicopter's exhaust, the civilian version of the infamous Bell UH-1 Iroquois, commonly known as the "Huey," exposed the location of the aircraft. The glowing image allowed the sniper to adjust his aim for the proper lead.

When the aircraft passed perpendicular to his location, he squeezed the trigger until the rifle broke. He repeated the process again and sent another projectile toward the now-doomed helicopter.

As the thermal image of the engine began a slow rotation, he knew his target had been hit. With the rear tail rotor disabled, the torque from the main rotors sent the vehicle into an uncontrolled spin. An experienced pilot would have been able to overcome this event, but this particular Iranian pilot did not possess the necessary skills.

The spinning aircraft disappeared over the neighboring mountain peak, and the sniper lost visual.

Taking his eyes from the scope, the man flipped his night-vision goggles down, found the two empty shell casings, and placed them in a utility pants pocket. Standing, he could hear the struggling helicopter in the distance. He imagined the panic inside the passenger area as the increasing desperate struggle by the pilot became apparent. The passengers, numerous Iranian government officials, would soon realize their crimes against their citizens had come to an abrupt end. In the darkness, he mumbled, "Karma can be a bitch."

As he walked north from his hide, he glanced back to the south and saw a glow in the mist off in the distance. Ten seconds later, he heard a low rumble. The culmination of the disabled tail rotor and the hapless helicopter crashing into the Elburz Mountains.

Keying his radio mic, he said, "Slash one tango."

He heard one click in his earbud.

Part I

Chapter One

WASHINGTON, DC

Present Day

William Fischer, better known as Will to his friends, did not resemble the stereotypical Hollywood spy. But at one time, he roamed the streets of Europe as one of the more successful operations officers the CIA ever produced. These days, if someone needed to know details about matters inside the hallowed halls of the George Bush Center for Intelligence located in Langley, Virginia, all they needed to do was ask Will. Since retiring, he maintained contacts both inside the building and outside. Most of these contacts would meet him in various diners, taverns, or dive bars around the DC area. After decades spent abroad, he seldom ventured out of Maryland, Delaware, or Virginia.

On this particular Monday evening, Fischer sat alone at a table in a small Italian eatery five blocks from his house. He justified his habit of walking to and from the café by claiming the exercise did him good. With his bill settled and a half-full glass of the Irish ale demanding his attention, a slender woman sat across from him. He recognized the crystal blue eyes and the blonde hair that fell riotously around her face and shoulders.

Lowering the glass from his lips, he smiled. "Well, lass, it's been a while."

"Yes, William, it has. You haven't changed."

"Nonsense, I'm older and fatter."

"Maybe, but you still keep your rusty-brown hair unruly." She leaned forward. "I always loved the way you refused to trim those bushy eyebrows and your walrus mustache. Just like I remember."

He studied her through the smudged lenses of black horn-rimmed glasses. "You didn't come all the way to North Potomac to tell me I haven't changed, Sam. Why the visit?"

A gentle smile appeared on her lips. "Can't an old friend just stop by and say hi? Besides, I've missed you." She studied him a moment. "I've always loved your wardrobe. It's what I call thrift shop chic: rumpled corduroy sport coat, khaki pants two inches too long, scuffed loafers, and a wrinkled white oxford shirt."

"They're comfortable and you're stalling." He paused, clasped his hands in front of him, and leaned forward over the table. "Look at my manners. Can I get you something?"

"No. I'm not here to eat. I ran across something someone in your position might find useful." She palmed a small object on the table and slid it toward Fischer, keeping it hidden by her hand. "Do not keep this in your house. Use the information wisely."

Covering the object with his own hand, he slipped it off the table and placed it in his front pants pocket. "How bad is it?"

"Explosive. Just having this material could be dangerous for you. Read the information and you'll understand why."

She hesitated. "I'm giving it to you so you can warn the appropriate individuals."

After a couple of chuckles, Fischer lowered his glass and set it on the table. "Sam, my life has been in danger ever since I set foot in that damn building over in Virginia for the first time."

Samantha Edgar placed her hand on his arm. "Not as much as having this info. You need to watch your back carefully."

"You know something I don't?"

"Nobody knows more than you do, Will. That's the problem. Have you spoken to Joseph recently?"

The older man shook his head. "Not since he retired. Why?"

She started to say something but caught herself.

He drained his glass and returned it to the table. "Never figured you to be a worrywart. What's wrong?"

She stood. "I've already said too much. Watch your back, Will." She turned and disappeared into the crowd inside the bar.

The waitress strolled by. "Can I get something for your friend?"

"No, she just stopped by to say hello. Thanks for asking."

"My pleasure. See you tomorrow night?"

He stood. "I certainly hope so."

The warning from the former CIA case officer who just left his table left him a bit unsettled. Having not seen her since his days in Ukraine, the sudden appearance and emphatic warning seemed a bit odd.

Shaking off the feeling, he debated taking an Uber home, but who in their right mind would agree to a five-block ride? He walked out of the restaurant and gathered his thoughts. In his many years working for the agency, he had been threatened more than once. Most threats were simply nothing more than someone blowing off steam. But for someone like Samantha Edgar to go out of her way to hunt him down and give him a warning? He slipped his hand into his pants pocket and felt the small flash drive. His curiosity about the information on the computer storage device grew stronger by the second.

He walked back to his house, constantly looking over his shoulder.

A lifelong bachelor, Fischer lived in the Washington, DC suburb of North Potomac west of the busy I-270 corridor leading to Frederick, Maryland. His modest ranch-style home, having been paid off for years, held the mementos of a long career as a CIA operations officer. His current source of income came from being a consultant. A fancy way of saying he charged a lot of money for information others needed.

He took pride in the fact his information was always good, and his regular clientele depended on his expertise.

Fischer followed his normal daily routine during the next fourteen days. These activities included phone calls and poring through the pages of the most influential online news feeds around the globe. Being multilingual, a fact few of his friends or clients knew, he kept up with world events and the clandestine efforts to change them. The only exception to his regular habits, staying inside his house. Apart from an excursion to a bank and the mailing of a package to an old colleague, he did not venture out.

After fourteen days of using Grubhub and DoorDash,

the warning from Samantha Edgar faded into his subconscious, and he once again took a stroll to his favorite Italian hangout. The minute he stepped out of his house, he noticed an unfamiliar vehicle parked across the street. After a moment's hesitation, he considered going back inside. He then remembered his neighbor across the street recently purchased a new SUV, and this must be it. With a quick shake of his head, he set out for the diner. Being paranoid did not become him.

The uneventful walk to the diner and the subsequent safe return home brought a feeling of normalcy.

After unlocking the front door, he stepped inside and relocked it.

Searing pain and then blackness engulfed him as he slid to the floor.

A bright light stirred him back to consciousness. He blinked several times in an attempt to shade his eyes. His efforts failed as he realized his arms were bound to a chair.

A deep voice growled from behind the light. "I hope you enjoyed your nap."

Fischer knew not to say anything.

"I suppose you are wondering why this is happening, aren't you, William?"

The voice sounded familiar, but he could not place it at first. He remained quiet.

"Well, I'll answer your unasked question. You need to find another hobby besides being a noisy chatterbox about agency affairs."

"I find it fascinating."

"You might find it as such, but it's unhealthy for you."

"Is that a threat?"

"A promise."

Fischer took a deep breath. "What do you want?"

"Information."

"About?"

"Someone gave you information you shouldn't have. Where is it?"

"I have no idea what you are talking about."

The slap made his ears ring. "Wrong answer."

"Who are you?"

"I hope you aren't expecting an answer."

"Thought I'd try." The last statement confirmed he knew the speaker.

"Well think about *this*. You need to give me the information back, and I need Joseph Kincaid's location?"

"I have no idea what you're talking about."

"I'm sure you do. I couldn't find it here in your house. Last chance, where is Kincaid?"

Fischer shook his head.

"Very well. The next time you hear from me, you won't like the outcome, Will."

"Sticks and stones, mate."

No reply. The front door clicked shut. Then, as silence filled the room, so did the smell of natural gas. He tugged harder at his bound limbs. They did not budge. An hour later, the hands of a cuckoo clock on the wall of the living room reached eight and twelve. The resulting explosion shattered the tranquility of the quiet neighborhood in North Potomac.

Chapter Two

SOUTHWEST MISSOURI

The sound of tires approaching outside the open hangar caused Wolfe to stop working on his aircraft's port engine. Directing his attention to the asphalt drive, he grabbed a shop towel to clean his grease-covered hands. He replaced the cowling of the exposed engine on the Beechcraft B55 Baron and walked out of the hangar.

A gun-metal-gray Range Rover Sport slowed to a stop and an elderly man dressed in a navy blazer, white oxford shirt, pressed khaki chinos, and scuffed loafers exited the vehicle. The guest, who resembled the actor Morgan Freeman more than a little, waved. "Good morning, Michael."

"Mornin', Joseph. This is a pleasant surprise."

"Hope you're not too busy."

"Nope. Want some coffee?"

"Yes. Plus, I need to speak to you and Nadia."

Wolfe raised an eyebrow. "About?"

"Let's talk inside."

They walked the fifty yards to a custom-built home

north of the hangar. The two buildings were located on the northern end of a sixty-two-acre plot of land. Once inside, Wolfe brewed a pot of coffee while Joseph sat at the breakfast nook table.

"Nadia will join us after she gets Ben down for his nap."

"How is the young tike? Isn't he about four years old now?"

"Just turned and he's doing great." Wolfe leaned against the kitchen counter. "How's Mary doing?"

"We received good news from her oncologist. The tumors are gone, and she appears to be in full remission."

"That's great news."

"Yes. We have to keep monitoring it, but she's in good spirits."

Nadia came into the kitchen, and Joseph stood to give her a hug. "Did I overhear Mary's in remission?"

"Yes."

"That's a relief." She settled into a chair at the table. Wolfe placed a cup of coffee in front of her and one before Joseph.

He sat across from his friend and held his mug with both hands. "Okay, what did you need to talk about?"

"Do you remember my friend, William Fischer?"

Wolfe nodded.

Joseph produced a key and an index card from within his navy blazer. He laid them on the table. "A week ago, I received these in a package with the return address of a UPS Store in North Potomac. There was a note inside telling me if anything happened to him, I was to collect the contents of a safe deposit box." He pointed to the key. "Using that key and the instructions on the card. By the way, I didn't find his name anywhere on or inside the envelope. I knew Will sent it because of a code word he and I used back in the day, printed at the top of the note."

Picking up the key, Wolfe said, "I take it something happened to Will."

Joseph continued. "A gas explosion destroyed his house two days ago, with him inside. Police are calling it an accident. However, one of my contacts within the agency told me Will's body was found tied to a dining room chair. Michael, it was no accident."

"Doesn't sound like it."

"Another thing, Will mentioned in the note I was not to retrieve the contents. I'm too well-known in and around DC."

Looking over his coffee cup, Wolfe took a sip and said, "There's a protocol for gaining access to a safe deposit box, Joseph."

"I'm aware of that. The index card has instructions on the process."

"So, you want me to go to Washington, DC and retrieve whatever's in the safe deposit box."

"Yes."

"I'm retired, or did you forget?"

"I'm aware of your current status." He paused for a moment. "I wouldn't ask you if the circumstances were different. But, right now, you and Nadia are the only two individuals I trust to retrieve whatever's in the box."

"You know an awful lot of people, Joseph. Surely, there's someone else?"

"The individual I spoke to indicated the CIA has changed over the past year. Many in current management are self-absorbed and only interested in their own advancement. The people in the field don't know who has their backs at the moment."

Wolfe examined the key again. He glanced at Nadia. "Okay with you?"

"We owe Joseph a lot, Michael."

"Yes, we do. Very well. When do you want me to leave?"

"As soon as you can file your flight plan." He paused a brief moment. "There's another reason I prefer you do this, Michael. You can fly into a small place like Potomac Airfield, and no one will know you're in the Washington, DC area."

"Fine with me." He studied the index card for a few moments. "What's in the safe deposit box?"

Joseph shook his head. "Not sure, but it appears he might have been murdered over the contents."

"You want me to check out his house?"

"I don't advise it. From what I've been told, it was leveled in the explosion and resulting fire. Probably not worth the chance of being seen by someone or having your image captured by a security camera."

"Then I can leave early and get back the same day."

"I was hoping you'd do it that way. When do you think you could be back?"

"Depends on how long it takes to obtain access to the safe deposit box, but I would say late afternoon."

"I'll be here when you get back."

He left at dawn and made a fuel stop in Lexington, Kentucky. Michael Wolfe arrived in the Washington, DC area by eleven a.m. A rental car provided by Enterprise waited for him at the airport fixed-base operator's office. An hour later, he presented the safe deposit box key and his ID to a TD Bank branch representative.

The young lady nodded and went to a file drawer next to her desk. She pulled the card to the box. "This is unusual. I'm supposed to ask you to recite a nine-digit number."

Wolfe shrugged. "It's Washington." He recited the numbers from memory.

She chuckled and said, "Perfect. I'll take you to the box."

When they both inserted their keys, the door opened, and Michael pulled out the long rectangular box.

"I'll be right outside when you're done." She exited the secure area while he placed the box on one of the pullout shelves scattered among the drawers. Inside, he found a bubble-wrapped object. He removed the protective outer plastic and found a 128-gigabyte flash drive. He stuck it in his pocket and returned the box to its appropriate slot. Stepping out of the secure area, he thanked the young lady and returned to his rental car.

At exactly 6:13 p.m., he touched down on his 3000-foot asphalt runway and taxied into the open hangar. Joseph leaned on the front quarter panel of his Range Rover and waved as Michael taxied past.

After shutting the Baron down, he exited and handed the flash drive to Joseph. "Nothing in the box but this."

Holding it up in the fading light of mid-October, Joseph said, "Let's see what's on it."

Nadia stood on the back deck of their home. As they approached, she said, "What'd you find?"

Joseph held up the flash drive. "Would you do us the honor of seeing what's on this?"

Five minutes later, she stared at the laptop screen and said, "It's encrypted."

Wolfe chuckled. "How long is the encryption key?"

"Looks like nine digits."

He recited the numbers he gave the lady at the bank.

She entered the numbers into the encryption key. "Nope. Now what?"

Wolfe pursed his lips and turned his attention to Joseph. "Was Fischer paranoid?"

"No, but he took security seriously."

"Huh." He remained quiet for several moments. "Try the numbers backward."

Nadia nodded and typed the numbers. The contents of the drive spilled onto the laptop's screen. They saw an Excel spreadsheet, a Word document, twenty jpg files, and an MP3 audio file.

Joseph leaned back in the chair and furrowed his brow. "Huh." He stared at the screen for a few moments. "Nadia, let's have a look at the pictures."

Chapter Three

SOUTHWEST MISSOURI

The information held on the flash drive amounted to a series of photographs and transcripts of numerous overheard conversations. The pictures appeared to be random landscapes and cityscapes with little or no relationship to each other.

As Nadia scrolled through the pictures, Joseph remained quiet. Wolfe sipped coffee, trying to answer the question of why these particular pictures. None related to the other. Finally, Wolfe said, "This is like going through travel brochures for places to visit. Not one of these images has anything to do with the others."

Joseph said, "I agree, Michael. Nadia, what do you think?"

"Something's wrong with these images. If you examine the file sizes, they're too big for the type of picture they are. Let me try something." She typed on the keyboard and then studied the properties of the pictures. "Just as I thought. Each picture has about two hundred characters embedded within the code. It will take some time, but I can extract the words."

Both Joseph and Wolfe sat quietly as Nadia copied and pasted. An hour later, she sat straight. "Basically, it's a list of names, employment organizations, and locations."

Setting his coffee cup down, Joseph asked, "Whose names?"

Looking up, her eyes were wide. "The names are agents with the CIA, MI6, and the Mossad."

"Are you sure, Nadia?"

"Positive. Here's my name, Nadia Picard, with my old address in Tel Aviv." She studied the screen for a few moments. "Plus, there are several names I recognize from my days with the Mossad. William Fischer's name is here, along with his physical address." She read a little further. "Michael, what alias did you use when you were doing jobs for the Mossad?"

"Daniel Lyon."

"It's here with the notation location unknown."

Joseph rose and stood behind Nadia. His gaze remained on the screen as his brow furrowed. "I recognize a lot of the names."

Nadia turned in her chair and stared up at Joseph. "How many?"

"Over half.

"Of the ones you recognize, who are they?"

"Over the years, I've worked with them. Some very closely. I don't like the implication of this."

Wolfe looked at his wife and then at Joseph. "Seems kind of strange Fischer would take the trouble to hide names with steganography and then not tell us why."

The older man had not taken his eyes off the computer. "I would have to agree, Michael. And why names of individuals I've worked with throughout the years?"

Turning to his wife, Wolfe asked, "What are the date stamps on the files?"

"Good question." She consulted the computer screen for several minutes. "If William gathered the names, he did it over a long period of time. The pictures ranged from three to six years ago."

"Which could mean, either William has been slowly putting this information together, or someone gave him the files."

The older man folded his arms. "His compiling this list makes no sense. He knew you and Nadia were married and living here in the States. That alone tells me there's a strong possibility someone gave him the data and he hid it." Joseph paused for a moment. "There's a possibility he was killed to get the information back."

Wolfe walked over behind Nadia. He stared at the screen for several moments. "This looks like a hit list. Names and addresses, if known. I notice your location is labeled unknown, Joseph."

"Not too many people know where I live. Outside of you two, there are less than half a dozen. I'd like to keep it that way." He paused for a moment. "Who could check on this quietly?"

"What about Jerry Griggs?"

"He has his hands full with his new job."

"How about Carla?"

Joseph's eyebrows rose. "Now, that might be a possibility."

"Do you know how to contact her?"

He shook his head. "Jerry always handled it."

"No worries, I know how."

Two Days Later
Miami

Seagulls screeched overhead as Wolfe trudged through the sand on the southern tip of Florida, the Atlantic Ocean to his immediate right. He held his sandals in one hand as sand caressed his bare feet. An old colleague from his days in the CIA walked next to him.

She glanced up at him. "Thought you retired."

Wolfe smiled. "I did, Carla."

"Then why are you doing this? I always assumed you were smarter than that."

"I'm doing a favor for Joseph."

Carla Webb nodded. "Ah, got it." Pencil-thin, the diminutive woman appeared susceptible to being blown away by a strong wind. However, her appearance betrayed the fact she could be as tough as nails and equally as deadly. "So, why the surprise visit to my little slice of heaven, here in Miami?"

"How in tune are you to the goings-on in Washington?"

She chuckled. "Why do you think I'm in Florida? I'm currently persona non grata."

Wolfe furrowed his brow. "Since when?"

"Since the coup that ousted the old guard."

"Wasn't aware of one."

"You were smart. You got out before the bloodletting."

Wolfe stopped walking and contemplated the woman. "Give me the fifty-thousand-foot assessment."

"That's what I've always admired about you, Michael—no time for bullshit."

He remained silent as they continued their stroll.

"When President Griffin appointed the new director, he apparently failed to check her resume. Griffin hasn't made too many mistakes, that I've noticed, but he made a whopper on this one. Emma Elliot's been in management with the agency for a while, and she's an expert in hiding her true colors. In the early years of her career, she was incompetent and devoid of ethics during her short tenure in the field. Not sure who she slept with, but she was transferred to Langley before her thirtieth birthday."

"Never heard of her."

"Not surprised."

"Go on."

"When Dwight King decided to retire, rumors grew like mushrooms after a summer shower."

"Concerning?"

"Who the heir apparent would be."

"Let me guess. Emma Elliot wasn't on the short list."

"Not even an honorable mention."

"What happened?"

"Your guess is as good as mine, Michael. Since she was appointed director, retirements have doubled. I volunteered for this assignment before the shit hit the fan. So, hopefully, I can weather the storm here until Griffin comes to his senses."

"What are you doing?"

"Monitoring radio and internet traffic coming out of Cuba."

Wolfe laughed. "Someone has to do it."

"That's what I keep telling myself." She studied the sand as they walked. "But you didn't fly all the way to Miami to listen to me complain."

"No. I came to see if you know why Will Fischer was murdered."

"Why do you think I would know?"

"Because you two were friends and you know things."

"You want facts or rumors?"

"Both."

"Langley's the reason the police are claiming it to be an accident. Something about national security and the best interests of the country."

"Standard BS."

"Ya think?"

"Is there anyone at Langley you still trust?"

She didn't answer right away. Finally, she said, "Not anymore."

"Okay, then, what are the rumors?"

"They are all over the board. My favorite one is about Fischer being a mole for the North Koreans."

With a frown, Wolfe glanced down at the woman. "Why's that your favorite?"

"Because it's so obviously stupid it defies reason. There's one I think more likely. He stumbled upon some dark fact the CIA had kept secret for decades."

"Huh." He stayed quiet for a moment, then said, "What do you think?"

"Like I said, knowing Will, I prefer the dark-secret theory myself."

"Got any details?"

"Only speculations."

"I'm listening."

"In the final days of the chaotic Soviet withdrawal from Afghanistan, they lost track of several small nuclear bombs."

"That was almost four decades ago, Carla."

"Hard to believe, isn't it. Supposedly, a couple of enterprising Soviet generals enhanced their retirement accounts by selling them to the highest bidder."

Silence fell over the two beach strollers as Wolfe debated what to tell her. Finally, he said, "I don't think that was the reason, Carla. It seems Will was given information someone wanted back, and they killed him over it. Have you ever heard about a hit list of retired CIA, MI6, and Mossad personnel?"

Carla contemplated the sand where they walked. "Let's circle back to that deep-dark-secret rumor. Who's on the list?"

"According to information Will left behind, his name was on it as is Nadia's and mine. Nadia is identified with the last name Picard, and her location as Tel Aviv. I'm identified by an alias I used at one time. My location was labeled as unknown."

"Does the information mention why the names are on the list?"

"No. Joseph Kincaid worked with many of them at one time during his long career. Even the numerous Mossad and MI6 operatives."

"Huh. That gives credence to something I heard a long time ago." She looked up at Wolfe. "You know the CIA will deny the existence of the list."

"Why?"

"If you don't know why something exists, deny it does."

"So, you think someone within the CIA put the list together?"

She shrugged. "I didn't say that. But over the years, Joseph worked with a lot of different people and not everyone liked him."

"Yeah, I know."

"Is there anything I can do to help?"

"Maybe."

"Name it."

"If I give you the list, can you noise around to see how many of them are still alive?"

"Do you think it's a hit list, Michael?"

"Not sure what I believe at the moment. But William hid the information away from his house and informed Joseph, if anything happened to him, where to find it."

"You're going to find out who killed William, aren't you?"

He smiled. "No. I'm retired and I want to stay that way. I'm trying to find answers for Joseph. He doesn't trust anyone in Washington right now."

She chuckled. "He's a smart man. So, let's say I find more of the individuals on the list dead. What then?"

"We try to determine why?"

"Thought you didn't have any desire to get back into the game."

"I don't."

"Need some help?"

"Don't you have a job?"

"I'm bored, Michael. I can do the Cuba thing in my sleep."

A slight grin crossed his lips. "Find out what you can. If the news is not good, then we can talk about next steps."

The diminutive woman chuckled. "You are getting back into the game."

Chapter Four

SOUTHWEST MISSOURI

Nadia watched Wolfe taxi the Baron into the open hangar and shut off the engines. Their son, Ben, tugged on his mother's arm the second he saw his father inside the aircraft. As soon as the propellers stopped turning, she freed his arm and watched him run to where Wolfe stood outside the plane.

Reaching down, he scooped up the little man and said, "I think you've grown since I left this morning."

"Did you bring me anything, Daddy?"

"Sorry, not this trip." Wolfe hugged his son and then let him down. The boy turned and ran back toward the house.

Nadia now stood inside the hangar. "How was your trip, Michael?"

Shutting the door to the airplane's cabin, he turned to her. "There's been a seismic shift in upper management at the CIA."

"Such as?"

"It started when President Griffin appointed a new

director. Since then, a large portion of the senior administrative staff has retired."

Nadia frowned. "Where does that put Carla?"

"Out in the cold, so to speak. She realized what was coming and volunteered to move to the Miami area to keep track of Cuba."

"Interesting. Did she confirm the information on the flash drive was a hit list?"

"Carla didn't know for sure." Wolfe pressed a button on his key fob. The hangar door lowered as they walked toward the house. "She did mention rumors are floating around about Will's death. One of them assumes he stumbled onto something the agency desperately wanted to keep secret."

"Which, in a round-about way, suggests the agency is trying to keep the list off the street."

"Or find out who put the list together."

"Glad we're retired."

He chuckled. "Me, too. But why are both of our names on it?"

"I have no idea. But they don't seem to know where we are either. Which is good, in my opinion."

"Yeah, but how long before they do?"

"Are you worried about it?"

Wolfe shrugged. "It depends. Carla is checking to see if anyone else on the list is dead. If there isn't, it might be old information."

"Then why was William killed?"

"That's the question we need to answer."

Joseph Kincaid gripped his coffee mug with both hands as Wolfe summarized his meeting with Carla. When the ex-

CIA operative finished, Joseph said, "I didn't realize so much had changed since I retired."

"No way you would be expected to, Joseph. You were busy helping Mary."

The older man sipped his coffee and set the mug down. "Too many years of being in the thick of things. I've lost my patience for the high drama within the agency." He paused and displayed a slight smile. "Coming home was the right decision for us."

Wolfe nodded.

"Which brings us back to the topic of the flash drive. To whose attention should it be directed?"

"Joseph, I'm not sure letting them know we possess the device is a good idea."

The older man studied Wolfe for a few moments. "They should be investigating the list, if in fact, it led to the death of William."

"My concern is why Nadia's and my name are on it. Plus, Nadia hasn't been stationed in Tel Aviv for seven years. Carla is going to check with her sources and see if she can learn whether any of the other individuals on it are dead or retired."

Contemplating a spot on the kitchen table, Joseph pursed his lips. "What if the origins of the list are unknown?" He turned his attention to Wolfe. "And William isn't the first name on the list to be eliminated."

Studying his friend, Wolfe raised an eyebrow. "Could it have been an underground project before King?"

"Then, why is it surfacing now?"

Standing, Joseph walked to the coffeepot and refilled his mug. He stopped before replacing the carafe. "Why those names? And why are there so many individuals I've worked with?"

"We're asking the right questions. How we find answers is another matter." Wolfe looked at Nadia. "Is there any chance more information is imbedded somewhere on the flash drive?"

She shrugged. "Maybe, but I wouldn't know how to access it, Michael."

"Who would?"

She smiled. "Alexia."

"Call her."

Nadia stood and went to their bedroom. Wolfe turned to Joseph. "Do you still have the president's ear?"

With a nod, Joseph said, "We speak two or three times a week. Why?"

"How's Jerry doing?"

"He's a work in progress, I'm told."

"The reason I ask is, you might want to have a private conversation with him about the flash drive."

"I agree, but not until we know more about it. Does Nadia still have a back channel to Uri Ben-David?"

"They still talk. But not in his capacity as director of the Mossad. Their relationship is more like a doting father and his daughter. He treats Ben like a grandson."

"Do you think he would reveal what he knows about this with her?"

"Not on the phone."

"Wise." The elder man took a sip of coffee. "How would you two like to take Ben to Israel to see his surrogate grandfather?"

Wolfe chuckled. "You getting back into the game, Joseph?"

"No, I want another source for the information before I take it to President Griffin. That way I can keep Will Fischer's name out of it."

"Why?"

"Dead men can't defend themselves."

Four Days Later

A black Audi A4 sedan featuring dark tinted windows waited in the pickup lane at a secure diplomatic entrance to Ben Gurion Airport in Tel Aviv, Israel. Escorted by two heavily armed security guards, Wolfe, Nadia, and Ben were delivered to the vehicle out of sight from other travelers. All courtesy of Uri Ben-David, Israel's newly appointed director of the Mossad.

Inside the car, a man sat in the front passenger seat. He turned and smiled. Brown eyes, inherited from his mother, viewed the world behind rimless glasses resting on a prominent nose. His thinning short gray hair completed his resemblance to a retired college professor.

The little boy sitting next to his mother said, "Papa!"

"How is Ben today?"

"Where's Nana?"

"Waiting at home. She's anxious to see you."

"I want to see her now."

Uri smiled. "Soon, Benjamin, soon."

Nadia said, "Thank you for picking us up, Uri."

"More time for me to spend with young Ben." He turned to the driver. "Take us to my apartment."

"Yes, sir." The muscled man sitting behind the steering wheel checked his rearview mirror and pulled away from the curb.

Uri Ben-David turned again in his seat. "How was your flight?"

Nadia said, "Thank you for having our tickets waiting for us in Atlanta."

With a wave of his hand, Ben-David replied, "It is the least Israel can do. Our country will remain in debt to both of you for a long time."

"Nevertheless, we appreciate your courtesy."

Wolfe said, "How's the new job going?"

"Not that much different than the old one." He sighed. "Unfortunately, more frequent meetings are part of the daily routine."

Wolfe nodded. "One of the reasons I enjoyed field work. Fewer meetings."

Thirty minutes later, sitting on the sofa in Ben-David's apartment, Ben Wolfe slept on the lap of his surrogate grandfather. Looking up from the boy, the director asked, "What were you unable to discuss on the phone, Michael?"

"Joseph received a package in the mail with a key taped to an index card. On the card were directions on how to gain access to a safe deposit box in a suburban bank near Washington. Those instructions also told Joseph not to personally collect the item in the box. He needed to send someone else."

"Let me guess, that someone was you?"

Wolfe nodded and continued. "I flew in, retrieved the contents, and flew back on the same day. The contents were a flash drive. Many of the files on the drive were jpeg files with embedded messages."

Ben-David frowned. "A list of names, correct?"

"Yes."

"Who had the information?"

"Do you remember a CIA case worker named William Fischer?"

"Yes, he and I knew each other well."

"Do you know he is dead?"

Ben-David turned his head toward a window. He stroked the little boy's hair and glanced down at him. "No." He took a deep breath. "When?"

"He died from a gas leak in his home. The place burned to the ground. He was tied to a chair in the living room."

"Oh dear."

Wolfe reached into his pocket and produced a similar drive. "This is a copy of the original. It's encrypted as well. It's for you, if you want it."

Ben-David offered his hand and Wolfe stood to hand it to him.

The director asked, "What else is on it, Michael?"

"Transcripts of numerous overheard conversations and multiple recorded phone conversations."

"Do they explain the names?"

"No."

"Do they reference any of the names?"

"No. We think there's more information embedded within the files, but we have no way of determining if there is."

"And you need help?"

"If you are so inclined."

"Whose names are on the list?"

"William Fischer's, Nadia's, and mine, although it's one of the aliases I used when I was running around Europe for the Mossad. The problem is, many of the individuals on the list worked with Joseph at one time or another during his tenure with the CIA."

Ben-David looked at Nadia. "Let me guess, your last name on the list is Picard?"

"Yes, and it gives my location as Tel Aviv."

"Let me see the list?"

Nadia handed him a folded sheet of paper.

He unfolded it, held it in the hand not occupied by his godson. Wolfe watched as the Mossad director scanned the page. He refolded it and handed it back to Nadia.

"I could say I don't recognize any of the other names, but I would be lying. You two are like family to me, so I'll be truthful."

Nadia shot a quick glance at her husband and then returned her attention to Ben-David. "How bad is it, Uri?"

"Well, it brings up a recent episode I would like to forget."

Chapter Five

TEL AVIV, ISRAEL

With Nadia visiting old friends to introduce Ben, Wolfe spent their first full day in Israel working old contacts. One of those individuals, Josef Rubin, had acted as his spotter during his time working for the Mossad. Josef now held a high-level job at Israeli Weapon Industries or the IWI.

When he arrived at the IWI building, he received a VIP welcome and an immediate escort to Josef's corner office on the fifth floor.

"Shalom, Michael. It is so good to see you again."

"Shalom, Josef." Wolfe looked around the man's office. "You've done well for yourself."

"Yes, I have been extremely fortunate. What brings you to Israel?"

"Nadia wished to visit some of her cousins and introduce them to our son, Ben."

The smile on Josef's face grew large. "A son. Michael Wolfe has a son?"

"Yes. He just turned four."

"This is a joyous day, my friend. I, too, am a father."

"Yes, I heard. Two daughters."

"Both, thank goodness, take after their mother; they are both beautiful. Here is a picture." The IMI executive walked to his desk and offered Wolfe a gold-plated frame.

"They are beautiful, my friend. Your wife remains as pretty as I remember."

"Motherhood has been good for her." Placing the picture back on his desk, Josef crossed his arms. "Uri Ben-David told me you have questions for me."

"A few. If you feel uncomfortable answering them, please do not feel pressured to tell me."

A nod was the response. "I will answer those I can."

"Does the name William Fischer mean anything to you?"

Rubin shook his head. "Not really. Why?"

"What about the name Herschel Katz?"

Rubin hesitated. His eyes narrowed, and he crossed his arms. "The name is familiar, but I can't place it."

"How about Azaria Sieff?"

The Israeli gunmaker frowned. "Michael, what is this about?"

"What happened to Sieff?"

"Azaria Sieff died six months ago in a single-car accident."

"What about Herschel Katz?"

"Michael, I must ask what this is about?"

"Did Uri tell you?"

"No. But he asked me to be truthful with you."

"What about Katz?"

Rubin took a deep breath and then blew it out. "Katz was an undercover agent who infiltrated the Hezbollah in the West Bank. He stopped communicating with us a few years after I left the Mossad. He was assumed to be dead. We never recovered a body or heard what happened."

"When did this occur?"

"A year or so ago."

"Why would his name be on the list? The other names are more current."

"I can't answer that. Where are the other names from?"

"All are either from the CIA, MI6, or the Mossad."

The ex-spotter stared at his old comrade. "Is my name on the list?"

"Yes, Josef, it is."

The man sat behind his desk and picked up the picture of his wife and daughters. After gazing at it for a few moments, he sat it down. "So why are yours and Nadia's names on the list?"

"That's what I am trying to determine."

"How many names are already dead?"

"With the addition of the two I asked you about, we've learned of three others."

Josef tilted his head and frowned. "Are you working for the American CIA again, Michael?"

"No, I'm retired."

The frown his friend displayed morphed into a sly smile. "Coming from anyone else but you, Michael, I would have laughed at the attempted lie. Why are you interested?"

"I'm trying to assist a friend of mine. William Fischer reached out from the grave to give my friend the list."

"Who's the friend?"

"Joseph Kincaid."

The ex-Mossad operator contemplated the man across from him. "If I help you, will you assist me with one of my projects?"

"Depends."

"We are developing a new sniper rifle system, and I would like for you to test it."

Wolfe's mouth twitched. "You could have mentioned that in the first place. When?"

"I can take you to the firing range today."

Offering his hand, Wolfe said, "I believe we have a deal."

South of Tel Aviv, IMI's firing range occupied twenty acres of barren land snuggled against the shores of the Mediterranean Sea. Surrounded by three-meter-high chain-link fence topped with Concertina wire, the actual firing range sat behind a twenty-meter earthen berm. The only way to spy on the goings-on inside this fortress would be with a drone or satellite.

Wolfe examined the rifle handed to him by Josef Rubin. He held it in both hands, felt the balance, and then aimed it downrange to check the scope. Rubin remained quiet as he watched Wolfe study the weapon.

After several minutes, the retired sniper said, "It's based on the IWI Dan .338, isn't it?"

"Very good, Michael. Yes, it is. However, we've made a few improvements."

"This one is more balanced than the other Dan .338's I've shot."

"We've been able to increase the accuracy range to 1600 meters."

Raising his eyebrows, Wolfe glanced at his friend and then went back to the rifle. "What's the estimated accuracy at that distance?"

"We've bench tested it to less than 1.0 MOA."

"Bench tested? I've never seen a bench rest in the field."

"Exactly. That's why I want you to test it at 1600 meters. We'll see if our engineers earned their pay."

Wolfe raised his ear protection headphones. He walked over to the firing line and found the 1600-meter target. After adjusting his shooting glasses, he lay prone and fine-tuned the scope.

After a few additional minutes of working on the telescopic sight, he squeezed off a round. The metallic clank of a hit reached their ears five seconds later.

Josef looked over from his spotter's scope. "Two inches below."

Wolfe adjusted the scope again and squeezed off another round.

"Center circle. See what kind of a spread you can create."

After three more shots, Josef took his gaze away from the scope, a large grin on his face. "From this distance, I'm guessing it is more accurate than our engineers predicted at 1600 meters."

Wolfe stood. "Let's check it before we go farther. Nice rifle, Josef."

"Thanks, Michael. Let's walk down range while we talk."

When they were a hundred meters from the firing line, Josef said, "Azaria Sieff was one of Israel's IDF's most accomplished snipers, as was I for the Mossad. Katz infiltrated Hezbollah a year before COVID spread around the world. The messages we received from him were regular until the middle of 2022. I left the Mossad before then. We don't know if he caught the disease or was discovered. He just disappeared."

"Kind of unusual, isn't it?"

With a nod, Wolfe's old spotter said, "Hezbollah has a tendency to return bodies. It's their way of telling us they uncovered a spy. They didn't this time."

Wolfe kept his attention on the target area as they grew closer. "So, you think he might have been a double agent."

"Yes. Either that or COVID got him."

"If he was a double agent, how much damage could he have caused?"

"Don't know. I personally never met the man. I had, however, heard about him."

They arrived at the target area. Bending, Rubin looked at the metal plate and smiled. "Our engineers earned their pay on this one. How hard was it to keep the spread so tight?"

"Not very. Like I told you. Nice rifle."

Rubin stood and looked back toward the shooting platform. "Michael, you mentioned the names on the list were only CIA, MI6, and the Mossad."

"That's correct."

"Do you have any theories on why yours and Nadia's names are on it?"

"None whatsoever. But I did find it interesting how we were identified."

"How was that?"

"Nadia Picard living in Tel Aviv and me as Daniel Lyon, location unknown. I got the feeling the list might have been generated with old intel."

Rubin studied the ground as they walked. "When you and I worked together, you were a sniper for the Mossad, correct?"

"Yes."

"And Nadia trained as one, right?"

Wolfe nodded. "I forgot about Nadia's training."

"Want to reassess the list?"

"I think we have to."

As they walked back to the range's firing line, Rubin said, "I have something for you before you go."

Wolfe arrived back at Uri Ben-David's apartment in Tel Aviv just as the sun slipped beneath the waves of the Mediterranean. Nadia and Uri sat at the kitchen table, Uri helping Ben with his dinner.

When he entered the kitchen, Wolfe said, "Never thought I would witness Uri Ben-David being domestic with a small child."

With a chuckle, the older man glanced at Wolfe. "I have two boys, Michael, or did you forget?"

"Didn't forget. Didn't know."

"Both are grown and married, but neither have children, yet. I look forward to grandchildren someday."

"Josef recognized two names on the list. One, Azaria Sieff, died in a traffic accident. The other, Hershel Katz, disappeared in the West Bank."

"I thought he might be helpful." Uri offered the young Wolfe a cookie. The boy took it with gusto. Ben-David continued. "What are your thoughts on the matter?"

"Rubin made a few observations I think we need to evaluate."

"Such as?"

"Azaria Sieff was a sniper with the IDF. Josef's name is on the list, and he served in the same role for the Mossad. My name is there, as is Nadia's. She trained as a sniper, Uri."

"What about Katz?"

"Josef only told me he disappeared."

Ben-David frowned. "Yes, that was the incident I spoke about earlier. My fear is he might have been a double agent." He remained silent for a few moments. "You think being a sniper is important for being on the list?"

"My bet is it's critical for your name to be there. If I wasn't retired, I'd think seriously about trying to learn the truth. I don't like the fact Nadia and I are on it."

"You may be retired from the CIA, but I have no knowledge of you retiring from the Mossad."

Wolfe crossed his arms. "Nadia and I left Israel, Uri. It was kind of obvious."

Without taking his eyes off of Ben, Uri said, "Not to me, and I'm the director."

Eyes round as saucers, Nadia cast her husband a questioning expression.

He said, "Do you want to explain your comment, Uri?"

"What's to explain? I want you and Nadia to take a few days or weeks and look into this matter. Young Ben, here, can stay with my wife and me at our house in Haifa. She has already told me she would love to spend some time with him. She gets lonely while I am here in Tel Aviv. I believe he would be spoiled rotten in just a few days."

Wolfe glanced at his wife and saw her give him a slight nod. He turned to Uri. "A week. No more."

"Knowing how you and Nadia work together, it won't take that long." Ben-David offered the younger Wolfe another cookie. While the child ate, the head of the Mossad said, "I received a phone call this afternoon."

"And?"

"Who in the States knows about this list?"

"Joseph, Nadia, and myself. Why?"

"It seems the new CIA director scheduled a meeting with Joseph. When your president found out, he hit the ceiling. I also heard the meeting did not go well."

Raising an eyebrow, Wolfe said, "Jerry Griggs?"

Uri shrugged. "Maybe."

Chapter Six

White House

Jerry Griggs, the current national security advisor to President Roy Griffin, watched with concern as the president paced behind the Resolute Desk and ranted, his face crimson with anger.

"Does the woman not understand there are protocols when it comes to interviewing former presidential advisors, Jerry?"

"I wouldn't pretend to know the answer, sir."

"What was I thinking when I nominated Emma Elliot to the position of director of the CIA? What possessed me to do that, Jerry?"

"Is this question rhetorical, or are you seeking my real opinion, sir?"

Griffin stopped pacing and glared at his advisor. "The question was rhetorical."

"Good, because I really don't want to answer. You wouldn't have liked my response."

The redness in his cheeks faded, and a slight smile came to his lips. "Joseph said you could be brutally honest at times."

"I try."

"So, what is your opinion of Ms. Elliot?"

"She has an excellent resume and interviews well."

"But?"

"Once you get past the fluff, she's got her own agenda. One I doubt you realize or would approve of."

Griffin returned to his chair behind the desk. "How did I miss it?"

"Sir, you needed a new director, and a few members of congress led you astray."

"You didn't say anything. Why?"

"I was new around here; the new paint in my office wasn't even dry. Sorry."

The president straightened in his chair and tried to hide his smile. "Why did she want to talk to Joseph? Do you know?"

"I can only speculate, sir."

"Well then, speculate. I'm listening."

"Ms. Elliot believes Joseph still possesses more influence with you than she does. And she doesn't like it. I don't believe any meeting between her and Joseph would do anyone any good. It might even hasten global warming."

After a small chuckle, Griffin said, "She's correct, I trust Joseph. I haven't made up my mind about her yet."

"Mr. President, she will be hard to pry out of the chair."

"Okay, Jerry, you seem to know more about her than I do. What's her secret agenda?"

"To surround herself with yes-people. I'm sure you weren't aware, but there have been an above average number of senior managers retire since she was sworn in."

"No, I wasn't aware of this."

"Since I'm no longer employed there, I don't have first-hand knowledge. But I do know the top layer of CIA management has been decimated with less qualified individuals being promoted into those positions. In my opinion, the United States is less secure because of it."

Leaning back in his chair, the president drummed his fingers on the desktop. "Do you think they've been forced out?"

"No question in my mind, sir."

Griffin pushed a button on his desk phone. A voice said, "Yes, Mr. President?"

"Bob, find Emma Elliot and get her here ASAP. Clear my calendar until I meet with her."

"Yes, sir."

"Oh, and, Bob, I want you available for the meeting as well."

"Very good, sir."

The call ended. Turning his attention to Griggs, Griffin said, "Jerry, find the attorney general and get him over here. I need to know what my options are in regards to getting Ms. Elliot out of her position."

Tall, handsome, slender, and prematurely bald, Jerry's green eyes usually sparkled with mischief. Today, he silently questioned his decision to take the position after his mentor, Joseph Kincaid, resigned to attend to his wife's cancer diagnosis.

Six-foot-two, with above average basketball skills, he turned down numerous Division II scholarship offers, waiting on one from his Division I hometown school of

Vanderbilt. When this opportunity did not occur, he post-poned his education to follow his father's path into the Army. Four years and a stint as a Ranger later, he returned to Vanderbilt and graduated summa cum laude.

On the eve of his graduation ceremony, a man named Joseph Kincaid bought him dinner for the sole purpose of recruiting him to join the CIA. A week after receiving his diploma, he arrived at "The Farm" for his clandestine service training. Now, with ten years of experience trudging around Europe, and three years on a desk at Langley, he held the position of national security advisor to the president of the United States.

The arrival of Emma Elliot could be heard throughout the West Wing of the White House. Closing his eyes and shaking his head, he stood and headed for the Oval Office.

He entered the office and heard, "Mister President, what is the meaning of dragging me here for a meeting? We have critical events occurring around the world that need my attention."

President Griffin, in his normal, calm voice said, "Ms. Elliot, I assure you, this meeting will be just as critical, if not more so."

She glared at Griffin then softened her expression. "My apologies, Mr. President."

Griffin scrutinized her from his desk. He motioned for Griggs to sit on the sofa across from the CIA director. At that same moment, Attorney General Theo Barrett entered and sat next to Griggs.

The president started. "Thank you all for coming on such short notice." He directed his attention to the CIA director. He gave her a slight smile and clasped his hands in front of him on the desk. "I apologize for skipping social niceties, but what the hell are you doing at the CIA, Ms.

Elliot? I understand there has been a wholesale departure of your most experienced upper management."

The woman's eyes narrowed and she started to stand, but stopped and straightened herself on the sofa. Raising her chin, she said, "Not sure what you are referring to, Mr. President. We've had a few—"

"A few? The number I was given today indicates 60 percent of your senior leadership team have announced their retirement in the past two weeks. Sixty percent! Normal turnover at that level within the agency, on an annual basis, has never exceeded 15 percent. Are you running them off?" He focused on her for a second and then continued. "I certainly hope not, because if you have, that will be grounds for your dismissal."

Her wide eyes offered the best insight into the emotions she had to be experiencing. "I assure you, Mr. President, I have not, as you suggest, run them off. My management style and philosophy may not have set well with some of the older staff. But I certainly did not demand their resignations."

"What did you say to Mr. Joseph Kincaid, Ms. Elliot?"

"I sought his counsel on who might replace the departing staff members."

"Careful, Ms. Elliot. I have a long history with Mr. Kincaid, and that is not what you two discussed."

"Well, sir, since you seem to know more than I do about meetings I conduct, why don't you tell me what we conferred on?"

Her glare at the president made Griggs wonder where this exchange would lead.

Leaning forward on his desk, Griffin frowned. "You basically told him to keep his nose out of agency business."

She straightened, her back at least twelve inches from

the sofa cushion. "That is not what I told him. I merely mentioned that since he no longer worked for the federal government, conversations with any government official might not be considered appropriate."

He slammed his palm on the desk. "Ms. Elliot, you are in charge of protecting the US from foreign threats. Not domestic friends."

"Nevertheless, sir, I believe I need to take action when I deem it appropriate."

The president stood. "Very well, Ms. Elliot. Consider yourself on notice. If I hear of any additional resignations, I will be forced to take action to protect the interests of the United States. Is my meaning clear?"

The CIA director stood and straightened her shoulders. "Extremely clear, Mr. President." She turned and stormed out of the Oval Office.

Looking at the two remaining occupants sitting on the sofa, Griffin smiled and said, "Well, that went better than expected."

Chapter Seven

Veteran MI6 operator Harry Butler sipped on a rather eloquent espresso and watched waves crash against the docks below where he sat. He glanced at his watch and noted the individual scheduled to meet him was five minutes late.

Casually surveying his surroundings, on the eastern shores of the Adriatic Sea, he knew Vlorë to be the third most populous city in the country of Albania. It served the country as both a major seaport and industrial center. In addition, it remained a popular destination for tourists. Albania also held the title of world leader in coffeehouses per capita.

Nestled in a district favored by locals and tourists, one of the multitude of coffeehouses was Bujar's. A family-owned establishment with a spectacular view of the Bay of Vlorë, they offered outdoor seating and were famous for their baklava.

With the background din of the harbor and the various customers conversing near the table where he sat,

Butler started to think he had been stood up for the meeting.

He checked his watch again and stood. Protocol dictated meetings with contacts more than five minutes late were to be abandoned. A humming above his head drew his attention. The last image he saw before his world went black was a dark object with four spinning blades.

MI6 Director Jonathan Chapman read the memo and slammed a fist on his desk. "When?"

His assistant, Liam Hayes clasped his hands behind his back. "Six hours ago."

"For gawd sake, why wasn't I informed earlier? And why was he in Albania, of all places?"

"We just got the information, sir. Butler's last report indicated he had a lead on our two missing MI6 agents. We assume he'd set up a meeting with the source."

"But we don't know, correct?"

"No, sir, we don't. The explosion occurred five minutes after his scheduled meeting time. Eyewitnesses told police there were two tables occupied on the patio. One man sat alone, and the other had four customers nearby. Description of the lone customer indicates it was Butler. Five people, including the owner and his wife, were inside the café. There were no survivors."

Chapman stared at the memo. "Ten people."

"Yes, sir."

"What was he doing prior to going to Albania?"

"He was in Israel meeting one of his contacts within the Mossad. They've also lost agents recently."

An eyebrow rose on Chapman. "Do tell."

"Yes, sir. One in a single car accident, which Butler reported as suspicious, and the other missing in the West Bank. He's presumed dead."

"Damn."

Hayes kept his eyes on the director but remained quiet.

Putting the memo down, Chapman said, "Thank you, Liam. That's all for now. Please hold my calls."

"Very good, sir." The assistant turned with a perfectly executed military about-face and shut the door as he left the director's office.

Chapman turned his attention to the phone on his desk. He picked up the receiver and dialed a number memorized several years ago. The international call was answered on the third ring.

"Good afternoon, Jonathan."

"Hello, Uri. Am I catching you at a bad time."

"Not at all. What can I do for you?"

"I don't suppose you would have a few moments for a face-to-face tomorrow, would you?"

Ben-David hesitated. "Where?"

"We have a safe house in Cyprus. Say, noon tomorrow?"

"What's this about, Jonathan?"

"Can't divulge much right now, but it concerns both of us. At least the masters we serve."

"Very good. Send me the details and I'll be there. Is this private, or should I bring some of my staff?"

"Let's keep it as private as possible. However, it does concern some of our American friends."

"Ahh…" He paused for a moment. "Speaking of Americans, two of our mutual friends are visiting. Would this meeting have anything to do with them?"

Chapman did not respond for a moment. "Is their last name the same as a predator?"

"Very good, Jonathan. It is indeed."

"By all means, let them join us. They are indeed the Americans I mentioned."

Island of Cypris

Royal Air Force base Akrotiri, Cypris, was constructed in 1955 and still administered as a Sovereign Base Area for the United Kingdom. The air base, home to No. 84 Squadron and the No. 903 Expeditionary Air Wing of the RAF also played host to United States Air Force assets when needed.

Uri Ben-David's Gulfstream G550 landed at RAF Akrotiri at a few minutes past 10 a.m. The aircraft taxied to a secure area of the airport and was met by a black Range Rover with darkened windows. Three individuals walked down the airstairs of the Gulfstream and entered the vehicle. It sped off to an RAF secure building.

Once inside, Jonathan Chapman shook the hand of Wolfe and said, "Nice to see you again, Michael. I thought you and Nadia retired."

"We did."

Raising an eyebrow, Chapman glanced at Ben-David, who shrugged. The MI6 director said, "I see." He paused for a moment and offered Nadia his hand. "I'm glad the two of you are here. Some developments have occurred that might be of interest to you, Michael."

Wolfe kept his expression neutral. "What might that be?"

"A list of names that includes both you and Nadia."

Nadia involuntarily reached for her husband's hand. He grasped it and tilted his head. "What kind of list?"

"Something one of our MI6 agents uncovered during a routine trip to Washington, DC."

"Was this list given to him by a man named William Fischer?"

Chapman said, "No. But I take it you are already familiar with this information."

"Maybe."

Ignoring the caution in Wolfe's voice, Chapman continued. "One of our agents was in Albania yesterday morning when he met a rather gruesome demise. He was following a lead concerning the list."

Ben-David said, "We've had two agents on the list disappear. One in a car accident, the other vanished in the West Bank."

Wolfe addressed Chapman. "Were you aware of William Fischer's death?"

The MI6 director stared at the retired CIA operative. "No, I was not."

"He died when his house exploded due to a natural gas leak."

"Oh dear."

"Nadia's and my name are on the list as well."

"Yes, I am aware of that."

"Do you know why?"

"No. We haven't been able to determine a connection with any of the names."

"Nadia and I believe we know."

Chapman raised an eyebrow. "Care to enlighten me?"

"Was your agent in Albania a former sniper?"

The MI6 director remained quiet.

Wolfe frowned. "From your response, I'll take that as a yes. Who was he?"

"Harry Butler."

"I knew Harry. He was an excellent marksman."

"That's why I invited you and Nadia to this little get-together."

A tall gentleman entered the room. Chapman said, "This is my assistant, Liam Hayes."

Both Wolfe and Nadia nodded toward the man.

"Liam, these are the two individuals I spoke to you about."

"Nice to meet both of you." He handed a piece of paper to Chapman. "There's been a development in the Butler incident."

After scanning the page, Chapman looked up at his assistant. "A drone?"

"Yes, sir. Our experts are telling me it was a civilian model. The operator would need to be within two hundred meters to control the unit. It wasn't a remote, like we first suspected."

Wolfe folded his arms. "In other words, they knew he would be there."

"Damn." Chapman kept his eyes on the page for several more moments. He turned to Ben-David. "Uri, can you tell us more about the deaths of your agents?"

The director of the Mossad said, "Yes, I think I should." Uri Ben-David remained standing as everyone in the room found a place to sit. After clearing his throat, he started his narrative.

"It started with Azaria Sieff. We sent him to Beirut to follow up on a tip from within Hezbollah. In hindsight, we should have recognized it for what it was, a way to expose one of our operatives.

"Supposedly, Sieff was to meet his source to gain knowledge of an upcoming attack on one of our ultraorthodox settlements in East Jerusalem. The Palestinian Authority claims jurisdiction over the land and wants the settlers out. Sieff was there to learn details about the attack.

"He never made it to the meeting. Witnesses to the accident claim he was driving erratically and ran off the road. But we recovered the car and his body. Upon examination, paint found on the left side of his car came from a Toyota pickup. Thousands of these vehicles are used by Syrian-backed Hezbollah militants on a daily basis.

"We finally determined he was assassinated. There never was an informant. We were duped into sending him into the West Bank. A decision that got him killed."

Chapman nodded. "Much the same as our man in Albania."

"Exactly, Jonathan." He took a breath and continued. "However, the details of Hershel Katz's disappearance are different." Ben-David stood and walked to a coffeemaker and poured a cup. When finished, he turned to face everyone in the room. "Katz came to us as an immigrant from Germany. He was fourteen when his parents moved to Israel. After serving his mandatory two-and-a-half years in the military, he joined the Mossad. Twenty-four months into his service, he had yet to distinguish himself. His performance ratings were mediocre to low average. But he spoke Palestinian Arabic flawlessly. So, his superiors started using him as an errand boy. Running missions into Gaza and the West Bank. He excelled in this capacity."

Wolfe asked, "Any signs he was a double agent?"

"None. But there were rumors he was seeing a Palestinian woman in Ramallah."

Chapman stood and joined Ben-David at the coffee machine. "I say, old boy, did anyone try to confirm this?"

The Mossad director said, "After he disappeared, we tried to find her. Never did, not even a trace."

After taking a sip of his newly poured coffee, Chapman pursed his lips. "You think he disappeared on purpose?"

"We don't know."

Nadia frowned. "Then we need to know what the significance of being on the list means. Besides the fact many of these individuals were trained as snipers."

Leaning forward in his chair, Wolfe put his elbows on his knees. "Wait a minute. Did either of your men know or deal with William Fischer, Uri?"

Chapman turned to his assistant. "Damn. Liam, check to see if Butler worked with Fischer. If I remember correctly, both were in Germany at the same time."

"Yes, sir." Hayes stood and left the room.

Ben-David tapped his finger against his coffee cup. "Excuse me, I need to check on something." The Mossad director pulled his cell phone out and stepped out of the room as well.

"What are you thinking, Michael?"

"Jonathan, Fischer was in Germany a lot and I ran a few ops there myself." He turned to Nadia. "Did you ever operate in Germany?"

"Once. At the beginning of my stint with the Mossad. Why?"

"If the Mossad agent Azaria Sieff operated in Germany, we have the starting point of a connection. What it is, who knows, but at least we have a start."

Ben-David returned to the room. He said, "According to our file on Sieff, his parents came from Germany. Plus, he spoke fluent German. Katz also claimed to be from Germany when he migrated."

Chapter Eight

Emma Elliot possessed one trait her predecessor lacked. A total disregard for the feelings of others. In addition, she cared not who she pushed aside to reach her own goals, even if it was the president of the United States. With this attitude and achieving her goal of being named director of the CIA, she set her sights on a newly acquired goal. The downfall and dismantling of the presidency of Roy Griffin.

Her assistant sat in front of her desk and listened to the unhinged diatribe her boss spewed. "How dare he criticize my decisions on personnel. This is now my agency, and I will run it the way I see fit."

Her assistant, Samantha Edgar, nodded. "Yes, ma'am."

Elliot stood and turned to the window behind the desk, her hands clasped behind her. She took a deep breath. "Have you been able to locate the home of Joseph Kincaid?"

"Not yet. He has hidden his residency so effectively, even the agency does not know where it's located."

The director turned. "I find that hard to believe, Ms.

Edgar. You haven't turned over enough rocks. I must send him a not-so-subtle reminder he is not to meddle in the internal affairs of this agency."

"He hasn't worked for the agency in a long time, ma'am."

"Ms. Edgar, Joseph Kincaid was the de facto director of this agency for decades. He may no longer live in Washington, but he still has deep ties. If any of those individuals still work for the agency, they need to resign or retire. I will not have him running interference from afar."

"What do you wish me to do, ma'am?"

"Must I tell you how to do everything? You have carte-blanche access to all CIA records. Use that power to root out those sympathetic to Kincaid's influence. I want them gone from the agency. Plus, I want to know where he lives."

Samantha Edgar stood. "Yes, ma'am." She turned and left the office.

Elliot returned to staring out the window behind her desk. She mumbled to herself, "Why must I suffer fools like her."

Somewhere Over the Mediterranean Sea

Wolfe watched the blue waters of the Mediterranean slip beneath the Gulfstream G550 during the one-hour flight back to the Ben Gurion Airport in Tel Aviv. Nadia sat next to him, her seat back and eyes closed.

She straightened her seat and looked at him. "You've been quiet."

"Thinking."

"I figured as much. About?"

"How and why Germany could be the link between all of the names on the list."

"Have you been there often?"

"Couple of times." He turned to her. "When were you there?"

Diverting her eyes from him, she mumbled, "I don't remember."

With a chuckle, Wolfe patted her thigh. "Bullshit."

Taking a deep breath, she regained eye contact with him. "Do you remember your first few missions for Uri?"

"Yeah. Most were in Germany. Why?"

"I was your backup and guardian angel."

"Huh. Didn't know that."

"You weren't supposed to. That's when I fell in love with you."

"Uh…" Wolfe kept his gaze on her, reached for her hand, and squeezed. "You've never mentioned…" After several moments of silence, he said, "Nadia, Asa Gerlis claimed to be from Germany, didn't he?"

"Yes, I believe so." She stopped, "Michael, you don't think he's still alive, do you?"

"No. We both watched Gerlis die in the front yard of that house in southern France. But something about him and Germany is gnawing at the back of my mind."

She remained quiet.

He turned back to the window. The sea passed slowly thirty thousand feet below them. "How much of Gerlis' past is still considered confidential, I wonder?"

"It's not a subject many members of the Mossad like to discuss, Michael."

"Yeah, well, tough. I need to see his file."

"The man to ask is sitting a few rows back."

Standing, Wolfe made his way back to where Uri Ben-David sat.

"It's classified, Michael."

"I figured that much, Uri. But there's a connection between Gerlis and the list. I feel it."

Ben-David considered Wolfe for a few moments. "How?"

"Where did Gerlis come from?"

"When he first applied, he said Germany. But there are those in the Mossad who believe he was born in one of the former satellite nations of Russia."

"But no one knows for sure?"

"Correct."

"Uri, the questions about the list and all the names on it may have answers in Germany."

"Why do you say that?"

Taking a deep breath, Wolfe let it out slowly. "Don't laugh when I tell you this."

"I'll try not to."

"Emma Elliot."

Ben-David did not see humor in the statement. He narrowed his eyes. "Explain."

"When did all the drama about the list start?"

After not responding for several moments, he said, "Right about the time Dwight King announced his retirement."

"Exactly. Emma Elliot's name appeared out of nowhere as a dark horse candidate for the job. Why? Where did she come from?"

"Our information indicated she was a low-level functionary who failed as a field operator. Her support came from several senators who lobbied Griffin to appoint her."

"I heard the same story. So, the question would be, why did they support her?"

"You would have a better source on that than I, Michael."

"Can I use a secure phone when we land?"

"I believe it can be arranged."

"I need to get ahold of Jerry Griggs, Joseph."

"Why, Michael?"

"I'd prefer not to answer that question at the moment. I need background on Emma Elliot."

"He'll ask why."

"I know that. The reason is a little convoluted. The names on the list may be associated, not only to you but to some event or place in Germany."

Joseph remained silent for a few moments. "William Fischer ran a bunch of assets in Germany before the Soviet Union collapsed."

"We've established numerous individuals on the list have something to do with Germany. Both Nadia and I do. As does a dead agent with MI6 and two from the Mossad."

"What does this have to do with Emma Elliot?"

"Most of the deaths started immediately after Dwight King announced his retirement."

"Michael, don't you think that's a kind of a stretch?"

"I know it's thin, but I don't like coincidences. The closeness of the two events makes me ask questions."

Joseph did not immediately respond. Wolfe waited, patiently, for his friend to mull over the question. Finally, he heard, "Very well. I'll ask him to call you. Where are you going to be?"

"For now, Israel. Here's the number." He repeated the number twice. "It's a secure satellite phone Uri is allowing Nadia and I to use while we're in-country."

"I won't ask why. Expect Jerry to call as soon as he can."

"Thanks, Joseph."

Samantha Edgar closed the door to her apartment and secured the door with the four locks installed. Once in the bedroom, she stepped out of her high heels and headed for the bathroom. She removed her skirt and blouse as she stared into the mirror. "You're the one whose ambition got you into this mess." Her reflection did not answer.

Turning on the shower, she removed her undergarments and stepped in when the water steamed the mirror. She let the hot water wash away her makeup, and hopefully wash away her guilt at causing William Fischer's death. It did not.

Finally, she sank to the floor of the shower and the tears flowed.

"I'm sorry, Will. I didn't know the bitch was crazy."

She remained on the floor hugging her knees to her chest until she could cry no longer.

Time passed slowly as she lay in bed staring at the ceiling. Sleep would not make an appearance until a little after 3 a.m. When the alarm went off at 7 a.m., she hit the snooze button and rolled over. "I'm taking a personal day. Fire me if you don't like it."

At 8:10 a.m. she got up, cell phone in hand, and called the HR department at Langley. Ten minutes later, she had approval for personal time off to take care of a family emergency.

With the dread of facing Emma Elliot at some point during the day removed, Samantha Edgar started making calls. By noon, she had a meeting lined up with a reporter from *The Washington Post* and an airline ticket for Boise, Idaho.

Celine Ramone, an investigative report for *The Washington Post*, waited, as requested, at a Starbucks in the Baltimore/Washington National Airport. She sipped on a Blonde Vanilla Latte and watched passengers hurry by the coffee shop.

A woman appeared at the table. She said, "Thank you for meeting me here."

The reporter appraised the tall blonde as she sat across from her. "I'm curious. You said you worked for the CIA?"

Samantha Edgar said, "Recently retired."

"My editor will want proof."

The woman handed Ramone a thick manila envelope. "Proof of my identity is in this package. What you will also find in the envelope is documentation outlining a plot by the current director to remake the CIA into her personal army. She wants to embarrass and remove the current president of the United States from office. You will also find the transcript of a meeting she presided over outlining the plan she has to replace him with someone more to her liking."

The reporter stared at the woman and chuckled. "Really? Are you wasting my time, Ms. Edgar?"

The former assistant to Emma Elliot smiled and stood. "No, I'm not wasting your time, Ms. Ramone. If you would be so kind and check out some of the facts in these documents, I think you will find them accurate. Now, I have a flight to catch. I will call you in five days to see how you've progressed with your investigation."

With those words, Samantha Edgar stood and vanished into the crowded terminal foot traffic.

Celine Ramone opened the package and skimmed the contents. Unimpressed, she stood, found a large waste disposal receptacle and dropped the envelope inside. Without another thought of considering the information viable, she exited the airport for her car.

Chapter Nine

The desk phone on Jerry Griggs' desk buzzed. He checked the caller ID and noticed it was an outside number. He picked up the receiver and answered, "Griggs."

"Good afternoon, Jerry."

"Joseph, what a surprise. How's Mary?"

"In remission, thank goodness. How's the wind blowing up there?"

"They've issued gale warnings."

"Sorry to hear that. Hope you're in a safe harbor."

"No better than when you were sitting here."

"You remember Michael Wolfe?"

"One doesn't forget someone like him."

"He needs a favor."

"For him, anything."

"His request is simple, Jerry. Just call him."

"Where is he?"

"For the moment, Israel."

Griggs did not comment for a few seconds. "What's he doing there?"

"Trying to discover more about the list."

"Give me his number. I'll call from a secure phone."

The call ended, and Jerry drummed his fingers on his desk. Finally, he stood and walked out of his office. He passed his assistant's desk and said, "Got an errand to run for the boss. Be back in thirty minutes or so."

She glanced at him as he breezed by. "Okay, Jerry."

After getting into his car, he exited the White House grounds and made his way through traffic until he found an empty parking slot on Pennsylvania Avenue. He stopped the car, retrieved his personal cell phone, and dialed the number given to him by Joseph.

The call was answered on the third ring. "Wolfe."

"Michael, it's Jerry."

"That was quick. Can you talk?"

"I'm on a cell phone given to me by JR Diminski. Does that answer your question?"

"Perfect. What do you know about Emma Elliot?"

"Other than how she managed to thoroughly piss the boss off this morning?"

"Really, how?"

"By being her cute and cuddly self."

"Jerry, I don't know the woman. What does that mean?"

"Sorry. The boss didn't know her either. Three senators met with him the day Dwight King announced his retirement. The meeting lasted about an hour. The only other person in the room was Bob Short. The next day, he nominates her for the position at the CIA."

"So, you don't know what they discussed?"

"No, that occurred my first week on this job. I didn't even know where the bathrooms were."

"Huh." He paused. "What did she say that pissed off the president?"

"She basically told him to keep his nose out of agency business."

"I'm sure that didn't go over well."

"You're right, it didn't. He's now questioning his decision."

"You could be doing your boss a favor by gathering detailed background on her."

Griggs heard a car's horn blare. He glanced in the rearview mirror and saw a driver shaking his fist at a pedestrian crossing the street.

"What the hell was that, Jerry?"

"Car horn."

"Where are you?"

"Parked on Pennsylvania Avenue. I didn't think it wise to call you from the White House."

"Smart."

"Do you know more about Elliot than you're saying, Michael?"

"No, but I've got a lot of questions."

"Such as?"

"Does she have ties to Germany? Has she been out of the country in the past year? How did she go from obscurity to director of the CIA in the blink of an eye?"

"I don't know. Michael, what does Germany have to do with this?"

"It's a connection that might be important. There are six names on the list confirmed dead, another is missing but presumed to be dead. All have ties to Germany, including Nadia and myself. Ms. Elliot's appearance on the scene only a few weeks before the first name on the list died bothers me."

"You mean Fischer?"

"Yes."

"It could be a coincidence."

"I don't like coincidences, Jerry. Coincidences can get you killed."

"Okay, Michael. What do you need from me?"

"Someone in DC has to know more about her. Find them. When you do, let me know. I'll head back and talk to them."

Griggs did not say anything for a few seconds. "Is Joseph in danger?"

"I don't know. But he and William Fischer were friends. He's been in Germany more times than any of us can count. Plus, at one time or another, he's worked with the majority of the individuals on the list. Is he in danger? My guess would be yes."

"What about you, Michael?"

"Nadia and I are on the list. Don't forget you're now the national security advisor. Were you ever in Germany?"

"Aww, shit."

"That's what I thought. How long?"

"Four years."

"I think you have as much skin in the game as any of us. Find someone who knows about her."

Griggs glanced at the clock on the dash. "Hey, Michael, I've got to get back. Anything else?"

"No, see what you can find and get back to me. We're going to be in Israel for a few more days."

The call ended, and Griggs drove back to the White House.

———

When Michael ended the call, Uri Ben-David asked, "He did not know anything, did he?"

"I didn't expect him to, Uri. But if anyone can find something out in DC, it's Jerry Griggs."

"I heard you mention something about Emma Elliot and the president."

"Jerry didn't go into details, but it seems she and the president went toe to toe. I don't know Griffin that well, so I'm not sure how he would respond to her talking back to him."

"I've met him a few times. Fair-minded and strong-willed. If she was speaking about something she felt strongly about, he'll be fair. But…"

"What's the but about, Uri?"

"If she's just trying to protect her turf, he'll push back."

Wolfe tilted his head. "What did your agency tell you about her?"

"Her appointment caught us off guard. We know very little about her."

"Kind of dangerous for the Mossad not to know anything about the current CIA director."

Ben-David smiled. "Let's see what Jerry Griggs comes up with."

That Evening

Having called his wife to tell her he needed to work late, Griggs sat at a table in the back of a dreary dive bar in a less-than-desirable section of Alexandria. The sticky tabletop made him wonder if anyone ever cleaned it.

At exactly eight, the door to the tavern opened, and a diminutive woman with curly black hair walked in. She spotted Griggs and made a beeline toward his table. "Wasn't our last meeting in a dump like this?"

"Yes."

"You sure don't know how to show a gal a good time, Griggs."

"How's Miami?"

"Hot and humid. How's being the national security adviser?"

"About the same: hot and humid. I need a favor, Carla."

"Of course you do. You always need a favor. What's it this time?"

"I need a deep dive on Emma Elliot."

One of the waitress's set a draught in front of her. She took a sip before she answered. She grimaced and said, "Places like this must get a discount on bad beer." She set the beer down. "A friend of ours asked me the same question a few days ago."

"What did you tell him?"

"I didn't know anything then. However, I've been busy."

Griggs used both hands to clasp his untouched beer. "Such as?"

"She's a mystery wrapped in an enigma."

"Really, Carla, a cliche?"

"In this case, it's not a cliche. She joined the agency right after graduating from Carnegie Mellon. She majored in economics. Here's a tidbit, she was not recruited."

"She wasn't?"

"Nope. As they say in college sports, she was a walk-on. Records indicate she was turned down when she applied the first time. A senator from Pennsylvania intervened, and she was accepted. She didn't excel during her training, either."

"Who was the senator?"

"Calvin Hendricks. Why?"

"Huh." Griggs finally took a sip of beer. He made a face and sat the glass aside. He returned his attention back to Carla. "He was one of the senators who met with the president prior to her being nominated for the position."

"I didn't know that." She remained silent for a moment. "Jerry, doesn't Pennsylvania have a large German population?"

He nodded. "Yeah, one of the larger ones."

Carla said, "Her birth certificate indicates she was born in Germantown. Both of her parents immigrated from Germany and are now deceased."

"Huh. Michael may be right. Germany might be the key to Emma Elliot."

"What are you talking about?"

"He asked me if she had ties to Germany."

"Shit, Jerry. She may still have relatives there."

"It's possible. What else did Michael talk to you about, Carla?"

"Yeah, some kind of list he's on."

"He and Nadia. I suppose he told you who all was on the list."

"Yeah, he gave me a copy."

"We recently learned at least six of the names on the list are dead and one's missing. The dead ones were assassinated, like Fischer."

"Aww, shit. Now what, Jerry?"

"Want a job with the White House?"

She raised her eyebrows.

Chapter Ten

WASHINGTON, DC

Griggs placed the sheet of paper on the president's desk.

Griffin read it and looked up. "Is it legal for the White House to hire someone like her?"

"As long as her position falls under the National Security Council umbrella, it is."

"What about her career with the CIA?"

"She's been relegated to a dead-end position in Miami. In her words, 'Anything's better than this place.' I've worked with her a number of times over the years. She's excellent at her job. I might add, Joseph recommends her as well. Plus, when Elliot learns she worked for Joseph, her career will be over."

The president smiled. "Who do you want her to work for, Jerry?"

"Me."

Returning the sheet of paper, he said, "Make it so."

"Thank you, sir."

As he turned to walk out, Griffin asked. "Jerry, did you

say she would be fired from her job if Elliot finds out she worked for Joseph?"

He stopped and turned toward the president. "Yes, sir."

"Did she tell you that?"

"No, sir. Rumors on the street indicate Elliot is ridding the agency of anyone who might have said good morning to Joseph at any time or worked for him in any capacity."

"But it's only a rumor?"

"Well, sir, I've not seen it in writing. But…"

"Track it down. If you learn it's official policy, she's gone."

Griggs gave the president a mischievous grin. "I'll do my best, sir."

Back in his office, he dialed a number on his desk phone.

The call was answered before the first ring ended. "Jerry?"

"Yeah, Carla. How soon can you move back to DC?"

"Did the president say yes?"

"He did. You'll work for me."

"What's today?"

"Wednesday."

"I'll be there Friday. I'll send my resignation letter to HR as soon as I hang up."

"I take it you've already written one?"

"What do you think?"

With a chuckle, Griggs said, "See you on Monday. I'll get the paperwork started here. You'll need to report to the guard house at the West Wing entrance. I'll let them know to expect you."

"Got it." Silence fell over the phone call. "I spoke to Samantha Edgar."

"And?"

"She's the one who gave the list to William."

"Did she say why?"

"She thought it would help protect him. Obviously, it didn't."

"Oh, boy."

Carla stayed quiet for a few moments. Then she said, "Thanks, Jerry. I owe you big-time."

"Don't mention it. Glad to have you on my side."

The call ended, and Griggs took his cell phone out and sent a three-word text message. *She's on board.*

Joseph read the text and immediately deleted it. He stood and retreated to the huge back deck and surveyed the wooded area behind his house. Events were starting to occur in rapid succession. In the past, when cascading actions presented themselves, he always had the ability to foresee the outcome. Not this time.

Grabbing the wooden rails, he secured himself as a wave of vertigo swept over him. He closed his eyes against the swirling sensations and tried to steady the weakness in his legs.

Mary appeared on the deck and hurried to his side. "Are you having those feelings again?"

He nodded, not trusting himself to speak.

"Why don't you lie down, Joseph."

Glancing at his wife, he smiled. "They've passed."

"Maybe so, but I'm worried these episodes are occurring closer together. Are they stronger or about the same?"

"The same. They go away almost as rapidly as they appear."

Taking his arm, she said, "Let me help you into the house. I think it's time you saw a doctor about this."

He walked wobbly toward the sliding glass door. "Yeah, I think you're right."

Steadying him by the arm, she walked beside him, his gait hesitant. When they reached a sofa, he collapsed and seemed to black out for a moment.

She said, "Joseph?" He stared at her with a blank expression. She repeated, "Joseph?"

After blinking several times, he said, "Call Doctor Harmon. Something's wrong."

"When did these symptoms start, Joseph?"

Siting on the end of the examination table, the retired CIA operative directed his attention to the doctor and then at Mary, who sat against the wall. "Off and on since I retired, but now they're occurring on a regular basis."

Doctor Vince Harmon, a former Marine physician, contemplated his old friend for a moment and then consulted the computer screen he sat next to. "How much coffee are you drinking?"

"About the same."

With a grin, the doctor said, "Cut back. Your usual amount would make most people bounce off the wall."

"Okay."

"What about brain fog?"

"No."

Mary cleared her throat. "Uh, Joseph, tell the truth."

He glanced at her, and said, "Normally, I can look at a problem and know how to solve it. Solutions aren't coming to me like they used to."

The doctor frowned and returned his attention to the computer screen. "Your blood chemistry is normal, though your blood pressure is a tad high. What about headaches?"

"No. Just the lightheadedness."

"Do you get out of breath easily?"

Taking a deep breath, the patient nodded. "A little."

Harmon stood and used his stethoscope to listen to the blood flow in Joseph's neck. He remained quiet as he listened. He then checked the other side. "Well, I think we need to get an angiogram scheduled."

"Why?"

"Precaution more than anything. For someone your age, you're in excellent health, Joseph. But I prefer to be proactive rather than reactive.

"You heard something in my neck, didn't you?"

The doctor gave Joseph a sly smile. "Not really, but something is obscuring your blood flow. I want to know what."

Joseph said, "All right. When?"

"If I have my way about it, tomorrow."

———

Light brought a sensation of floating. His eyes fluttered open, and the first images were blurred. This passed quickly as he surveyed his surroundings.

A young nurse appeared beside him and said, "I see you are waking up, Mr. Kincaid. I'll let the doctor know."

He drifted back to sleep.

"Joseph, can you hear me?"

His eyes fluttered open, and he saw Dr. Harmon above him. "Yes, how'd the angiogram go?"

"They put a stint into your ascending carotid artery.

The obstruction may not have caused your lightheadedness, but my guess is it did."

"I thought the cardiologist would have been here."

"He'll be by in a while. I was making rounds and thought I'd check in on you." He lightly tapped Joseph's forehead. "Besides, we need to keep all those state secrets you have up there safe."

"Thank you, Dr. Harmon."

"Don't mention it. As soon as you get out of post-op, you can see Mary and another one of my patients."

"Who?"

"Michael Wolfe's been here since you went in for your angiogram. He's kept Mary company."

Joseph took a deep breath. "How long before I get out of here?"

"Not long. Be patient."

An hour later, Mary held Joseph's hand while Wolfe stood next to his bed. "Feeling better?"

Looking at his friend, Joseph said, "Thanks for coming. I thought you were in Israel."

"I was. Nadia and Ben are still there. She's making the rounds, introducing our son to all of her aunts, uncles, and cousins."

"Does she miss Israel?"

"She won't say anything, but I think she does a little. So, what happened? Mary said you were having occasional fainting spells?"

"That's what she calls it. It was more of a loss of focus and concentration. The legs felt like rubber."

"Glad they caught it. We need you sharp right now, Joseph."

Narrowing his eyes, he looked at the ex-CIA sniper. "What's wrong?"

"The events around William Fischer's death are escalating. When we get you home, I'll explain it better."

"What's the 'we' about?"

"That's why I'm here. To help Mary get you home."

———

The Next Day

"Okay, Michael, I'm home. Time to tell me what's going on."

"Jerry told you Carla works for him now, right?"

"Yes."

"Well, she's already earning her salary."

"Good." Joseph sat at the kitchen table. Wolfe sat across from him.

The retired sniper asked, "How well do you know Emma Elliot?"

"I don't know her. I still can't understand why Griffin nominated her."

"A lot of people within the CIA agree with you. Did you know that 60 percent of upper management has retired since she became the director?"

"No, I didn't."

"President Griffin is livid. There's going to be a show-down between him and Elliot. Probably in the not-too-distant future."

"You mentioned Carla's already making a difference."

"Yeah. Do you know Samantha Edgar?"

Joseph stalled for a moment. "I know William was very fond of her. Why do you ask?"

"Carla knows her, too. She was Elliot's assistant."

An eyebrow rose on the recently discharged patient. "Interesting."

"It gets better. Where did the flash drive found in the safety deposit box come from?"

"I assumed Fischer came across the information from various sources. Why?"

Wolfe gave him a grim smile. "Samantha Edgar gave it to him."

The older man sitting at the kitchen table straightened. "Do you think the information is fake?"

"No, I think it's very real. Carla said Samantha is terrified of Elliot. She also considers her a danger to the security of this country. On top of all that, she disappeared."

"Disappeared?"

Wolfe nodded.

"On her own or…"

"No one knows. She took some time off for a family emergency and has not been seen since."

"What I remember of Samantha, she doesn't scare easy."

"That's what Carla said."

"I hope nothing bad has occurred."

"I have a source checking out airline flights from the Washington area. We should know by tomorrow if she flew out."

"JR?"

"No, Alexia."

Joseph stared out the large window in the room at his back lot. "Did Samantha tell Carla why she gave the drive to William?"

Wolfe nodded.

Chapter Eleven

SOUTHWEST MISSOURI

Mary placed a steaming cup in front of Joseph on the kitchen table. "The doctor said you need to cut back on your caffeine. Try this."

Looking up with a grimace, he said, "I hate tea, you know that."

"It's green tea, dear. Decaffeinated."

"Wonderful." He took a sip and closed his eyes. "Also, flavorless." He gripped the cup with both hands before he turned his attention back to Wolfe. "Now, why did Samantha Edgar give the flash drive to Fischer?"

"She felt the contents would help protect him."

Joseph studied the tea in his cup and then took a deep breath. "Obviously, it didn't."

"No, it didn't. There seems to be another issue. The new director sees you as a major threat to her."

Joseph stared at Wolfe for a few seconds, shook his head, and sipped his tea. "That seems a bit delusional. Why would she think of me as a threat? I'm retired."

"Carla asked Samantha the same question. She didn't

have an answer. Apparently, Elliot has a huge chip on her shoulder about you and anyone who worked directly for you or assisted on one of your projects. Samantha believes those are the individuals who made the list."

Joseph took his eyes off the tea and looked at Wolfe. "That's crazy. I've worked with a lot of good people over the years, and I've seen the list. But I've never met half of them. There has to be another reason."

"I thought as much. Does the name Harry Butler ring a bell?"

"Yeah. I worked with him in London."

"He was killed by a drone explosion in Albania. He wasn't collateral damage. The drone targeted him specifically."

Taking another sip of his tea, Joseph kept his gaze on Wolfe. "Who else?"

"Azaria Sieff with the Mossad."

Joseph did not respond right away. After a few moments, he raised an eyebrow.

Wolfe tilted his head. "You know something, don't you?"

"Maybe."

"Want to tell me?"

"Sure." Joseph set the tea aside and said, "You know, this tea isn't so bad."

"You're stalling."

"Yes." He clasped his hands together. "Not one of my stellar accomplishments." After taking a deep breath, he started on his narrative. "A number of years ago, before I settled in this area and started the home security company, I met Calvin Hendricks. He was the sheriff of Baltimore County, Maryland. At the time, he possessed a cocky and brash personality. Somehow, he discovered I was a recruiter for the CIA and approached me at a law-enforcement conference."

Wolfe crossed his arms. "This should be good."

"It isn't. Anyway, he cornered me in the hotel bar one night and proceeded to regale me with his exploits as sheriff. I believed about half of it. But there was enough interest I asked him to send me a resume. He did, and I checked some of his references."

"Let me guess, his references didn't like him."

"On the contrary, they did. But none were senior law-enforcement officials. The names he gave me were all old college buddies. When I contacted sheriffs in neighboring counties, they all said they knew him but would not comment further. The chief of police in Baltimore had a few harsh words about him."

"I assume you told him you couldn't recommend him."

"Yes, I told him so. I thought that would be it. That's when it got ugly."

Wolfe leaned forward at the table. "How so?"

"He accused me of being prejudiced."

The retired sniper laughed out loud. "He what?"

"Not only did he accuse me to my face, he wrote to the then CIA director. He and I came up through the agency together. He laughed it off, told me not to worry about the matter. I think the mistake the director made was handing it to a deputy director to get back to Hendricks."

"What was the deputy director's name?"

"Dwight King."

With a chuckle, Wolfe said, "Oh, this gets better with every word."

"Dwight later told me Hendricks was insulted a deputy director was assigned to get back with him. Not the director himself. He promised he would have payback for the slight."

"Did he?"

With a shrug, Joseph sipped his tea. "Who knows? Hendricks lost his next election."

"Let me guess. You had something to do with that."

Joseph grinned. "He lost by a landslide."

"So, Hendricks blames you for losing his sheriff's position?"

"I wouldn't know. I didn't even know he was a senator until you told me a few minutes ago."

"But it might explain his zeal for getting Emma Elliot into the director's chair."

"Michael, I don't see that as a catalyst. There has to be another reason."

"There could be, Joseph, but I've seen individuals seek revenge for less reasons."

"Yes, the human ego can be fragile at times. What about this Hershel Katz? You mentioned a body was never found."

"No, Uri said that Hezbollah normally returns the body when they find a double agent."

Joseph stopped the tea mug halfway to his lips and put it back on the table. "What if this list has another meaning, and it's not about eliminating people who used to work with me?"

"I'm not following you, Joseph."

"My brain's been foggy, it was right there in front of me. If someone needs to vanish without a trace, how would you do it?"

Wolfe smiled. "Put his or her name on a list of people who are being assassinated. They disappear and, all of a sudden, they're no longer a suspect. They're assumed to be dead." He tapped this finger on the table. "There's one catch."

"That is?"

"Why did Samantha Edgar have all this information, and why give it to Fischer?"

"You're making my head hurt, Michael."

"No shit. Jerry said the same thing. He's got Carla trying to figure out where Samantha's loyalties lay."

Raising an eyebrow, Joseph looked at Wolfe. "Let me guess. You're going back to Israel to find Katz?"

"Or at least determine who he really is or was. If he is the one who killed Fischer, Butler, and Sieff, he needs to be stopped." Wolfe gave Joseph a weak smile. "Now that you're home and on the mend, I'll fly to Atlanta in the morning for a flight back to Tel Aviv."

"What about your being retired?"

"I am from the CIA. As Uri Ben-David told me, I didn't retire from the Mossad."

Tel Aviv
Two Days Later

Wolfe studied the personnel file of Herschel Katz given to him by Ben-David. He directed his attention to Nadia, who sat across from him. "This reads like Asa Gerlis' resume."

"That's what Uri said."

Returning to the file, he picked up one page. "He claimed to be from a small town in the Rhine Region called Karbach." He studied the report. "That's in western Germany, isn't it?"

His wife thumbed something into her phone. She studied it for a moment. "Yes, about 150 kilometers from the Belgian border. Why?"

"Gerlis claimed he came from Poland, but it was actually Kazakhstan. What if Katz's claim he was of Jewish heritage from Germany is as false as Gerlis' was?"

"Let me guess, Michael. You're going to Karbach to find out, aren't you?"

"My German is still pretty good. How's yours?"

She shrugged. "I haven't used it for a while. Probably rusty."

"Want to go with me so you can practice your German?"

"Uri's wife keeps asking when you and I are going to take some time off together. I think she would enjoy having Ben to herself for a few days."

"Well, see? There you go. Let's give her an opportunity to spoil him."

Nadia smiled.

Chapter Twelve

RHINE GORGE, GERMANY

After checking into the Romantik Hotel Schloss Rheinfels, Nadia and Wolfe drove the ten kilometers to the small community of Karbach. When they arrived, Wolfe said, "Bet we have to travel on to Emmelshausen to get census information."

"I bet you're right. This village is basically a wide spot in the road."

Wolfe looked over at her. "You've been in the US too long."

She chuckled. "I learned that from you."

"Apparently, I'm a bad influence. Let's find their version of City Hall and see what they say."

It took five minutes to determine the tiny community did not possess what they searched for. Instead, they stopped at a tavern catering to hikers.

In English-accented German, Nadia asked the woman behind the bar, "Where would we find information on folks born in this area?"

A large woman with blonde hair scrutinized her guest. "Who are you searching for?"

"A cousin of mine."

"I've lived here all my life. What's the name?"

"Katz."

She chuckled. "Lots of Katzes in the area. First name?"

"Herschel."

"Herschel Katz. Hmmm. Don't recall anyone of that specific name." She pointed to an elderly gentleman sitting at a corner table. "That is Manfred Katz. He's the patriarch of the family around here."

Nadia thanked her, and they strolled over to the table. "Herr Katz?"

The man set his beer down and smiled. "Ya. Who might you be?"

"My name is Nadia Wolfe." She waited for him to comment. When he did not, she continued. "We are seeking information on a man named Herschel Katz. He is supposed to have been born here. Would you know anything about him?"

"Ya, ya, sit. We have several Herschel Katzes here. Can you be more specific?"

Nadia sat in a chair next to him and offered a picture of Katz from his Mossad file. "This is the man we are trying to locate. His mother's name was Gertrude, and the father's Henrick. Would you know any of them?"

The man stared at the picture and then took a couple of sips on his beer. He appraised Nadia and then her husband who stood behind her. He shook his head. "Nien."

Wolfe took the picture back and said, "You hesitated, Herr Katz."

"I hesitated, young man, because I have never seen this man or known anyone by those names."

"Can you tell me where official records might be kept?"

"Emmelshausen would have public records. But I know all of the members of the Katz family in this part of Germany. The man in that picture is not from here."

Standing Wolfe said, "Danke, Herr Katz." He turned to Nadia. "Let's go." They both bid the elderly gentleman a good day and returned to their rental car.

As they turned onto the L213 for the eight-kilometer trip to the west, Wolfe said, "We aren't the first ones looking for records of Herschel Katz, Nadia."

"His hesitation took too long. What do you think we will find in Emmelshausen?"

"We'll either find nothing or a freshly minted record of Herr Katz's existence."

She pulled out her cell phone and started punching numbers into the device. After hitting the send button, she watched her husband. "Let's see what Alexia can find before we start asking questions."

"We probably should have started there."

"Yes, but we had no reason to suspect anything."

When Nadia ended the call, she said, "She's going to see if there is anything on Katz. Let me see the picture of him. I'll take a photo of it and send it to her."

Emmelshausen turned out to be a quaint community where they found a pizzeria ristorante and stopped for lunch. They sat inside and watched the inhabitants of the town pass by. Speaking French, they discussed their next moves.

Nadia nibbled on a slice of pizza and watched the street. "Let's say we find no trace of Katz here in Germany. What then?"

"No more effort than we've exerted, so far, I can't say. Let's see what Alexia finds before we make any major decisions. Changing the subject, have you ever been in Germany as a tourist?"

She shook her head. "Nope. I've been in Berlin and Frankfurt, but always working. You?"

"The same. What I've seen so far, away from the cities, I like. Reminds me a lot of the geography where our house is."

Nadia's cell phone vibrated. She checked the ID before answering. She greeted the caller and listened, not saying a word. Finally, she said, "Thanks, Alexia. Can you send it to my secure drop box?" She listened again. "I appreciate it. We'll be home in a few weeks."

She ended the call and turned to Michael. "Apparently, Herschel Katz's bio is a complete forgery. His real name is Armin Jazani. He's Iranian."

With a raised eyebrow, Wolfe asked, "How did she find him?"

Nadia said, "The picture. JR has some rather sophisticated facial recognition software. Alexia used it to scan CIA files. Apparently, Mr. Jazani belonged to a youth group associated with the Iranian Revolutionary Guard. CIA archives had a copy of his photo."

"Huh. That explains a lot." He paused and closed his eyes. "Ahhhh, shit."

"What's the matter, Michael?"

"I think I just realized what the list is really about?"

"Want to tell me?"

"Not until we get back to Israel. How he fooled the Mossad will be a question Uri will need to answer."

Nadia frowned at her husband. "Why not tell me now?"

"I need Uri to be there when I explain. Is Alexia sending what she found?"

"Yes, she's sending the information to our drop box. So, why not tell me about the list?"

"Right now, it's conjecture. I need to confirm something, then I can tell you."

"Okay. Do we have to go back right now?" She put her hand on his. "We can afford to spend a few days paying attention to each other. We're here, we have a lovely hotel room, and there's lots to see. Then we can fly back to Israel."

He patted her hand. "Thanks for reminding me."

Tel Aviv
Three Days Later

Uri Ben-David strode urgently through the halls of a nondescript building hidden within the city limits of Tel Aviv. Nadia and Wolfe followed. As of ten minutes ago, they were officially paid consultants to the director of the Mossad, and the director was not in a good mood.

When Ben-David burst into the room, everyone grew silent as he headed to the podium near the front. His new consultants arranged themselves against a wall in the back.

He surveyed the area and then cleared his throat. "We've discovered yet another mole within our ranks. The man we knew as Herschel Katz has been identified as an Iranian agent. His real name is Armin Jazani. He was trained by the Islamic Revolutionary Guard in covert activities." The director paused to let the information register with the individuals in the room. A low murmur within the gathered personnel broke the silence. He continued. "If you will remember, the Mossad was infiltrated more than a decade ago by an agent from Kazakhstan. He was permanently retired five years ago. Why is this happening again, people? What disciplines do we need to implement to prevent another occurrence in the future?"

The murmurs ceased, but no one offered a suggestion.

"I am mystified by these incidences and extremely disappointed in our recruitment policies. These men were exposed by the same two individuals, Michael Wolfe and his wife, the former Nadia Picard. They have agreed to help us improve our background checks for future recruits. They have also volunteered to help us find Armin Jazani."

A hand shot up on the wall opposite Wolfe and Nadia. "It was my understanding Katz was sent into the West Bank and either captured or killed."

The director nodded. "That was our understanding, as well. However, with the discovery of his real identity, we have revised our assessment of what happened in the West Bank. There is a strong possibility he passed through Gaza straight to Egypt to seek transportation to an unknown location. We have agents checking security videos at both the airport and docks."

A tall woman entered the conference room, walked to were Ben-David stood, handed him a file, whispered in his ear, and then left the same way she entered. Without a discernable sound.

The director opened the file on the podium, studied the contents for a few moments, and returned his attention to those gathered in the conference room. "It seems our Mr. Jazani's image was captured by a security camera at Cairo International Airport boarding an EgyptAir nonstop flight to New York City. This occurred thirty-one days ago." He directed his next question to Wolfe. "When did Fischer's house explode?"

"Twenty-two days ago."

Returning his attention to the file, he said, "Ladies and gentlemen, we need to use both our technology and resources to find Mr. Jazani. Not next week, not tomorrow, but yesterday. Do I make myself clear?" The buzz in the room intensified as heads nodded.

Ben-David left the conference room followed by Wolfe and Nadia.

Wolfe did not sit at the small conference table in Ben-David's office. He paced.

Nadia folded her arms. "Are you going to finally reveal your revelation in Germany, Michael?"

Turning toward the conference table, Wolfe looked at his wife. "Remember when Ian and I were gone for a few days in May?"

"Yes."

He faced Ben-David. "Want to explain?"

"Oh, that." He cleared his throat. "Nadia, Michael and Ian McGill traveled to Azerbaijan in May to carry out an assignment for Israel. When I proposed it to Michael, our goal was to punish Iran for their backing of Hamas and Hezbollah. We asked him and Ian to do it to help them resolve what they experienced during their three months in Iran several years ago."

She glared at her husband and then at Ben-David. "Why was I not told?"

"Plausible deniability. The task was highly classified. Only the prime minister, the US president, Joseph, and I knew about it. Michael and Ian planned it, provided their own transportation to the site, and coordinated their own ingress and egress. We didn't even inform the CIA. Now you, besides the original four, are the only ones who know about the mission."

Her eyes grew wide. "May 19. That was the day the Iranian president's helicopter crashed in the mountains."

"Yes, that is correct."

Wolfe said, "Now the list makes sense. The Iranians would be embarrassed if the world knew they lacked the ability to protect their president. They obviously know why the helicopter went down, so their solution is to eliminate all the snipers they have information on. But it appears they used old intelligence, thus the incomplete addresses."

"Michael, what if they find our house? What about that?"

"They'll find a rather nasty hornets' nest."

Chapter Thirteen

LONDON

The phone in Jonathan Chapman's office buzzed. He glanced at the data display identifying a call from Tel Aviv. He lifted the receiver. "Hello, Uri?"

"Good evening, Jonathan. I was hoping to find you in your office."

"Not unusual these days, my friend. What can I do for you?"

"I have a possible lead for you in the death of your man in Albania."

"I say, rather sporting of you, old boy. Who is it?"

"Check your inbox. I just sent a photo."

Chapman busied himself accessing his email and saw the message. He opened the photo and stared at the image. "The photo appears to be from an ID."

"It is."

"Who is it?"

"He is an Iranian who infiltrated the Mossad. He disappeared a year ago and only recently flew to the US."

"Islamic National Guard?"

"Yes, unfortunately."

"Do the Americans know this?"

"No, and that's what I want to talk to you about."

"How is this about our man in Albania?"

"Mutual friends uncovered this mess. He and his wife are consulting with me on the affair."

"I see."

"Can you send me any security videos you might have of the unfortunate incident?"

"Yes, expect them within the hour."

"We have information I do not wish to broadcast even over a secure network."

"I see. Do we need to meet again in Cyprus?"

"What a splendid idea, Jonathan."

Tel Aviv

Wolfe studied the computer screen, adjusting the speed of the video playback with the mouse.

Nadia rubbed her weary eyes. "I stared at that video for three hours and didn't see him. You still think he's there?"

"No, I don't think. I know. Where, is another issue. He might have been able to avoid any of the security cameras. But he's in the crowd, somewhere."

He paused the video and looked up at her. "Did Chapman send us any other videos?"

"No, you've viewed all of them, just like I have. You have to remember, Michael, Albania might not have the number of security cameras Tel Aviv or London possesses."

Drumming his fingers on the hotel room's desk, he noticed something. Using the mouse, he reversed the video and clicked play again. When he zoomed in on a specific section of the crowd, he pointed to an individual walking away from the scene. All the other spectators were facing the location of the explosion. "Bingo, look at this guy."

Bending over, Nadia examined the area where her husband pointed. "Pixels are a little sparse."

"Yeah, but you know how to overcome something that minor."

"Okay, let me sit there."

Relinquishing his seat to his wife, he let her manipulate the image. After five minutes, she said, "That's interesting."

"Kind of what I thought."

"Take off the hat, and it's Armin Jazani."

"It's him even with the hat."

"Don't be snide. How'd you spot him?"

"Everyone in the crowd was transfixed watching the removal of bodies from the café. He's the only one leaving the scene. His actions stood out."

Nadia made a screen shot of the video. "I'll send this to Alexia to confirm with facial recognition."

Wolfe wandered over to the window. He opened the curtains and watched the lights of ships moving along the coast of the Mediterranean heading toward port. "Do we know if there were any Ring cameras on houses surrounding Fischer's home?"

"That's a question I can't answer, Michael."

"Neither can I." He checked his watch, did the math. "It's close to dawn in DC. I'm calling Jerry."

A groggy voice answered the call after the fifth ring. "Griggs."

"You awake?"

"I am now. Who's this?"

"It's Wolfe. I need something."

Silence prevailed for a few seconds. When he spoke again, Griggs sounded more alert. "Okay, what'd you find?"

"You know about the Mossad mole, don't you?"

"Yes, thanks to you."

"We have access to a security video provided by your cousins across the pond."

"And?"

"We have a security video of him at the scene in Vlorë. He stuck around to see the aftermath of his handiwork."

"So, what do you need from me?"

"Any and all home security videos from the surrounding homes in Fischer's neighborhood."

"They didn't find anything on them."

"Jerry, the guy wouldn't have stood on the curb with a sign saying, *Hey I did it.* They didn't know who to look for. We do."

"Got it. West Potomac police did the investigation. CIA wasn't involved."

"Why?"

"No one knows. Probably because Fischer had been retired for a decade."

"Or because Emma Elliot already knew who did it."

"Huh." He paused. "Didn't think of that."

"Jerry, get any videos the police have to Nadia, ASAP."

"Got it. Are you still in Tel Aviv?"

"For the moment. We may take a trip to Cyprus tomorrow. Think the president would let you off your leash for a day?"

"Who's going to be there?"

"Both cousins."

"Hmm. Let me ask him. Send me the details about where and when. I can be very persuasive sometimes."

RAF Akrotiri – Cyprus

"Gentlemen, the president was adamant that Emma Elliot not be made aware of this meeting." Jerry Griggs smiled as he sat at the conference table.

Both Chapman and Ben-David nodded.

Wolfe and Nadia entered the room. While Nadia hooked up a laptop to a computer projector, Wolfe said, "I think all of you will find this of interest." He turned to his wife. "Ready?"

"Yes."

An image from the projector appeared on a blank wall at the end of the room. Nadia said, "This is from a Ring camera across the street from William Fischer's house." A Ford Escape sat parked in front of the house. Five seconds later, a man got out. The camera lost track of him as he disappeared out of the viewing angle. She continued. "Nothing suspicious here, right? A man parks his car and gets out."

Chapman asked, "Was that Jazani?"

She smiled and touched the mouse. A new video played. "Note the SUV is the same, but it's parked a few doors down from Fischer's. Only on this image, we get a clear view of the license plate." She stopped the video. "A friend of mine traced the vehicle to an Avis rental kiosk at Ronald Reagan International."

Ben-David asked, "Who rented the SUV, Nadia?"

The image of a South Carolina driver's license appeared on the screen. "Gentlemen, meet Charles Devon, the US version of Armin Jazani. Facial recognition confirms it's him."

Chapman stood and walked closer to the image being projected on the wall. "So, we can place this man at two locations, each associated with the death of an intelligence officer?"

Wolfe answered, "Yes."

Turning his attention to Wolfe, Chapman smiled. "Any idea of where this man is now, Michael?"

Crossing his arms, the retired CIA operative said, "No. We also need to establish if there is a connection between Jazani and Emma Elliot."

Griggs asked, "Senator Hendricks?"

"Very good, Jerry. We know that Jazani used the small town of Karbach, Germany to create his legend as Hershel Katz. Does Hendricks have connections to this town? We don't know yet."

"It would appear improper for the White House to do a probe into the good senator." Griggs looked at Chapman and then Ben-David. "Would either one of you two gentlemen have a suggestion?"

The director of the Mossad pulled out his cell phone, stood, and walked out of the room.

———

Thirty minutes later, Ben-David entered the conference room and returned to his seat. "What did I miss?"

Wolfe said, "Not much, Chapman's been on the phone, as has Jerry. What'd you find out, Uri?"

"We had some preliminary data on Hendricks. None of it good for Israel. So, Unit 8200 decided to dig a little deeper into the senator's background."

Chapman ended his call and said, "We know very little about him. Since he's always been friendly to the UK, we didn't waste resources finding out more. What'd you discover, Uri?"

"What we know so far is Hendricks came from the Germantown section of Philadelphia. His parents immigrated from Berlin in 1954. In 1958, he became the family's first child born in the States. He had an older brother who died in 2010. Both of his parents are deceased as well.

"His voting record in the Senate is anti-Israel for the most part. He doesn't verbally condemn Israel, but he doesn't go out of his way to support it."

Wolfe drummed his fingers on the table. "My bet is you'll find Emma Elliot making an appearance in his background somewhere as well."

Ben-David said, "Why, Michael?"

"A hunch. Hendricks persuaded President Griffin to appoint her as director of the CIA. There has to be a reason for him doing so. All we have to do is determine what that reason was."

Chapter Fourteen

WASHINGTON, DC

Senator Calvin Hendricks settled into his seat aboard the Senate subway for the two-minute ride from the Capitol to his office in the Dirksen Building. His mind was not on the trip but rather a text message received on his cell phone. *Return to office ASAP.*

As the chairman of the Senate Intelligence (Select) committee, he knew who sent the message.

As he walked into the reception area of his office suite, he said to his assistant, "Hold my calls, please, Tammy."

"Yes, Senator."

Once seated behind his desk, he responded to the message on his desk phone. The call was answered on the second ring.

"It took you long enough."

"Cut the theatrics, Emma. What's so important?"

"My assistant Samantha Edgar has vanished."

"Define vanished."

"She supposedly took some personal time for a family emergency but hasn't communicated with me for five days.

One of our agents paid a visit to her apartment. It's empty, except for the furniture. Her clothes, laptop, and cell phone are missing. Plus, she also checked Elliot's bank account. It was closed."

"When did this occur?"

"The day after her call to the HR department."

"Did you have your agent trace her cell phone?"

"I'm not stupid, Calvin. Yes. She told me the last time the phone accessed the cellular network was in Concourse A at BWI International Airport."

"Then she flew somewhere. Have your tech people check passenger lists."

"Don't you think I would have done that? There's no record of her flying anywhere."

"Emma, she worked for your agency. She'll have an alternate set of credentials to use."

Silence returned to the phone call. Hendricks waited for her reply. When it did not come immediately, he said, "Or did you forget that, Emma?"

"I'll have them check."

"In other words, you didn't think of it, did you?" When the new director didn't reply, he knew the answer. "What does she know?"

"She's been acting strange since Fischer died."

"Have you checked her relationship with the man?"

"Yes. Stop treating me like child."

"Then stop acting like one."

"How dare you—"

"Shut up, Emma. You're where you are because of me. I can also get you removed from your position. You need to stop whining and fulfill our agreement. Find her." He slammed the phone down, breaking the connection.

He glared at the phone and muttered, "Having her appointed CIA director might have been a mistake."

Somewhere in the Northwest United States

Five hundred miles northwest of Boise lies the port city of Tacoma, Washington. Samantha Edgar, now driving northwest on I-82, would arrive there by early evening. She had booked passage on a cargo ship scheduled to leave the port two days hence. Her destination, Australia.

She thought back on one of her last conversations with William Fischer before his death. A momentary pang of guilt struck her.

"How much do I owe you for these IDs, Will?"

Fischer smiled. "Because you're a friend, they're on the house. But I need you to do me a favor."

"Sure."

"Keep an eye on Emma Elliot. She's not a good choice for director."

Taking a deep breath, Samantha said, "I know. She seems to be way in over her head."

"She's more than that, she's dangerous."

"I know. That's why I asked you for these."

He gave her a reassuring smile. "Thinking of skipping town?"

"Not yet. But working for her makes me nervous. She's compiling a list of names for some reason."

Fischer's thick eyebrows shot up. "What kind of names?"

"I only got a glance at it. I didn't recognize anyone, except one. Joseph Kincaid."

"Can you get me a copy of the list?"

"Not sure. I can try."

"Do you know anything about steganography?"

"Yes, hiding messages so that the information is not visible."

"Very good, Samantha. It works best with digital photographs. You can hide the information within the digital code of the picture."

"I remember learning how to do that during my time at The Farm."

Fischer put a hand on her shoulder. "We've been friends for a long time, Sam. Be careful around Elliot. She's dangerous and not good for the agency."

"I'm beginning to understand your warning."

"Get me the list. Maybe I can determine what it's for."

She kissed him on the cheek. "I'll get you a copy as soon as I can."

———

It would be three months before she saw him again and then for only a few moments at the Italian restaurant to give him the flash drive. A tear slid down her cheek. She wiped it away with the palm of her hand and tried to focus on the road ahead as her eyes teared.

The following day, the Uber driver stopped at the port authority building to drop her off. She stared at the building and then turned her attention toward the busy port.

She said to the driver, "Have you ever wanted to do something, but something in the back of your mind tells you it's a bad idea?"

"Every day, lady, every day."

"The more I think about this trip, the more I realize it's probably a mistake. I'm basically running away."

The driver turned to the blonde woman in his back seat. "Bad boyfriend?"

She turned toward the driver. "A bad boyfriend I could handle. I'm talking about a bad career choice."

"Yeah, I've made a few of those. But none I wanted to leave the country over."

She turned her attention to the driver. "What kind of career mistakes?"

He shrugged. "Let's just say I got in over my head."

Samantha stared at the back of the man's head and then out over the water of the port. "Can you take me back to my hotel?"

"Sure." As he accelerated away from the dock, he said, "Change your mind?"

"Kind of. When you said you've never been scared enough to leave the country, it made me realize I'm running from something I can control. Thank you." She returned her gaze to the port and beyond. "I was running because I got scared."

"I've never been that scared."

"No, most people don't experience that kind of fear." She faced the front of the vehicle and said, "Thank you for talking to me. I realize my situation isn't that dire. I can handle it."

Checking his rearview mirror, the driver smiled. "Glad I could help."

"Trust me, you did."

Tacoma, WA

Samantha Edgar gazed at her image in the mirror. Her long blonde hair, now shorter and a pleasant shade of dark auburn, made her appear ten years younger. She sported a pair of blocky black glasses, and her normally blue eyes were now hazel, thanks to tinted contacts.

Picking up the prepaid Tracfone, she punched in a number.

The call was answered with a cautious, "Hello."

"Carla, it's Sam."

"Where the hell've you been, girl? You've got Emma Elliot shitting her pants trying to find you."

"Good luck with that."

"I hope you're not in the DC area. Because if you are, run far and run fast."

"I'm not anywhere near DC. That's why I called."

"Good. What's up?"

"Are you still in Miami?"

"Oh, hell, no. I'm working for Griggs."

"You left the CIA?"

"Yeah. No tears were shed either."

"I need to talk to you and Jerry. Can you arrange it?"

"Sure. When?"

"In a day or so. I need to change locations. I'll set up a personal Zoom account and will send a link. Plan on Friday."

"Got it."

"And, Carla?"

"Yeah."

"I finally figured out who's calling the shots, and it's not Emma Elliot. It's someone else."

"Who, Sam?"

"I'll tell you on Friday. I just figured it out a day ago."

Chapter Fifteen

TEL AVIV

Wolfe checked the caller ID, calculated the time difference in his head, and pressed the accept icon. "Kind of early for you isn't it, Jerry?"

"A lot going on here, Michael. When are you returning to the States?"

"Depends. Why do you ask?"

"Carla's been in touch with Samantha Edgar. She's left DC and wants to talk to her and me on a video chat. She indicates she knows who's behind the list."

"When's the call?"

"Two days, Friday."

The retired sniper did not reply immediately. Finally, he said, "I have a few things to settle here. We'll return in time for the call. Where's the meeting going to be?"

"We haven't decided. Carla doesn't want us anywhere near DC when we make the connection."

"Want to do it at my place in Missouri?"

There was silence on the phone for a few moments. "That's a hell of an idea, Michael."

"Get a message to her and let her know we'll supply the link for the meeting. Nadia knows how to mask our location. Something she learned from Alexia Gibbs. Plus, we have access to a more secure video chat application than Zoom."

"Not sure how we will get ahold of her. She called us."

"We'll work it out, Jerry. Just be at our place early on Friday."

"Got it."

The call ended and Wolfe turned to his wife. "I need to be back at our place by Friday. You want to stay here?"

She shook her head. "No, I've enjoyed the visit, but I miss our home. What's going on?"

"Carla heard from Samantha Edgar. Apparently, she knows something about the list."

"I'll call Uri and get us a ride." She paused. "What about Ben?"

"I'm not leaving him here, if that's what you're asking?"

Shaking her head rapidly, she said, "No, Michael, I'm not either. But I also don't want to put him in harm's way."

"With all the precautions we've built into the place, he's safer there than anywhere."

"Yes, I know. I just thought we'd put all of this cloak-and-dagger nonsense behind us."

With a grim smile, he said, "It does seem to follow us around."

Washington, DC

Calvin Hendricks entered his private, unlisted office inside the Capitol building. Identified with only a number, his offered extra square footage compared to those assigned senators with less seniority. Almost as soon as he shut the door, a knock sounded. He opened the door and allowed two individuals to enter.

"Thank you for coming, gentlemen. We may have a problem."

Senators Taylor Finley and Jayden Berry moved into the room as Hendricks locked the door.

Finley spoke first. "What kind of problem, Calvin?"

"Emma Elliot."

Berry settled into one of the leather wingback chairs. "Let me guess. She's not cooperating."

"No, she seems to have her own agenda. And this particular agenda may be an obstacle to ours."

"Why do you say that?"

"Her obsession with Joseph Kincaid is blurring her vision of the real task at hand."

Sitting in an identical leather wingback chair, Finley placed his elbows on the arms and made a steeple with his hands. "Then we get rid of her. She was always a place-holder at best, Calvin."

Sitting on one corner of his desk, Hendricks pursed his lips. "I agree with you, Taylor. But the problem is Griffin will probably not listen to us if we suggest someone else. My sources tell me he is not pleased with her performance and questions why we recommended her."

"Do we accelerate our plans against Griffin?"

"No, not yet." Hendricks stood and sat behind the small desk. "He's still way too popular. We need his poll numbers to plummet before we move against him."

"Is the asset still in place, Calvin?"

"Yes, Taylor, he is. But we cannot rely on him too often. We need to keep suspicion away from him for now."

The room remained quiet for a prolonged period of

time. Finley spoke first. "I understand Elliot's assistant disappeared."

Hendricks raised an eyebrow. "Where did you learn this?"

"A committee memo circulating this morning. I'm surprised you didn't see it, Calvin."

"I haven't been in my main office today. But I knew about her absence."

"Why didn't you tell us?"

"I thought Elliot was being paranoid and Edgar would return. She supposedly took time off for a family emergency."

"Well, I've heard Elliot's entire staff's been mobilized to find Edgar. No one knows where she is."

Berry smiled. "My chief-of-staff knows someone on Elliot's staff. I'll ask him to confirm."

"Excellent. Gentlemen, let's adjourn until we know more about Edgar's status. This might work in our favor with Griffin's polling numbers."

As Finley stood, he said, "How's that?"

"If we spin it correctly with our contacts in the media, we can make it appear Griffin doesn't have a good grip on the nation's security."

———

White House

"Why do you need to travel to Missouri, Jerry?"

"It has to do with the list, Mr. President."

"Are you consulting with Joseph?"

"No, sir. Michael Wolfe."

"I see." The president stood and walked over to the coffee service. "What's the issue?"

"Emma Elliot's assistant has gone missing. We think because she knows too much."

Griffin stared at his national security advisor. "Is Elliot responsible for her disappearance?"

"No, sir. Her assistant is fine. But she's gone into hiding. I'm going to Missouri to meet with her. She claims to know who is behind the list and its significance."

The president put the now-full coffee cup down and closed his eyes. "How many individuals on the list are dead, Jerry?"

"Twelve."

"How many Americans?"

"Half."

"Six Americans are dead because of this list?"

"Well, sir, we aren't sure it's because of the list or not. That's why I need to travel to Missouri. If Samantha Edgar can shed light on the matter, it makes sense to go."

POTUS lifted the coffee cup to his lips and sipped. He kept his gaze on Griggs. "How long will you be gone?"

"Kind of depends on what we learn."

With a raised eyebrow, Griffin said, "Very well. Tell Bob to make sure the Gulfstream is ready for you in the morning."

Griggs walked to the door. Just before he opened it, the president said, "Jerry."

Turning, he said, "Yes, sir."

"Tell Michael hello for me."

"I will, sir."

Tacoma, WA

Checking out of the fifth hotel in as many days, Samantha Edgar drove her rental car to the next one. This would be the location where she would conduct the video chat with Jerry Griggs and Carla Webb.

Now in the last room she would occupy in Tacoma, she tested the Wi-Fi and found it adequate for her needs during the next day's meeting. She also found a new email in the temporary Gmail account she'd set up several days prior. It was from Carla.

Change of plans. Do not use Zoom link you provided. We will send a link for a different application ten minutes before the meeting. You will need to sign in to a VPN of your choice prior to connecting with the new link. C. rugby

Relief swept over her. The word following Carla's initial was a secret between them. Both were closet rugby fans.

Chapter Sixteen

SOUTHWEST MISSOURI

The region known as the Ozarks extends from the Boston Mountains in Arkansas to the Missouri River in the north and the Mississippi River to the east. The Cherokee Trail of Tears passed through this region in the mid-nineteenth century. The area is known for its rolling hills, abundant rivers and lakes, dense forests, and laid-back lifestyles.

Within this region, southwest of a town called Ozark is a large plot of land featuring a thousand-yard asphalt runway for a totally refurbished and modernized 1979 Beechcraft B55 Baron. It also possesses a hangar and a contemporary home on the northern border of the property. Trees occupy the remaining acreage.

Michael Wolfe's B55 Baron touched down on the southern edge of the runway, and he taxied the plane to the hangar. He pressed a button on a device, and the door to the airplane's shelter slid open.

Nadia, in the passenger seat, turned and nudged the sleeping boy. "Wake up, Ben, we're home."

The four-year-old batted his eyes and sat up. He looked out the window and smiled. "Yeah, we're home."

Wolfe busied himself with shutting down the aircraft as Nadia and their son exited the cabin. During this time, Wolfe's cell phone buzzed. He checked the caller ID and accepted the call.

"We're back, Jerry. Just landed." Wolfe heard the sound of jet engines in the background. "I take it you guys are still airborne."

"Yeah, we'll be wheels down in two hours, according to our pilot."

"Okay, let me know when you're heading this way."

"Got it."

The call ended and Wolfe started to unload luggage from the storage compartment. On his way into the house, Nadia met him. "I hope Jerry and Carla are not going to be here anytime soon. We have *nothing* in the house. Not even coffee."

With a chuckle, he said, "Want me to go?"

"Nah, I'll take care of it. But I can be back sooner if you keep a watch over Ben."

"Consider it done."

She sighed. "How did we get so domesticated, Michael?"

He gave her a hug. "I guess we grew up along the way."

"Maybe. I'll be back in as soon as I can."

The Next Day

Alexia Gibbs and Nadia Wolfe were both born in Europe. Alexia in Spain and Nadia in France. Both married American men and now lived in the US. Their friendship began because of their shared background but grew over the years because both were intelligent and compassionate individuals. Each followed a different path to the United States, and each felt a strong kinship to the other.

By Western European standards, Alexia's five-foot-nine stature made her taller than the average female. Her path to the US was different than Nadia's. Born to parents in Spain who were staunch supporters of Catalonia, she grew up with a chip on her shoulder toward authority. Graduating from the University of Barcelona with an IT background, she moved to Paris to work for an ISP provider as a security analyst. She soon discovered the lucrative vocation of hacking.

During this period, she had called the Latin Quarter of Paris home. She made good money with her job, but even more with her hobby. However, greed got to her one night, drawing the unwanted attention of the French General Directorate for Internal Security, the DGSI. After a hastily arranged midnight flight out of Charles de Gaulle International Airport, she ended up in Mexico City.

There she hid from the authorities, earning a meager living with her computer skills and maintaining a pencil-thin physique. When she did venture out in public, she wore her tousled black hair short and dressed in loose-fitting clothes to hide her gender. As a naturally pretty woman, she utilized black Buddy Holly-style glasses and a Chicago Cubs ball cap.

Ten years into her exile, she made another mistake. She unknowingly became involved with a group of Russians. This incident eventually threatened her life. Weeks later, in a daring daylight raid, she was spirited away from under the watchful eyes of her Russian nemesis by a group of FBI agents and a computer hacker she only knew by his online name, Zardoz.

Now, five years after the incident, she had married one of her rescuers and wore her black hair long and flowing. Her clothing emphasized her slender athletic body, which she maintained by swimming in the lake near their home with her husband on a daily basis. She spent her spare time doting over him, their son, and their new house. As an IT professional, she helped guide the company she co-owned into one of the top computer security companies in the world.

Alexia hugged Nadia when she arrived at the rural Missouri home early on Friday morning. "It is so good to see you, Nadia. How was Israel?"

Her friend smiled. "Hot and dry. But the smell of rosemary was in the air, and I do love that about the country."

"I must go there sometime."

"What about going home to Spain? I never hear you talking about going there."

Alexia gave her friend a shrug. "Because, I have no desire to go back. My parents are gone, and there is absolutely no one there I care to visit. Besides, I love Jimmy's and my home on Stockton Lake. I'm happy there." She sighed. "I don't remember ever being happy in Spain or France."

"I have no fond memories of France either."

Alexia asked, "Where will the video call take place?"

"Michael suggested the conference room above the hangar. He has his satellite internet receiver there."

"Good. After I set up the computer, there will be no way anyone can trace the call back to here." She paused. "Where is Carla Webb?"

"She and Jerry will be here around nine. Why?"

"No reason. Jimmy told me she's an interesting person."

"She is." Nadia paused. "You and I will be out of camera range. Samantha is very paranoid about being found."

"Don't worry. JR and I discussed the details yesterday. We have a few tricks up our sleeves. If anyone is trying to find her, they will think she's on a different continent."

Tacoma, WA

Samantha Edgar took a deep breath and pressed the left button on her mouse. The new program installed several minutes ago immediately came to life with a split-screen image. The image of herself appeared on the right and a blank screen on the left. It flashed once, and she saw Jerry Griggs, Carla Webb, and an individual she did not recognize.

Jerry spoke first. "Hi, Sam. How you holding up?"

"I'm fine, Jerry. Hello, Carla."

Carla smiled and said, "This is Michael Wolfe. He's a friend of ours."

"I've heard the name. Joseph always spoke highly of you. It is nice to finally meet you, Michael."

Wolfe nodded at the camera. "It's nice to meet you as well, Samantha. I wish the circumstances were better." He turned to his right and back at the screen. "I just checked. Your computer's location indicates you are in a coffee shop in Cape Town, South Africa."

"Oh, my."

"Don't worry, Samantha. That's how it was planned."

Griggs spoke next. "Sam, you did a nice job on changing your appearance."

She shrugged.

Wolfe said, "I need to remind everyone that we need to keep this short."

With a nod, Griggs continued. "What can you tell us about Emma Elliot?"

"If she is allowed to stay as director of the CIA, she will make it a weak and ineffective agency. There are more resignations coming, Jerry. You have to tell the president he has to fire her."

Carla said, "You mentioned there was someone pulling her strings."

"Yes, I figured it out the other day. Think back on who recommended her."

Grigg's eyebrows rose. "Senator Hendricks?"

"Yes, and his two toadies: Taylor Finley and Jayden Berry."

Wolfe asked, "For what purpose?"

"I don't know. But Elliot is in way over her head. All she can think about is getting even with Joseph Kincaid."

Griggs frowned. "What does Elliot have against Joseph?"

"Once again, I don't know, but it's causing her to be on the verge of having a psychotic episode. The night before I left, she went into a rage about him. Her ranting made zero sense. She doesn't know I worked with him at one time. I want to keep it that way. That's why I left. She scares me, Jerry."

"Do you want us to protect you?"

Samantha shook her head. "No. I already have my car packed. All I have to do is shut off the laptop and I'm out of here. I'm leaving the area right after we finish. I have a pay-as-you-go phone and plan to change it at random intervals."

Carla nodded. "That's smart. Do you need money, Sam?"

"No, Carla, I don't. I'm in good shape right now. I've got a couple of alternate IDs and credit cards to go with them."

"That can't last forever."

"I know, but I'm good right now."

Wolfe glanced at the two women out of camera range. Alexia's attention was on a laptop while his wife watched her every move. Alexia suddenly fixed her attention on Wolfe. With a surprised expression, she made a frantic slashing motion across her throat.

The retired sniper said, "Shut your computer down, now, Sam."

The screen went blank.

Griggs turned to Alexia. "What happened?"

Alexia pursed her lips. "I'm not sure. All of a sudden, someone was only two ISPs away from closing in on her location. How, I don't know."

"Do they know she's in the United States?"

Still concentrating on her computer, she said, "I don't know how they got so close. They shouldn't have been able to."

Standing, Wolfe asked, "Who are they?"

"Good question. Let me check something." She typed on her laptop.

Wolfe turned to Griggs and Carla. "Do you have a way to contact her?"

They both said in unison, "No."

"Damn." He stared at the screen where the video meeting had occurred. "I hope she got the hell out of there."

Chapter Seventeen

SOMEWHERE IN WASHINGTON STATE

When the tall man identified as Michael Wolfe told her to shut the laptop down, she did. Samantha knew the man by reputation. His word was good enough for her. She closed the lid, picked up the machine, and hurried to her hotel room door. She listened for a moment and then opened it.

She saw no one in the hall outside her ground floor room. A door, four rooms away, led to the rear parking lot. With her belongings already in the car, all she needed to do was exit the hotel and drive away. Far away.

Fifteen minutes later, she pulled into the parking lot of a crowded Costco and sat quietly in her car. After taking several calming breaths, she opened the back of the laptop and removed the battery. Then, using her cell phone, she sent a text message to Carla to let her know she was okay, for the moment. Reassessing what had happened would come later. Right now, it was time to leave Tacoma. Turning south would lead her to California, while north meant Canada.

Thinking back to her days at The Farm, she surveyed

her surroundings and made note of the cars near her. She then moved the floor shift to reverse and eased out of the parking lot.

California offered crowds and isolated spots in the mountains. South, it would be.

Washington, DC

Not far from the hustle and bustle of the United States Capitol building is a spot on the Washington Channel off the Potomac River. Luxury yachts and recreational boats are docked in their personal slips next to upscale hotels and restaurants.

On one of the larger and more expensive yachts in the wharf sat a group of men, each enjoying a glass of single malt eighteen-year-old Glenlivet scotch. Calvin Hendricks contemplated the Washington Monument rising above the skyline to his north.

After taking a sip of his drink, the senator said, "Gentlemen, we may have a slight problem."

Finley raised an eyebrow. "What type of problem, Calvin?"

"Elliot's assistant, Samantha Edgar, has disappeared. Rumors as to why are varied. I believe she knows something she should not. She's an intelligent woman, much more so than Elliot. There is a chance she stumbled across information that allowed her to realize the true purpose of the list. Even if she hasn't figured it out, we cannot, and I will repeat myself, cannot, allow her to speak to the press or any congressional committee." He turned to the fourth individual sitting on the deck of the yacht. "Morgan, what can your agency do to help us?"

Major General Morgan Walker, Director of Signal Intelligence (SIGINT) division at the NSA, smiled and raised his glass of scotch. "Three steps ahead of you, Senator."

"Good."

"We believe her to be in the northwestern part of the States: Washington, Oregon, Idaho, or western Montana. We traced her computer to that area earlier today. Someone is helping her though. She was in the middle of an encrypted video chat when she suddenly shut her computer off and pulled the battery. Whoever they may be, they are very good."

Senator Berry narrowed his eyes and said, "Better than the NSA?"

"In some respects, yes. My team told me their location kept changing every fifteen seconds or so. One of my senior tech guys called them ghosts."

"Hmm…" Hendricks stared off toward the north. "Maybe we need to move our timeline up."

Morgan barely shook his head. "My suggestion is we don't. Doing so could cause us to be exposed. And, gentlemen, that is not something I wish to happen."

"None of us want that either, General. However, the longer we wait could cause the entire plan to fall apart."

"I disagree, Senator. In my experience, caution is always better than haste."

"Your objections are noted, General. If there are no other objections to moving our timetable up…"

None came. Hendricks looked at his two fellow senators. Both nodded.

"Very well. Gentlemen"—he raised his glass— "to the start of a new day in this republic."

They all clicked their glasses together.

———————

Alexia spent the rest of the day either on the phone with her partner, JR, or doing analysis on her laptop. The conference room above the hangar offered the group a total of fifteen hundred square feet. Wolfe kept his desk in one corner, with the conference table taking up the middle. Carla and Jerry utilized the time to work the phones to see if any of their contacts had additional knowledge of the list. No one did.

Wolfe motioned for Nadia to follow him to the lower level. When they got to the bottom of the stairs, he said, "I know everyone is asking how they found her. Did anyone ask if she was using an old computer? Or did she buy a new one?"

Nadia tilted her head. "I don't think anyone bothered to ask her."

"I didn't think so. If it is her personal computer, there's a strong possibility someone compromised it before she left DC."

"Michael, I don't think anyone even thought of that. Why don't you bring it up to Alexia?"

"In time. Right now, we need to figure out who back-tracked her connection." He glanced up the stairs for a moment. "And did they get close to locating us?"

"From what she saw, they were keyed in on Sam's location."

He put his hands on his hips and kept his gaze up the

staircase. "Whoever is trying to find her will realize someone is helping her."

She folded her arms. "What are you saying, Michael?"

"I'm not saying it did, but our offering to help Samantha may have exposed our location."

"Oops."

"Yeah, oops."

Griggs appeared at the top of the staircase. "Michael, you and Nadia need to get up here, now."

Wolfe took the steps two at a time with his wife hot on his heels. When they arrived in the conference room, Alexia was white as a sheet.

"Michael, I think I screwed up."

"What happened?"

She pointed at her laptop. "I was so intent on making sure Sam's location was hidden, I totally took my eye off of yours."

Taking a deep breath, the retired sniper asked, "Who found us?"

"The same organization that was searching for Samantha. The NSA."

Ian McGill, a Scotsman and former operative with the United Kingdom's elite Special Air Service shook Wolfe's hand. "Haven't seen ya for a while. How the hell are ya, laddie?"

"Fine. I take it you suffered no ill effects during our excursion across the pond?"

"None whatsoever.

"Where can we talk?"

"What's wrong, Michael? I haven't seen your serious side since our days trying to get out of Iran."

Wolfe gave his friend a grim smile. "I'm afraid I need to impose on your good nature and your expertise again, my friend."

Ian McGill's stint with the SAS helped him rise to the rank of sergeant major. His twenty-five years serving his country saw him in every hotspot the members of Parliament committed the United Kingdom to during those years. Now in his late forties and married to a local Missouri gal named Lori, he appeared ten years younger. He was also careful who knew where he lived. Michael Wolfe was one of the few individuals who did.

The Scotsman led his friend through the expansive house to the deck off the west side of the structure. "Will this work?"

"Yes, thanks, Ian."

"So, what kind of trouble have ya gotten yourself into this time?"

"Doing a favor for Joseph."

Raising one of his bushy eyebrows, McGill asked, "How can I help?"

"It's a long story."

"Ahh… Let me get us each a Guiness and then you can tell me your tale of woe."

After another Guiness for each, Wolfe finished his tale, and McGill stared up the hill in back of his home. The sun lay low on the horizon, and a cool breeze tousled the Scotsman's light-brown hair. He scratched his closely cropped beard and asked, "Where are you going to stash Nadia and the lad?"

"When it's time, they'll stay at Joseph's."

"Wise, my friend." He pondered his empty glass. "Lori should be home in a while. She'll want to know where her friend is."

"I know."

"What do you wish of me, Michael?"

The ex-CIA operative said, "My place is basically a fortress. No one can get on my land without me knowing about it. But I'm only one person. If multiple individuals invade from the west and south, I could be a bit outnumbered. I have various sniper hides on the upper level of the hangar. However, I can only man one at a time. Considering what I've seen from this group, so far, I think they'll send multiple intruders, late at night or early morning."

With a chuckle, McGill said, "I take it you don't expect them to ring the doorbell."

Wolfe gave his friend a grim smile. "No, I don't. William Fischer was taken by surprise inside his home. Something I still find hard to believe."

"Been a while since I played sniper, Michael. And I was never as good as you."

"It's like riding a bike, Ian. You don't forget."

"Aye, laddie. When do you want me there?"

Chapter Eighteen

WASHINGTON, DC

After returning to Washington, DC from the meeting in Missouri, Carla Webb made contact with several individuals she knew within the NSA bureaucracy. Officially, the mission of the agency was to monitor foreign signal intelligence or, in the vernacular of the agency, SIGINT. The one individual who agreed to meet with her demanded it be in Baltimore and nowhere near the DC area.

At 8:42 p.m., Carla sat in one of the many dark booths in an old dive bar in downtown Baltimore. Unlike similar bars around the DC area, this one served good beer. She nursed the glass as she waited for her contact to arrive. She was now eight minutes late.

When the time on her cell phone read 9:00 p.m., Carla stood to leave. At that same moment, the individual walked into the dimly lit establishment. The woman scanned the room, locked eyes with Carla, and slowly walked to the booth.

"Sorry I'm late, Carla."

"No problem, Misty. Thanks for coming. Want a beer?"

The woman shook her head. "Can't stay long. What kind of information were you needing?"

"Any scuttlebutt about the NSA looking for a runaway member of the CIA?"

Her guest's eyes grew round. "No one is supposed to know. How did you hear about it?"

The diminutive ex-CIA agent shrugged. "Rumors, mostly. My new boss asked me to check them out."

Misty stiffened and narrowed her eyes. "What new boss?"

"No one you would know."

The woman stared at Carla for a few moments. "You're not with the CIA anymore, are you?"

"Correct. I'm not."

Misty's ramrod-straight posture relaxed a bit. "I'd feel better if I knew who you are working for."

"Let's just say he works directly for the top guy in one of the branches of government."

"The president?"

"You said it. I didn't."

The woman gave Carla a frown. "Is that supposed to make me relax?"

"Why are you being so skittish, Misty? We've known each other a long time."

"I'll take that beer, after all."

When the server placed it in front of Carla's guest, Misty took a long pull and set the glass down. "Something weird is going on in the SIGINT section."

"Weird how?"

"Normally, everyone is easygoing. They have a select group of analysts working on an isolated project. All of them look scared and won't talk to anyone except their own group. It's very unusual."

Carla sipped her beer but did not respond. She kept her eyes on the woman across from her.

"I understand our work is confidential but, most of the time, we all kid around. Not these people. They barely say hello in the hallways. The rumor is they're searching for a CIA double-agent operating inside the United States. Someone who was high up in the organization, and that aspect of it is making them nervous."

"That's what my boss heard but couldn't get a straight answer from anyone."

Misty took another gulp of her beer. "The rumor is this individual could do serious harm to the security of our country, unless they're stopped."

"We didn't hear that part. What kind of damage?"

"No one is speculating."

"Any names being thrown around?"

"The only one I've heard is Sam. I bet there are more than a few Sams at the CIA."

With a nod, Carla said, "Yeah, I bet there are."

Fifteen minutes later, Carla returned to her car and sat behind the wheel. She debated whether to call Jerry or wait to talk to him in person. Griggs solved the problem for her. Her cell phone chirped.

"I was just about to call you, Jerry."

"What'd you learn?"

"Our neighbor has a whole bunch of folks searching for someone named Sam."

"Shit."

"At least we know who they're looking for."

"Carla, did Sam give you any hint of how we can get in touch?"

"I think she designed it that way. She'll have to call us."

"Okay, get some rest. We'll talk in the morning."

Langley, VA

Bob North, the deputy director of the CIA finished giving the DCIA his report and folded his hands in front of him on the conference table. The explosive response came, exactly as he expected.

Emma Elliot pounded her fist on the mahogany surface in front of her. "What the hell is going on around here? I am so tired of hearing excuses of why you can't find Samantha Edgar. She's one person. How hard can it be to find her?"

Executive Director Isabelle Brooks took a deep breath and frowned. "Emma, the CIA has other priorities besides trying to find one person. Besides, our operational charter forbids us from operating inside the US. Hand it over to the FBI. Let them find her."

"To hell with our charter." She pointed her index finger at Bob North. "There is nothing of higher importance than finding Edgar. Is that clear?"

North glared at her. "I—"

"Careful with your response, Deputy Director. This is an internal matter. We will handle it ourselves."

North closed his eyes, took a deep breath, and pinched the bridge of his nose. After blowing out the breath, he opened his eyes and glared at the director. "Why are you obsessed with finding Edgar?"

The head of the CIA stood, leaned forward, and placed her palms flat on the table. "Do I need to remind you two who the director of this organization is?"

North stood as well and glared at Elliot. "You've lost half of the senior staff, and you're on the verge of losing others. Get your priorities straight, Director. Or my next conversation will be with the director of national intelligence."

Elliot breathed hard and stared at the deputy director. "How dare you question my authority."

"Your authority comes from the president of the United States. From the reports I've been given, he is not exactly pleased with your performance so far."

The DCIA pursed her lips, stood straight, and screamed, "Consider yourself on report, Mr. North. Meeting adjourned." She turned and flung the door open. It banged against the wall leaving an indentation of the knob in the drywall.

North looked over at Brooks. "Did you get that recorded?"

"Yes."

"Get it to whoever you need to. The only way we're going to be rid of this woman is to go over her head."

Brooks stood and followed the DDCI out and returned to her office. Once inside, she shut the door and leaned against it. Staring at the ceiling, she shook her head and mumbled, "I see why you left, Samantha."

Taking several calming breaths, she could feel her pulse pounding. Standing still, she placed two fingers on her carotid artery and waited. Finally, her pulse rate slowed and she went to her desk. From the top right-hand drawer, she removed her personal cell phone. No calls.

She then took her CIA issued cell phone and transferred the recording of Elliot's rant to a flash drive. This she placed in her laptop bag. Then the recording on her cell phone was deleted. With all of this accomplished, she picked up her desk phone and dialed a number she knew at the White House.

———

The president's national security advisor checked the caller ID. He picked up the phone. "Griggs."

"Jerry, it's Isabelle Brooks."

"Well, hello, Izzy. What can I do for you?"

"Your boss still pissed at Emma Elliot?"

"You might say that, why?"

"I might have something for you. Are you free?"

"I'm not free, but I do come cheap. What's going on?"

"Remember the park bench where we used to meet near the Dupont Circle North Metro Station?"

"Yeah. The one where all the homeless people sleep."

"That's the one. How soon can you be there?"

Griggs glanced at his watch. "Fifteen minutes."

"I'll be waiting."

The call ended and the president's national security advisor stood. He walked out of his office and said to his assistant, "Got an errand to run. If the boss asks, tell him I'll be back in an hour."

"Okay, Jerry."

———

Griggs beat the executive director of the CIA to the park bench by five minutes. He stared at his phone, just like everyone on the street in Washington, pretending to read. His peripheral vison picked up the woman as she approached his location. Sitting on the opposite side of the bench, she studied her phone as well.

Without looking at her, he said, "It's been a while since we met here."

"I know. I miss those days. No responsibilities."

"What have you got?"

She put a folded copy of *The Washington Post* on the bench between them. "Check the sports section. There is something your boss will be anxious to hear."

"Like?"

"Emma Elliot, proclaiming she doesn't give a damn about the charter preventing us from operating in the US. She's using CIA personnel inside the US to search for Samantha Edgar. In fact, she told Bob North there is no higher priority than finding Samantha."

"Whoa, that is big news." He turned toward her. "Where is Samantha?"

"Good question. NSA thinks she's somewhere in the northwestern states. They missed her by ten minutes at a hotel in Tacoma. She's since disappeared again."

"How are they tracking her?"

"Elliot's paranoid. She had every member of her personal staff's laptops compromised. They can be tracked, regardless of any precautions they take."

"You're kidding me?"

"Nope. Sucks for Samantha. They'll catch up to her eventually, if the president doesn't fire the woman first."

"Izzy, why does Elliot have her hair on fire about Samantha?"

"She's claiming the woman is a traitor. Sold the Chinese some nonspecific national secret she won't reveal. It's all BS, Jerry. Samantha knows something about Elliot she doesn't want made public. That's all we can figure out."

A Cloak of Deceit

"Okay, I'll get this to the boss."

135

Chapter Nineteen

SOUTHWEST MISSOURI

The original twenty-five-acre plot Wolfe owned in Christian County resembled a trapezoid more than a rectangle. The eastern side, due to the presence of an asphalt runway, measured twice the length of the western border. Since the original purchase, the retired Marine sniper added two parcels of land to his real estate property tax statement. The exact acreage now totaled sixty-two.

Officially, the land belonged to an LLC registered with the Missouri Secretary of State's office. Since Wolfe and Nadia were the LLC, they owned the property. But with the help of a certain computer genius, anyone doing an in-depth search for the associates of this particular LLC would never discover who actually owned the property.

Plus, surveillance video from an army of commercial grade Go-Pro wildlife cameras provided the first line of defense against any intruder who might entertain the thought of sneaking up on the residence.

The second line of defense came from strategically placed trip wires around the property. With the abundance of wildlife in the area, these had to be serviced on occasion. Today was such an occasion.

Wolfe, dressed in hiking boots and camo hunting clothes from Bass Pro Shops, walked the northern border of his land. He knew where the cameras and trip wires were located. His mission on this day was to ensure the integrity of both systems.

As he turned toward the south on the western border of his land, he spotted the first indication someone had been exploring the periphery of his property. Clear indentations in the soil exposed boot prints outside the barbwire fence constructed to keep his neighbor's cattle off the western side of his property. Wolfe took pictures of the prints and followed them to the southern fence line. There, they disappeared.

After walking the periphery, he checked the various locations and repaired two trip wires set off by deer. He then changed batteries on three Go-Pro cameras showing low power. This would be his routine until further notice.

When he returned to the house, Nadia asked, "Any signs of intruders?"

"Not inside our property, but someone walked the western fence line and seemed way too interested in our side."

"That's interesting. How do you know?"

"Footprints would stop every twenty or so meters and point toward the fence." He retrieved a bottle of water out of the refrigerator and twisted off the cap. After drinking half of the contents, he said, "It might be time for you and Ben to stay at Joseph's place."

"Nonsense."

"I'm serious."

"So am I. Michael, I am not going to abandon you and our home. My place is here, by your side."

"What about Ben?"

"I have confidence in your ability to keep all of us safe."

He gave her a grim smile and took another long drink. "Make sure the safe room in the basement is stocked."

"Already have. I've even vacuumed the escape tunnel. Amazing how many spider webs I knocked down."

"That's a good sign. It means we haven't had to use it for a while."

She chuckled. "Ben ran back and forth in the tunnel, laughing and giggling, so many times I didn't have to make him take a nap. He laid down by himself."

Wolfe finished the bottle of water and slowly screwed the cap back on it. "Nadia."

"Oh, no. What'd you forget?"

"That we are parents and have an obligation to protect Ben. Protect him from all threats. We could have avoided this by my simply saying no."

"Michael, we made the decision together when Joseph asked for our help. Let's finish this and determine how we never have to get involved again."

---

2 a.m. the Next Day

Now on his fifth cup of coffee, Wolfe stared at the video monitor. Movement could be detected on one of the cameras in the southwestern quadrant of his property. The moonless sky, combined with the canopy of trees, blocked what little light came from the Milky Way ribbon overhead.

The low-light Go-Pro cameras picked up the movement, but distance did not allow discernable details.

He said, "Hey, Ian. I got something on one of the cameras."

The Scotsman stirred and grumbled. "Bloody hell." He swung his legs over the side of the cot and dry rubbed his face. "Whatta, ya got?"

Wolfe did not answer right away. A ghostly figure emerged from the gloom and looked directly at the camera. "Tall man, appears to be wearing NVGs and carrying an AR-15."

Fully alert, Ian McGill leaned over Wolfe's shoulder and studied the monitor. "Which camera?"

"Number three."

"Where's that?"

"Southwest corner, about fifty meters inside my property line."

McGill picked up a headset for their communication system. He adjusted the headband so the earphone fit comfortably and the microphone stayed close to his cheek. "I'm going to the south hide. Keep me posted on what the ghost does." Before he left, he retrieved his PM L96A1 sniper rifle fitted with a Sightmark 4K digital nightscope.

"Will do."

The hide McGill referred to was on the upper level of the hangar. Built by Wolfe over the course of the past two years, the hides provided an observation port for the surrounding terrain. A man could lie prone with a rifle and open a series of small windows. Those would allow a view of the tree lines to the south and west.

When he was in place, he said into his mic, "Where is he?"

"He moved to the east out of camera three's view. I'm watching camera four for movement."

"Keep me posted, so I can find the best window."

Silence filled his ear. After three minutes, McGill heard, "He's moving across four's field of view, still heading east."

"I'm moving to the center window."

"Good choice."

The two men did not communicate for ten minutes. The Scotsman surveyed the tree line with the scope. Nothing. He said into his mic, "I've got nothing so far."

"Not surprised. He hasn't moved for five minutes. Almost like…" Wolfe pressed the mouse, and all the camera views were displayed on the monitor. He could see headlights in the distance from the camera on the top of his house. At this time of night, there should be no traffic in this remote part of the county. "Got a bogey coming in from the north."

He reached for a switch and turned it on. This activated a light in the basement where Nadia and Ben would be staying.

His radio crackled. "What's wrong?"

"Vehicle on the road heading toward the house. Are you in the safe room?"

"Yes."

"Okay, keep your radio on."

Wolfe watched as the vehicle turned the corner and slowed before it drove past the house. He used the remote to turn the camera to follow. As soon as it traveled an additional sixty meters, it stopped and turned off the vehicle's headlights.

"Okay, everyone, we have a new player to the north. Ian, your guy should be visible to you."

"Got him. He just emerged from the woods. He's armed."

"Is he running?"

"No. Slow and deliberate."

Checking the rooftop camera, he saw a figure moving toward the house.

"Damn." He made a quick decision. "Nadia, you've got someone approaching. I'm not taking any chances. I'll head to the hide where he's visible."

"Ben and I are in the safe room."

"Stay close to the tunnel. Just in case."

Standing, Wolfe grabbed a Remmington 700 with a nightscope from his arsenal and moved to the north of the second floor where more hides were located.

Tracking the newcomer with the scope, he kept the crosshairs on the man's chest as the intruder circled the house. Just as the man climbed the stairs to the deck, a rifle shot rang out and then another.

The man, who was now on the deck, stopped, turned, and ran down the steps. He stopped briefly, which allowed Wolfe to target the individual's chest again. As he applied pressure to the trigger, the figure dashed to the north. The bullet missed him by a few feet and buried itself in the ground.

"Damn." Wolfe threw the Remmington's bolt to chamber another round but, by then, the figure was running hard toward the car. Targeting the man again, Wolfe gave him a good lead and squeezed the trigger. The bullet missed by a foot as the runner jinked to the left.

"Son of a bitch."

Before Wolfe could chamber another round, the figure disappeared into the tree line. Changing his aim point, he threw the bolt on the rifle again and fired three rounds into the vehicle parked on the road west of his house.

The third bullet hit the gas tank. An explosion and the resulting fireball lit up the early morning darkness.

Wolfe calmly said, "Report, Ian."

"One bogey down. I heard an explosion. What happened?"

"Vehicle disabled. We have one on foot."

Chapter Twenty

SOUTHWEST MISSOURI

Wolfe and McGill approached the downed assailant. Both wore night-vision goggles. Using caution, they approached the prone figure from two directions.

Maintaining his attention on the intruder, Wolfe said, "Keep your eye on the tree line. No telling where the driver is."

"Want me to check the vehicle?"

"Let's find out who this is first. Besides, if you were the other guy, where would you be right now?"

"Getting as far away as possible."

"Exactly."

The man lay face down in the grass next to the asphalt runway. Wolfe felt the carotid artery for a pulse. Nothing. "Where'd you hit him?"

McGil said, "Center mass."

Rolling the body over, Wolfe flipped his NVG's up and turned on a flashlight. He removed the black balaclava covering the face. "Shit."

"What's the matter, Michael?"

Standing, Wolfe looked at his partner. "This whole clus-terfuck just got complicated."

McGill knelt by the prone man. "Who is this guy?"

"He posed as a Mossad agent known in Israel as Hershel Katz. In reality, he was a double agent named Armin Jazani, he's Iranian."

"Son of a bitch. Guess we pissed them off."

"Yeah." Wolfe removed his cell phone from a pocket on his utility pants, found Jerry Grigg's number, and pressed the send icon.

By the time the sun lightened the eastern sky, Christian County sheriff's cars were too numerous to count. Their drivers concentrated on taking of pictures of the burned-out car, tracks the driver made, the man lying dead by Wolfe's runway, and pictures of the dead man's trek through the woodlands. Also present was Joseph Kincaid, who consulted with his friend, Blake Perry, the current sheriff of the county.

Perry looked at Joseph and asked, "You want me to keep this out of the media?"

"As best as you can, Blake. Someone from the FBI will be here shortly and will explain why it's important to keep a lid on this."

"I have a fugitive out there, Joseph. A fugitive with a gun who I would assume would have gladly used it on the Wolfe family."

"Yes, you do." The retired national security advisor saw Wolfe approaching and asked him. "What did you find, Michael?"

Wolfe handed the sheriff a piece of paper. "This is a still

from a security camera on the roof of my house. Note the license plate on the car, Sheriff."

"It's a US government plate." The sheriff returned his attention to Wolfe. "What tha…"

"I have the same question. Why was a US government official helping an Iranian double agent invade my home?"

Perry frowned. "An Iranian double agent. What the hell's going on here, Michael?"

"Good question." Wolfe handed the sheriff another piece of paper. "This is from a security camera on my back deck. He's wearing the same clothes as the dead guy. All black with a balaclava. Note the gun in his hand."

"Yeah."

"Know what it is?"

"I've seen them, but don't know the brand."

"It's a Heckler and Kock MP7A1 submachine gun. It's used by special forces for close-quarter assaults. The long tube is a suppressor. He was part of the assault team, Sheriff."

Perry frowned. "Those FBI men can't get here soon enough. I need to gather my guys and explain a few things."

He walked away, leaving Joseph and Wolfe by themselves. "What's going on, Michael? You act like you know more than you're telling."

"Why would someone use a government car for an assault like this?"

The older man did not say anything for a few moments, his attention on Wolfe. "My guess would be to draw attention away from who really planned it."

"Exactly. Who would you suspect?"

With a sly grin, Joseph said, "Off the top of my head,

I'd say Emma Elliot's a candidate. But you don't think so. Do you?"

"No. I have a funny feeling she's not that smart. Someone else is pulling the strings. The fact the National Security Agency was involved in searching for Samantha Edgar also bothers me. Alexia believes they were able to backtrack this location. That also concerns me."

"Why is the NSA involved?"

"I have no idea. Except they have the capabilities to monitor internet activity. Like Zoom meetings."

Joseph folded his arms. "The director of the NSA Signal Intelligence Division is Major General Morgan Walker. I knew of him but never worked with him. So, I have no idea where his loyalties lie."

Wolfe grinned. "Maybe it's time for Jerry to have a talk with him."

The older man pulled a cell phone out and punched in a number from memory.

Jerry Griggs knocked on the door of the president's personal office in a hallway off the Oval Office.

"Yes."

Opening the door, Griggs said, "Good morning, sir."

"Mornin'. What've you got for me today?"

"Here's the summary of all the important stuff that happened overnight."

President Griffin took the page and skimmed it. His eyes settled on the last item. He looked up at his advisor. "When did this occur?"

"About 2 a.m. Central Time."

"Is Michael's family, okay?"

"Yes, sir. However, there are a few facts I did not feel needed to be put in the official summary."

"I'm not going to like them, am I?"

"No, sir."

"Very well. Tell me."

Griggs recapped his discussion with Joseph and included the information that the burned-out car belonged to the NSA. The car had been previously reported stolen in the St. Louis area. "That's what they know so far. The man who drove the car has disappeared. Wolfe's property is rather remote, with only a few neighbors. Those properties have been searched, with no one found."

"Does the FBI need to get involved?"

"Already are."

"Good. Since you seem to be on top of this, what do you need from me?"

"A meeting with NSA Director Walker."

The president frowned. "What do you suspect, Jerry?"

"Uh…"

"Spit it out."

"Joseph and Michael are concerned the stolen NSA car is a false flag operation."

"What do you mean?"

"Michael explained it to me this way. What better way to divert attention from the NSA than by having their stolen car used in the assault on his property?"

"You're not making sense. Why would the NSA send someone to assault Michael's house and family?"

"Because the NSA is the agency searching for Emma Elliot's assistant, Samantha Edgar."

The president raised his hand, palm toward Griggs. "Wait a minute. What the hell are you talking about, Jerry?"

"It's complicated, sir."

"I'm a fairly smart guy. Humor me."

"It all started with a list of names given to a retired CIA operator."

After the sheriff's cars, the FBI agents, and Ian McGill left for the day, Wolfe studied copies of the security surveillance videos from his various cameras. The original files were given to the FBI at their insistence. But his system was programed to automatically make copies and rename the files. Thus, if a situation like today arose, he would still have copies for his personal review.

He started with the video of the man from the car stepping onto his back deck. All of his security cameras were high-definition, which allowed him to enlarge the images for greater detail. Concentrating on the shoes of the assailant, Wolfe discovered the man wore black New Balance training shoes. A simple web search gave him an example of the tracks this type of shoe would leave behind.

Additional scrutiny of the videos revealed the stolen car had been sitting on the road north of his house with its lights turned off for at least three hours. This explained why the sheriff's department never found a car used by Katz. He arrived in the same car as the missing man.

With this information in hand, Wolfe started his own hunt.

Two hours later, as the sun dipped below the western horizon, he had a better picture of what happened to the fugitive after the car exploded. He returned to his house and discussed it with Nadia.

"I think I know how the guy I chased off our deck got away."

They were sitting in their bedroom, Ben asleep in the room next door, with Nadia working on her laptop. She looked at her husband. "How?"

"His tracks stop two miles to the west. I found a spot with tire impressions on the shoulder and cigarette butts on the ground. This could have been the vehicle that brought Katz to the party."

Nadia closed the laptop. "Think about it for a second, Michael. They were planning to leave the government car somewhere."

"I didn't think of that, but you're probably right."

"Michael, that means at least three persons were involved in the assault."

"I know." He held up a Ziplock bag. "I collected the cigarette butts. DNA can be extracted from the saliva. If the guy is ex-military or a government employee, we'll know his identity."

She frowned. "Who can do the analysis without anyone knowing?"

"Joseph will know someone."

"What about Uri?"

Wolfe grinned. "That's even better." He glanced at his watch. "It's the middle of the night there. Let's talk to him in the morning."

"We also have to tell him what happened to Katz."

"Another reason to involve him. I collected blades of grass from where he died."

"At least, if it was Katz, Uri can close the book on him."

"And we can confirm it was him."

Chapter Twenty-One

TEL AVIV

Two Days Later

Uri Ben-David studied the piece of paper on his desk. "So, DNA confirms it was Katz?"

His assistant, Mosha Fishman said, "Yes, blood samples and DNA match."

"Any idea who the other man was?"

"Nothing in our databases or those of our friends in Interpol." He paused for a moment. "We were denied access to one."

Pinching the bridge of his nose, Ben-David closed his eyes. "I think I know which one, but go ahead and tell me."

"CIA."

"Let me guess, Emma Elliot blocked our access."

Fishman gave his boss a grim smile. "I was told we did not have a legitimate reason to check their databases."

"Thank you, Mosha. Please close the door when you leave."

"Yes, sir."

When the assistant left, Ben-David stood and turned to face the window behind his desk. The bluish-green of the Mediterranean, off in the distance, held container ships waiting for their turn to enter the Port of Tel Aviv. The implications of Elliot's refusal to cooperate sent a chill up his spine. Rather than wait for a convenient hour to call, he turned and picked up his cell phone.

Wolfe's eyes snapped open at the vibration coming from his nightstand. He grabbed the phone and checked the ID. He croaked, "Yeah—Wolfe."

"Sorry to wake you, Michael. This is Uri."

Blinking the sleep from his eyes, Wolfe took a breath and said, "What'd you find?"

"It was, indeed, Katz. We struck out on the other one. But you might want to have one of your sources check the CIA DNA database."

"Why?"

"We were told we didn't have a legitimate reason for the search."

"What does a legitimate reason mean? Professional courtesy should be enough."

"I agree. We think someone higher up nixed our request."

"Elliot?"

"We don't have proof, but that would be my assumption. Which raises our suspicions she knows exactly who the individual might be."

"Okay. Thanks for the update."

The call ended and Wolfe lay down.

Nadia snuggled up to him. "Was that Uri?"

He draped his arm over her shoulder. "Yes. The dead man was Katz."

"What about the other DNA?"

"No luck. He thinks Elliot blocked the search." He tightened his hug. "Which means, there is a greater than 90 percent chance the smoker is with the CIA."

"How can we make sure?"

"We'll get Jerry to do it. He still has contacts over there."

Call me — secure line — W

Jerry Griggs stared at the text message. The letter W could only mean one individual. Michael Wolfe. He checked his watch and found the time to be fifteen minutes before nine in the morning. An hour earlier in Missouri. He stood and walked out of his office.

Griggs often wandered the White House grounds with his head down and hands in his pants pockets. Other times, he would use these excursions to check something on his cell phone. Today, he found a bench in a quiet corner and dialed Wolfe on his personal cell phone. One equipped with an encryption algorithm designed by a friend of Joseph's.

Wolfe answered the phone on the first ring. "Thanks for calling, Jerry."

"I take it something happened?"

"Yeah, the Mossad confirmed by DNA the dead body was Katz."

"Well, that closes the matter."

"I don't think so. Not by a long shot. We have evidence two additional individuals were involved. We have DNA from one of them. Nothing in our friends' files or any of the files they were allowed to access, either. One request was denied."

"CIA."

"Bingo."

"Oh boy. And you want me to see what I can do?"

"Only if you feel comfortable doing so."

"I'm not comfortable with this entire scenario."

Wolfe remained quiet while Griggs ranted. When he stopped, the retired sniper said, "Are you finished?"

"Yes."

"Who can check the CIA DNA database?"

"You're not going to give up on this, are you?"

"No."

"Very well, Michael. Carla can do it. She still has a way into the CIA computer."

"I won't ask how."

"Probably best." Griggs remained quiet for a few moments. "Send the file. We might have a match by tonight."

"She'll need to be stealthy."

"It won't be her first time to break into the database, Michael."

The call ended and Griggs stood. He returned to his office and, five minutes later, he was on his desk phone telling Carla she had a new assignment.

Carla Webb, wearing baggy jeans, an oversized hoodie, dark sunglasses, and a black durag walked into a public library in downtown Arlington with a brand-new HP laptop under her arm. In a far corner of the facility, isolated from other patrons, she accessed the internet. Once she signed onto a certain website and supplied a specific password and identi-fication protocol, she requested match to a DNA profile.

Two minutes later, she received a photograph and a summary of the individual's profile. After taking a picture of the computer screen with her phone, she shut the computer off and stood. With the laptop tucked under her arm again, she walked out of the library. Boarding a bus a few blocks from the building, she sat in the back and extracted the battery from the computer.

With the picture now displayed on her phone, she studied the information and portrait. "Damn." She attached the file to a text message and pressed the send icon. "Damn, damn, damn."

Wolfe studied the picture sent from Carla. He looked at Nadia. "I can see why Emma Elliot didn't want Uri's DNA search to be run on the agencies files."

"What happened?"

He turned the phone so she could see. "That, my dear, is the individual who dropped the cigarette butts outside the vehicle while waiting to pick up the late Mr. Katz and our mystery guest."

She took the phone to study it closer. "Appears to be a typical forty-something male."

Taking the phone back, Wolfe said, "Yeah, a typical forty-something male who just so happened to, at one time, do contract work for the CIA."

She raised her eyebrows. "Did you know him?"

"Knew of him." He paused for a moment. "He was supposedly, at one time, a Marine sniper. But little was known about his background. He's also one of the men on the list given to Fischer. And one of the names identified as being deceased."

Nadia's head tilted ever so slightly. "Michael, this is starting to form a pattern."

"I agree." He walked to the coffee machine on the kitchen island. After he poured a cup, he turned and leaned against the counter. "I think this confirms my recent suspicions about the list."

"How's that?"

"Let's chase rabbits for a moment. Suppose someone wanted to create a diversion. A sleight of hand, so to speak."

Nadia gave her husband a slight smile. "Go on."

"Let's assume the Iranians did create the list as payback for downing their president's helicopter. Emma Elliot somehow obtained a copy. Seeing an opportunity, she adds a bunch of names to it and used Samantha to, shall we say, leak it."

With a frown, Nadia said, "That means Samantha is involved."

"Not necessarily. She might be, but her traveling to the West Coast suggests she's scared. My guess is she was duped into giving the list to Fischer."

"Isn't this a little complicated for Elliot? No one we've talked to thinks she's capable of devising a plan this intricate."

Wolfe considered his wife for a moment and then nodded. "There is that." He folded his arms and stared at a spot on the wall. "Ian's and my journey to the Azerbaijani mountains was sanctioned by Israel. Even then, it was compartmentalized within the Mossad. Who else could have known about it?"

"The person who gave the list to Elliot."

Her husband nodded. "Exactly. But the timeline's off."

"Not following you."

"The helicopter crashed in May. Let's say the Iranians found the reason for the crash and, wishing to avoid embarrassment, hastily put the list together from old intel. Thus, the wrong addresses. Then they activated Katz by giving him the list."

"Michael, Katz had already disappeared into the West Bank before the helicopter crash."

"Like I said, the timeline is off."

Nadia looked at him with a cocky smile. "Maybe there was a woman involved."

"Or, the Iranians suspected the Mossad was getting close to their agent, so they pulled him."

"That would explain a lot, Michael. Since Katz was already considered dead, they could use him to deliver the list. But to whom?"

"Who's searching for Sam?"

"The National Security Agency."

"Exactly. What agency monitors electronic messages?"

She gave her husband a grin. "The National Security Agency."

"Exactly. And who's the director of signal intelligence for the NSA? Morgan Walker."

"So, Walker knows about the list and shares it with Elliot? Why? That doesn't make sense, Michael."

"No, it doesn't. But Walker would have a relationship with the chairman of Senate Intelligence Select Committee."

"Calvin Hendricks."

"Who just so happened to suggest to President Griffin to appoint Elliot as CIA director."

"What's their end game, Michael? Why go to all this deception?"

"I have no idea. Remember, we were chasing the proverbial rabbit when we started this conversation. At the moment, all we know for certain is two individuals on the list tried to kill us. My bet is the third guy's name's there as well."

"Whoever these men are, they are not doing it for free, Michael. Somebody is paying them. Knowing who, would help."

"Exactly. Who do we know that might have the ability to follow the money?"

They both said, "Alexia," at the same time.

Nadia pulled her cell phone out and made a call.

Chapter Twenty-Two

KENWOOD, CA

North of Sonoma, California is an unincorporated area known as Kenwood. Here, Samantha Edgar found a nice, but small, Airbnb cottage for less money than a hotel room. Secluded, with little to no traffic on the access road, it seemed the perfect place to hide for a while. Vineyards and the foothills of Sugarloaf Ridge State Park could be seen from her northeast-facing kitchenette window.

Registering for the cottage using one of her alternate identity credit cards, she felt safe for the first time in six months. She looked forward to a slower pace versus her frenzied nonstop change of locations since leaving Washington, DC.

On the day after her arrival, she slept for fourteen hours straight. Afterward, she lounged around the bungalow the rest of the day reading a novel found on a bookshelf in the living area. The third day brought a desire to explore some of the local wineries. There, she acquired several bottles of an interesting chardonnay. On the way back to her bungalow, she stopped at a local farmers market and bought provisions for two or three days.

During this time, she did not turn on her cell phone or access the internet. It felt like freedom. She did not know what was going on in the world, nor did she care. No one knew where she was.

On the fifth day of her stay in Kenwood, she made a mistake that almost cost her life. Her image was captured on a Bank of America security camera attached to an ATM.

Major General Morgan Walker heard the ping of an incoming automated text message. He opened the file and read the alert. Without emotion, he deleted the communication and reached for his cell phone.

When the call was answered, he said, "Target is in Kenwood, California."

"Method of ID?"

"Security camera feed from a Bank of America branch. Verified with facial recognition software."

"Got it." There was a pause. "Your orders?"

"Terminate with discretion."

The call ended. Walker returned to the current project on his desk.

Two Days Later

The quiet and laid-back lifestyle in Kenwood lulled Samantha into letting her guard down. After a day trip to

Sugarloaf Ridge State Park, she arrived at her cottage a little past 11 p.m. Her training at the CIA Farm instilled in her a habit of taking precautions after being away from a place of residence for any length of time. So, she drove by the cottage. Nothing. She then circled the block searching for any vehicle that seemed out of place.

After a sleepless night, she rose to make coffee. She checked the clock on the coffeemaker, 5:02 in the morning. As she filled the carafe with water, she glanced out the window above her sink. A dark-clad figure dashed between two other cottages. Now fully awake, she abandoned the idea of making coffee and found her recently acquired pay-as-you-go cell phone. Switching it on, she input a number and pressed the send icon.

A female voice cautiously answered, "Hello?"

"No names. Just listen."

"Okay."

"I'm in California wine country. I need to be somewhere else fast."

After a slight pause, the voice said, "I can arrange."

"When?"

"Today."

"This is a burner phone. I'll call you back."

The call ended, and Samantha Edgar hurried to her bedroom and threw clothes into her duffle bag.

"Wolfe."

"Michael, it's Carla."

"Kind of early for you, isn't it?"

"I've heard from our friend."

Bringing his attention to full alert, he said, "When?"

"A minute ago. How fast can you fly to California wine country?"

"If the jet's available, I could be there by noon Pacific Time."

"Find out if it's available and call me right back."

The call ended, and Wolfe dialed a number. It was answered on the second ring.

"KKG. This is Stewart."

"It's Wolfe. Is the Honda available?"

"For you, yes. Anybody else, no."

Wolfe smiled. "I have a slight emergency. Can you file a flight plan for me?"

"Sure, when and where?"

"Today. Hang on, let me check something." He thumbed search terms into his phone. He found what he needed. "Napa County Airport."

"You, got it, Michael."

He checked his watch, did the math in his head, and called Carla back.

"Yeah."

"Have our friend at the Napa County Airport at 11:30 a.m. She'll need to go to the FBO and give her name as Samantha Wolfe."

"Got it."

"Is she driving a rental?"

"Don't know. I can ask."

"If she is, have her dump it. She'll need to take a bus, not an Uber, to the airport."

"I'm sure she can figure it out."

"Good."

The call ended and Wolfe grabbed his go bag. Just

before he walked out of the back door, he kissed Nadia and said, "Going to California to pick up Sam. I'll be back before dark."

"I'll have the guest room ready."

He smiled and shut the door.

As Samantha slipped out the back door of the small Airbnb rental, Astronomical Twilight had technically begun. With the sun still eighteen degrees below the horizon, the surrounding area remained in darkness. But the sky had begun to brighten. She needed to be away from the cottage before dawn.

Staying in the shadows and blocks away from Sonoma Highway, she made her way north. As the foothills to the east became visible with the coming day, she found a secluded space in one of the wineries dotting the landscape in this part of California. She pressed the send icon on her phone.

The call was answered on the first ring. Carla said, "I've got you a ride."

"Where?"

"Napa County Airport. You need to be there by 11:30 this morning. Can you make it?"

"I have to. Who's picking me up?"

"Our friend, the predator."

"Thank you. I owe you."

"Use your first name and his last name when you get there."

"Got it."

The call ended, and the only problem Samantha faced was getting to the airport on time.

By seven thirty, the older of the two watchers grew impatient. "Something's wrong."

His partner scowled. "What makes you say that?"

"Don't know, it's a feeling. I'm gonna check the house." The driver opened his car door.

With a shake of his head, the passenger lit another cigarette. "You need to relax, Carl." He blew smoke out from his first drag and watched the driver make his way toward the house.

Before he could finish the cigarette, Carl came running back to the car and slid into the driver's seat. "She's gone. The car's still there, but she isn't."

"Shit." The smoker threw the butt out the window and buckled his seat belt. "Now what?"

"Since we don't know how long she's been gone, I haven't got a clue."

"Get back on Sonoma Highway. Maybe she's walking."

"Until a better idea comes along, we'll try that."

Samantha walked south through the residential area of Kenwood. On her second day of visiting wineries, she discovered a small boutique specializing in merlot. The woman who owned the winery enjoyed their conversation and invited her back. When she walked by, she saw the proprietor tending her vines.

"Hi, Margie."

The woman looked up, smiled, and said, "What are you doing out so early, girl?"

"Oh, just walking."

Margie walked closer. "Why the duffle bag?"

Samantha summoned tears and let one slip down her cheek. "Nothing I need to bother you with."

"Nonsense. Can I help?"

"Do you know if there is a way for me to get to Napa County Airport? Without calling an Uber?"

"Well, now, I'm not sure. Why do you need to go?"

"My boyfriend is mad because my brother's coming to visit. So, he took off with my car. I need to be there before noon."

The woman smiled, again. "Men can be so aggravating at times. I need to go to Napa today for some cuttings. I could take you?"

"I'll pay for the gas."

"Nonsense. I'll enjoy the company."

Samantha, touched her arm. "Oh, Margie, how can I ever thank you?"

Carl drummed his fingers on the steering wheel. "Where could she have gone?"

The smoker flipped another butt out the window. "Is there an airport around here?"

"Hell, if I know." He opened his smart phone and did a Google search. "Yeah, it's called Napa County Airport. Why?"

"How far?"

"Thirty-four miles, about forty minutes, why?"

"She could have grabbed an Uber or something. Since we can't find her..." He checked the time on his phone. "It's eleven, and we haven't spotted her yet. My guess would be she's arranged for a flight."

With a shrug, Carl said, "Better than sitting here with our thumbs up our butts." He put the car in gear, and they headed south.

Chapter Twenty-Three

NAPA COUNTY AIRPORT

Wolfe leaned against a small coffee bar in the airport's FBO, sipping a cup of steaming brew, his attention on the front door. The entrance opened and Samantha Edgar breezed into the regional airport's business office.

She scanned the room, smiled when she saw him, and hurried to his side. "Thank you for coming."

"No problem. Any luggage?"

"What you see is what I've got."

"Coffee?"

"No thanks. Just a quick ride out of here."

"That's not going to be a problem. Follow me."

She followed him to the HondaJet and climbed into the cabin. When he was sitting behind the jet's yoke, he started his pre-flight checklist. She nervously scanned the parking lot.

Carl pulled into the airport complex and drove down Airport Road. The smoker searched the jets on the tarmac and pointed to one. "The HondaJet. It's idling like it's getting close to taking off. Get closer."

The driver parked in a slot with a clear view of the jet. The smoker got out and trained binoculars on the plane. "I can't see the pilot, but there's a woman in the passenger seat."

"Is it her?"

"Can't tell. The plane's turning, heading for the runway. Is there any way you can get onto the tarmac?"

"Hell no, dude. I'm not messing with the FFA."

The smoker watched as the plane turned onto a runway. As the plane accelerated, he got a glimpse of the pilot. "Son of a bitch."

As the HondaJet left the ground and went wheels up, Wolfe turned to Samantha. She occupied the co-pilot's seat. "Don't touch anything."

"Didn't plan to."

"So, what happened?"

She glanced at him and then back out the windshield. "I made a mistake."

"It can happen. What'd you do?"

"I've been careful. Cash for everything, battery out of my phone unless I need it, and I've been moving every two or three days."

"So far, so good."

Taking a deep breath, she said, "I was tired of constantly changing locales and stayed a little too long at an Airbnb in Kenwood, California."

"I will assume you didn't check in under your real name."

She chuckled. "No, didn't do that. This morning, I saw a couple of men walking around my cabin, paying way too much attention to it. One approached way to close to my front window. That's when I decided to sneak out."

"How could someone find you, Samantha? It sounds like you took all the precautions needed."

"Michael, I don't even know who's looking for me. At first, I thought it would be the CIA. But those two weren't from the agency."

"We're speculating it's someone within the NSA."

"Oh shit."

Wolfe took a quick glance at his passenger. "What?"

"I went to an ATM in Kenwood."

"Well, that could do it. Particularly if they are monitoring security cameras."

"Which means, if I walk into an international airport, a security camera will take my picture, and they'll know about it."

"Why do you think I asked you to meet me at Napa County Airport?"

"Thank you." She chose not to mention the men she saw in the parking lot as they took off.

"When we get to the airport in Springfield, I'll taxi into the hangar and then you and I will transfer to my Jeep. It's already inside the building. No security cameras. We have them, but they'll be turned off when we arrive."

"You keep saying 'we.'"

"Yeah, I'm a part-time corporate pilot for a company called KKG Security."

"Part-time?"

"I fly the corporate jet when the regular pilot is otherwise occupied."

"Got it."

"Sam, why did you leave DC?"

Staring out the starboard window, the fugitive CIA agent sighed. "Fear, confusion, frustration. You name it, I felt it."

"Because of Elliot?"

She nodded. "And other things."

"Want to explain?"

"Since you are ex-agency, you'll understand. When most of the senior management were forced out—"

"The common understanding is they resigned or retired."

She shook her head. "Nope. They were given ultimatums. Then, with Jerry Griggs and Carla Webb gone, I had absolutely no one left I could trust."

"You could have resigned, like the others."

"I was told, in no uncertain terms, that would not be possible."

"Or?"

"Ms. Elliot is not a stable person, Michael. She has moments of lucidity, but most of the time she lives in a fantasy world where she's more powerful than the president."

Taking another quick glance at his passenger, Wolfe said, "Since when?"

"The moment she walked in the door." She paused for a moment. "Here's the other scary part of this mess. She's being controlled by someone else."

"Who?"

"I don't know. But I do know they're in government." She stretched, yawned, and leaned back in the chair.

"Sam, we've got a three-hour flight. You look exhausted. Go to the back and try to get a few hours of sleep."

"Thank you. I believe I will."

FBI agent Mark Steelman offered his ID to the Airbnb owner.

Martha Cooke studied it while he held it in front of her. Satisfied, she said, "How can I help you, Agent Steelman?"

"The individual in cabin A. Do you know when she will return?"

"Sorry, Agent. I don't make a habit of keeping track of the guests' comings and goings. She's paid up through this coming Wednesday. Why? What's she done?"

"I'm not at liberty to discuss that." He put the ID back into his sportscoat pocket. "Is she registered under the name Samantha Edgar?"

Martha frowned. "No. She registered under the name Elizabeth Johnson and paid with a credit card under that name. What's going on here, Agent?"

"She's a fugitive. Can we see inside the room?"

The innkeeper tilted her head. "If I don't allow you?"

"I'm afraid we'll get an open-ended search warrant for the entire property. I doubt you would want that, would you, Ms. Cooke?"

"No, I don't believe I would. Wait here. I'll get you a key to the cabin."

She disappeared while Steelman waited.

A minute later, she handed it to him. "Let me know what you find. If you see she's left, I'll clean up."

As he walked away, the FBI agent, mumbled, "Fat chance of that, lady."

With his gun in his left hand and the key in his right hand, he unlocked the door and nodded toward his partner.

His partner opened the door and both entered, Steelman first, their guns in front of them. "FBI—hands where we can see them."

The tiny cottage was empty. All of her clothes were gone, but the refrigerator still held fruit, vegetables, bottled water, two bottles of local wine, bagels, and a half-consumed tub of cream cheese. Steelman holstered his gun and placed his hands on his hips.

"Shit, Charlie. She's gone. The tip was good, just not in time."

"Maybe she left a computer behind." He took off toward the bedroom. Five minutes later, he reappeared, shaking his head. "No such luck."

"Great, just great." He scanned the room. "All right, gather what you can, and we'll see if she left anything important behind."

A tone told Jerry Griggs his phone received a new text message. He glanced at it and opened the message.

Our friend is safe – W.

With a smile, he put the cell phone back in his pocket and stood. He walked down the hall and knocked on the president's private office door.

"Come in, Jerry. It's open."

He entered the office and smiled. "How'd you know it was me?"

"You have a distinct walk, and your knock is always a question."

"Nice to be predictable."

Griffin leaned back in his office chair. "What's on your mind?"

"Samantha is safe and tucked away in the Ozark hills. You can schedule your meeting with Emma Elliot at any time."

"Before I do, I need you to prepare a list of candidates who would be willing to take the position of DCI. No flakes this time."

"Not asking Senator Hendricks for recommendations, I take."

Griffin chuckled. "No. I want the list put together by tomorrow morning. When I meet with her, both the attorney general and the DNI need to be in the meeting."

"Got it."

The Following Morning

"Do you have the list?"

"Yes, sir." Jerry Griggs handed the folded piece of paper to the president.

Griffin accepted it and grinned. "There's only one name here."

"He's also the only person you can trust to put the CIA back together after little Ms. Elliot broke it."

"Will he, do it?"

"For you, yes, I believe he will. Mary's cancer is in remission and, if you ask him to take the position for a year, he'll make the agency hum again." Griggs gave the president a crooked smile. "I also believe some of the individuals Elliot drove out would return just so they could work for him."

"When's our meeting with Elliot?"

Glancing at his watch, Griggs said, "In an hour."

"Very good. Let's make sure she waits for at least fifteen minutes."

"I like your style, Mr. President."

Chapter Twenty-Four

WASHINGTON, DC

Emma Elliot sat on the sofa in the Oval Office. Jerry Griggs sat across from her and read an open file. They were the only ones in the room.

"I have other things to do besides wait for the president, Mr. Griggs."

He smiled and said, "As do I, Ms. Elliot, but he is the president of the United States. His time is just as valuable. He will be here shortly."

"You can call me Director Elliot."

Griggs thought, *not for long*. Glancing at his watch, he noticed sixteen minutes had elapsed.

At that moment, the door to the hallway leading to Griffin's private office opened and the president entered, followed by Attorney General Dale Delgado and Director of National Intelligence Hallie Goodman.

Griggs stood. Elliot did not.

The president sat at the Resolute Desk while Delgado sat on the same sofa as Griggs, and Goodman placed herself at the opposite end of the couch occupied by Elliot.

The president said, "I won't beat around the bush, Ms. Elliot—"

"It's Director Elliot."

Griffin's demeanor turned dark. "Not anymore. You were relieved of your duties as of sixteen minutes ago."

"You cannot fire—"

Delgado interrupted. "Actually, he can."

"I'm a cabinet member and approved by the Senate, Mr. Delgado. Only they can fire me."

"That's not exactly true. In the 1926 ruling by the Supreme Court in Myers v. United States, members of the cabinet serve at the pleasure of the president."

Hallie Goodman said, "And the president is not pleased with your performance."

Elliot stood abruptly. "I don't have to sit here and listen to this."

Griffin said in a stern voice, "*Sit down* and shut up."

Her eyes grew round, and she sat.

The president continued. "We have a recording of you speaking to Executive Director Isabelle Brooks. After she reminded you of the CIA charter, you said, and I quote, 'To hell with the charter. This is an internal matter. There is nothing of higher importance at this moment than finding Edgar. Is that clear?' Do you remember that outburst, Ms. Elliot?"

Elliot stared at the coffee table in front of her.

The president looked at the DNI. "Ms. Goodman, would you read the statement that Ms. Elliot will be giving to the press."

"With pleasure, Mr. President. *After careful consideration, I have decided to step down as the director of the Central Intelligence Agency. I want to thank President Griffin for the opportunity to serve in this position.*"

All Elliot could do was blink as she shifted her attention to the DNI.

The president said, "It's short and to the point. If you don't agree, I will announce at this afternoon's press conference that you were fired for incompetence. Your choice, Ms. Elliot."

The woman held her hands together in her lap, returned her stare to the coffee table again. She mumbled, "All my plans, gone. They're gone. It's just not fair."

Griggs rolled his eyes and stood. He went to the main door to the Oval Office and motioned two Secret Service agents in. "Would you escort Ms. Elliot to the circle drive? A car is waiting to take her to her apartment."

After Elliot left the office in the company of the Secret Service, Griffin turned to Delgado. "Dale, would you contact the FBI agents you have standing by at Langley to clear out Ms. Elliot's office? They are to seize all of her personal files and search for any improprieties."

"It would be my pleasure, Mr. President." The attorney general stood and left through the same door as Elliot.

Griffin turned to the DNI. "Hallie, would you brief the other agencies under your jurisdiction about the situation? Ask them to provide you with any communications they might have received from Elliot."

She stood. "Yes, Mr. President."

When Griffin and Griggs were alone, the president turned his attention to his national security advisor. "What did Joseph say?"

"He agreed but wanted to discuss it with you first."

"I just hope I don't work the man to death."

"He said the same thing."

When the former director of the CIA arrived at the door to her apartment, her hands automatically turned the key and the knob. She entered the nicely appointed apartment and stumbled to her bedroom where she collapsed on the bed.

Her eyes remained open as she stared at the wall next to her bed. She remained in a catatonic state for the next few hours. Finally, the ringing of her cell phone brought her back to reality. She raised herself slowly and sat on the side of the bed. The ringing stopped for a few moments and then started again.

Fumbling around in her purse, she found the device and accepted the call. "Hello."

Her greeting was answered with silence.

"Hello."

The silence continued.

She glanced at the caller ID. The word *Unknown* could be seen on the screen. She ended the call and dropped the phone on the bed.

The ringing started again. She grabbed the phone, pressed the accept button, and yelled, "What the fuck do you want?"

"Is that the proper way to answer a phone, Emma?"

"What do you want, Hendricks?"

"I heard you got fired this morning."

"Yeah, so what?"

"That doesn't go well for our plan, now does it?"

"It wasn't my plan either."

"I do hope you had the good sense not to say anything about our arrangement."

"What do you think? Of course not."

"That's good to know."

Elliot fell back onto the bed and stared at the ceiling.

"Get my job back, and I won't go to the press with all your dirty laundry, Calvin."

"Tsk, tsk, Ms. Elliot, that's an unfortunate attitude."

"Yeah, well, it's the only attitude I have right now."

"Very well." The call ended.

She glared at the device several seconds and then threw it through the open bedroom door. It crashed against the hallway drywall, making a sizeable dent.

By the time dusk settled over the DC area, Emma Elliot's disbelief had morphed into blinding anger. She locked the door to her apartment and took the elevator to the parking garage level. One of the perks of her job, as the DCIA, allowed for a car and driver to pick her up each morning for the ride to Langley. So, her car remained parked in the garage below the apartment tower.

As she walked down the second-floor parking deck toward her slot, she heard tires squeal behind her. Turning, she froze as a large vehicle accelerated toward her. She recognized the driver only seconds before the SUV struck her.

The mass of the big vehicle propelled her body forward into one of the support pillars. Her head struck the concrete first, splitting it open. As the truck passed, the driver glanced at the damage caused by the impact. He smiled as he accelerated away from the incident. Emma Elliot took her last breath as her body slid to the oil-stained concrete floor.

The next morning, headlines in *The Washington Post* screamed *Scandal in the Griffin Administration!* Cable morning talk shows brought out their stable of talking heads to pontificate and dispense their conspiracy theories. The theories they spewed were so far from the truth, it made Jerry Griggs's head spin.

He sat next to the president as the deputy director of the CIA gave POTUS the morning brief. When he finished, Griffin asked, "What's known so far about Emma Elliot's death?"

"Not much, sir. Our driver dropped her off at her apartment complex and waited until she entered the building. Security cameras in the hallway show her letting herself into her unit five minutes later."

"What about the cameras in the parking garage?"

"They were turned off during the time of the incident."

"So, it wasn't an accident?"

"No, sir. DC police and the FBI are calling it a suspicious death."

Griffin nodded. "Thanks, Bob."

The DDCI stood and left the oval office. The president turned to Griggs. "Your thoughts, Jerry?"

"I have no proof of this, but I'd say somebody needed to shut her up before she talked to the press."

"Those were my thoughts as well."

"Sir, this raises questions we need to consider."

"Such as?"

"Someone else was manipulating Elliot. If that's the case, they aren't done yet."

The president sat in a hard-back rocking chair made famous by John F. Kennedy during his administration. Griffin placed his elbows on the arms, making a steeple with his hands. He tapped his lips. "Why now?"

"Excuse me, sir."

"Why now? Why is all of this drama happening now? What sparked it?"

"Sir, you've had a particularly scandal-free administration. Could it be a coincidence?"

Tilting his head, the president said, "Jerry, you believe that about as much as I do."

"You're right, sir, I don't believe it's a coincidence, either. Maybe Joseph can figure out what's going on. He arrives today."

The president sighed. "Can't be soon enough."

Somewhere Over the Eastern United States

Joseph Kincaid turned to the pilot of the Baron B55. "I appreciate you flying me to Washington, Michael."

"Not a problem, Joseph. Are you sure you want to take on the responsibility of running the CIA?"

"Kind of seems like a natural progression to me."

Wolfe grinned. "Yeah, it does. What was Dr. Harmon's opinion?"

"He gave me the green light after I promised to limit my coffee intake."

"Sounds like him." Wolfe directed his attention out the front windshield. "What were Mary's thoughts?"

"Totally against it. But she understands the need. I promised her I would take it as a temporary assignment."

"Just like you did when you agreed to be Griffin's national security advisor for a year. That turned into what? A four-year gig."

"She brought that up as well, Michael."

Wolfe grew quiet as the city of Louisville, Kentucky passed underneath the twin-engine plane. Finally, he said, "Want me to stick around for a few days?"

Joseph turned to his friend. "I wouldn't want to impose on you."

"Nadia and I discussed it last night. We're both worried about you. Plus, you and I both know the death of Emma Elliot was not an accident. Someone needed to keep her quiet. When I picked up Samantha in California, she told me someone else was pulling Elliot's strings. But she didn't know who. That person's still out there."

"Jerry Griggs told me the same thing."

"Then my offer still stands. Want me to hang around for a while?"

"If you wouldn't mind."

"Consider it done."

Chapter Twenty-Five

The suspicious death of Emma Elliot made headlines for two days. Without a person of interest being identified, the story disappeared from the news cycle. Once attention by the news media died down, Senator Calvin Hendricks picked up his desk phone and dialed the White House number. When the switchboard answered, he said, "This is Senator Hendricks. May I speak to the president?"

"Certainly, Senator. Let me see if he is available."

Five minutes later, Griffin said, "To what do I owe the pleasure of your call, Calvin?"

"I guess we've all heard of the terrible accident Director Elliot suffered. I want to make an appointment with you to discuss our recommendations for her replacement."

"Well, Senator, I appreciate the call, but I've already made my decision. I'm bringing a former CIA legend back to help the agency to recover from the chaos instilled by Ms. Elliot. Once he has accomplished his mission and helped the organization be more responsive to the nation, I will be more than happy to listen to your recommendations."

Hendricks did not respond for several seconds. "I see. Are you saying you will ignore my committee's recommendation?"

"Nothing could be further from the truth. I'd be happy to hear your recommendations, but like I said, it would be after my appointee has accomplished my goals. The agency lost too many senior managers during Elliot's tenure."

"My committee didn't see it that way, Mr. President. We thought she did an excellent job of streamlining an old and bloated bureaucracy."

"I'm afraid we will have to disagree on that point, Senator."

"May I ask who you will nominate for the position?"

"Someone who has a stellar reputation and has been approved by the Senate for a previous appointment. I already have the blessing of the majority leader. I will announce it at a news conference tomorrow."

"I must insist on knowing who you are nominating, Mr. President."

"You can insist all you want to, Senator. I will announce it at the news conference."

"You are aware any candidate you appoint has to be approved by my committee."

"Senator Hendricks, the majority leader has assured me the nominee will not have to go through any committee due to his reputation and the imminent need to replace the former director."

"I must protest, Mr. President. My committee is the first line of defense to keep unsavory individuals out of leadership at the CIA."

"I didn't want to say this, Senator, but your committee failed to recommend a qualified candidate in Ms. Elliot.

Watch the news conference, Senator." Griffin ended the conversation.

Hendricks stared at the receiver and then slammed it hard on the phone's cradle. "Damn."

———————

President Roy Griffin hung up the phone and chuckled. "I probably won't get Hendricks' vote next November."

Joseph Kincaid frowned. "I don't enjoy putting you in this position, Mr. President."

"It's my fault. I'm the one who took Hendricks' recommendation without checking her resume. Besides, the majority leader is looking forward to doing an end run around Hendricks. He told me the senator has started to irritate him with some of his ludicrous demands."

The two men were meeting in the president's private dining room on the second floor of the family residence. Joseph stared at his cup of decaffeinated green tea. Griffin carefully watched his former national security advisor. After several moments of silence, Joseph set his cup on the table and said, "Roy, do you think Hendricks is behind this so-called list?"

A slow nod was his answer. "I'm afraid I do. Jerry seems to think so, as well."

"What's his endgame?"

"I don't know. Griggs has someone doing a deep dive on the man."

Joseph tapped his index finger on the table. He studied his teacup for a moment and then turned his attention to Griffin. "Do you trust Michael Wolfe, sir?"

"With my life."

"As do I. May I make a recommendation?"

"That's why you're here."

"Turn Michael and his wife Nadia loose on this matter. They have connections literally around the world. If there is something dirty in Hendricks' background, they'll find it."

The president took a sip of coffee and kept an eye on his friend. "You obviously suspect something, Joseph, or you wouldn't mention the senator by name."

"It's more of a feeling than a suspicion."

"I've learned to trust your feelings. What do you need from me?"

"Promote Michael and Nadia from their U.S. Marshal identities to Homeland Security investigators. It gives them authorization to take their search international and carte-blanche authority to find out what Hendricks is up to."

The president picked up the handset of his phone again and said, "Barbara, please find the secretary of Homeland Security and ask him to join me in the Oval Office as soon as he can."

Griffin listened and then said, "Thank you, Barbara." When he replaced the handset, he turned to Joseph. "I've missed having your insight around, my friend."

The Next Day

Wolfe studied the ID wallet. It contained laminated credentials with his picture, declaring Patrick Ryan to be an investigator for Homeland Security. The case held an accompanying badge opposite the identification card. He then opened an identical one for Nadia in the name of Holly Harper. He turned his attention to Joseph. "Exactly what are you expecting us to do?"

"Senator Calvin Hendricks recommended Emma Elliot for the DCI position. The president wants to know why. The woman was out of control from the beginning. The good senator called the president to request a meeting so he could recommend a replacement almost before Ms. Elliot's body was cold. Why?"

"I take it Hendricks wasn't pleased with your being named the acting director of the CIA."

"The president didn't tell him. You have to remember, I got under Hendricks' skin some years back when I didn't recommend him for a position within the CIA."

"Thought you were better at winning friends and influencing people."

"Trust me, Michael. Calvin Hendricks is not a friend, nor do I want him as one. He's a dangerous man. The president needs you and Nadia to find out exactly how dangerous."

"Restrictions?"

"Only one. Don't get caught."

With a chuckle, Wolfe said, "Goes without saying." He put the two wallets in his back pocket and then crossed his arms. "I take it you suspect something."

With a nod, Joseph said, "I do. Jerry agrees with me. Hendricks is the source behind the list."

"That's kind of a stretch, isn't it?"

"Think about it for a minute. We've already seen that Hershel Katz was a double agent for the Mossad. He disappeared and then was killed during an invasion of your property. Why was he there?"

Wolfe remained quiet as he listened.

Joseph continued. "Then Emma Elliot refuses to allow DNA samples to be compared to CIA personnel. Which identified the cigarette smoker as an ex-CIA contract agent."

"Okay, Joseph, you've got a point. Why would Hendricks be involved?"

"That's what the president needs you and Nadia to find out."

"Did everybody forget she and I are retired? Plus, we have a young son to take care of."

"I'm very much aware of that. But the fact both of you are officially retired means no one will suspect the two of you are trying to dig into Hendricks' motivations."

"If we say no?"

Joseph folded his arms. "You won't. I know both of you too well. Besides, you didn't give the IDs back. You stuck them in your pocket. Which means you want to do this for the president."

Wolfe removed the ID wallets from his back pocket and studied them for a few moments. "I hate being predictable."

———

The Next Day

An off-the-beaten-path coffee shop in downtown Chevy Chase, Maryland offered a clandestine spot for Wolfe to meet Carla Webb. As was his habit, he arrived early. To his surprise, Carla sat in a far corner with a grin on her face.

Arriving at the table, he sat and said, "I forgot you and I were trained by the same individual."

"He was a good mentor."

"Are you sorry you left the agency, now that he's the director?"

"Who said I left?"

"Got it. Jerry told me you have some info on Hendricks?"

She pushed a flash drive across the table. "Interesting information in the file labeled 2010."

"Oh."

"Hendricks traveled to Brussels during the summer of 2010 on a fact-finding junket concerning NATO. He went by himself."

Wolfe raised an eyebrow. "Isn't it unusual for a senator to go overseas on one of those alone?"

"Extremely."

Wolfe contemplated the small device. "What else is on here?"

"A bunch of juicy tidbits."

"Such as?"

"The year before President Bryant died of an aneurism, Hendricks formed an exploratory committee to see what kind of support he would have running for president. Since Griffin held the title of VP when Bryant died, he was sworn in as president. Being the last year of Bryant's eight years, Hendricks had planned to be the party standard bearer at the convention. But as Griffin's favorability numbers rose and the senator's fell into the single digits, his supporters abandoned him. He's had a chip on his shoulder ever since."

Wolfe sipped his recently delivered coffee. "Huh."

"Did I mention, as chairman of the Senate Intelligence Select Committee, he has access to everything the DCI can access?"

"What's your gut telling you?"

"I'm just an analysist."

"BS. You're one of the best operatives Joseph ever recruited. You have an opinion. What is it?"

The diminutive woman shrugged.

"Spill it, Carla."

"Remember the cartoon *Peanuts*?"

"Yeah."

"There's a character in the cartoon with dust swirling around him."

"Pig-Pen?"

"Exactly. Hendricks is like Pig-Pen. Chaos surrounds him." She paused for a moment to sip her coffee. Finally, she said, "If I were you, I'd start in Brussels. Something happened there, because Hendricks' politics changed dramatically after the visit."

"Really."

Carla sipped her coffee and nodded.

Part II

THE CONSPIRACY

Chapter Twenty-Six

LYON, FRANCE

Interpol Headquarters

Wolfe offered his ID and badge to the man standing in front of an ornate oak desk. The man, as tall as Wolfe and twenty pounds heavier, accepted the credentials and studied them for a moment. He handed them back to the retired sniper and accepted Nadia's. These he scrutinized for the same length of time as Wolfe's before handing them back to the woman.

"When did you go to work for Homeland Security, Mr. Ryan? Thought you were with the CIA, and your name was Michael Wolfe."

"Not much gets past you, Peter."

Peter DeVos chuckled and offered his hand. As the two men shook, he said, "Good to see you again, Michael. What's with the Homeland Security IDs?"

"Window dressing. This is my partner, Holly Harper."

DeVoss offered his hand, and Nadia shook it. "What brings American Homeland Security to Interpol?"

"Ms. Harper and I are gathering information on a man named Calvin Hendricks. We wanted to stop by as a courtesy and see if you have any background on him."

"Name's not familiar. Should I ask who is he, or what he did?"

"Both. Calvin Hendricks is a US senator who may have been compromised by a foreign entity."

The Interpol agent walked back to his chair behind the desk and tapped the space bar on his computer's keyboard. "Where did this supposed entrapment occur?"

"NATO summit meeting in Brussels, 2010."

"I see. Please, have a seat. This might take a few minutes."

Wolfe and his wife sat in cushioned Queen Anne leather chairs placed in front of DeVos' desk. They watched the Frenchman type, study the screen, type again, and then check his results.

"In 2010, there wasn't a meeting in Brussels. That year's summit was held in Lisbon, Portugal."

Both Wolfe and Nadia glanced at each other. She immediately returned her attention to the Frenchman and said, "Monsieur DeVos, do your records show any kind of meeting at NATO Headquarters that year?"

"Nothing out of the ordinary." He typed again and leaned forward. His eyes grew round. "Hello, here's something." He studied the laptop screen for a few moments. "One of our agents reported that an American politician claimed he had been robbed during a meeting held in his hotel room. The American's name was Calvin Hendricks. He said he met a woman at the bar of the Rocco Forte Hotel. He reported she accompanied him to his suite and before they could, uh, let's say, conduct business, she robbed him of over a thousand euros."

Leaning forward in his chair, Wolfe asked, "Why did an Interpol agent question him and not the local police?"

DeVos smiled. "Because the man claimed the woman was from Belarus, Serbia, and he wanted Interpol involved."

Nadia asked, "Was the woman ever arrested?"

Shaking his head, the Frenchman kept his eyes on the computer screen. A sly grin grew on his lips. "No. In fact, no one matching the description he gave could be located. Security cameras in the hotel did not record an incident, as described. Plus, no witnesses could be located who saw the senator and the woman together. According to the police in Brussels, the case is still open. And this is interesting, the American never followed up with the Belgian authorities."

Wolfe's left eyebrow rose. "Peter, isn't that a little suspicious?"

"Yes, my friend, I would agree. There never was a woman, or a robbery. It was done to establish an alibi of where he was that day."

"Kind of what I'm thinking." Wolfe stood and offered his hand again. "Thanks, Peter. Can we contact you again if we have any questions?"

"Sure, Michael."

As Nadia stood and they turned to leave, DeVos said, "Uh, Michael."

He stopped and looked over his shoulder. "Yes?"

"Be careful where you use your ID. A lot of people still remember you from our days in Europe."

A slow smile came to Wolfe's lips. "Got it. Thanks for the tip."

Wolfe drove their rented Volvo SUV north on the A6. Their decision to drive versus flying helped them keep a low profile and maintain flexibility on where they might need to travel.

Nadia stared out the window of the SUV at the passing French countryside. "Do you think Ben's okay?"

Her husband said, "I doubt he's had time to miss us. Uri told me his wife had way too many activities lined up. He figured they wouldn't have time to accomplish half of them before we get back."

She kept her gaze locked on the passing scenery. Finally, after taking a deep breath, she said, "Did running into Peter DeVos compromise our aliases?"

"I don't believe so. At one time, he worked for the French Directorate-General for External Security. He and I worked together for a year rounding up Russian double agents. We got to know each other fairly well. I'm not worried about him revealing my real identity. I know where the bodies are buried in his career." Wolfe glanced at her. "And, he knows, I know where the bodies are buried, literally. So, will he compromise our aliases? Nope, he'll back me up."

"You sure?"

"Yes. He told me to be careful. That's his way of saying he'll keep my real identity under his hat. But I can't get sloppy. If I do, he'll make sure I pay for it."

She did not respond, keeping her eyes on the countryside. "I miss Ben."

He reached over and patted her thigh. "I do, too. But he is getting exposure to life in Israel. Something you have mentioned several times we needed to do."

"I know, but I wanted to be the person showing him the country."

An exit sign for a rural road flashed by. Wolfe changed lanes and left the A6. A kilometer later, he turned the SUV onto a small dirt road and stopped. He turned to Nadia. "Let's turn around, head back to Lyon, grab a flight to Israel, pick up Ben, and go home."

She stared at him. "You're serious."

"Extremely."

"We promised Joseph."

"We also retired several years ago. And no one seems to remember we did or, for that matter, care."

"I know. Have you been happy?"

"That's not the issue. The issue is we have a responsibility to Ben."

She took a deep breath and let it out slowly. "Yes, I'm very aware of that."

Wolfe continued. "We've played spy for the majority of our adult life, Nadia. We aren't that young anymore. I don't want to regret not being there for Ben. My father was gone most of the time when I was his age. It's hard for me to even remember him."

She turned toward him. "I don't remember you even mentioning your father."

He shrugged. "Nothing to talk about. Like I said, I barely remember him."

"What happened?"

The retired CIA operative took a deep breath. "Mom never told me. One day, he didn't come home, and she never mentioned him again."

"What was his profession?"

"Something to do with law enforcement. Once he was gone, Mom discarded everything she had that reminded her of him."

"Did you ask about him?"

"At first. When I did, she would tear up, shake her head, and not answer. I finally stopped asking. That's why I don't want to be away from Ben any more than I have to. He needs to know who his father is."

Taking a deep breath, she asked again, "Michael, have you been happy?"

"About having Ben in our life, yes."

"About us retiring?"

He wrapped his arms over the steering wheel and rested his chin on them. "I enjoy being a corporate pilot."

"Are you happy not doing what we used to do?"

He stared off into the distance. "In a way."

She smiled and put a hand on his shoulder. "I miss being able to accomplish something not too many people have the skills to do."

"Thank you. That's a better way to phrase it."

"What we're doing right now is a bit more exciting than driving to the local grocery store to do the weekly shopping."

He didn't answer.

"Yes, I miss Ben. But we have a chance to help Joseph. We owe him that."

Wolfe turned to her. "I agree." He started the SUV, put it in gear, and drove toward the next entrance ramp to get back on the A6. Brussels remained four hours away.

Belgium

Gazing out their hotel room window, Wolfe studied the building containing the headquarters of the North American Treaty Organization off in the distance. "Nadia?"

"Yes."

"Did you ever work in Brussels?"

"Yes."

"When?"

"During the time you worked for the Mossad."

He turned toward her. "The only work I did for the Mossad in Belgium was when they sent me to eliminate an Iranian bomb maker."

"Yes, I know."

"How?"

She went to him and placed her arms around his waist and her head on his chest. "I was your backup."

"I didn't have backup."

"Yes, you did. You just didn't know it."

He returned the embrace and placed his chin on her head. "Is that when…"

"Yes. I fell in love with you."

He closed his eyes. "How many times were you, my backup?"

"Most of your assignments."

Breaking from the embrace, he took her by the hand and led her to the bed.

Chapter Twenty-Seven

CIA HEADQUARTERS, LANGLEY, VA

Joseph Kincaid walked the halls of the George Bush Center for Intelligence saying hello to the men and women who worked there. Most he knew and those he did not, he stopped and conversed with for a few moments.

He ran into an old friend who would not let go of his hand. She said, "Thank gawd, you're back. This place has gone to hell since you started working for the Griffin administration and Dwight retired."

"Thank you for sticking around."

"I was on the verge of leaving."

Untangling himself from her handshake, he asked, "I appreciate you staying, Tamara. What did she do to cause your concern?"

"She kept demanding an update on an operation involving Calvin Hendricks."

Joseph kept a neutral expression. "I take it we don't have an operation involving the senator."

"No, sir. When I told her so, she flew off the handle and told me I was useless as an associate director."

"Not the best response from an HR point of view. Did she offer any details?"

"No, she would storm off mumbling under her breath. She asked me the same question four days later. It was like we'd never had the original conversation. I think the pressure was getting to her."

"Possibly." He thanked her again for staying. As soon as she walked away, he hurried back to his office on the sixth floor.

Jerry Griggs sat behind his desk working on a summary for the president when his personal cell phone vibrated. He checked the ID and accepted the call. "Griggs."

"It's Joseph."

"How's your first day going, Mr. Director."

"Have you heard from Michael?"

Griggs did not answer for a few moments. "No. Why?"

"Can you get me in to see the president today?"

"Head this way, I'll make sure he has time."

Forty-five minutes later, Joseph and Griggs sat in President Griffin's personal office. "Okay, Joseph, what's happened?"

"Sir, during a casual conversation with one of the associate directors, she relayed an incident where former Director Elliot asked her about an operation involving Senator Hendricks."

Griffin remained quiet for a few moments and then asked, "Why would a US senator be involved with a CIA operation?"

"That was my question as well. I've checked, all of Elliot's files are sealed."

"Joseph, you're the director. You have access."

"I'm the acting director, Mr. President. I don't feel comfortable accessing them until I'm confirmed. Did the FBI find anything in her apartment?"

"That's a question for Ryan Clark."

Joseph was ushered into FBI Director Ryan Clark's office at 1:15 p.m. Shaking the hand of his old friend, Joseph said, "Thank you for taking the time to see me, Ryan."

"Congratulations on being named DCI."

"I'm afraid the jury is still out on the matter." Joseph settled into a chair in front of Clark's desk. The FBI director sat behind it. Joseph said, "I won't take much of your time, but when your agents searched the apartment of Emma Elliot, did they find anything suspicious?"

Clark frowned. "Such as?"

"Files on Senator Calvin Hendricks."

"They found a lot of files that should not have been there. In fact, I had it on my to-do list to call you after you settled into the job."

"Have you seen the files?"

"Summaries."

"It's important, Ryan. Can I see the summaries?"

Clark reached for his desk phone and punched in a three-digit number. He said, "Riley, bring in the file we discussed yesterday from Elliot's apartment." Silence. "Yes, that one. Thank you."

Not fifteen seconds later, an attractive middle-aged

woman entered the office, placed the file on Clark's desk, smiled at Joseph, and then exited.

Clark handed the file to Joseph. "You'll find this contains information concerning an unidentified US senator who may be working behind the scenes to disgrace President Griffin."

After scanning the multiple pages in the file, he asked, "Have you discussed this with the president?"

Shaking his head, Clark said, "Waiting on an investigation by two senior agents to determine if there is any validity to the information."

"Is the identity of the individual mentioned?"

"No. But you obviously know or suspect who it is."

"There is a good chance it's Calvin Hendricks."

The director did not say anything for several moments. "Well, that explains why Hendricks has called numerous times demanding the files seized at Elliot's apartment be transferred to his committee."

Joseph smiled. "I take it you have not complied with his, uh, request."

"No, and I don't intend to do so. If we can verify Hendricks is the senator in question, I'll turn the matter over to the attorney general."

"Ryan, Michael Wolfe is in Europe investigating an incident involving the senator. Hendricks claimed to have been robbed in 2010 at a NATO summit in Brussels. The problem is, the summit was held in Lisbon, Portugal that year."

"A fact like that is easily verified. That's kind of dumb on the senator's part."

"I would agree it's a dumb mistake, unless he was trying to misdirect any inquiry of his whereabouts and actions in 2010."

Clark tapped his lip with his index finger. "What else have you got?"

"That's why Wolfe is in Europe. He and his wife still have contacts throughout Europe, and it keeps the CIA out of the inquiry."

With a chuckle, the director asked, "Who's he supposedly working for now?"

"Homeland Security."

"Uh boy." Clark accepted the file back from Joseph. "Let's stay in touch. I'll talk to the attorney general about getting a court order to put Hendricks under surveillance."

"Make sure you do it quietly, Ryan. He's looking to undermine the Griffin administration. If he gets a whiff of your investigation, he'll call a news conference, scream bloody murder, and blame the president."

With a sly smile, Clark said, "Not my first time, Joseph."

Chicago

The man who emerged from the jet bridge at O'Hara International Airport turned left outside the gate. He hurried down the concourse to a coffee bar facing the departure lounge where his connecting flight would originate. Five minutes later, a tall, middle-aged man sat at an adjacent table to his right.

Senator Calvin Hendricks said to the newcomer, "You're late."

"Talk to the airline. I haven't been on an on-time flight this month."

"What happened at Wolfe's property?"

"It was a clusterfuck. Who planned it?"

"Katz."

"Well, there you go. He paid the price for his stupidity."

"You didn't answer my question."

The man at the next table grumbled. "Apparently, he failed to check out the security surrounding the property. The place is a fortress, with trip wires and security cameras throughout the woods surrounding the house and hangar. Wolfe's got sniper hides on the top floor of his hangar. He probably knew where we were from the minute we stepped onto his property."

"Unfortunate."

"For Katz."

"Yes, yes. We have a problem. With Elliot's death, our eyes and ears are gone from inside the CIA."

"That's your department, not mine."

Hendricks glared at the man for a few moments. "Everything is on hold until we get this situation resolved."

"Better not place my payment on hold."

Rolling his eyes, the senator took a deep breath and let it out slowly. Through gritted teeth, he said, "With you, it's always about the money."

"Not doing this for my health."

"We need the CIA and the FBI focusing on the list again. Got any ideas?"

"You forget why I was hired. It wasn't to provide, as you say, ideas. Figure it out yourself."

Hendricks glared at the man sitting at the next table. Finally, he stood. "My flight is getting ready to depart. Keep yourself available." He walked out of the café, crossed the terminal, presented his boarding pass, and disappeared into the jetway.

Chapter Twenty-Eight

BELGIUM

The small bistro, located in the Grand-Place square, offered covered outdoor tables, much like similar establishments in Paris. Construction started on the outdoor space in the 11th century and continued for the next 600 years. In 1695, during the Nine Years' War, a majority of the structures were destroyed by French artillery. Only the tower, of what eventually became the Brussels Town Hall, remained. Since then, the area has been rebuilt and modified. Now, the Grand-Place is an important tourist destination and considered one of the world's most beautiful squares.

With the town hall to their left, Wolfe and Nadia surveyed the foot traffic in the cobblestone paved area. Nadia sipped an espresso, while he enjoyed a cafe americano. She touched his arm. "There's Jean-Paul."

Turning his attention in the direction she indicated, he recognized the man from pictures he studied before their arrival in the plaza. "Your turn."

She stood and set off to intercept him. When she was a few meters from him, she spoke in Parisian-accented

French. "Excuse me, monsieur. Do you have a moment?" She displayed her Homeland Security credentials.

The man contemplated her for a moment. "What is this concerning?"

"My partner and I have some questions we think you can help us with. Would you join us for an espresso?"

The man looked at Wolfe and smiled. "Yes, Ms. Picard, I would enjoy that."

He followed her to their table. Wolfe stood and shook hands with the man. Switching to English, Wolfe said, "Sorry for the intrusion on your day, Jean-Paul."

Jean-Paul Lussier smiled. "Uri told me you two might find me. What should I call you?"

Wolfe pointed at his wife. "Holly Harper, and my name is Patrick Ryan, at your service."

Lussier clasped his hands together. "I personally prefer your real names. What brings you to Belgium?"

Nadia said, "You've heard about Hershel Katz?"

Leaning back in his chair, the Jewish Frenchman hesitated. "Oui."

"He's dead."

"Word on the street indicated he was a double agent and made his way to America."

"He did." Nadia continued. "He died on Michael's and my property in the middle of the country."

"Good. I met him once. Did not care much for him."

Wolfe said, "Which brings us to why we are here and under assumed names."

"Uri told me a little, but maybe you should fill in the gaps."

Five minutes later, after summarizing their reason for being in the country, Lussier remained quiet for few moments. "2010 was a long time ago. If there were security videos, they would be long gone. The hotel where he claims to have stayed might still have records, but they would be digital and archived by now."

"Uri indicated you might have a contact within the Belgian Federal Police."

"I might."

"We'd like to talk to him."

"His name is Noah Peeters, Michael. And he is not a fan of the United States. I doubt he would be truthful with you."

"Would he talk to Nadia? She still speaks fluent French."

"Maybe. But you two will need a legitimate reason to ask him about a case a decade and a half old."

"What's the terrorist situation here in Brussels, Jean-Paul?"

"Tenuous."

"Tell him there is a possibility the incident in 2010 may be linked to a plot to weaken the Mossad, MI6, and the CIA."

"He won't care about the CIA."

Wolfe gave the Mossad agent a slight smile. "He might want to reconsider that point of view. If memory serves me, the CIA has given his government more tips on terrorist attacks planned for Brussels than MI6 and the Mossad combined. What will his country do if they no longer have the benefit of those early warnings. Homeland Security is asking for a small favor."

With a grin, Lussier stood. "How do I get in touch with you two?"

Nadia told him.

As he walked away, Nadia turned to her husband. "Kinda stretched the truth a bit, didn't you, Michael?"

Watching the Mossad agent disappear into the crowd on

the square, Wolfe shrugged. "Did I? We don't know what Hendricks has planned. Maybe what I said is in the realm of possibility."

She chuckled before taking another sip of her espresso.

Nadia and Wolfe were escorted into the office of Captain Noah Peeters of the Belgian Federal Police. Both were surprised how young the man appeared. Tall, athletic, dark hair, and a chiseled face. He stood when they entered but did not smile, his hands behind his back.

The man spoke in French. "Credentials, please."

Both offered their Homeland Security IDs. Nadia said in French, "Thank you for seeing us."

The man accepted the wallets, examined them, and then handed them back.

Wolfe also spoke in French. "We know you are busy. We only require a few moments of your time."

Peeters' scowl softened. "You both speak French?"

The couple said in unison, "Oui."

A smile seemed to almost crack the stern face. "Finally, educated Americans." He switched to English. "How can I help you today?"

Nadia answered him in French-accented English. "We are seeking information on a US senator who claimed to have been robbed at the Rocco Forte Hotel by a woman he met in the hotel bar. The date would be October, 2010."

The captain's eyebrows rose. "You sound like you have roots in France."

"My father was an international businessman, and I was raised in Paris."

"Ahh." He turned to a keyboard sitting in front of a large monitor. "Let me check our records."

The captain typed, studied, and then typed some more. Turning his attention back to Nadia, he said, "What was the exact date?"

"October 22, 2010."

"Hmm."

Both Wolfe and Nadia remained quiet.

"I see here, it remains an open investigation. No witnesses were found and a suspect never identified."

Wolfe said, "That was our understanding as well."

"Agent Ryan, did you say the victim was a US senator?"

"Yes."

"He's identified here as an employee of the United Nations."

"Does it give his name?"

"Calvin Hendricks."

"Calvin Hendricks is a United States senator who took office in January 2005. What form of identification does your report indicate he used?"

"Passport."

"Not a UN ID?"

"Not that the report mentions."

"How is the suspect described?"

Peeters scrolled the mouse and read something on the screen. He said, "Tall, slender, blonde with blue eyes, no specific height or weight, spoke with what the victim described as a Serbian accent."

"In your opinion, Captain Peeters, could an American distinguish the difference between a Serbian accent and a Russian accent?"

"I'm not an expert, Agent Ryan, but I would say no.

They are both Slavic languages but with key differences a non-native speaker might miss."

"So, the Serbian woman might be a Russian. Would that be a safe assumption?"

Peeters seemed to relax for the first time since they arrived. "Yes, but we have no way to prove it."

Wolfe stood. "We don't need to prove anything. The fact Hendricks identified himself as a member of the UN and the possibility the woman might have been Russian is all the information we need."

As the rented Volvo headed south on the I-6 out of Brussels, Nadia turned to her husband. "How do we prove Hendricks' involvement with the Russians?"

"Apparently, he's gotten a little more sophisticated with his meetings than the one in 2010. It was clumsily covered up with the Serbian woman story." Wolfe paused for a moment. "How much location data is stored in cell phones, Nadia?"

"According to Alexia, it depends on the carrier. Most keep it for five years. Why?"

"It would be interesting to see where Hendricks has traveled in the past five years. As a senator, he has an excuse to go overseas whenever he feels the need."

"I would think public records of his activities would exist."

"If we had access to his senate records, we could cross-reference cell phone data on his actual location. If there is a discrepancy, we would know what to look for."

"I wonder if Alexia could get the information?"

Wolfe gave his wife a smile. "Give her a call. See if something like that would interest her."

Chapter Twenty-Nine

SOUTHWEST MISSOURI

Alexia Gibbs' day job kept her busy, with little time for extracurricular activities. The process of chasing a money trail for her friend Nadia Wolfe occurred after her husband and son were in bed asleep.

So far, the trail remained elusive. Senator Hendricks appeared to have a clean record when it came to publicly available financial transactions. The key word in her search being "appeared." On this particular night, she followed a transaction link she had not found before, to a numbered bank account in the Cayman Islands. Discovering the bank account opened the floodgates to a whole new side of the senator.

Without awareness of the time, she used her cell phone to contact her friend. The call was answered on the second ring.

"Hello."

"Hi, Nadia, it's Alexia."

"Isn't it kind of late for you?"

A momentary silence on the phone was followed by,

"Sorry. I didn't know what time it was. Do I need to call back?"

"Nonsense, it's almost eight in the morning here in Paris, which is the middle of the night for you."

Ignoring the comment, Alexia said, "I've been following Hendricks' financial transactions, like you asked."

"What'd you find?"

"Where do you want me to start?"

"That bad?"

"Well, he's a saint if you only look at public records. Once you get below the veneer, he's running a criminal enterprise."

"How so?"

Alexia pulled up her notes from earlier in the evening on her computer screen. "First, he has three separate cell phones he pays from the numbered account. None of which are in his name, but with the same carrier."

"That's kind of dumb."

"I agree with you, Nadia."

"Can you monitor any calls on those cell phones?"

"I am shocked at the question." She chuckled.

"Good. What else did you find?"

"The account sends automatic disbursements to five different bank accounts on a biweekly basis. The amounts are always five figures but vary in value. The largest of the distributions goes to an account in the same Cayman bank. Guess who owns it?"

"Hendricks."

"Correct, Nadia. The balance in this account is over seven figures."

"Who owns the other four?"

"I'm still working on that, but all four are in a bank in Dubai."

"Alexia, you'll probably find that Armin Jazani owned one of those four accounts. He's now deceased."

"That information might help me uncover all four of them. Thanks for the heads-up. Now, want to know who's funding Hendricks' numbered account?"

"I can't wait."

"Central Bank in Minsk, Belarus."

The phone call went silent for a considerable length of time. Finally, she heard. "Alexia, where's that money coming from?"

"Their neighbor to the east."

"We've got him. Do you know where Hendricks is right now?"

"He flew into Chicago yesterday and made a connection to London. He's staying at the Hyatt Place, Heathrow, room 434."

"How long is the reservation?"

"He flies out tomorrow night, London time."

"Hold on." The phone went silent for two minutes. Nadia came back on. "Michael says we are only six hours from London. We're heading that way. Call me if Hendricks moves."

London

Wolfe exited the elevator on the fourth floor. He checked the sign for the direction of the room he sought and turned in that way. As he passed room 434, he noticed a Do Not Disturb sign on the exterior door handle. He continued toward the end of the hall where he turned around and walked back toward 434. He stopped, knocked, and waited.

No response. He knocked again. Still, no response. Looking up and down the hall, he pressed the key card against the reader. The door clicked, and he entered the room.

The sound of a shower could be heard behind the closed bathroom door. Taking a quick survey of the room, he saw clothes on the bed and a suitcase in the closet. The stainless-steel bag tag identified the owner to be Senator Calvin Hendricks.

From his wallet, he took a clear silicone disk out and slipped it between the business card and the solid side of the identification holder. Just as he finished, the shower shut off. Wolfe returned to the door and let himself out.

Ten minutes later, he slipped behind the Volvo's steering wheel and said, "Done."

Sitting in the passenger seat, Nadia stared at her phone. "We have a good signal. What's the range on the disk?"

"Kilometer." He turned toward her. "Was Alexia able to find any more about his itinerary?"

"All she could find was on his official senate website. He has a dinner meeting tonight and then flies to Munich tomorrow morning."

Glancing at his watch, Wolfe settled into his seat. "Now we wait."

Their wait lasted a brief forty-six minutes. Hendricks exited the hotel and slipped into a Mercedes four-door sedan parked by the lobby door. Wolfe saw this through his side-view mirror. When the car passed them, he started his and followed.

The Mercedes headed east toward London. Keeping a safe distance behind the sedan, Wolfe noticed the driver made several maneuvers designed to determine if someone followed. The retired CIA agent knew the tricks and kept their presence from being discovered.

He turned to Nadia. "Whoever is driving him hasn't been trained too well."

Keeping her attention on the car they followed, Nadia said, "Why is Hendricks riding in a car with a driver who is making obvious counter-tailing turns and switchbacks?"

Wolfe did not answer her right away. Finally, he said, "Good point. Not your standard Uber driver, is it?"

"Not in the slightest." She pulled out her phone and punched in a number. When the call was answered, she said, "Hi, Alexia. Can you check an international license plate?" She listened for a moment and then relayed the number for the Mercedes. The call ended. "She'll get back to us."

Ten minutes later, Nadia's phone chirped. "What'd you find?" She listened. "Interesting, thanks. I'll let you know later." She ended the call. "I'm now questioning the intelligence and judgement of Senator Hendricks. The car is leased to the Russian embassy here in London."

Shooting a quick glance at his wife, Wolfe shook his head. "Obviously, the good senator feels he is above everything. He can't be this foolish." He frowned. "Or can he?"

She pointed as the car they followed made a left turn into a famous restaurant on the outskirts of London. "Would Hendricks recognize you?"

"Don't know. Being in his position within the senate, there's a chance he might have seen my picture."

"Kind of what I thought. No need to take the chance. I'll go in."

Wolfe drove the Volvo past the portico just as Hendricks walked into the establishment. He backed into a parking slot at the back of the lot. He turned to his wife. "Try not to make eye contact with him."

With a chuckle, she said, "I've done this before, Michael. Don't worry."

He smiled. "I know, just be careful."

She returned the smile, gave him a quick kiss on the lips, and exited the vehicle.

Entering the high-end restaurant, Nadia approached the host and reverted to a thick French accent. "Monsieur, I apologize for the intrusion. I am horribly late for a dinner engagement. May I search for my party?"

"What is the party's name?"

"Hendrickson."

"Let me check." He searched his chart and then shook his head. "I'm sorry, no one by that name. I do have a Hendricks."

Nadia said, "No, that is not him."

The host smiled. By this time, several guests were lined up behind Nadia. "Why don't you walk through to see if he is here. Please don't disturb our guests."

"Merci, Monsieur." She walked into the dining area and immediately scanned the diners. Without seeing the senator, she turned her attention to the private booths area on the left. In the very back corner of the room, she saw him. He faced a man with his back to Nadia. When she passed them, she glanced behind and almost stopped walking. The senator's dinner companion turned out to be Sergey Ivanov, the top Russian case officer in the United Kingdom. Keeping herself in character, she returned to searching for her imaginary date.

Walking back the way she came, she hesitated and managed to take several pictures of the senator and the SVR handler. She retreated to the restroom to make sure the pictures were clear. While not perfect, they were good enough to identify the Russian. In addition, she did not think Ivanov would be fooled with a second trip through the dining room. She waited a few minutes before leaving the stall and the restaurant.

Wolfe watched the minutes pass on the dashboard clock. When it showed twenty minutes had elapsed, he opened his door at the same moment she exited the restaurant through the front entrance. At a casual pace, she made her way toward the car.

When she slipped into the passenger seat, she said, "You won't believe who he's meeting with."

"Nadia, at this point, I'll believe anything."

"You know him."

"Nadia—who is it?"

The smile on her face told him the name would be interesting. "Sergey Ivanov."

Wolfe laughed out loud. "You're kidding?"

"No, they had a few vodkas and then ordered dinner. Very chummy."

"I do hope you took pictures."

Her grin told him she had.

"Send them to Jerry. He'll know who Ivanov is."

Chapter Thirty

WASHINGTON, DC

Jerry Griggs heard the tone of an incoming text message. He picked up his cell phone. The new one read, *check email, interesting meeting NW*. The only NW he knew would refer to Nadia Wolfe. He accessed his personal email account and found one from a Gmail account labeled *ladypredator@*. When he opened the attachment, he studied the two individuals in the photo. He recognized the senator and the man he was talking to. With a grin, he picked up his phone and called the director of the FBI.

Ryan Clark arrived at the White House a few moments before a car ferrying the attorney general to the meeting pulled in behind him. Both men were escorted to the situation room where the new acting CIA director and the secretary of Homeland Security already sat.

President Griffin pointed to two empty chairs and said, "Take a seat, gentlemen. Thank you all for coming so late in the day. But I felt it necessary because we may have a serious problem." Looking at his national security advisor, Griffin said, "Go ahead, Jerry."

Griggs stood and laid a photo in front of each of the attendees. "The picture I am providing to each of you is that of Sergey Ivanov. He is the Kremlin's man in the UK and one of their top intelligence officers in the SVR. In other words, he handles all of their most important spies."

Joseph Kincaid held the photo for study and said, "He's a buddy of the Russian president as well. They grew up together in the KGB."

Now, with another stack of pictures in his hands, Griggs set the next one in front of the attendees. "This picture was taken four hours ago at a restaurant on the western outskirts of London. Note who is sitting with Mr. Ivanov."

A chorus of, "son of a bitch," spread around the table.

The NSA nodded. "Exactly. Senator Calvin Hendricks having a friendly glass of vodka and a medium-rare steak with Russian's top spy in England."

Attorney General Dale Delgado closed his eyes and pinched the bridge of his nose. "Can we assume this is not a chance meeting for the good senator?"

Griffin clasped his hands together. "There's more. Continue, Jerry."

Now seated at the conference table, Griggs said, "We have received information that Senator Hendricks has a bank account in the Cayman Islands with just under ten million dollars. Source of those funds is a bank in Belarus."

A communal groan rose in the room.

As he studied the photos, Delgado asked, "Who took the pictures?"

Joseph Kincaid answered, "We have a team following the senator. He's been on our radar for a while now."

"Mr. President?"

"Yes, Ryan."

"Do we need a team of agents on a plane for London?"

"I think that would be a wise move. Jerry can give you his hotel information. If they leave immediately, they can be there before he checks out in the morning." Griffin turned to Delgado. "Can you arrange for a warrant for Hendricks' arrest to be signed by a judge within the hour?"

"Yes, sir."

"Make it so. The warrant can be scanned and emailed to the agents in-flight. They should have a printer available so it can be printed. I would love for them to arrest him in his underwear."

Clark stood and left the room.

Griffin turned his attention to the remaining men at the conference table. "We need to assess how extensive the damage could be with the Russians having Hendricks in their back pocket."

Secretary of Homeland Security Eric Perez took a deep breath and let it out slowly. "Mr. President, I believe we can expect the damage to be cataclysmic."

"Why do you say that, Eric?"

"Hendricks is the chairman of the Senate Intelligence Select Committee. He is regularly briefed on a variety of subjects by the heads of my departments."

"That's why I asked the question, Eric. Gentlemen, we have a lot to accomplish. Security protocols need to be changed and strengthened immediately."

Ryan Clark reentered the room. "The agents will be wheels up in thirty minutes."

"Who is on Hendricks' committee?"

Perez said, "Senators Taylor Finley and Jayden Berry are key members."

Turning to Clark, Griffin said, "Put them under surveillance immediately."

"Yes, sir."

The president stood. "Gentlemen, let's get to work. I don't have to stress how critical this situation has become."

London

The pounding on Hendricks' hotel door started at exactly 6:05 a.m. GMT. At first, he ignored it, but then heard, "Calvin Hendricks, FBI. Open the door."

Frowning, he shuffled to the door and peered out the security fish-eye peephole. Two men in suits stood there. FBI badges hung from their necks on lanyards. He asked, "What's the meaning of this interruption?"

"Open the door, Senator."

"Not without proof of who you are."

As he watched through the peephole, the agent standing in the back pressed his cell phone to his ear. When he took the phone down, he said, "You will be getting a call from the Senate Majority Leader. Answer it."

At that second, Hendricks' phone vibrated. He rushed back to the nightstand and stared at the caller ID. It was from a number in Washington, DC he knew belonged to the leader. He answered, "Hello."

"Hendricks, do you recognize my voice?"

"Yes."

"Good. Open the damn door."

"What's going on, Carl?"

"Open the gawd damn door and find out."

The call ended. The pounding started up again, and Hendricks unlatched the security lock.

Wolfe and Nadia stood off to the side of the FBI agents as they filed into the room. Once Hendricks was placed in handcuffs, the husband-and-wife team strolled into the room. Hendricks stared at Wolfe and demanded, "Who are you?"

Holding his Homeland Security badge and ID, he said, "Patrick Ryan, Homeland Security."

Nadia showed her ID. "Holly Harper." She turned to the FBI agents. "Gentlemen, would you do the honor of searching his room?"

The taller of the two agents nodded and yanked the senator's suitcase out of the closet, while the other agent explained Hendricks' Miranda rights.

When he was done, Hendricks screamed, "I demand to know the reason for this."

Nadia walked up to him and showed him the picture she took on her cell phone. "Remember your dinner last night with Sergey Ivanov?"

The senator did not respond.

"Mr. Ivanov works for the Russian SVR and just happens to be their top spy recruiter. Did you know that, Mr. Hendricks?"

"I don't know the man."

"Then, why were you having dinner with him?"

"He claimed to be a man interested in doing business in my home state."

"Not according to records pulled from the NSA. They have you and him talking on a regular basis over the past two years. You were always out of the US on one of your many overseas trips when you spoke to him."

While this conversation went on, Wolfe examined the senator's cell phone. Using tips given to him by Alexia Gibbs, he scrolled through the phone numbers. One in particular seemed to be called more than others. Taking the phone, he stepped out into the hall and called Griggs.

The president's national security advisor answered. Wolfe said, "Jerry, I need you to do your magic and see who this number belongs to." He told him the number. "Thanks. Call when you know something."

When Wolfe stepped back into the hotel room, he closed the door. The tall FBI agent showed him a phone. "Found this in the lining of his suitcase."

"Looks like a satellite phone."

"It is. But it's not from the USA. It's Russian."

Turning his attention back to the senator, who now sat on the unmade bed, Wolfe said, "Senator, you've been a naughty boy."

Hendricks glared at him but said nothing.

Somewhere Over the Atlantic

Wolfe and Nadia hitched a ride back to the US on the FBI Gulfstream. Hendricks sat at the front of the cabin in a seat by himself, his hands and feet cuffed. The two FBI agents were busy on cell phones talking to colleagues about the evidence found in the suitcase and the senator's backpack.

Nudging his wife, Wolfe showed her a text message from Jerry. *Phone number is attached to the Russian cell phone provider MegaFon. Owner listed as Ivan Ivanovich.*

With a chuckle, Wolfe said, "That's the Russian equivalent of John Smith."

"Figures." She paused. "Michael, will any of this be enough to put Hendricks in jail?"

"No, but it will probably give the senate enough reason

to expel him. Either way, he's no longer in a position to compromise the US government."

"So, how does all of this relate to the list? And, for that matter, what's so important about the list?"

Running his fingers through his hair, Wolfe shook his head. "I honestly don't know."

She laid her head on his shoulder. "When are we going back to get Ben?"

"I spoke to Uri before we got on the plane. Ben seems to be thriving. He's picking up Hebrew rather fast." He leaned his head over to touch hers. "Uri said he does miss us. Unfortunately, right now it is better for him to be there than with us. I'm not convinced we aren't still in the crosshairs of a sniper's rifle."

Lifting her head, she asked, "Why?"

"Everything Hendricks did was sloppy. It's like he wanted to be caught." Wolfe stopped and raised his head. "Or, and I didn't think of this until just now, somebody wanted him to get caught."

"Now that you mention it, you're right. Was he a decoy?"

"Possibly, because something else is going on here, Nadia."

"What if somebody else within the government is compromised?"

"It would explain a lot." He pulled his cell phone out of his back pocket and punched in a number.

Chapter Thirty-One

WASHINGTON, DC

Federal District Courthouse

"Mr. Breckenworth, how does your client plead to the charges of espionage?"

"Your Honor, my client pleads not guilty."

The judge turned to the prosecutor. "Any recommendations?"

"Your Honor, Mr. Hendricks should be considered a flight risk. The people request his passport be revoked and he be held without bail."

The judge turned to the defense attorney and asked, "Any comments?"

"Yes, Your Honor. My client is innocent and has no desire to run away from these ridiculous allegations."

"Very well." Returning his attention to the defense team, he said, "Mr. Harris, the man does not have a criminal record and is a duly elected member of Congress. Your request for the defendant to be held without bail is denied. However, his passport must be surrendered. I set bond at one million dollars." He slammed his gavel and stood. Turning, he exited the courtroom, and the stunned district attorney stared at the now-closed door with an open mouth.

At the back of the gallery, Wolfe and Nadia stood and hurried out of the courtroom. They stood off to the side and watched the crowded courtroom empty.

The retired CIA operative folded his arms. "That was a mistake by the judge. Hendricks will have bail posted within the hour and be dead within forty-eight."

"Why do you say that, Michael?"

"Emma Elliot didn't survive the first night after she was stripped of her CIA director title."

"You think someone will try to kill the senator?"

He shrugged. "Not try. They'll get it done and make it appear to be suicide."

Nadia subtly pointed toward the door of the courtroom. Hendricks' attorney emerged and became immediately surrounded by reporters. From their advantage, individual questions were garbled by the din of twenty people trying to be heard.

The herd quieted as Dwight Breckenworth said, "The senator is innocent. The charges against him are politically motivated by the current administration. He will be proven innocent in a court of law."

More shouting ensued, with one loud enough to be heard over the din. "Is it true, Hendricks is planning to challenge President Griffin for his party's nomination?"

The lawyer raised his hands, palms toward the reporter. "Senator Hendricks is a loyal supporter of the current president. He has no plans to challenge his party's nominee."

Wolfe stopped listening. "The final piece of the puzzle just fell into place, Nadia."

She looked up at him. "How so?"

"The list is a sham. It was made to draw attention away from the real goal, disgrace Griffin, and pave the way for Hendricks to run for president. If he is elected, all of a sudden, the USA has a president who's been compromised by the Russians. Let's get out of here before traffic gets snarled up."

Driving away from the district courthouse, Wolfe tapped his finger on the steering wheel.

Glancing over at her husband, Nadia said, "Every time you tap your finger on the steering wheel, you're mulling over something."

"I may have been a little hasty about what I said earlier."

"You mean what you said at the courthouse?"

"Yeah, I thought I had it figured out. But the more I think about it, the more things don't add up."

"I agree. If the Russians were planning on Hendricks challenging Griffin, why the sloppy tradecraft? If they were really trying to compromise a potential candidate to oppose President Griffin, I would think they would have been a little bit more discreet about the meeting between Ivanov and the senator."

The ex-CIA operative did not respond for a while as he drove toward their hotel room near Reagan National Airport. "Did Joseph say when Hendricks' two senate buddies were to be interviewed?"

"Tomorrow afternoon. Why?"

"When we get to the hotel, let's see if we can get invited to watch."

Nadia smiled.

The Next Day

Senator Taylor Finley sat in an interview room at the J. Edgar Hoover Building on Pennsylvania Avenue. An attorney sat next to him as they waited for the agents assigned to his case to arrive. The lawyer turned to his client. "Don't say anything unless I authorize it."

Finley shot the man a sharp glare. "I haven't done anything."

"Save it for the interview."

Clasping his hands together, he said, "It's true. I didn't know Hendricks was dealing with the Russians."

At that moment, the door to the room opened, and a tall gentleman accompanied by another man entered. Neither the lawyer or Finley stood. The two men sat and offered their credentials.

"Special Agent in Charge Mike Garcia, FBI. This is Homeland Security Agent Patrick Ryan."

"My client knows nothing about Calvin Hendricks' involvement with a Russian spy, gentlemen. I demand his immediate release."

Garcia smiled. "He's not under arrest, Counselor. We're merely seeking information."

"Good. My client will be as cooperative as possible. He will not be answering self-incriminating questions."

The FBI agent nodded. "Very well. Agent Ryan, do you have any questions for Senator Finley?"

Wolfe gave the senator a slight smile. "What is your relationship with Senator Hendricks?"

Finley glanced at his attorney, who nodded slightly. "He and I are on the same committee."

"For the record, what is the committee?"

"Senate Select Committee on Intelligence."

"Your duties?"

"I'm one of the members."

"Hendricks is the chairman, correct?"

"Yes."

"How many trips overseas does he take a year?"

The attorney leaned over and whispered into Finley's ear.

The senator said, "I've been advised not to answer your question, Agent Ryan."

Wolfe turned and stared at the attorney. "Why would that question incriminate your client, Counselor?"

"His answers would be speculative at best. He would have no way to know Hendericks' schedule or his activities outside of the senate, Agent."

With a nod, Wolfe turned to the FBI agent. "Your turn, Agent Garcia."

The FBI agent asked questions for another fifteen minutes. Finley only answered two of the numerous ones presented to him. Finally, the SAC folded his hands. "You've been less than helpful, Senator Finley. My instincts tell me you are lying to Agent Ryan and me. Are you?"

The senator narrowed his eyes and glared at them. "I answered the questions I could. No, Agent Garcia, I am not lying to you."

A knock at the door caused the FBI agent to stand and open it. A man in a navy suit handed Garcia a sheet of paper. He read it and asked, "When?"

The newcomer said, "About two this morning."

"Thanks, Matt." Shutting the door, Garcia passed the note to Wolfe. After scanning the page, he folded it and handed it back to the FBI agent.

Garcia said, "Counselor, I have just been informed that Senator Calvin Hendricks fell to his death from the top floor of the Grand Hyatt's atrium last night."

Finley's eyes grew round, and he stared at Garcia and then at his attorney.

The lawyer said, "Gentlemen, may I have a few moments alone with my client?"

Both Wolfe and the FBI agent stood and left the room.

———

Thirty minutes later, the lawyer called Garcia and Wolfe back into the room. When they sat, the senator asked, "When did this happen, Agent?"

"About two this morning."

"Was it an accident?"

Garcia smiled. "I'm not at liberty to discuss details at the moment."

The lawyer said, "Agent, my client's life could be in danger. Was this an accident?"

"Why would your client's life be in danger if he knew nothing about Hendricks' extracurricular activities?"

Wolfe said, "No, it was not an accident. Hendricks was pushed. He also had a blood alcohol content of .35. Someone pumped him full of liquor and helped him over the railings."

Finley stared at Wolfe for a long time.

The ex-CIA operative said, "Sounds like something the Russian president likes to make happen, doesn't it? Only, this time, the incident occurred in this country to an American politician."

The respiratory rate on Finley increased. He turned to

his attorney. "I don't care what you say. I'm telling them what I know and seeking protective custody."

Wolfe listened to Finley outline the project.

"The concept was to have the list circulate within the intelligence community to raise suspicions about President Griffin's control over the intelligence community. When Dwight King retired, Calvin felt it was our chance to move the project even further along. When we recommended Elliot to Griffin, we knew she was incompetent. But we also discovered she was paranoid, which helped our plan even more."

"So, what exactly is the list?"

"Hendricks told us it was a lot of random names. Some were to help certain people disappear. Whether that happened or not, I have no idea."

Wolfe did not comment on this part of the senator's narrative. He let the man continue.

"Calvin stopped relaying details to Jayden Berry and me after Emma was fired. When Joseph Kincaid became the acting DCI, he retreated into a shell. He didn't like Joseph for some reason. Whatever it was, he never explained why."

"Let's go back to the list, Taylor. You're telling me it meant nothing? Just random names?"

"That was my understanding. Except for a few individuals who would use the list as a cover to disappear."

"Did he ever mention where the list came from?"

"No."

"What about Jayden Berry? What does he know?"

"Less than I do. He wasn't at all the meetings with Hendricks. He was kind of a gofer for our committee."

The meeting went on for another thirty minutes. When they were done, Wolfe thanked the senator and followed Garcia out. As they walked away from the interrogation room, he asked Garcia, "What do you think, Mike?"

Garcia took a deep breath and let it out slowly. "I think he was lying his ass off."

"Yeah, I got the same feeling."

Chapter Thirty-Two

WASHINGTON, DC

Wolfe walked into the hotel room and heard Nadia talking on her phone. She motioned him over to the chair where she sat and said, "Ben, your daddy's here. Do to you want to talk to him?" Nadia put the phone on speaker and handed it to her husband.

"Hi, Ben."

"Hi back. Mommy said you were busy today. Doing what?"

"Talking to a lot of people. I hear you're learning Hebrew."

"Yeah. Want me to say something?"

"Sure."

"Bi li glida."

"Do you get ice cream a lot?"

The little boy giggled. "Yes, but I'm not supposed to tell you."

Nadia said, "It's okay, Ben. Just as long as you eat your vegetables as well."

"When am I coming home, Mommy?"

A tear welled up in Nadia's eye. "Soon, Ben. Are you homesick?"

"A little. I miss our forest and you and Daddy."

She looked up at her husband.

He said, "Ben, do you want us to come this weekend and get you?"

"This weekend we're going to a fair. So, after the fair, maybe."

"Okay. We'll call your doh-dah and make plans."

"Yippee."

The call ended a few minutes later. Before he could say anything, Nadia hurried into the bathroom and shut the door. Putting his ear to the door, Wolfe could hear her crying softly. "It's okay to miss Ben, Nadia." He waited. She did not answer. "Nadia, talk to me, princess."

The door flew open. She wrapped her arms around his waist and buried her head against his chest. He could feel her body shake as she sobbed.

He stroked her hair, placed his cheek on the top of her head, and remained quiet.

After five minutes of silence, she looked up at him. "Make love to me tonight, Michael. Then, tomorrow, we will return to Israel and get our son."

He led her to the bed and they collapsed, embraced in each other's arms.

As they lay in bed, still holding on to each other, Nadia said, "You haven't called me princess for a long time."

"A mistake on my part."

"Yes. I agree."

He raised up on an elbow and gazed at her. "I don't like

how we both fell back into this life of spies and international mischief as fast as we did. I thought we put all this crap behind us."

"We did."

"Then what happened?"

She placed her hand on his cheek and said, "Your love of a just cause. It's who you are. And it's one of the many reasons I love you."

He lay back down with his hands behind his head. She placed her head on his chest and his arm immediately slipped around her shoulder.

She said, "I'm probably the reason we did. I said we owed Joseph a lot."

"We do. More than we can ever repay."

"I also know we'll continue to help him if he asks."

"Yes. One of us will. Me."

She remained quiet for several moments. "Why do you say that?"

"Because if we've learned anything over the past few weeks, it's that our priorities have changed. We have a son. A son who we sometimes conveniently seem to forget. We then tried to turn back the clock and go on some wild adventure. We need to get ourselves and Ben back home."

He felt her head nod on his chest. He also felt wetness where her cheek touched his chest.

When she tilted her head up to look at him, he saw tears pooling in her eyes.

His hand wiped her cheek. He said, "I've been thinking we need some additional security at the house."

"Such as?"

"A dog."

"What kind?"

"German shepherd."

She tried to hide it but could not. A real smile crossed her lips. "I like the idea. I know Ben would. Who will train him?"

"Or her. An old buddy of mine used to be a dog handler in the military. He has a kennel now and trains dogs for police departments. I talked to him a year ago when I first started thinking about it. He told me he would love to find one for us. The breed is extremely intelligent and loyal to their family."

She brushed her bare breasts against his chest and put her head on his shoulder.

He brought her into an embrace and made love to her for the second time that evening.

Central Missouri
A Week Later

Wolfe shook the hand of his friend. "How've you been, Mack?"

"Fine, Michael, just fine. And yourself?"

With a shrug, Wolfe said, "You know me. I can't seem to stay out of trouble."

Mack Brown laughed out loud. "Yeah, I can see that." He pointed to Nadia and young Benjamin as they strolled among the kennels. "Nice-looking family, my friend."

"Thanks. Something I never thought I would have."

Brown remained quiet as he watched young Ben Wolfe stop and say hello to some of the dogs. "I think I've found you a good match."

"Really? That was fast."

"Not really. I learned about the situation a few weeks

ago and made a few inquiries after you called. She's a four-year-old German shepherd I trained as a police dog. She and her handler were in an automobile accident about a month ago. They both survived, but the handler is paralyzed and can't work with dogs anymore. The department decided to retire the dog rather than give her to an inexperienced officer."

Keeping his hands in his pockets, Wolfe nodded as they walked toward a section of Brown's kennel. "Understandable."

"The dog's name is Nova."

"I like that. It means new in Latin."

"Yes, it does. If you agree, I'd like to introduce your son and wife to her in a few moments."

Raising his eyebrows, Wolfe said, "She's here?"

"Yeah, I've been kenneling her, waiting for you to get up here. I've had a few days to observe her. She's a good dog, but…"

"Why the hesitation, Mack?"

"She seems a little depressed. Not sure if it's because of the accident or if she misses being around people."

"If you're placing a human emotion onto a dog, it's called, anthropomorphism."

Brown smiled. "You haven't been around German shepherds much, have you?"

"Not really. The ones I have been always amazed me."

"In my opinion, they're smarter than a lot of the humans I've had to deal with."

With a chuckle, Wolfe said, "I can see that."

They arrived at the kennel where Nova slept. Wolfe knelt down and quietly said, "Nova."

The dog's head jerked up. She immediately rose and walked over to where Wolfe held the back of his hand to the kennel door. Nova sniffed and then sat down. Her tongue came out. She panted and displayed what resembled a smile.

"She likes you."

Turning to his friend, Wolfe asked, "How can you tell?"

"She didn't bark. She always barks at new people."

Wolfe stood and waved at Nadia and Ben to join him. He turned back to Brown. "Let's see how she reacts to the family."

Ten minutes later, with Nova chasing a tennis ball thrown by Ben, the kennel owner said, "She's already bonded with your family, Michael."

"I can see that." He turned to Nadia. "What do you think, princess?"

She smiled then looked up at him. "I think she's a perfect addition to our family."

"She never growled or barked." Turning to his friend, Wolfe said, "How much to adopt her, Mack?"

"The price is a good home."

"We can provide a great home with plenty of room for her to run. But I need to pay you something."

"Sorry, nonnegotiable."

"What about a donation to the kennel?"

Brown smiled. "That, I can let you do. But before you leave, we must go over a few basic commands you will need to keep reinforcing."

"When?"

"Now."

The drive home started late after four hours of working

with Nova. Now she lay on the back seat, her head resting on Ben's lap. Both were sound asleep.

Nadia turned to check Ben and the dog. She then reached for Michael's hand. "Thank you."

He glanced over at her, his left hand on the steering wheel. "For what?"

"For being you. I've never seen Ben so happy."

"Nova seemed to accept him as hers from the very start. Think she'll like our place?"

"What's not to like? Open spaces, no traffic, and a precocious four-year-old boy to play with." She paused. "Do you think she will add some security?"

"Once she gets used to the layout, she'll guard it with her life. It's the nature of the breed."

Looking back at Ben and their dog, Nadia said, "I'll feel better about Ben being outside as long as Nova's with him."

"Yeah, there is that."

Chapter Thirty-Three

BERLIN, GERMANY

Russian Embassy

Smoke rings emerged from the man's mouth as he amused himself while waiting for the SVR agent.

Sergey Ivanov entered the office and waved his hand. "Must you pursue that disgusting habit inside? Besides, there is a no-smoking rule in this building."

"Then you should have arranged for this meeting to be outside, Sergey."

"Not a wise choice for you, my friend."

The man grinned as he sat in a leather wingback chair in front of an ornate desk. "Hendricks is dead, per your request."

"Excellent. How?"

With a sly smile, the smoker said, "Sudden deceleration on a hotel lobby floor."

"Did it appear to be an accident?"

He shrugged.

"Those were your instructions. Make it appear to be an accident."

"He had so much alcohol in him, he probably would have died anyway."

"Did your image appear on any security video?"

Another shrug.

"Dammit, Dimitri. You were told to not have your image captured by a camera."

"I had a flesh-colored balaclava on. All anyone will see is a blurred face. Relax."

"That is not the point. The Americans will treat it as a murder now."

"So? The Americans are scared of their own shadows. They will cover their ass and tell the foolish public he fell over the railing."

"You're not as young as you were when the Berlin Wall fell. You need to be more careful. You're no good to me dead."

"One day, my dear, Sergey, you will grow tired of me. When that happens, I plan to have already disappeared. Then, I will show up when you least expect me."

"Is that a threat, Dimitri?"

"Threat? No. Promise? Yes."

Ivanov grinned. "That's why I like you. You're a cold-hearted bastard."

The former East German policeman sucked on his cigarette and blew the smoke at the SVR agent. "What's next?"

"I need you back in the States. Go in through Canada and wait for more instructions."

"Wolfe?"

"Maybe."

"Then, I am going to need more help. The man you sent was an idiot."

"Why do you say that?"

"He did not do his homework. Wolfe has built himself a fortress, even though it does not appear to be one."

"Well, I am not sure we need to do anything about him for the moment. Besides, the American president is not doing anything to aggravate our benefactor."

Petrov tilted his head. "I'm curious. Who is our benefactor, comrade?"

"At this stage, you don't need to know."

"Why?"

Ivanov paused for a moment. "You have been properly compensated for your efforts, have you not, Dimitri?"

"Compensated, yes. Properly, is open to debate."

"Should I be worried about your commitment?"

The man dropped his cigarette on the wood floor and ground it out with the heel of his shoe. "I am committed to whoever pays me the most, Sergey. So far, you do not have any competition. Try to keep it that way." He stood and walked out of the office.

Washington, DC

Jerry Griggs' long, quick stride hurried him toward the private office of the president of the United States. He knocked on the door and, without waiting for an answer, slipped inside.

"Thanks for coming so quickly, Jerry."

"No, problem, sir."

"Has there been any progress on the death of Senator Hendricks?"

"Not really. Security video from the hotel shows a shadowy figure assisting the senator over the rail, but the facial features were obscured."

"I was afraid of that. So, it was a murder."

"I'm afraid so, sir."

"I don't like the Russian president's tactics for cleaning up his mistakes being used here in our country."

"Joseph is working on a theory but won't discuss it until he has more information."

"Good. Keep me informed." He put his glasses on and returned his attention to the papers on his desk.

"Yes, sir."

Griggs knew the words *keep me informed* were the president's way of saying dismissed, but he stood at parade rest and waited.

"Was there something else, Jerry?"

"Uh, yes, sir."

Griffin smiled, removed his glasses, and swiveled to look at his NSA. "Okay, what is it?"

"You have an appointment with the Russian consul this afternoon."

"Yes, I'm aware of it. Why?"

Swiping the screen of the tablet he held, Griggs showed the president a photo. "This was taken this morning at ten, Berlin time. The individual is leaving the Russian embassy in Berlin."

Replacing his glasses, the president took the small computer and studied the picture. "Am I supposed to recognize this man?"

"No, sir. But he is a person of interest in several unexplained deaths here in the US."

"Sounds like a problem for the FBI." The president paused. "Wait a minute, are you suggesting he's the shadowy figure helping Senator Hendricks over the hotel 9th floor railing?"

"That's a possibility. But he is a person of interest in the death of Emma Elliot. He came to our attention when evidence was discovered he was involved in the attack on Michael Wolfe's house several weeks ago.

"Who is he?"

"His name is Dimitri Petrov. We don't know what name he's using presently. At one time, he was a teenage rising star in the East German Stasi, but the fall of the Berlin Wall derailed his career."

"Jerry, that was thirty-five years ago."

"Yes, sir. He wasn't on anyone's radar until several cigarette butts were found near Michael's home. DNA from those discarded butts identified the smoker as Petrov. Using this information, the FBI identified the person who rented the car used in the hit-and-run death of Ms. Elliot. The name used on the ID was false, but the picture was matched by facial recognition to the Stasi ID of Petrov."

Studying the picture on the tablet, Griffin did not speak for several moments. "So, you're telling me we have a former East German Stasi agent running around the country killing American citizens."

"That about sums it up, Mr. President." Griggs paused. "Uh, sir?"

"Yes."

"There is also a possibility he was a contract employee for the CIA at one time."

"Oh, this just keeps getting better." The president pinched the bridge of his nose and swiveled to face the window in his office. He took a deep breath and said,

"Okay, call Joseph and see if he might have a few moments for me before the consul gets here."

"Yes, sir." Griggs turned on his heel and rushed back to his office.

Griggs and Joseph met the president in the private dining room. They sat across from him and waited for him to finish his lunch.

"Thanks for coming, Joseph. Would you like something to eat?"

"No, thank you, sir. What can I do for you?"

"Did Jerry tell you what he told me about this Petrov character?"

"Yes, sir."

"What're your thoughts?"

"I think the FBI needs to put a national BOLO out on him. He seems to be able to slip in and out of the country at will."

Griffin looked at Griggs. "Make the suggestion, Jerry."

"Yes, sir."

"What else, Joseph?"

"I understand you have a meeting with the Russian consul this afternoon."

"I do."

"May I ask what it is about?"

"It was at their request, more whining about the sanctions."

Joseph nodded and placed a folder on the table in front of the president. "My suggestion is to tell him we know about Petrov. He will disavow knowing anything about the man. Then tell him if the FBI captures him, it will be all over the media. Also, let him know we have undeniable evidence the man is a Russian asset and tied to several murders inside the US. All of that is in the folder."

A slow smile appeared on the president of the United States' lips.

President Roy Griffin's thoughts were occupied by the information in the CIA brief on current Russian activity inside the United States. The more he read, the more his anger and concern grew. He glanced at the grandfather clock on the office wall. His appointment with the Russian consul would occur within minutes.

A knock on the Oval Office door drew his attention. Secretary of State Albert Doyle escorted the Russian consul general of Washington into the room. The president stood, shook his hand, motioned to one of the chairs in front of the Resolute Desk, and returned to his own chair. "What can I do for you this morning, Mr. Pavlovich?"

"Mr. President, my president has asked me to request all economic sanctions currently in place be lifted. This would be in the best interests of both our countries."

"The United States is doing fine, sir. We have no intentions of lifting the sanctions until Russia complies with international law."

"I must protest…"

Griffin raised his hand with the palm toward Pavlovich. "Stop." He opened a manila file and placed two pictures in front of the man. "Tell your president that the United States is aware of the assassin he sent. We know who he is and, unless he is withdrawn immediately, we will be forced to place him under arrest and prosecute him to the fullest extent of US law."

"Mr. President, my government is not in the habit of sending, so-called assassins to other countries."

With a chuckle, Griffin shook his head. "Mr. Pavlovich, please do not insult my intelligence. The United States is well aware of your country's attempts to influence events around the world. I am very serious about Dimitri Petrov. Recall him immediately, or we will expose him in a most embarrassing way. Do I make myself clear, sir?"

Pavlovich stood and gave the president an insincere smile. "I am unaware of any such person named Dimitri Petrov, but I will relay your concerns to my president."

Chapter Thirty-Four

SOUTHWEST MISSOURI

Nova blended into the Wolfe family like she had been with them her entire life. Ben played with her until both were exhausted and Michael handled the daily training refreshers. Her thin frame, which she displayed when they first picked her up, now featured additional muscular tone. Her stamina also improved with her added strength.

One evening, several weeks after adding Nova to their family, the German shepherd lay in the middle of the living room floor, head up, front paws crossed, eyes closed, and panting. Wolfe looked up from the book he read and noted how content the dog appeared. "Nadia, Nova sure seems to be at home."

She turned her attention to the dog and smiled. "She didn't take long to feel at ease."

"Did you get a chance to glance at her pedigree Mack sent?"

Shaking her head, Nadia said, "No, I haven't. What does it tell us?"

"She'll be four in two months. From what I can tell, she comes from a long line of working police dogs. She also displays the family trait of black-and-tan coloring. Plus, both her father and mother outlived the average life expectancy of the breed."

"She's a beautiful dog."

Wolfe nodded. "I think so, too. If we keep her healthy with good food and exercise, she might live with us until Ben is out of high school."

"I hope so. She sure has taken to Ben."

"Yes, she—"

The large canine sprang to her feet and stared at the front door. A low growl emerged from her throat.

Wolfe turned to his wife. "Something's wrong. Go stay with Ben, and I'll handle this."

Nadia rose and hurried to the back of the house where Ben slept in his room.

Nova's growl grew deeper in her chest, her attention fully on the front door. Walking into his library next to the living room, Wolfe unlocked the top right-hand drawer of his desk and extracted a Glock 19. He picked up a magazine with hollow-point bullets and slammed it into the handle of the gun. He charged the weapon and returned to the living room. Nova still stood in the middle of the room. Her stare fixed on the front door.

"Come."

The canine immediately went to Wolfe's left side, her head inches from his thigh. The outside noise grew louder as a vehicle rumbled along the asphalt road. The sound moved from right to left at a snail's pace.

Turning, he said, "Follow," and hurried toward the kitchen. Nova did not stray from his side as his pace quickened. He grabbed a flashlight from the countertop and reached for the back door. Both he and Nova stepped out onto the large wooden deck at the back of the house.

To Nova, he said, "Seek."

The dog tore out into the darkness. Wolfe followed. They turned to the right toward the west side of the house. Moving toward the front, he noticed three figures standing beside what appeared to be an older pickup parked in the street. In the glow from the headlights, he could tell they did not hold guns. However, one of the members held what appeared to be a pry bar.

By the light of the moon, he saw Nova crouched near a forsythia bush. Staying in the shadows, he crept along the side of the house, keeping his focus on the suspicious men. He could hear what seemed to be a heated debate about their next steps.

He knelt next to Nova and stroked her head. "Good girl." The dog remained silent, her attention on the intruders.

When the intruders walked toward the house, Wolfe said, "Contain." Nova broke from her hiding place, barking and growling as she rushed toward the three men.

"Holy shit, where'd the dog come from?"

One guy ran back toward truck, but the other two stood still as Nova rushed toward them. The man on the left raised the pry bar, but Wolfe stepped out from behind the bush and turned on the flashlight. "Drop the bar."

Nova stopped but continued to bark and keep her distance.

"Who the fuck are you?"

"Doesn't matter. Drop the bar."

"You need to be more careful, mister. There're three of us, I only see one of you and the dog."

Wolfe pointed the Glock into the air and pulled the trigger.

The sound of the gun made the man with the pry bar drop it. The other man said, "Let's get out of here."

Wolfe said, "Guard."

Nova sprang toward the two men and gave them a menacing growl.

They both threw their hands up. "Okay, mister. We're out of here. No harm, no foul."

"Wrong. Hands on the truck and assume the position."

Forty minutes later, Christian County deputies had the three vandals handcuffed, each sitting in the back of three different sheriff cars. One of the deputies, who Wolfe knew, walked up to him and chuckled. "These guys have been harassing folks around here for several months. First, they vandalize the place and take whatever they can find in the yard. If someone interrupts them, they assault the victim. A few elderly folks have been seriously hurt. Thus far, no one's been able to give us an accurate description of them. How'd you curtail these clowns?"

Wolfe pointed to Nova. "New member of the family."

"Beautiful dog."

"And former police K9."

"I'll remember that, Michael."

"I hope you do."

Near Alexandria, VA

The B55 Baron taxied to a stop in a designated parking area at Potomac Field across the river from Alexandria. A Chevy Equinox pulled up next to the plane as Wolfe extracted his overnight bag from the luggage compartment in the nose of the aircraft.

He entered the vehicle and turned toward the driver. "Thanks for picking me up, Carla. How's working for the White House?"

"Jerry leaves me alone, so it's pretty good. So far."

"So, why schedule me to land at Potomac Field? Kinda out of the way, don't you think?"

"He and Joseph don't want anyone to know you're in DC."

"Okay. So, what's the emergency?"

"They know the identity of the individual who left the cigarette butts near your place."

Wolfe raised an eyebrow. "Who is he?"

She grinned. "I'll let them tell you."

Five minutes later, she steered the SUV into the driveway of a house at the end of a cul-de-sac with a For-Sale sign in the front lawn. She pressed the button on a garage door opener and drove into the vacant side of the garage with a Jeep Cherokee already parked inside.

With the garage door down, she said, "Now we can get out."

"What's with the cloak-and-dagger routine, Carla?"

She shrugged and motioned for him to follow her into the house. They entered a small laundry area with a washer on one side, the dryer on the other, and emerged into a spacious kitchen with an island. There, he found both Joseph Kincaid and Jerry Griggs standing, coffee mugs in hand.

Joseph offered his hand to his friend. "Sorry for all the misdirection, but Jerry and I thought it best."

Jerry said, "Can I get you a cup of coffee, Michael?"

"Yeah." He accepted the mug as it was handed to him. "Okay. What's going on?"

Griggs showed him a picture. "Do you know this man?"

It was obviously a military ID photo. Wolfe studied the image of a young man, possibly twenty, but no more. "He's vaguely familiar. Who is it?"

"His name is Dimitri Petrov. Does that ring a bell?"

Taking the photo, Wolfe continued to examine it. He finally shook his head. "No."

"Where were you on November 9th, 1989?" Joseph sipped his coffee.

Putting the photo down, Wolfe turned toward his friend. "A month from graduating high school and attempting to get into Jessica Fox's pants. Why?"

With a chuckle, Joseph said, "I remember you graduated high school a semester early."

"Yes, I did. However, I did not succeed in seducing Jessica Fox."

"Regrets?"

"None."

"Good. November 9th, 1989 was the day the Berlin Wall fell. It is also the day a young, up-and-coming Stasi agent disappeared."

"Dimitri Petrov?"

"Very good, Michael. Does the name mean anything to you now?"

"No. I joined the Marines in February of 1990. So, I was a long way from Berlin, Joseph."

"When did you start working for the CIA?"

"You know the answer."

"Humor me, please."

"I graduated from Georgetown in the spring of 1999. You recruited me just before, remember?"

"Ah, yes. One of my better recruitments."

Wolfe allowed a small grin to grace his lips.

The acting CIA director said, "During your time with the CIA, you were stationed in Berlin for a few years, correct?"

Hesitating for a few moments, Wolfe said, "Don't tell me. I've dealt with this Dimitri Petrov before, haven't I."

"I'm getting there. He was born in St. Petersburg the same year you were born. Because his parents were big supporters of the Soviet Union, they were given lucrative jobs in East Berlin. Dimitri went to private schools and joined the East German secret police agency, the Stasi right after he graduated. When the wall fell, his parents returned to Russia, and the young man disappeared."

"Where was he?"

"We don't know for sure, but, in 1992, it is believed he moved to Moscow and worked in the Boris Yeltsin administration. We think that's where he met the current president of Russia. Because of his fluent German, he found his way back to Berlin. In what capacity, we don't know.

"You may have run across him at some point. The two of you were there at the same time. Intelligence on the man indicates he knows who you are and your reputation."

"Why would he be familiar with me?"

"Because he's a trained sniper. Just like you."

Chapter Thirty-Five

Holding the picture in his hand, Wolfe asked, "How did you identify him?"

Jerry warmed his cup of coffee, turned, and leaned against the kitchen counter. "The cigarette butts you found close to your house."

Looking up, the retired sniper raised an eyebrow. "The Stasi closed shop over thirty years ago. How did you get DNA samples from them?"

Nodding at his former boss, Jerry said, "Ask him."

Wolfe turned. "Okay, Joseph. How'd that happen?"

"Uh, let's put it this way. When the Stasi were disbanded on June 30, 1990, several of us broke into their headquarters and stole a lot of personnel files. DNA was just starting to be an important part of forensics at that time. We lucked out and obtained a treasure trove of blood samples on file. Some of them were degraded, but we managed to get samples on about 60 percent of the agents. Petrov was one of the 60 percent."

Griggs said, "When the FBI traced the vehicle that

struck Emma Elliot back to the owner, they found it to be owned by Hertz. The picture on the fake driver's license used to rent it was Petrov's. Facial recognition told us his name. Then Petrov was photographed coming out of the Russian embassy in Berlin a few days ago. That's when all the pieces fell into place. We also think he assisted Calvin Hendricks over the railings at the Grand Hyatt."

"So, the Russians have a trained assassin running around the United States. Is that what you're telling me?"

Joseph nodded. "It's exactly what we're telling you."

"If he was photographed in Berlin a few days ago, do you know where he is now?"

"No."

"Is anybody searching for him?"

"The FBI is making it a national priority. Plus, President Griffin is putting pressure on the Mexican and Canadian governments to alert their border guards."

"Gentlemen and lady, that means absolutely nothing." Wolfe pointed to the picture he still held. "This guy looks like a clean-cut all-American male. Put glasses, longer hair, and a beard on him and no one is going to notice him."

Folding his arms, Joseph said, "I happen to agree with you. That's why you're here."

Wolfe's glare went from Joseph to Jerry then back. He glanced at Carla, who had remained suspiciously quiet during the exchange.

"I'm retired, Joseph. Nadia and I made the decision after our recent trip to France. It was a mistake for us to think we could play this game again." He laid the picture down and directed his attention to Carla. "Please take me back to the airport. If I leave now, I can get home before the sun sets."

Joseph gave his friend a smile. "I understand your

desire to lead a normal life, Michael. Particularly with Benjamin getting older." He paused. "But there's a chance Petrov may make another attempt on the lives of you and your family."

"Why?"

"They did before."

"And Katz died doing it."

"Petrov knows your defenses now. He won't make the same mistakes. Besides, he's a trained sniper. He could hide in the trees on your land, and you'd never know he was there."

"Don't bet on it."

"Are you willing to take that chance? What if Ben is outside and becomes the target. What if it's Nadia? I don't see you taking that chance, Michael. Or am I wrong?"

The veins in Wolfe's neck pulsed. "Dammit."

"The deterrents and precautions you've installed can only go so far. Particularly with the type of training Petrov received."

Silence fell over the four occupants of the kitchen in the empty house with a For-Sale sign in front. Three individuals kept their gaze on one man while he thought through the problem.

Wolfe narrowed his eyes and looked at Joseph. "What the hell does any of this have to do with that damn list?"

"We don't know for sure. But I can speculate."

"By all means." His voice dripped with sarcasm. "Please do."

"As you have suggested, the list appears to be of known snipers who would have the training to shoot down the Iranian president's helicopter."

"Yeah. I remember the conversation."

Jerry spoke next. "Before you made the suggestion, we

hypothesized everyone on the list was associated with Joseph in some fashion."

The acting director of the CIA said, "I've never heard of half the names."

Picking up the narrative, Jerry continued. "One of our IT guys at the White House ran the names through a search engine."

Wolfe folded his arms. "And?"

"Nothing. He couldn't find a tangible relationship between them, except that many of the names were men and women trained as snipers. Other than that, nothing."

"But you don't believe that's the reason for the list."

"No, we don't."

"Obviously, you have a theory."

Carla spoke for the first time since entering the kitchen. "There is speculation the list was put together to divert our attention."

Turning his attention to her, Wolfe said, "To divert it from what?"

Griggs said, "We don't know."

Joseph remained quiet, listening to the exchange.

Rolling his eyes, Wolfe said, "If I'm going to get involved again, you need to make more sense than you're currently making."

"I have to agree with you, Michael." Joseph gave his friend a grim smile. "We have few facts. We don't know the significance of the names, who put it together, or why Samantha Edgar felt compelled to give it to William Fischer."

"Have you asked her?"

"We can't find her. After you got her out of California, she vanished."

"She spent one night with us. Nadia took her to the

Greyhound bus terminal in Springfield the next day. Samantha told us she was going home." He paused and tilted his head. "No one can completely vanish."

With pursed lips, Griggs said, "Sam can. She was trained by the best."

Wolfe folded his arms. "Who?"

"William Fischer."

Turning to Joseph, the retired sniper said, "Wasn't she Emma Elliot's assistant?"

A nod was his answer.

"Then how do we know Samantha didn't put it together?"

Joseph said, "We don't."

Turning to Carla, Wolfe asked, "You and Samantha were friends, do you have any idea of where her home is?"

She started to say something but stopped. Pulling out her cell phone, she scrolled through some numbers and then stopped. Looking up, she asked, "Where is area code 337?"

Wolfe smiled. "I have a good friend with the same area code. It's southwestern Louisiana."

"That's the area code of Samantha's personal cell phone."

"Then that's where you need to start. Since Samantha felt compelled to give the list to Fischer, she should be able to tell you why."

Carla said, "Let me see what I can do to find her."

Sulphur, LA

Living under the name of Emily Sanders, an alias acquired during her time with the CIA, Samantha Edgar rented a small ranch-style home on the northern city limits of Sulphur, LA. Since her arrival two weeks ago, she had not met any of her neighbors, nor did she plan to.

With funds running low, she applied for a job at a local attorney's office and was hired as a legal assistant. Considering she held a law degree from Tulane, she passed the interview with flying colors.

In addition to a job where she would not have to mingle with the public, she changed the color and length of her hair and wore glasses instead of contacts. She vaguely resembled the woman who, at one time, walked the hallowed halls of the George Bush Center for Intelligence in Langley, Virginia.

The time approached six in the evening when the doorbell rang. Cautiously, she peered out the small window in the front door. A diminutive black woman stood there with a bottle of chardonnay in her hand.

Opening the door, Samantha said, "Well, I should have guessed if anyone could find me, it would be you."

Carla Webb slipped into the living room. "You weren't easy to find, girlfriend."

"I hope you're not here to take me back to Washington."

"Nope. I don't even plan to tell anyone I found you."

Shutting the door, Samantha said, "I'll get some glasses."

Five minutes later, the two women sat at a small kitchen table bought at a yard sale the previous weekend. Carla started the conversation. "So, what's this disappearing act all about?"

Taking a deep breath and then a long swig of wine, Samantha said, "I was paranoid and scared."

"You know Hendricks and Elliot are dead, don't you?"

"Yes."

"Joseph Kincaid is the acting CIA director."

The woman raised her eyebrows. "Really, since when?"

"Two days after Elliot died."

"Huh."

"Want to come back now?"

She shook her head. "No way."

"Care to tell me why?"

"Major General Morgan Walker."

Chapter Thirty-Six

SULPHUR, LA

The conversation at the small kitchen table came to a sudden halt. Carla Webb, the glass almost to her lips, lowered the wine and stared at her friend across the table. "The NSA Director of Signal Intelligence?"

"One and the same."

"Excuse me, what does he have to do with this mess?"

"He's the originator of the list."

Carla cocked her head to the side. "He was?"

"Yes. Actually, General Walker recruited Hendricks into the conspiracy a long time ago."

"Really? Then, what's the purpose of the list?"

Samantha finished the wine in her glass in one gulp. "After the helicopter crash killed the Iranian president, a group of CIA analysts got together and gamed out several scenarios on what the Iranians might do. The concept of Iran developing a list of assassins who might have shot the helicopter down came out of one of those sessions. So, when Emma Elliot ascended to the CIA directorship, Walker determined he could convince her to act out against

Iran. Hendricks and his toadies would raise the alarm about how dangerous Iran was becoming and use the list as proof. He would then take that message to the media. Hendricks would lead the charge of pointing fingers at President Griffin. They would accuse him of being weak on the Tehran regime."

"That wouldn't work, Sam."

Taking a deep breath, Carla's friend let it out with a huff. "That's just the first part, Carla. General Walker believes the current president is too popular and will abolish the two-term limit."

"How can Walker believe that. The 22nd Amendment to the Constitution sets out the terms of a presidency."

"He believes Griffin is so popular, he'll be allowed to amend the constitution."

"Then he's delusional. So, what's with the list?"

"The original list was modified by Walker to include individuals he believes are the key to Griffin achieving his goal. In his fever-induced dream, he believes the president will use both friendly persuasion and lethal force."

"That's crazy, Sam."

"Doesn't matter. It's what Walker believes."

"How has Walker kept this crazy scheme from being exposed to the public?"

"Because he had Hendricks running interference for him."

"One more question, Sam. There are names on the list of foreign agents. How would he know they could assist?"

"Walker is the director of the NSA's Signal Intelligence group. He has access to all kinds of information." She poured herself and Carla another glass of wine. "I asked myself the same question when I first obtained a copy."

"How did you obtain your copy?"

Samantha Edgar just smiled but did not answer.

Taking a sip of her freshly poured wine, Carla then said, "Got it." She remained quiet for a moment. "What are you going to do? Stay in Louisiana?"

"I grew up in Lafayette. My folks are gone, but I have good memories of the area. Plus, I'm working at a law firm, which will allow me to rebuild my cash reserves."

"What if someone finds you?"

"I doubt anyone actually cares where I am."

"Then, why draw attention to yourself by running?"

Her answer became a shrug.

"Sam, you're not making any sense. Why the cross-country trip then the disappearing act to Louisiana?"

"Carla, the rise of Emma Elliot perpetrated by a group of senators who did not have the best interests of the country at heart, disillusioned me. Working for the government, particularly the CIA, is a fool's errand. I'm done with it."

The diminutive woman stood. "Sorry to hear that, Sam. If you need anything, you know my number." She walked back to the front door, opened it, and left as quietly as she had arrived.

———

"Jerry, something's not right with Samantha."

"What's that, Carla?"

She held the cell phone to her ear as she watched the isolated ranch house down the street at the end of a cul-de-sac on the outskirts of Sulphur, Louisiana. "I can't put my finger on it, but she's kind of hiding in plain sight. She's using one of her CIA-provided alternate identities in a town less than a hundred miles from where she claims to have grown up."

"I thought you told me she would be hard to find."

"She should have been."

"But?"

"It took me exactly one hour to find her. With a little effort, anyone can find her."

"Did she say anything about the list?"

"She claims General Walker put it together because he thinks Griffin will try to suspend the constitutional amendment about only serving two terms. The names are supposedly individuals who can and will use force to help the president."

Griggs laughed out loud on the end of the phone call. He said, "You're kidding?"

"Nope, that's what she told me."

"I take it you didn't believe her?"

"No, I didn't. I'm now thinking everything she's ever told me has been a lie, Jerry. Except the fact she grew up in Lafayette. I already knew where she spent her childhood. She's up to something. What, I don't know."

"Okay, Carla. What're your plans?"

"Hope you don't need me in DC. I'm gonna follow her around for a few days."

"Hopefully, I don't need to tell you to be careful."

"She won't know I'm here."

Southwest Missouri

After parking the Baron in the hangar, Wolfe went through his shutdown checklist. When finished, he stepped out of the plane. Immediately, the family's newest member greeted him. She stared up at him with her tongue out, panting, and an expression he associated with a smile. He knelt down and rubbed her head. "Hello, Nova."

Benjamin came skidding into the open space, out of breath. "Hi, Dad. Nova knew your plane and sat on the deck watching until it disappeared inside. Then she took off like a rocket."

"I told you she was smart."

"Real smart. She hasn't left Mom's side since you've been gone."

Wolfe tilted his head and knelt down next to the German shepherd. "Really. Nice to know." He rubbed the dog's head again. "Good girl."

She continued to pant.

When they entered the kitchen from the deck, Wolfe saw Nadia leaning over the kitchen counter, studying a book. She straightened and smiled. "Glad you're home. Nova's been sitting at the back door and staring out at the hangar."

Walking over to his wife, Wolfe gave her a hug and then kissed her. "Glad to be home." He pointed at the book. "What's that?"

"*The Joy of Cooking*, I found it in a used bookstore."

With a frown, Wolfe said, "You don't need a cookbook." He touched her temple. "You already possess an excellent repertoire of recipes up there."

"Have you ever noticed I never make anything American?"

"American cooking. I didn't know there was such a thing. Unless you mean fried chicken and hamburgers."

"No, silly, I mean something like chicken pot pie or smoked ribs."

"How hard can it be?"

"From what I've read, not too. Ben suggested it."

Glancing at his son, who sat at the kitchen island smiling, Wolfe asked, "What made you ask about chicken pot pie?"

Ben shrugged. "When I was in Israel, Aunt Nuri asked me if I had ever had chicken pot pie. I didn't know what she was talking about."

Wolfe chuckled. "I'm afraid we have stifled your culinary experience. Made properly, it is excellent."

Nadia slipped her arm around his waist. "Good, because we're going to have a properly prepared chicken pot pie tonight. But I'm making the crust my way."

The cell phone in his back jeans pocket chimed. He checked the caller ID and sighed. "Oh, wonderful—it's Jerry."

———

Stepping out onto the back deck, Wolfe accepted the call. "I just got back. What's up?"

"Carla found Samantha."

"Where?"

"Sulphur, Louisiana."

"Huh. Where's that?"

"Due west of Layfette about a hundred miles."

"Okay. Why'd she run?"

"Carla questioned her, but thinks everything Sam said was a lie."

"Let me guess, Jerry, you want me to go down there and talk to her as well."

"Thanks. I was hoping you'd volunteer."

"That's not what—" He paused. "What did she lie about?"

"About everything. Carla thinks she's hiding something."

"That's vague. Like what?"

"Her involvement with NSA's General Walker. Who she claims is the one who made the list."

"Did she give a reason?"

"Yeah, get this. It's a list of people who will help the president rescind the 22nd Amendment. That way he can serve more than two terms."

"That's bullshit."

"Ya think? That's what Carla thought, too."

"Send me the address, I'll fly down tomorrow morning."

"I'll tell the president. Thanks again, Michael."

Chapter Thirty-Seven

SULPHUR, LA

Wolfe sat behind the wheel of his rented Toyota Camry. Carla sat next to him in the passenger seat. They watched the same house.

"She hasn't been outside since I spoke to her yesterday morning."

"Is there a back entrance?"

"Yes. I have a motion-detecting GoPro camera mounted on a tree in the woods behind the house. She hasn't left the premises."

"Okay."

"Michael?"

"Yeah."

"Could Samantha be involved with this General Walker?"

"What makes you think so?"

"She didn't act like herself yesterday. I've known her for at least a decade, and she's always struck me as a straight shooter. No BS or drama."

"I don't know her all that well."

Carla stared at the house. "I think she's lying about the reason for the list."

"It did sound a bit lame."

She turned her attention to the driver. "Any speculation about what's going on?"

Wolfe didn't answer, he pointed. A car passed their position and pulled into the driveway of the house they had under surveillance. "Who might this be?"

Raising her binoculars, Carla studied the vehicle. "Male."

Swiping his cell phone to activate it, Wolfe pressed the phone icon. He punched in a number and pressed send. After a brief pause, he said, "Hi, Alexia. I need a favor. Could you check registration on a KIA Sportage?" He then gave her the license number. "I can wait."

He glanced at Carla. "I have a funny feeling."

Returning his attention to the phone call, he remained quiet. After five minutes, he said, "Got it. Thanks, Alexia." The call ended.

Carla trained her attention on him. "Well?"

"It's a rental."

"Makes sense. Who rented it?"

He gave his passenger a grim smile. "A good friend of the late Calvin Hendricks. Jayden Berry."

The diminutive woman chuckled as she stared through the binoculars. "The plot thickens."

The front door of the ranch-style home opened, and Samantha Edgar exited with a backpack slung over her shoulder. Casually dressed in jeans and a loose sweater, she closed the door, put her key in the lock, and checked to make sure it was secure. Turning, she walked briskly toward the passenger door of the KIA. Both Wolfe and Carla ducked below the window as the SUV drove by. Once it passed, he started the Camry and followed.

Fifteen minutes later, the Sportage merged onto I-10 heading west. Wolfe kept his distance but followed.

Consulting her cell phone, Carla said, "We've got Beaumont and Houston ahead."

Wolfe tapped his finger on the steering wheel. "I noticed she had a backpack and appeared dressed for a plane flight."

"Possibly fleeing the country."

"Houston's two hours away. Call Jerry and see if he can find out if she has a ticket to somewhere."

"She's living under the name Emily Sanders. Do you think she'd use that name to fly?"

"She's got several IDs, right?"

"I know of at least three."

"Have him check all three."

"Got it." She made the call.

Hobby International Airport, Houston, TX

Jayden Berry watched Samantha Edgar finish her journey through the TSA line and enter the central concourse on Level 2 of the Hobby airport. Satisfied she was safe within the terminal, the good senator turned to head back to his vehicle.

As he headed toward the ground transportation exit, a man of average height joined him on the left and matched his stride.

The newcomer smiled and asked, "Are you Jayden Berry?"

Slowing his stride, he looked at the man and then stopped. "Who's asking?"

The man opened an ID wallet, showed him his badge, and said, "Homeland Security Agent Patrick Ryan, sir. Would you come with me?"

"Do you know who I am, Agent?"

"I'm very aware of who you are, sir. If you want to keep this quiet, please accompany me."

"I will not. I am a US senator. I demand to know what this is about."

Two other individuals walked up to where the two men now stood. Both took up positions behind the senator.

After glancing over both shoulders, he returned his attention to the agent. "Who are these people?"

"Agents Teressa Noval and Randy Trowel, FBI. Now, do you want to make a scene, or will you follow me?"

Stealing another look at the two agents behind him, he turned and glared at the man in front of him. "Are you sure you want to harass a US senator, son?"

"Not harassing. Merely giving you an opportunity to avoid a scene." His attention turned to the two FBI agents and said, "I believe this is now your arrest, agents."

Trowel grabbed the senator's left hand and slapped one end of the handcuffs on while Agent Noval said, "You have the right to remain silent…"

Five minutes later, Senator Berry sat in the TSA office at Hobby airport, handcuffed and fuming. "How dare you arrest a US senator in public like that. I'll have your badge."

Wolfe stood in front of Berry. His arms folded. "Somehow, I doubt it. The woman you accompanied to the TSA checkpoint was Samantha Edgar. She is currently wanted as a person of interest in the death of Senator Calvin

Hendricks. A few moments after she cleared security, she was arrested by FBI agents."

"I don't have a clue who you are referring to."

Wolfe held the cell phone so the senator could see. "This was taken when you picked her up at her house in Sulphur, Louisiana." He swiped the phone. "This one taken as you spoke to her just before she entered the TSA queue. Care to rephrase your last statement?"

Berry stared at the phone and took a deep breath. "I want a lawyer."

"Probably a wise decision, Senator. But not right now."

Samantha Edgar stared at Wolfe and Carla as they entered the TSA detention room. The retired CIA operator held a boarding pass in his hand. "Really, Samantha, Aruba?"

Her surprise turned to anger as she glared at Carla. "I thought I smelled treachery."

Carla walked over to her. "Did you forget I knew your other nom de guerres?"

"Apparently."

Wolfe asked, "What's your relationship to Senator Berry?"

"I want a lawyer."

Leaning over to stare her former friend in the eye, Carla said, "Senator Berry is being questioned in the other room. What'd ya bet, he covers his ass and throws you under the bus?"

Folding his arms, Wolfe added, "As a sitting senator, a judge will probably listen to him versus a CIA employee who's been on the run. Oh, did I mention, you've been fired for abandonment of post and dereliction of duty?"

The detainee's gaze switched from Carla to Wolfe several times before she said, "Make me a deal and I'll tell you everything I know about General Walker and the list."

The Woodlands, TX

The FBI transferred Samantha Edgar to a house north of Houston in the community of The Woodlands. Since being seized by the DEA from a member of a Mexican drug cartel, the home served the purpose of housing federal detainees without exposing them to local jails.

Into this setting, among numerous neighborhoods of high-end homes, members of law enforcement utilized the four-car garage to go and come without bothering the surrounding unsuspecting citizens. Because of this, agents were prohibited from parking in the street. The house, maintained by a lawn service three days a week and a live-in housekeeper, appeared to be occupied by a reclusive, well-to-do businessman. No one from the house disturbed those living next to it and, in turn, no one bothered them.

The day after arriving, Samantha Edgar received a visit from Joseph Kincaid, Acting Director of the CIA, and Director of the FBI Ryan Clark. Escorted directly from the airport to the house, their driver parked inside the garage and, after the overhead door closed, got out for an interview with the detainee.

Chapter Thirty-Eight

THE WOODLANDS, TX

Michael Wolfe waited in the kitchen for the arrival of the two directors. He dropped his charade as Homeland Security Agent Patrick Ryan and spoke with them before the interview with the ex-CIA employee.

Joseph Kincaid shook hands with Wolfe. "Has she said anything?"

"No. She wants a deal before she'll talk."

Clark said, "I have the AG standing by. If her information is worthwhile, we can work something out."

Nodding his head in the direction of the dining room, Wolfe said, "She's waiting at a table in there. She's dropped her charade as a victim."

"Is she expecting us?"

"No. She knows it will be someone with authority, but not exactly who."

They followed him into the adjoining room.

Samantha Edgar sat at the table. FBI agent Teressa Noval stood behind her, making sure she stayed put. When Joseph Kincaid entered the room, the ex-CIA agent stiffened. She followed him with her eyes until he sat across from her.

She said, "Why are you here, Joseph?"

"Because you've screwed up big-time, Sam."

Diverting her eyes to the tabletop, the detainee said, "I know."

"Want to tell us about it?"

"Not until I have a deal."

Clark said, "We need to know if you are blowing smoke or have something of importance to tell us."

She glared at the FBI director. "Oh, it's important. You might even consider it critical. That's all I'll say until I have something in writing."

The FBI director shook his head and stood. "Apparently, this was a waste of yours and my time, Joseph. Let's get back to the airport."

Edgar smiled. "Nice bluff, Director. All I'll tell you now is it has to do with the future of this country and the presidency."

Continuing to stand in front of the woman, Clark folded his arms. "Go on."

"It also involves a very high-ranking employee of the NSA. That's it. Nothing more until I have a deal."

Clark pursed his lips and stepped out of the room. Joseph drummed his fingers on the table. "I'm curious, Samantha, why?"

She looked at him and then at Wolfe standing behind the director. "Because the president nominated that idiot Emma Elliot, and the senate confirmed her. Of all the qualified candidates within the agency, he chose her."

With a slight smile, Joseph said, "Did one of those qualified candidates include you?"

Her eyes narrowed. "It most certainly did."

"Is that why you sacrificed William Fischer by giving him the list?"

Not changing her glare, she shook her head. "No, that was an unfortunate turn of events."

Leaning forward and slamming his fist on the table, Joseph Kincaid growled. "William was a friend, I'm not sure he would have called it an unfortunate turn of events."

She only shrugged.

Wolfe placed his hand on his mentor's shoulder but remained quiet.

Taking a deep breath, Joseph sat straighter. "Thank you for the reminder, Michael."

Clark walked back into the room. "The AG indicates, depending on what you have to say, he won't charge you with treason. However, he makes no guarantees beyond that."

"That's not good enough, Mr. Director."

"Afraid it's all you'll get until we can determine how valuable your information might be. It's your decision, Samantha. If you cooperate, he'll be lenient. If not, he'll throw everything but the kitchen sink at you. Your choice."

The woman's face remained defiant for several moments. Finally, it softened, and she nodded. "Very well. What do you want to know?"

Joseph asked, "What exactly is the meaning of the list, Samantha?"

"There was more on the drive than just a list of names."

"We know that."

She tilted her head. "I'm surprised at you, Joseph. You're normally quicker on the uptake than this."

"Humor me, Sam."

"Did anyone read the transcripts?"

"Yes. What about them?"

"I take it no one recognized the importance of the pictures, either."

The acting CIA director remained quiet.

She clasped her hands together and interlaced her fingers. "NSA's Director of Signal Intelligence Major General Walker has identified, through the NSA's surveillance capability, individuals within the US who want to rewrite the constitution or do away with it completely. The pictures identify their location, and the transcripts give a road map to their plans."

"We read the transcripts. They seemed innocent enough."

She gave Joseph a grim smile. "Those people knew their calls were being monitored. That's one of the reasons they're involved. They talked in code. Someone needs to reread them with what I'm telling you in mind."

Clark spoke next. "Do you know what they have planned?"

"No, but there's a concern within the agency that it will be bigger than the January 6th assault on the Capitol building. Much bigger and in multiple locations. This time, the mob will be well armed."

Wolfe said, "Are these people citizens, Carla?"

"Some are, some aren't. They organize through social media and the dark web."

Clark turned to Wolfe. "Where's the flash drive?"

"Jerry Griggs, has it secured."

The FBI director said to Joseph, "I think it's time to get it into the hands of the FBI."

"Griggs will only give it to you. No one else."

"I can live with that." Turning to Samantha, he said, "Why has Walker not given this information to the FBI?"

She shrugged. "I don't know."

"Don't know or don't want to say?"

"The latter."

Clark turned to the FBI agent standing behind Samantha. "Agent Noval, handcuff Ms. Edgar, and then escort her to the agency vehicle in the garage. We'll be along shortly. She has an appointment with the Department of Justice as soon as we return to Washington."

"Yes, sir."

After Edgar left the room, Clark turned to Joseph. "I need positive proof Walker's involved before the agency can act. Then there's the problem with Senator Berry. Is he involved?"

Joseph said, "He still thinks Michael is with Homeland Security. Let him handle it."

Turning his attention to Wolfe, the director said, "Are you willing to do that, Michael?"

The retired Marine nodded.

A second-floor bedroom contained only a table and two chairs. In one of them sat Senator Jayden Berry, his hands cuffed behind him. He looked up and snarled as Wolfe entered the room. "Where's my lawyer?"

Wolfe smiled and sat across from him. "He hasn't arrived yet?"

"Did anyone call him?"

"No."

"Agent, you are messing around with a US senator."

"Maybe for now. Did I show you a picture the last time we spoke?"

"I don't want to see a picture. I want a lawyer."

He placed a printout from a hotel security camera on

the table in front of the senator. It showed a shadowy figure pushing Calvin Hendricks off the balcony. Wolfe said, "Bet you were told he was drunk."

Berry stared at the picture but remained silent.

"He was. But someone assisted him over the railing." Tilting his head, Wolfe asked, "You didn't know that, did you?"

The senator shook his head as he stared at the photo.

"I don't know who you think you're dealing with, but they don't care if you're a US senator. Nor, do they play by the rules. Emma Elliot was murdered. As you can see, Hendricks died by their hands as well. Is that what you want for your future?"

"No." His voice weak and barely above a whisper.

"Who's paying the bills, Senator?"

"Don't know what you're talking about."

Taking a deep breath, Wolfe's demeanor changed abruptly as he leaned forward. He growled, "Don't play dumb with me, Berry. I've been dealing with these types of characters longer than you've been in politics. If they feel you are a danger to them, your life expectancy can be measured in hours, not years." Leaning back, he folded his arms and stared at the man sitting across from him.

In a weak voice, Berry said, "I have nothing to say. I have rights and I want a lawyer."

"I think the correct term is, you had rights. You've been classified as a domestic terrorist."

A worried expression crossed Berry's face.

Wolfe sneered. "Is it sinking in yet?" He paused. "Remember the legislation you sponsored five years ago limiting the rights of a domestic terrorist?"

A nod from Berry.

Wolfe stood. "Karma can be a bitch sometimes."

As he turned to leave the room, Berry said, "Major General Morgan Walker."

Turning back, the retired Marine sniper said, "Excuse me?"

"You heard me."

"What about General Walker?"

"Follow the money."

Returning to his seat, Wolfe tilted his head. "Humor me for a moment. Sometimes I'm a little slow. Follow what money?"

"Walker has a bank account in the Caymans. He's never said who funds it, but that's where the individuals working for him get their fees."

"How many individuals work for him?"

Berry shrugged. "That information was kept from Finley and me. We were basically gofers."

"Somehow, I doubt that, Senator."

Chapter Thirty-Nine

WASHINGTON, DC

A black Mercedes sat parked on a gravel road running parallel to an isolated tributary feeding the Potomac River. Trees were the predominant feature of the landscape, broken only by the water and the ancient road. One man sat in the Mercedes. His demeanor bordered on the darker side of the human experience.

Major General Morgan Walker, a senior manager at the National Security Agency, sat in the car, his anger growing by the second. The individual who requested his attendance at this out-of-the-way location, would soon be fifteen minutes late. Being a career military man, punctuality remained a virtue. Tardiness a sin.

By the light of a quarter moon, he saw a darkened shape slowly approaching his position. Walker's hand rested on a Kimber 1911 .45 ACP pistol in the passenger seat. The other vehicle stopped, and a figure exited.

Walker gripped the Kimber and also stepped out of the car.

The shadow said, "Walker?"

"You're late."

"Couldn't help it."

"Then plan better. What did you need to discuss?"

The shadow approached Walker's position and stopped. The glow from a lighter igniting a cigarette revealed the face of Dimitri Petrov for a split second.

Walker relaxed only slightly and said, "You called this meeting."

"Certain individuals are getting nervous. What about the two senators?"

"They are under surveillance."

"Are you sure?"

"What's that supposed to mean?"

Petrov took a long drag on his cigarette. He blew the smoke out his nostrils and said, "Are you aware that Berry is not responding to phone calls?"

"How would you know? We agreed I am his only contact."

"Obviously, you've been negligent. Did you know he went to Louisiana?"

Walker remained silent.

"He transported Edgar to a Houston airport. There, we lost track of them."

"Who's we, Petrov?"

"Friends."

Walker raised the 1911 and pointed it at the newcomer. "Our deal was for you to keep your goons out of the US."

Petrov shrugged. "Your assets don't seem to be capable of keeping tabs on them."

Narrowing his eyes, Walker said, "Do you have a point

to this conversation? If you don't, I'm leaving." He turned and started to walk back to his car.

"Samantha Edgar is in the custody of the FBI and scheduled for a meeting with the attorney general tomorrow."

Stopping in mid-stride, Walker looked back. "When did this happen?"

"Thought you had control over the situation, General."

"Answer the question."

The cigarette glowed in the dark as Petrov inhaled again. "It happened right after Berry dropped her off. She was arrested inside the terminal and then disappeared. Berry hasn't answered his phone since."

Walker remained quiet for a few moments. "I'll check into it." He turned to walk back to his car.

Petrov said, "If they are in custody, you know what needs to be done, don't you?"

Without replying, Walker slipped behind the wheel of his Mercedes and started the engine.

Samantha Edgar listened to the lawyer assigned to her. Since her cross-country trek, her financial resources were strained to the point she needed a public defender. A concept she found distasteful. But she had to admit, this particular woman knew what she was doing.

"Samantha, I need you to tell me everything, otherwise, I won't be able to defend you. I'll explain it this way. I'm not in the mood or frame of mind to be lied to. Since you are a trained attorney, you understand how this works. I'm going to ask you one time and one time only. Are you involved with the activities surrounding the death of William Fischer, Emma Elliot, and Calvin Hendricks?"

"I am aware of why they were killed."

"Were you directly involved with their murders?"

"No."

"How do you know about the why?"

"I saw a memo I was not supposed to see."

Lillian Frazer stared at her client for several moments. "Uh, before we go further, what was your security level, Samantha?"

"I was the director's assistant. Pretty damn high."

"You understand it's been withdrawn, right?"

"I assumed it would be."

"Excuse me. I need to make a few phone calls. I'm not comfortable proceeding without checking with the DOJ."

"I figured you would. I'll still be here."

The room's size barely qualified as a conference room. The six-foot table and six chairs took up most of the floor space. She sat on the side opposite the door with her hands cuffed and in front of her. She took a deep breath and closed her eyes. Additional cleansing breaths followed until she relaxed.

She stayed in this Zen-like state for five minutes until she heard the door open. She opened her eyes and stared at a large man standing in the doorway.

He said, "You won't be in here forever, Ms. Edgar. Be careful about what you say. Consider yourself warned." The door then closed, and she remained alone, again.

A minute passed before Lillian Frazer returned. Before the attorney could sit, Samamtha glared up at her and said, "My life has just been threatened by someone I've never seen before. I thought this was a secure facility. If you want my cooperation, put me in protective custody and arrange a meeting with Michael Wolfe."

The Next Day

Leaning against the doorframe, Wolfe folded his arms and contemplated Samantha Edgar. Her glare told him she did not believe she was safe yet. "Okay, they have armed FBI rapid-response agents surrounding this facility and two outside your door. What else do you want?"

With her arms wrapped around herself, she shook her head.

He said, "Okay, why me?"

Her expression changed only slightly. "Because you don't bullshit anyone."

"A matter of opinion. But I'll take that as a compliment."

"William was my friend. He and I had spent a lot of years rummaging around the back alleys of Europe. He had my back, and I had his. I had nothing to do with his murder."

"No one has accused you of it."

"Oh, yes, they have. Joseph so much as told me so."

"Samantha, the fact you gave him the flash drive and then disappeared after his death kinda caused a lot of fingers to point. Mainly at you."

"I know. Not the smartest thing I've ever done. But when I heard of William's death, I panicked."

"Understandable." He paused. "Your interview in Houston with Clark and Joseph didn't do you any favors, either."

She shrugged.

"Are you gonna tell me your story, or did I just waste half a day getting here?"

"Michael, I don't know the whole story. But I do know General Walker is someone who needs to be investigated."

"Why?"

"Emma Elliot wasn't scared of standing up to men like President Griffin. But she was terrified of General Walker."

"Again, why?"

"I don't know. Her entire demeanor changed when his name was mentioned."

Wolfe remained quiet for several moments. "Did that happen with any other individuals?"

Samantha shook her head. "Only Walker."

"Huh." He tilted his head and said, "I've never heard of him until all this mess started. Do you have any background on the man?"

"What little I know is from a CIA profile. He grew up in Orange County, California. After his parents died, he lived in Fort Collins, Colorado. He received an appointment to West Point where he graduated at the top of his class. Rapid rise through the ranks of officers and made colonel before his fortieth birthday."

Raising an eyebrow, Wolfe said, "What was his specialty?"

"Intelligence."

"Figures. Go on."

"He spent ten years in Europe with NATO, came back to the US when he got his first star, and has worked for the NSA since."

Wolfe pursed his lips. "Any details about his years at NATO?"

She shook her head.

"Where would I find those records?"

"Pentagon, I suppose."

"Is he liked there?"

"Couldn't tell you. Unlike some of his contemporaries, he never served any time there. He is supposedly one of the top experts on signal intelligence in the US."

"Family?"

"I saw no records of any."

"Maybe I need to find out a little more about Major General Walker."

"Just make sure he doesn't know what you're doing, Michael."

Chapter Forty

After parking in front of a nondescript brick building on the city's southwest side, Wolfe and Nadia entered. They climbed the staircase to the second floor where they found Alexia waiting for them next to her cubicle. The two women hugged while Wolfe stood off to the side.

When they finished, Wolfe said, "We appreciate you doing this for us."

"Not a problem, Michael."

"Where's JR?"

"He's actually taking a week off. This is the first time I can remember him doing so. Let's go to the conference room. We're the only ones here today."

Wolfe surveyed the area. The cubicle farm no longer existed. Instead, the building's second level held five offices, a soundproof conference room, and a restaurant-quality coffee station. Alexia led the way to their meeting area.

Once the door was shut and everyone took a seat, Alexia said, "Interesting individual, this General Morgan Walker."

Raising an eyebrow, Wolfe said, "In what way?"

"You told me he grew up in Orange County, California, right?"

"That's what I was told."

She smiled ever so slightly. "Morgan Edward Walker was born on June 1st, 1970, which would make him in his fifties, today."

The retired Marine nodded. "That would fit with his military rank."

"His mother and father were killed in an avalanche in northern California while on a skiing vacation. That was the winter of 1975. Walker was an only son and had been staying with a family friend."

"Where were the parents from?"

Alexia gave Wolfe a mischievous grin. "They were foreign exchange students from Iran who arrived in the early 60s. Both were engineers and stayed to work in the aerospace industry that was growing rapidly because of the Apollo program."

"If the parents died, where did the boy go?"

"Fort Collins, Colorado. He lived with his father's brother and wife. Both were professors at Colorado State University."

"I take it both of them were Iranian, as well."

"Yes. You have to remember during the sixties and seventies, Iranian students were highly sought after by universities due to being taught English as a second language. The Shah was extremely important to the US as a trading partner, but also a strategic location for American influence in the Middle East."

Wolfe considered Alexia for a moment. "Any information on the aunt and uncle?"

She nodded. "They died of natural causes a decade ago.

Before you ask, both bodies were cremated."

"Figures. Let me guess, not much is known about them, either."

"Not even pictures."

"Did they have children?"

"I hacked the personnel records of where they taught. Guess what?"

Wolfe folded his arms. "They aren't there."

"No, the records are there, but only academic records. Next-of-kin information was suspiciously absent."

Nadia spoke for the first time. "I have not seen a picture of General Walker. What does he look like?"

Alexia turned her laptop around so they could see the NSA identification photo of the general.

Wolfe chuckled, and Nadia leaned forward to study the image. She said, "He could pass as a typical American from California."

Alexia said, "I agree, a large concentration of Iranian immigrants settled in California. Particularly after the 1979 revolution, and most were highly educated. The brain-drain of those years still affects Iran to this day."

"How the hell did he get the name Walker?"

"Immigration records show the parents' name as Yazdani. But the father legally changed it to Walker just before the son was born."

"So, he tried to Americanize his family."

"That's how it appears to me, Michael."

Furrowing his brow, Wolfe said, "Any rumors about his political ideology?"

"None I could find. He spent five of his ten years in Europe at the NATO air base near Izmir, Turkey."

Wolfe stared out the conference room window and tapped his forefinger on the table. "Izmir is not that far from

Iran. Is that a coincidence? Or something he managed to arrange for a purpose? Most postings last three years or less. Why five? There has to be a reason he spent five years that close to his parents' homeland." He paused. "Is there a way to dig deeper into his time spent at Izmir, Turkey?"

Alexia's attention went to the computer screen and then Wolfe and Nadia. She repeated the process three times. Finally, she said, "Interesting challenge. I'd have to think about it for a little while."

Reaching into his pocket, he extracted the flash drive retrieved from William Fischer's safe deposit box. He handed it to Alexia. "This is the original flash drive. The one I gave Griggs was a copy. I was told the transcripts and photos have meaning."

She accepted the small device. "Okay. Such as?"

"I was told the pictures reveal the location of conspirators and the transcripts give more detail to their identity. I'm not sure I trust the individual who told me. But if there is a code and we can break it, maybe we'll learn who these people are."

After staring at the flash drive for a few moments, she placed it in a USB slot. "Since we know Walker is from Orange County, let's see if we can determine the location of each picture."

While she worked, he and Nadia stepped out of the conference room to the coffee service area. While Wolfe poured his wife a cup, he asked, "You've always had a good intuition about situations like this. What do you think?"

Taking the cup from her husband, Nadia studied the contents and then took a sip. "My questions would be, how big is the conspiracy, what is the goal, and why now?"

Wolfe didn't answer right away. He watched Alexia work through the soundproof glass. "All good questions." He raised the coffee cup to his lips. Before he took a drink, he lowered it. Turning to his wife, he said, "Promoting Emma Elliot to the directorship of the CIA may have been the catalyst for why now. I have a strong suspicion Samantha Edgar has lied to us from the start. If the flash drive has the key to the conspiracy, how did she get the intel without being part of the plan?"

"Have you asked her?"

"No."

"Well, to me, that should have been the first question you asked her."

"Well, considering she's a guest of the FBI, it might be tough to get an answer."

Nadia had started to say something when Alexia frantically waved them in. When they appeared at the door, Alexia smiled. "I found the key to the pictures."

Fort Meade, MD

Walking the halls of the Fort Meade, Maryland headquarters of the National Security Agency, Morgan Walker ignored those who passed him. The meeting he would have in a few minutes needed his full concentration. He entered and found himself the last one to arrive. He knew all of the men and women sitting on one side of the conference room. Only one chair faced them, and it was empty.

Eric Perez, secretary of the Department of Homeland Security, glared at him. "Sit down, Walker."

"Yes, sir."

Next to Perez sat Director of National Intelligence

Barbara Hurel. On Perez's left, the director of the National Security Agency, Lieutenant General Mark Schultz, gave him a neutral glare.

After Walker arranged himself in the chair across from all of his bosses, he said, "Is there a problem?"

Schultz said, "You might say that. When was the last time you spoke to Senator Calvin Hendricks?"

Sitting ramrod straight, Walker narrowed his eyes. "Six months ago, at one of his incessant committee hearings."

"You've not spoken to him since?"

"No, sir."

DNI Hurel pursed her lips. "Be careful with your facts, General."

"I am always careful with the facts, Director Hurel."

Perez gave the general a sarcastic smile. "The DNI is referring to a few disturbing pictures captured of you and Hendricks speaking on a park bench two days before his untimely death. Care to comment?"

"Difficult to comment when I have not seen the picture, nor do I remember the circumstance of it occurring."

"Are you denying you were there?"

"AI can create an abundant number of realistic images, Secretary Perez."

"This is not an AI generated photograph. It has been analyzed by the FBI. The photo is real, and the person in it is you."

"Once again, without seeing the evidence, I am disinclined to reply."

General Schultz drummed his fingers on the tabletop. "Walker, do you know Samantha Edgar?"

"I believe she was the assistant to CIA Director Emma Elliot. I have seen her in meetings, but as far as knowing her, I do not."

"She has implicated you in some sort of conspiracy involving Elliot and Hendricks."

Clasping his hands together, Walker smiled and said, "And what conspiracy would that be, General Schultz?"

"That's what we are trying to determine. So far, you've been uncooperative with this inquiry."

"Sir, it's not that I am trying to be difficult. The facts are I have no clue as to what you are talking about. What is the nature of this conspiracy you mentioned?"

"We have no details. Just innuendos."

"Well, there you go. Another conspiracy theory with no basis in fact. Like I said, I have not spoken to Senator Hendricks except in a committee hearing six months ago. Regardless of any photographic evidence, it just hasn't happened. As far as the Edgar woman, I have not personally met her. If someone said I have, well, they were lying."

"What about Senators Taylor Finley and Jayden Berry? Do you have regular meetings with these two men?"

"The only contact I've ever had with them is through the senate committee Hendricks led. I've never spoken to them outside of a hearing."

Secretary Perez said, "Thank you for clearing this matter up, Morgan. Sorry to have dragged you down here."

Chapter Forty-One

SOUTHWEST MISSOURI

"Knowing Walker is from Orange County, California helped identify one of the images. Cross-referencing the address on his birth certificate with Google Maps, one of the pictures on the flash drive is the house his parents owned until their deaths."

Wolfe rubbed his chin. "That was easy. What about the transcribed conversations, Alexia?"

"Those were a little harder to understand. But it's a basic cipher. If you assign a number to each letter of the alphabet and look at the first sentence, the number created by the letters of that specific sentence are the key to the message." She showed one of the transcripts on the wall.

Nadia stood, walked over, and studied the projected picture. "How so?"

"Let's say, if your first sentence is *how are you*, you can assign numbers to those letters. They give you the position of the important words within the rest of the text. So, in our example, the numbers would be 8, 15, 23, 1, 18, 5, 25, 15, and 21. With this information, you go to the transcript and assign numbers to each of the words in the message starting with the second sentence. The numbers from your first sentence tell you the sequence of the real message. Sounds complicated, but it isn't. I wrote an algorithm to do it automatically."

"What if the message is longer than twenty-six words?"

"The first twenty-six words, starting with the second sentence, are essential to the message. Any words after them are basically nonsense."

Displaying a grin, Wolfe asked, "Sounds complicated to set up. How would someone construct the message?"

Alexia shrugged. "AI has no trouble composing a message like I've described."

"Huh." He studied the message projected on the wall. "So, what did you learn from these messages?"

"I believe you figured it out some time ago. We just didn't have any way to confirm it. Iran is behind the list. Walker's Iranian ancestry made him the key individual to recruit. Which they did while he completed his tour in Turkey."

The retired Marine sniper sat and studied the message. "What is their goal?"

Alexia changed the PowerPoint slide on the wall. "This is the only message that contains any references to the ultimate outcome."

Wolfe read it silently. "Well, looks like I need to take a trip to Washington."

Langley, VA

The arrival of Michael Wolfe at CIA headquarters created a buzz among the seasoned personnel who knew about the retired Marine's exploits during his tenure with the agency. Closed-door meetings were nothing unusual in the building. However, his presence and the appearance of the top brass from the FBI intensified the speculation and rumor mills.

At exactly 1:00 p.m., the director's conference room's door closed, and everyone in attendance directed their attention to Wolfe. He stood next to a PowerPoint slide projected on a large screen. The presentation started with him summarizing how the cipher, on the so-called phone transcripts, worked.

After he finished, Joseph Kincaid asked, "Now that you've explained the cipher, what's the bottom line on the transcripts, Michael?"

"After the crash of their helicopter carrying the Iranian president, they embarked on a trail of revenge. They knew their helicopter went down due to a sniper's bullet, but not the identity of the sniper. Their solution to the problem? Announce to the world the accident occurred due to a mechanical malfunction. Then use new and old intel on the CIA, MI6, and the Mossad to identify individuals who might have ordered the mission and anyone trained to be a sniper in those Western intelligence agencies. Thus, the diversity of names on the list. From information received from our MI6 and Mossad cousins, there have been three former snipers from MI6 assassinated in the past three months and one Mossad agent. The death of Emma Elliot and Senator Hendricks can also be linked to this action by the Iranian Revolutionary Guard Corps."

He paused to let his audience consider the implications of the information.

Joseph Kincaid asked Wolfe, "Do we know if the source of the list is Iranian or one of their proxies?"

"The author was not identified by the information given to William Fischer. So, we don't have an answer at this time."

A hand shot up in the back of the conference room, a woman Wolfe did not recognize. "So, we don't have proof this is an actual Iranian plot. Do we?"

"At this point, no. But the evidence points in that direction."

Another hand. Wolfe pointed to the man next to the woman.

"Why bring this to the attention of both the CIA and FBI?"

FBI Director Ryan Clark stood. "The fact individuals on this list have already been murdered, along with Senator Hendricks and Director Elliot, demand an official FBI investigation. One we have already started. I might remind everyone in this room who might question the legitimacy of this information, we have already seen actions taken against individuals identified in the data. In my opinion, we have ample reason to pursue this matter further. Until we know different, we will act like the plot is real." Clark's gaze swept over the assembled managers. He continued, "Any questions?"

The conversation devolved into a discussion about the cipher before Joseph brought the meeting to a halt. He finished by saying, "Thank you for coming this afternoon."

Everyone stood and filed out of the room except Wolfe, Clark, and Joseph. When the conference room door closed, and they were alone, Clark said, "I have three teams of agents keeping General Walker under surveillance."

Joseph said, "I'm told he hasn't been in his office for

several days. When I tried to invite him to the meeting, his assistant told me he was touring data collection sites."

The FBI director slowly nodded. "I wondered why no one questioned his absence."

Wolfe collected his flash drive from the laptop and listened to the exchange between the two other men. He said, "Someone will tell him about the meeting. Even though his name was never mentioned. He's a smart individual and will realize how close we are to exposing him. I say, bring him in. If not, he'll disappear."

Clark folded his arms and looked at Joseph. "What do you think?"

"Michael raises a valid point. With the evidence we have, which isn't much, what would you charge him with if you did arrest him?"

"Sedition. Let me present your evidence to the attorney general. If he says go, we can have an arrest warrant ready before the end of the day."

Joseph nodded. "Very well. Keep me informed."

Wolfe handed Clark a flash drive similar to the one he used for the presentation. "This is a copy of what I just presented. There's a file called *General*. It contains everything we know about him. Including the group's long-term plan."

Accepting the device, the FBI director asked, "What's in it?"

"The Iranians believe Griffin may be the one who ordered the downing of the helicopter. As revenge, they are planning to destabilize his presidency. Then the Iranians will use oil revenues to financially support someone more sympathetic to their regime."

Clark frowned. "They want to choose the next president?"

Wolfe pointed to the flash drive. "It's all there."

"What about the laws prohibiting foreign influence in our elections?"

"Walker told them he could find ways around them."

"So, they're backing him?"

"Don't know. It's not specified in the transcripts. But I think we can surmise that's the plan."

The acting director of the CIA asked, "Have they identified who shot the helicopter down?"

"No."

"That's good."

Folding his arms, Clark said, "Are you not telling us something?"

Wolfe shook his head. "The individual who shot the chopper down is an unknown."

"Good, let's leave it that way." He walked out of the room.

Turning to Wolfe, Joseph said, "Do you think Walker will know we're on to him?"

"Absolutely positive he already knows. He'll slip his FBI tails and be in the wind by dark."

"Do you know something I don't?"

"At first, I didn't recognize the woman who asked the question. After she did, it dawned on me one of the translated transcripts referred to her."

Pinching his nose with his fingers, Joseph said, "She's the deputy executive director of the Asian and Middle East section."

"I didn't put the pieces together until after she asked the question. It appears you need to do a little house cleaning, Joseph."

"Yes, I do. Starting with a deputy executive director."

"Thought you weren't going to make those types of decisions as the acting director."

"I spoke to the president this morning."

"And?"

"He told me to act like I'm a confirmed director. This place is in need of rebuilding."

"President Griffin knows how to get the best out of you, doesn't he?"

"Yes, but he's right. The CIA needs new blood. Want a job?"

Wolfe shook his head and said, "Hell, no."

Chapter Forty-Two

SOUTHWEST MISSOURI

Four hundred feet in the air, the small drone's electric motors were barely audible. With moonrise several hours away, the drone was also invisible by anyone on the ground below.

Nadia worked on her laptop in the office she and Wolfe maintained in the house. With Ben already tucked in and sound asleep, she could work without interruption. Nova curled up in the middle of the room, also asleep after a busy day of guarding the young boy.

The German shepherd's head jerked up, and she emitted a low growl deep in her throat.

Nadia turned around. "What's the matter, Nova?"

Now on her feet, she kept her attention on the ceiling and barked once.

"Protect Ben."

The dog took off toward the small boy's room. Nadia unlocked the top drawer on her desk and withdrew her Glock 48. She slammed a ten-cartridge magazine into the gun's handle and charged the weapon before heading toward the house's main entrance.

Stepping out onto the front porch, she listened for any vehicle noise. Hearing none, she shut the door and threw the dead bolt. Moving swiftly to the back entry, she heard nothing when she stood on the deck. She reached into her jeans' rear pocket and extracted her cell phone. Pressing an icon on her home page, she waited for the call to be answered. "Ozark Security. How can we be of help this evening, Mrs. Wolfe?"

"I'm not sure. But something disturbed our German shepherd enough she gave me a warning."

"I'll have a car there is ten minutes."

"Thank you."

The call ended, and she mumbled, "Now, let's see if whoever is out there can wait ten minutes." She moved back to Ben's room. Nova sat next to the bed of the still-sleeping young boy. Approaching the dog, she stroked its head and said, "Good girl."

The dog's attention remained on the ceiling.

The drone operator watched the video feed from the small drone to the monitor on the controller. He checked his flight time and knew he had at least thirty more minutes of battery power. His rented pickup sat parked a mile north of the Wolfe property on the main access road to the remote property.

The client did not reveal the reason for the assignment, only that it needed to be a night survey of the area. Mainly the house and what appeared to be a barn behind it. He lowered the small drone's altitude to fifty feet and circled the barn area. The camera picked up the image of an asphalt street east of what appeared to be a large garage door. Realizing the significance of the discovery, he maneuvered the small unmanned aerial device down the length of the runway. It ended just short of a tree line.

Satisfied with the video of the landing strip, he steered the small device back to capture more images of the hangar and house. Lowering the aircraft to an altitude of ten feet, he concentrated on capturing details of the building's exterior.

Nova stood at the back door and whined. She looked back at Nadia and barked once. Not sure what she was trying to communicate, Nadia opened the door, and the dog tore out toward the hangar area.

She stepped out onto the deck and heard a low buzzing sound from the direction of the runway. In the low light of the stars, she could see Nova running silently toward the south on the asphalt. The dog leapt into the air.

Because of distance and low light, Nadia could only see shadows. But the dog shook whatever she held in her jaws, violently.

With the camera pointing toward the building, the operator saw movement to the north of the drone's location and moved the camera to determine what caused the movement. At that exact moment, the video feed vibrated rapidly and then stopped. The startled man glanced out the front windshield of the pickup and noticed flashing lights in his rearview mirror.

His hand went to the key to start the engine, but the other vehicle pulled alongside, and a bright spotlight illuminated the interior of his truck. He shielded his eyes and heard an amplified voice say, "Step out of the vehicle with your hands where we can see them."

"Shit." The man's first thought raced back to the fact he was not being paid enough to risk going to jail, so he opened the door and stepped out, his hands above his head. With the spotlight shining directly into his eyes, he was blind to what was going on around him. He sensed more than saw a large man appear next to him and spin him around. He was then slammed against the truck and his hands cuffed.

"What's the meaning of this? I wasn't doing anything."

Another man entered the truck and withdrew the drone's controller. "What are you doing with this?"

"Taking night pictures."

"Right. Hate to tell you this, dude, but you've been busted."

Christian County Sheriff Blake Perry watched the pickup driver on the video monitor of the interrogation room. He turned to the woman on his right and asked, "Ever see him before, Nadia?"

She said, "No, Blake I haven't."

He picked up the small drone and examined it. "Never knew a dog could snatch one of these things out of the air."

"Nova has talents we haven't discovered yet."

The sheriff looked back at the dog sitting next to the

small boy who kept his hand on her back. "No, sir. I've never heard of a dog doing such a thing."

With a smile, Nadia said, "Michael plays Frisbee with her all the time. To her, the drone was probably just a Frisbee making noise."

"Probably." He placed the drone on the desk and said, "I'm gonna ask him a few questions. You stay here and listen."

When Perry entered the interrogation room, the man stiffened.

"I'm the sheriff of this county. What the hell were you doing spying on one of our citizens?"

The man remained quiet.

"You didn't have any identification on you, son. Want to tell me who you are?"

A shake of his head was the suspect's only response.

"Quiet type, huh?" Perry stood. "Well, since you won't talk to me, I'll talk to you. Not sure you realized what you did out there. But the house you were spying on belongs to a good friend of mine. That person also has friends in the military and the federal government. There's gonna be a shit-pot load of FBI agents crawling down your throat by the end of the day. I seriously doubt they will be as nice as I am."

He stood to go.

The drone operator said, "Name's Bob Wright. I own a drone mapping company, and I was hired to photograph the house and land."

"At night?"

The man shrugged.

Perry grinned. "Nice try. I don't believe a single word of that hogwash. Hope you had a big dinner last night. I don't have the budget to feed someone who won't tell me his real name." With that statement, the sheriff walked out of the room.

He returned to the video monitor where Nadia stood. "When did you say Michael would be back?"

She glanced at the time on the monitor. "He should be landing in about a half hour."

"Good. I'm anxious to hear what he has to say about this little incident."

Later That Same Day

Michael Wolfe observed the prisoner, once again in the interrogation room, while Sheriff Perry stood next to him.

"We checked his fingerprints. His name is Delbert Garcia. Small-time hood from Chicago. According to a detective I spoke with this morning, he's an unsuccessful crook. Every time he's pulled a job, he gets caught. About a year ago, he disappeared, and they hadn't heard anything else about him. As far as they knew, he'd moved on."

"Has he said anything?"

"Only what I told your earlier."

"Huh."

"Do you want to talk to him, Michael?"

"Sure, but don't record it."

Perry frowned. "What've you got in mind?"

"Nothing illegal. I'm just going to scare him a bit." Wolfe walked around the corner and entered the interrogation room.

The prisoner looked up when Wolfe entered the room and sat across from him. "Who the hell are you?"

"The guy who owns the house you were photographing last night."

The prisoner raised an eyebrow but remained quiet.

Wolfe continued. "Did the person you work for tell you who lives at the property?"

A shake of his head was Garcia's response.

"Too, bad. You might have thought twice about accepting the job. You see, I'm a retired Marine sniper. One of the best they've ever trained. That's not a brag, it's a fact. Now I work for the government. I'll leave it to your imagination as to what I do for them. At times, it includes my special training."

Garcia shrugged.

With a grin, Wolfe said, "We know a little about you now: your name, address, shirt size, habits, and hangouts. Guess what?"

With a shrug, the prisoner said, "I'm not gonna play your game."

"That's fine, I'm gonna tell you what I know anyway. Your name is Delbert Garcia, you live in a run-down apartment building in the Grand Crossing area and, when you're in Chicago, you hang out in a bar called Dusty's Place. Want me to continue?"

Another shrug. But Garcia's body betrayed his projected indifference. He started bouncing his right heel on the floor and diverted his gaze away from Wolfe.

Leaning forward, Wolfe clasped his hands together. "Tell me who hired you, Delbert."

Perspiration formed on the prisoner's lips as he returned his attention to the retired Marine. "Man, you're gonna get me killed. I can't tell you that."

"Then you've got a predicament. You see, if you don't tell us, we'll have to release you. If you are released, I'll assume you'll need to go back to my house to continue your surveillance."

"No, no, no, I'm done with that shit."

"I don't believe you."

"No, man, really. I'm done."

Wolfe sat back in his chair. "If we release you, you'll never know when your last breath will be taken. Unless you tell us, who hired you, you'll never know when I'll have you in my rifle sights."

"Ahhhh, man…" He intensified his bouncing heel. "He was Russian. He introduced himself as Dimitri. That's all I know."

"See? That wasn't so hard."

Chapter Forty-Three

MIAMI

NSA Director of SigInt checked the rearview mirror in his rented Chevy Equinox. The Ford Explorer remained three vehicles behind him in traffic. Regardless of which agency might be following him, the drivers and models changed, but they all remained three cars behind Walker's SUV.

Three days of being followed. Whoever they were, they were good, but he knew what to look for. A new car or truck each day, but it maintained the same distance and switched off with another vehicle every thirty minutes.

He guessed the followers were FBI. But they could also be with the CIA or even his own agency, the NSA. As these thoughts raced through his mind, his cell phone chimed, indicating the arrival of a text message. At the next stoplight, he read the message.

Chances high, you and list have been compromised. Suggest appropriate measures on your part. C

He slammed his palm on the steering wheel and muttered, "Damn."

Checking his follower, he pulled ahead as the light

turned green. Advancing his speed, he increased the number of vehicles separating him and whoever kept him under surveillance. As he moved into the heaviest traffic of his journey, he waited until he could make a sudden left turn in front of a long line of approaching cars.

Ten minutes later, he felt comfortable he was no longer being followed. Since returning to his hotel would be stupid, he headed toward an entrance ramp for northbound Interstate 95.

***

Miami

FBI Agent Ted Romel finally made the left turn and accelerated. But his quarry was nowhere in sight. He turned to his partner, Susan Feltz. "Call it in. We've lost him. Maybe he'll go back to his hotel."

"What are the odds?"

"Not good. I think we've been burned."

***

Washington, DC

At exactly 10:10 p.m. on a Wednesday night in October, one hundred FBI agents descended on twenty-five private residences. Each team of four agents was given the task of arresting one of twenty-five federal government employees identified either by a flash drive given to William Fischer by Samantha Edgar or the testimony of an arrested small-time hood from Chicago. Five of those individuals would later be released due to a lack of evidence. But the employment of all twenty-five with the federal government came to an abrupt end.

The only person on the list whose whereabouts were unknown became Major General Morgan Walker. After eluding three teams of FBI agents in Miami, he simply disappeared off the face of the earth. When his bachelor home in McLean, Virginia was searched, investigators found files hidden in a false basement wall. These files led the FBI to five more conspirators.

Once in custody, these five individuals were more than happy to discuss what they knew.

Six and a half hours later, Walker pulled into a locally owned motel just outside of Brunswick, Georgia. After checking in, he found a Walmart and replenished his left-behind luggage, clothing, and personal items. He also purchased a pay-as-you-go cell phone with cash.

As an NSA employee, he knew exactly how to disappear, both in the electronic sense and the trackable sense. At ten that evening, he dialed a number on his new phone. It was answered on the third ring.

"Hello."

"It's me. What's happened?"

"Apparently, they raided your home. They know just about everything."

"Damn."

"A federal agency has three teams following you."

"Not anymore."

"Good. I suggest you disappear."

"Why?"

"The FBI put a national BOLO out on you. Stay in the shadows until this blows over."

"What about you?"

"If they know about you, it won't take long for them to figure out who I am. I'm leaving in the morning."

"How will I get ahold of you?"

"You won't. This needs to be our last call."

Walker heard banging on the phone. "What's that?"

"The door. It's probably too late for me to leave. Destroy the phone you're using."

After the comment, the line went dead. Walker immediately took the back off the phone and removed both the battery and SIM card.

FBI Director Ryan Clark read over the arrest summaries early the next morning after a long, sleepless night. He picked up the phone and dialed a number he knew by heart.

"Good morning, Director. Were last night's festivities successful?"

"Yes, thanks to the hard work of over a hundred agents. Are any questions being asked this morning regarding the absence of several CIA employees, Joseph?"

"No. However, I suspect the news media will get wind of the arrests soon enough. Have you heard from the president?"

"Yes. He called to get an update at four this morning."

There was silence on the call for a few moments. Clark said, "Joseph, you have his ear better than I do. Maybe a short news conference announcing what happened would be appropriate."

"Already ahead of you. He'll read a statement about the plot at ten this morning. He will blame Iran, offer proof of their complicity, and announce heavy sanctions against the regime. The US consul to the United Nations will ask for the Security Council to impose further sanctions on Iran's economy."

"Good. I have a meeting with the NSA director in fifteen minutes. He's concerned about the disappearance of Walker."

"He should be. What are you going to tell him?"

Clark chuckled. "The truth."

"He won't like it."

"Too bad. Four of his people were arrested last night, with the head of the conspiracy still missing."

"I've worked with him before." Joseph paused. "He'll understand the decision to keep the information from him."

"I'm more concerned about Walker getting out of the country."

"Ask for his assistance. He can help monitor that."

"I know, that's what I'm planning to do."

"Good luck, Ryan."

"Thanks, Joseph."

The call ended, and Clark checked his watch. It was time to head to the conference room.

The Following Day

Michael Wolfe trudged through the western part of his property. This section remained thick with native Ozark trees, dogwood, maple, oak, and an assortment of nut-bearing specimens. Nova navigated the underbrush next to him. His mission, on this particular excursion, was more to clear his mind than actually accomplish a specific task. Having Nova join him increased the peace of mind he felt when he set out on hikes like this one.

He stopped and listened to the sounds generated by the creatures who dwelled within the woodlands. Except for birds and the occasional squirrel rummaging through fallen foliage, the forest remained quiet.

Reaching down, he scratched the dog's head. "Not sure there is anywhere else in the world I'd rather be, Nova."

He could hear the canine panting. Glancing down, he could tell she was concentrating on a spot to the right of their location. She stiffened, getting ready to sprint, when he said, "Stay." The dog relaxed and sat. He kneeled beside her, keeping his hand on her back, and followed her line of sight. He saw a female deer standing still and looking in their direction fifty yards from their position.

"Good girl, Nova."

The vibration of his cell phone broke the spell, and the deer scampered off. Standing, he retrieved the device and checked the caller ID. It was Joseph. Taking a deep breath, he accepted the call. "This is Michael."

"Hope I didn't catch you at a bad moment."

Not in the mood to explain, he said, "We're good. What's up?"

"How soon can you get to Washington?"

"I thought I explained to you the last time I was there that I would not be returning."

"You did, but I chose not to listen."

"What's wrong?"

"General Walker eluded his FBI shadows and is now in the wind. No one knows where he is."

"And how is that my problem?"

"The problem is he knows where you live and probably suspects you were the one who broke the cipher on the flash drive."

Wolfe did not respond.

"The FBI arrested twenty-five members of the conspiracy two nights ago. When the agency searched his house, they found a false wall in his basement."

"I take it they found something."

"You could say that. They found the keys to the whole plot."

"What agencies were involved, Joseph?"

"CIA, NSA, and the Pentagon, although, none were above the rank of colonel, and three members of Congress. Not including Emma Elliot and the two senators associated with Hendricks."

Remaining quiet for several moments, Wolfe finally asked, "How high up did the conspiracy go?"

"High enough, the FBI is still interviewing associates of the individuals."

"What do you need of me?"

"We know Petrov is still out there. Where, we don't know. Our guess is he'll hook up with Walker at some point."

"Uh-huh."

"You know where this is going, don't you, Michael?"

"Yes, you want me to find both of them?"

"Walker will know the FBI is after him. He'll take appropriate precautions. He also knows how to stay off the grid. You have the resources to find him."

"You're kidding me, right? How do I have the resources?"

"Alexia and Nadia make a good team. Plus, since neither one of them works for a government agency, no one in the government will know what they're doing."

"Except you."

"Michael, I can make certain computers resources accessible to them, if needed."

"I'm not speaking for either of them. You'll need to make the pitch. If they agree, I'll find Petrov and Walker. But I'm not coming to Washington."

"That's fine. Glad you're on board."

"What happens when I find them?"

"I'll leave that to your discretion."

"No questions asked?"

"No questions asked."

Part III

PULLING BACK THE CLOAK

Chapter Forty-Four

KANSAS CITY

Morgan Walker watched pedestrians stroll up and down 47th street on the Kansas City Plaza. The high-end restaurant featured an outdoor dining area on the roof of the one-story structure. Nestled between two taller buildings on either side, the area afforded diners a comfortable place to dine outside. The exception being during the frigid Kansas City winters.

Waiting for a guest to join him, Walker did not mindlessly watch the crowd. He searched for familiar faces or anyone paying too much attention to his presence. He saw neither.

A man pulled a chair out across from him at his table and sat. "You could have picked a less conspicuous location, Walker."

"It's called hiding in plain sight, my dear Dimitri. As long as we don't draw attention to ourselves, no one will give a shit who we are."

"Whatever."

"What happened to the drone operator?"

"I don't know the details, but he's in FBI custody and probably telling them everything he knows."

"Which is?"

"Not much. I gave him a first name, but that's it. He's a two-bit hood from Chicago who happened to be good with drones. Beyond that he's worthless."

Walker turned and surveyed 47th street. "At least we know where Wolfe lives. But I was hoping the drone video would show us where the booby traps are located."

"Were you aware the FBI arrested most of the cast members in your little play?"

Turning his attention back to Petrov, the general nodded. "I knew about one. How many were arrested?"

"Twenty-six."

Slamming his fist on the table, Walker hissed, "Damn."

"Don't draw attention to yourself."

"They got everybody, but one." He turned away from the former Stasi policeman. "How did they identify them?"

"I don't know for certain, but I was told they searched your home. Twenty-four hours later, they started making arrests. They even escorted three congressmen off the House floor. The news media is showing that particular video constantly."

"Is my name being used?"

Petrov shook his head. "No, your name has been kept out of the media. Why, I don't know."

"Damn."

"I assume you have identification showing you to be someone else?"

Walker turned his attention to the street. "Of course."

"Good. I would use it from now on, just in case." Petrov stood. "Do you have a phone?"

"Got a new one this morning."

Placing a business card on the table, Petrov prepared to leave. "That's my new cell number. Don't use the old one again."

Picking it up, the former general placed it in his shirt pocket. When he spotted Petrov exiting the restaurant on the sidewalk below where he sat, he placed a call on his new cell phone. It was answered on the fourth ring.

A female voice said, "Hello."

"No names. I take it you did not get picked up."

"I'm not associated with the others, remember?"

"Are you safe?"

"I'm not at my residence, if that's what you're asking."

"Good. Don't go back."

"What do you know that you haven't told me?" The woman's voice turned icy.

"They found my files. It's the only conclusion I can come up with. If they did, they will eventually identify you."

"Damn you, Walker. Don't call again."

The call ended before he could repeat, "No names."

Southwest Missouri

The small café sat on the north side of a busy east-west highway. Few parking spaces were left when Wolfe pulled into the lot. Not recognizing any of the vehicles, he wondered if he might be the first to arrive. When he ducked into the restaurant, the man he was to meet was already at a table in a far corner, a cup of coffee on the table in front of him.

The man's eyes followed Wolfe's progress across the

dining room. When he sat, Wolfe said, "Didn't see your vehicle."

"Sold it. Driving a good old American Ford F150, now."

A waitress set a cup of coffee in front of Wolfe. "What can I get ya, hon?"

"What's my friend having?"

The middle-aged woman chewed hard on her gum. "Eggs over easy, grits, and bacon."

Raising an eyebrow, the retired Marine glared at his companion. "I'll have whole wheat toast and scrambled eggs."

The waitress scribbled on her pad and hurried off. Wolfe took a sip of his coffee and contemplated his friend. "Damn, Ian, let me understand this. You bought a Ford F150 and eat grits for breakfast? Aren't you getting a little Americanized?"

"Beats the hell out driving a damn Land Rover and eating haggis and black pudding. Besides, Land Rovers are a bit pretentious around here. I like blending into the background."

"Guess you're right. How've you been, my friend?"

"I hope you're not here to talk me into going to Iran again?"

"No, Sergeant McGill, I'm not. In fact, I told those who might ask a favor of us to go to hell."

"Good for you." He took a sip of his coffee and then continued. "What's so urgent?"

"An American general named Walker and a Russian who calls himself, Dimitri Petrov."

"Why?"

"Our little excursion into the mountain range on the borders of Azerbaijan and Iran."

"Do these men you mentioned know who did it?"

"No. Neither do the Iranians. But they've taken it upon themselves to make sure the ones who did do the deed are never identified. They made a list of suspected snipers and hired this Petrov character to eliminate all of them. Nadia's and my name are on it."

"Where are these two gentlemen?"

"That's the reason for our breakfast this morning. They've disappeared."

"Aye, laddie, now I understand. As long as I don't have to leave the US, I'm in."

"I hoped you would be."

The waitress brought their food.

When she left, McGill took a bite and stared at Wolfe. "By disappeared, what do you mean?"

"Poof. No trace of them. Walker was with the NSA and Petrov is a former Stasi policeman."

"Great. What else haven't you told me?"

"Only the best parts." He proceeded to tell Ian McGill the whole story.

The hour grew late as Wolfe waited for Nadia to come to bed. The retired Marine stared at the ceiling fan slowly turning above him. With his hands behind his head, he listened to her singing in the shower. His thoughts drifted to the realization he had spent more time with her than any other human being. Her coming to bed, smelling of roses or lilacs, made all the nonsense they had endured over the years, worth it.

When the shower shut off, he waited. Eventually, the bathroom door opened, and she moved silently to her side of the bed and slipped under the sheets. Instead of her normal T-shirt and running shorts, she wore nothing. She snuggled against him, her warmth radiating against him.

She whispered into his ear. "Make love to me tonight, Michael."

He rolled over and granted her request.

An hour later, she asked, "When are you and Ian going to start searching for General Walker?"

"It kind of depends. You and I are meeting Alexia and Carla Webb tomorrow. She'll be in town to brief us on everything the CIA and FBI know about him. I explained to them I'm not comfortable leaving Ben with anyone right now, so the meeting needs to be here."

She snuggled closer to him. "I feel the same way."

"After the drone incident, Nova needs to be around Ben as much as possible."

She raised on one elbow and stared at him in the darkness. "Why? Is something going to happen?"

"More precautionary than anything. I didn't realize how sensitive her hearing is. She might be the difference between us knowing about a threat and reacting before it's too late."

Nadia glanced at the digital clock on the nightstand and then lay back down. "It's getting late. What time will Carla be here?"

"Around 10 a.m."

"Then, we need to get some sleep."

"As I recall, it was your idea to postpone doing so."

Punching him lightly on the arm, she said, "You didn't have to agree with me."

"Oh yes, I did."

On the second floor of Wolfe's hangar, next to the conference room, resided a small office with a sophisticated computer system designed by Nadia's friend, Alexia. It monitored all of the security cameras placed strategically around his property. In addition, it provided the computer hacker, when she was visiting, access to her computer system at her company's office.

Ian McGill arrived first for the meeting and found Wolfe on the ground floor doing maintenance on the Baron. "Planning on taking another trip, laddie?"

Wiping his hands on a shop towel, the retired Marine said, "Not until we know Walker's whereabouts."

"Been thinking about that."

"Uh-oh."

With a grin, the Scotsman said, "Why not draw him to us?"

Tilting his head, Wolfe asked, "Now there's a good idea. How?"

"That's the part I haven't figured out yet. But with all the brain power here today, maybe someone else can make a suggestion."

By noon, Wolfe's conference room buzzed with activity. Carla Webb and Alexia huddled on one side of the table as the diminutive CIA agent reviewed what she knew about General Walker. Nadia studied Alexia's efforts on her laptop, while Wolfe and McGill made contingency plans should Alexia's efforts prove fruitless.

At 12:34 p.m., Alexia said, "Michael, you and Ian need to see this."

Standing, both men walked to the other side of the table and peered at the laptop screen.

Wolfe asked, "What am I looking at?"

Pointing to what appeared to be a security camera shot, she said, "This is in Kansas City. You might recognize this as the Plaza. Forty-seventh street to be exact. See the man sitting at the table next to the restaurant's sign?"

"Yeah. What about him?"

"Check out who's sitting across from him."

Lowering himself to get closer to the screen, he said, "Kinda resembles Morgan Walker."

"That's because it is. His hair's a different color, but facial recognition software claims it's him. The fellow in the chair across from him is Petrov."

Straightening, Wolfe folded his arms. "When was this taken?"

"Last night."

"How did you…oh, never mind. So, they were both in KC as of yesterday."

"Correct." She typed on the keyboard for a few seconds. The image changed, and he saw a man with his head down walking on the sidewalk. "This is him forty minutes later walking west on 47th, minus Petrov."

Putting his hands on his hips, Wolfe focused on the laptop screen. "Okay, now I need to know how you found him?"

With a sly grin, she explained. "Carla had the idea. Hack into the largest commercial security system and run a facial recognition routine." Pointing to the security image, she said, "That was the result."

"Can it be done on a national level?"

"Sure, but there's a time crunch. Most of those collectives only keep the videos for a week or so. Too much data.

But, in some cases, the videos are kept longer when a crime is committed at a client's business. Then the video is sent to the police."

"Understandable."

"But, since the drone incident, we decided to try the surrounding big cities. Easier to get lost and stay hidden in a large municipality." Alexia paused for a moment. "We did Tulsa, Memphis, and St. Louis first, then KC. We found him in KC."

Wolfe folded his arms and tapped his lips with a finger. "Okay, it works. How does that help Ian and I intercept them?"

She grinned. "Joseph said he would give us all the help we need. Correct?"

"Yes."

"Since we know he was in KC last night, have NSA run voice recognition on all cell phone calls transmitting from the area of the Plaza. Once they find it, we will have his cell phone number."

Tilting his head, Wolfe grinned, pulled his cell phone from his jeans pocket, and punched in a number.

Chapter Forty-Five

SOUTHWEST MISSOURI

The Next Morning

The speakerphone on the conference table in Wolfe's second-floor office space emitted the voice of Alexia Gibbs. She said, "There is a recording of a voice identified as Walker using a prepaid cell phone. There is a woman on the call who has not been identified. Her phone is also a burner."

Nadia sat at the conference table typing on a laptop. She said, "Did she have an accent?"

"All I was told was mid-central United States. Possibly Chicago or St. Louis."

Wolfe drummed his fingers on the table. "Do they have a location for Walker's phone?"

"They don't. But I have an idea. I'm about halfway to your place. I'll see what I can do when I get there. Is Ian planning to be there?"

"He can be in twenty minutes. Why?"

"If my plan works, you two might need to take a trip."

"I'll get the Baron ready."

"I'll be there in about thirty minutes."

The call ended, and Nadia looked up from the laptop. "I watched everything Alexia did yesterday, and I still don't understand the process."

"It's okay, princess. You'll get it."

She gave him a grateful smile. "I know. I'm being impatient."

Ben and Nova appeared at the top of the stairs. "I'm hungry. So is Nova."

Walking toward the stairs, Wolfe patted the small boy on the head. "I've got to go downstairs. I'll fix both of you something."

"Yay." Ben turned. "Come on, Nova. Time for breakfast." The two scampered down the stairs as Wolfe followed.

Ian McGill arrived exactly two minutes before Alexia pulled into the driveway. They were both met by Wolfe at the hangar's opening. "You two go on upstairs. I need to finish a few chores down here before I join you."

Ten minutes later, as he worked on the plane, Ben appeared at the bottom of the stairwell and yelled at him. "Daddy, Mommy needs you upstairs. She said to hurry."

Wiping his hands on a shop rag, he bound up the stairs two at a time, followed by his son. When Wolfe entered the conference room, both Alexia and McGill were bent over the conference table studying a large map.

Nadia looked up from her laptop and gave him a satisfied grin. "I believe we've found Walker."

Continuing to wipe his hands, Wolfe walked over to where she sat. "Where?"

"All this gave me was a GPS location. Ian's helping Alexia interpret the latitude and longitude."

"Well, he would be the right person to do so."

McGill straightened and gave Wolfe a broad smile. "Well, laddie, guess where the good general has himself hidden?"

"I wouldn't have a clue, Ian. Where?"

"Remember, last year, where you took me pheasant hunting?"

"Yeah, north of the Cedar Bluff Reservoir on the Smoky Hill River in Kansas."

"If I'm reading the map correctly, about four klicks north of the Cedar Bluff State Park is an old motel. His phone was pinged there twice before he shut it off."

Wolfe moved closer to the map and saw where McGill pointed. He studied the roads and traced Kansas 147 north to I-70 and then east. He tapped a town called Hays. "There's a regional airport there that can handle the Baron. They also have car rentals." He glanced at his watch. "I'll file a flight plan while you reserve a vehicle. See if you can get an SUV or something similar."

"Got it."

The retired Marine walked over to his wife. "Let's hope Ian and I can find him. Keep searching. If anything changes, let me know."

She looked at him like it might be her last time. He saw her expression. Bending over, he kissed her. "Don't worry. I'll be back."

"Promise?"

"Promise."

Hays, Kansas

The four-wheel drive Ram 1500 crew-cab pickup, now parked next to the Baron B55, appeared larger than the plane. Wolfe loaded his suppressed Barrett M82A1 50 caliber rifle into the back seat, along with a Remington 700. His go bag sat on the floorboard next to Ian's duffle.

When they finished loading the Ram, Wolfe walked over to the FBO and paid for the Baron to be hangared and prepped for a quick return to Springfield.

Thirty minutes later, Wolfe drove the truck through the town of Hays, north toward 1-70.

McGill commented, "I remember this from our trip last November. Flattest damn country I've ever been in."

Wolfe glanced at his passenger. "You've never been to Qatar, then."

"Oh, I've been there, but for some reason this part of Kansas seems flatter."

"Which makes our task a little harder. If Walker is holed up in this motel, I'm gonna have to be a long distance from it to be hidden. You'll have to be fairly close to make a positive ID."

"Aye, laddie. I know. How far do you need to be?"

"At least a thousand meters."

"Good thing I brought our comm gear."

Without a response, Wolfe made the exit to south Kansas 147. Six miles later, they passed the motel. He said, "Okay, we need to do a little recon and see if he's still here."

"How do you propose we do that?"

"You, my friend"—he pointed to the west of the hotel— "will drop me off out there. When I'm set up, you'll check into the motel. You will be my eyes and ears. I only noticed about ten rooms. See how many are empty. Once we know, we can figure out a plan."

Thirty minutes later, laying prone behind his Barrett M82A1 one thousand meters to the west of the hotel, Wolfe checked the view through his scope. By moving from side to side, he had a clear view of all ten front doors. He keyed the mic on his comm set. "Showtime, go."

McGill responded with one click of his mic. He walked into the hotel office and found a tall man wearing a tan shirt and jeans. McGill said, "Got any vacancies?"

"Sure. How many nights?"

"Two. Scouting hunting spots."

"It's the right time of year. Kind of slow right now. I've only got one other quest."

"Thought you'd have more this time of year."

The man shook his head. "Nah, this is my slow season. Give it another two weeks and I'll be full. Say, fella, from that accent, you're not from around these parts, are ya?"

"Nope, Scotland. Been living out east and searching for someplace a little less crowded."

"Well, it ain't crowded around here." He handed him a metal key with a big plastic fob attached identifying the room number. "I've put you on the opposite end of the building. My other guest likes quiet."

"Fine with me. Thanks."

McGill walked out of the office and back to the Ram truck. When he got in, he keyed the mic. "Tango is in the last room, away from the office."

"Got it."

Once in his room, McGill looked out the back window.

Prairie grass and not much else comprised the scenery. He slipped out the window, staying close to the back wall. He found the last room and placed a silicone disk on the window. When he was back in his room, he tested the small listening device and was rewarded with the sound of a television.

Afternoon turned to dusk, and dusk turned to night. All McGill heard was the television in the room he monitored. Then, around nine, he heard a phone. The voice speaking in the room was muffled and did not stay on the call long.

He keyed the mic to his comm link with Wolfe. "Tango may be leaving. Heads-up."

"Roger."

———————

Lying prone for long stretches of time had never bothered Wolfe. However, age and lack of practice made his wait less comfortable. After walking around in the dark, he heard McGill radio him. He got back behind the Barrett and said, "Roger."

With his scope now aimed at the front door of the suspect's room, he waited patiently.

McGill did not transmit again until Wolfe saw the lights go out in the room. "Tango preparing to leave."

"Roger."

The only vehicle in the lot, besides the Ram pickup, appeared to be an older model Honda Accord. While Wolfe did not find this to be unusual, it did give him a slight sense of concern. What kind of vehicle would an on-the-lam general drive? The question was rhetorical and without an answer.

"Stand by."

Wolfe did not reply as he concentrated on the door. It opened, and a figure stepped out. Without lights inside the room, the figure was undiscernible.

"Talk to me. I have no details."

"Stand by." A short pause and then, "Male, approximately fifty, short gray hair. Wait one."

Wolfe tracked the suspect as they walked toward the Honda, his finger applying slight pressure to the trigger.

When the door opened, the interior light lit up the suspect. "Stand down. Not our tango."

Wolfe eased the pressure on the trigger and looked up from the scope to see the Honda drive away toward the south. He keyed his mic. "Can you access his room and see who this guy is?"

"You read my mind. I'll slip in through the back."

"I'll cover for you."

"Roger."

Ten minutes passed then fifteen. No word came from McGill as Wolfe waited. Only one vehicle had passed during this time. An old Ford pickup rumbled north.

Twenty minutes into his wait, the retired sniper heard, "Something's not right, here."

"How so?"

"I found a driver's license and an NSA badge for Morgan Walker, but the guy getting into the car was not Walker."

"Could it have been Petrov?"

"I memorized both pictures. It wasn't Petrov either."

"Take a picture of the IDs and get out of there."

"Roger."

Wolfe maintained his prone position. Only, this time, he scanned the highway going south with his scope.

Chapter Forty-Six

CENTRAL KANSAS

By 1 a.m., the Honda remained absent. McGill picked up Wolfe a few moments later and drove back to the motel.

Wolfe said, "I think I'm going to wait inside the guy's room. The fact he has Walker's ID means he knows something."

"Want company?"

"I need you outside to let me know when he returns."

"Makes sense."

"How'd you get in?"

"Back window was unlocked. I left it that way."

Wolfe smiled. "Thanks, I'll take advantage of it."

Time passed slowly as Wolfe waited in the room. During this time, he rummaged through the man's personal items. He found Walker's driver's license and NSA badge and placed them on the bed. A cell phone lay hidden by clothes in the man's luggage. This, he displayed next to the IDs.

Finding nothing else, he sat in a chair facing the door and waited.

At exactly 4:12 a.m., he heard a squelch in his earbud. "Tango returning."

Wolfe stood and placed himself next to the door. "Is he alone?"

"Appears to be. He's parked." There was a pause. "Yeah, he's alone."

"Keep watch."

"Roger."

Silence returned as Wolfe waited for the door to open. He heard the key in the lock and then the door swung open. An average-size man, approximately 5 foot, 10 inches tall entered. The smell of liquor and stale cigarettes accompanied him. He flipped on a light, froze, and stared at the articles on the bed.

From behind, Wolfe slammed the door and grabbed the man's right hand. He placed it into a tight rear wrist lock.

"What the fuck?"

Wolfe responded, "Shut up."

The suspect struggled to break the hold, but Wolfe applied additional upward pressure on the arm. The suspect screamed, "Who are you?"

"Shut up, or I'll be your worst nightmare." He twisted the man's arm.

"Hey, that hurts."

"It's supposed to."

Bending the arm farther, the man rose on tiptoe. "Hey…" He paused. "I get it."

The man stopped struggling, and Wolfe eased the tension. "Why do you have Morgan Walker's IDs?"

"Found them."

The retired Marine applied more pressure. "Wrong answer."

"Ahhhh…" The man hissed. "You're gonna break something."

"No, but I can wrench your arm out of its socket. "Now, why do you have Morgan Walker's IDs?"

The man remained silent, until Wolfe twisted harder. He heard a snap, and his captive screamed. Wolfe released the arm, grabbed the other wrist, and put it into the same hold. The injured limb hung useless.

"You broke my arm?"

"If you don't talk, I'll do the same thing to this one."

"All right, all right."

Wolfe increased the pressure. "Talk."

"We swapped IDs. That's why I'm hiding out in this gawd-forsaken fleabag hotel in the middle of fucking Kansas."

McGill slipped into the room and saw the confrontation. "Need any help, laddie?"

"Nah, this guy's going to cooperate, aren't you?"

"Yeah, yeah, yeah. Let go of my arm."

Easing the tension on it, Wolfe said, "What's your name?"

"Bob Alexander."

"Okay, Bob Alexander. I don't believe you. Wanna try again?"

"Hey, the guy and I resemble each other. He paid me ten thousand to do so."

"What's your address?"

"North Kansas City." He then recited the street address.

Wolfe looked at his partner and said, "Check it out."

"Got it." McGill left the room.

Releasing the man's arm, Wolfe spun him around. "Why?"

"Why what?"

"Why switch IDs?"

"Hell, if I know."

"You give him a cell phone, too?"

Alexander nodded.

"Number."

The man recited it.

"Okay, sit."

"What are you gonna do?"

"Tie you up, then a few of my friends are gonna arrive and keep you company."

"Ahhhh—man. Who're your friends?"

"FBI."

"Shit."

With the suspect detained by FBI agents, McGill drove the Ram back to Hays while Wolfe talked to Joseph. "Tell Clark there's something not kosher about this Alexander guy in room 10. Also, ask him to keep it quiet. I don't want Walker to know his cover is blown."

"I'm sure that won't be a problem."

"Alexia and Nadia have a line on the mystery guy's cell phone. They've traced it to KC International where Walker used the ID to rent a car. We have the make, model, and license. I don't anticipate it being hard to track him."

"Just remember." Joseph paused. "He's dangerous and probably feels cornered."

"I hope he does. That's when he'll start feeling pressured. Then he'll make mistakes. We can use those mistakes to get to him."

Joseph remained quiet for several seconds. "What about Petrov? Any clues?"

"If he's smart, he's left the country. I'm a little surprised Walker hasn't left as well."

"We have his passport."

"That's never stopped anyone who's determined to leave the country. We'll keep you posted."

"Be careful, Michael. Like I said before, he's a dangerous man."

The call ended, and Wolfe turned to McGill. "Let's hope the FBI can sit on this Alexander character until we find Walker."

"What are the odds, laddie?"

"The pessimist in me says not very good."

"Aye, kind of what I thought."

Morgan Walker used the cell phone he received from Robert Alexander and sent a text to the number Petrov gave him at their last meeting. After ten minutes and no reply, Walker pulled the battery from the phone. Frustration caused him to hit the steering wheel of the Honda Accord with the heel of his hand.

A new thought occurred, and he returned the battery to the cell phone. He dialed a number.

"I hope you have a good reason for calling."

"You aren't answering your text messages."

"What do you want?"

"Where are you?"

"You of all people should know not to ask a question like that over a cell phone."

"I'm tired of waiting. Are you in the country or not?"

"I've decided you are not worth the risk. You've managed to screw everything up through incompetence and stupidity. I'll take my chances on my own." The call ended.

Breathing became difficult as Walker stared ahead. With his chest heaving, his thoughts became confused. Only one of his team remained, and she refused to help. So be it. He would proceed on his own. His ultimate goal of over-throwing President Roy Griffin and the aftermath of doing so, seemed more of a dream than an actual plan.

Putting the rental car in gear, he drove out of the KC International airport complex and found north I-29 and then west on I-80. His next stop would be the foothills of the Rocky Mountains at Fort Collins, Colorado.

Southwest Missouri

Wolfe landed the Baron on his runway during the fading light of sunset. Exhausted, having not slept the night before, he bid McGill a good night, shut down the Baron, and told himself he would do his maintenance in the morning.

After McGill drove off, he entered the house through the deck door and was immediately greeted by an excited four-year-old boy and a black-and-tan German shepherd. After hugs and scratches, he deposited his go bag in the laundry room and emerged to find Nadia holding a beer.

She handed it to him. "Welcome home."

He hugged her before accepting the bottle and said, "I

find being away from you and Ben an unpleasant experience."

"Good. It means you are now fully domesticated."

"No need to be mean."

She chuckled. "So, what did you find out?"

"We didn't find Walker, but we found a man who resembles the general in ways only a brother might. I need you to dig up anything on a Bob Alexander or Robert Alexander."

"I can start by getting Walker's personnel file from the NSA human resources department."

Raising an eyebrow, Wolfe said, "You know how to do that?"

"Not yet. Joseph has given Alexia and I a back door into their system for emergencies such as this."

"I thought Alexia told us Walker was an only child."

"Yes, she did."

"But, after his parents died, he lived with an aunt and uncle in Fort Collins. Did she find any information about them having children?"

"I remember the conversation. She didn't even mention their names."

"I wonder."

"What, Michael?"

"If Walker's parents changed their last name, maybe the aunt and uncle did as well. They were professors at Colorado State University."

"We can sure check."

After getting Ben settled for the night, Nadia worked her laptop with Wolfe behind her drinking his beer. After using the link supplied by Joseph, she accessed Morgan Walker's personnel records. They found the notation in his file about growing up in Fort Collins after the death of his parents.

"I'll be damned, Nadia. Look at that." He pointed to

the name of his emergency contacts and their relationship to him. "It appears our General Walker has two cousins. One named Robert Alexander and the other Sara."

"Sounds like you ran into him in Kansas."

"It sure does." He paused for a moment. "Why does the name Sara Alexander sound familiar?"

Nadia recognized it as well and was already doing a search of the name. When the results appeared she said, "It sounds familiar because she is President Griffin's communications director."

"Son of a bitch." Wolfe glanced at his watch and then pulled out his cell phone.

Chapter Forty-Seven

WASHINGTON, DC

Joseph Kincaid's personal cell phone buzzed at 10:34 p.m. With a frown, he checked the caller ID and answered immediately. "I take it you found something, Michael?"

"Yeah. What is the name of Griffin's communications director?"

"Sara Alexander, why?"

"Is she from Fort Collins, Colorado?"

"Yes, I believe she is. What about her?"

"Ian and I ran into her brother in Kansas earlier today. He had General Morgan Walker's ID and cell phone. Guess who has his?"

"Shit."

"Yeah, that was my first reaction. It turns out, they are Walker's first cousins on his father's side. Secret Service needs to isolate her until I can get there to question her."

"I believe it would be better if Ryan Clark has a few of his trusted agents do that, Michael. Once she's in custody, you can question her using your Homeland Security alias."

"Fine with me. Can you handle getting this taken care of?"

"My next call will be to the president."

"I knew I could count on you. Thanks, Joseph."

At exactly 11:27 p.m., Sara Alexander was escorted out of her apartment under the watchful eyes of two female FBI agents. Once she disappeared inside the black Suburban SUV, she no longer held the position of White House communications director. Her absence the following day would be explained as needing to spend more time with her family.

At noon the next day, an average-height-and-weight male entered an interrogation room where the former White House aide sat. He introduced himself as Homeland Security Agent Patrick Ryan.

She said, "Why am I under arrest, Agent?"

"The fact is you are not under arrest, Ms. Alexander. You are being held due to your association with one Morgan Walker."

"I know of no such person."

Wolfe showed her a copy of Walker's military ID. "Ring any bells?"

Her eyes grew round for only a split second, then she caught herself and shook her head. "No."

"I see. Let me remind you of why you should remember this man. He is your biological cousin on your father's side. The two brothers immigrated to the US just before the Shah of Iran was overthrown. Their last name was Yazdani. Your father changed his name to Alexander and the brother changed his to Walker. Does that sound like something you've been told before?"

The woman shook her head.

"Anyway, this man"—Wolfe tapped the photo of the general— "met your brother in a small motel in the middle of nowhere Kansas and exchanged IDs. It's remarkable how much your brother and the general resemble each other." When she did not respond, he continued. "Your cousin is a fugitive. He has been charged with sedition and plotting to overthrow the US government."

"He's not a traitor, he's a patriot."

"I see. So, you do know him?"

She nodded.

"Where is he?"

"I have no idea."

"When was the last time you spoke to him?"

"It's been months."

Wolfe pressed a button on his cell phone. The conversation between Walker and her replayed. When it finished, he said, "That phone call was recorded three days ago."

She remained quiet.

"Ms. Alexander, you are facing life in prison or even the death penalty, if convicted. The evidence I've seen so far is fairly compelling as to your guilt. Now, any idea where I can find him?"

She clasped her hands in front of her, arms flat on the table. Her gaze did not deviate from the tabletop. "No."

Standing, Wolfe said, "That's too, bad. Cooperating with us would be considered a positive development."

Shifting her gaze to Wolfe, she said, "Look at the old family cabin in the Rocky Mountains."

"Where is it?"

"I'm sure someone has searched my apartment by now."

"They have."

"There is a safe deposit box key in my personal desk. It's taped to a card with instruction on access to the box. The deposit box contains the deed to the property. The location can be gleaned from it."

"Convenient."

"The cabin belongs to the family."

Wolfe turned to leave the room. Before he opened the door, she said, "You never asked why?"

Turning toward her, he said, "I personally don't care."

"My father and his brother were forced out of Iran. It was their home."

"Like I said, Ms. Alexander. I don't care." He closed the door as he left.

Wolfe sat at a conference table with the director of the FBI. Clark said, "Your friend from Kansas has been very helpful."

"He's not my friend." Raising an eyebrow, Wolfe asked, "How so?"

"When we explained to him why his cousin made the ID swap, he found religion. Apparently, Robert Alexander doesn't possess the mental agility of his sister. Walker's been taking advantage of him for years."

"Sorry to hear that. Does he know where the general is?"

"He's of the same opinion as the sister. He's probably retreated to a hunting cabin their father owned and willed to her on his passing."

"Does Bob remember where it is?"

"He told us he was never allowed to go. Safety with guns and all that." Clark paused. "Since you held up your end of the bargain and found him, want to complete the task?"

"Not particularly. Why?"

"Professional courtesy."

"The president still wants the FBI to be hands-off on this, doesn't he?"

Clark clasped his hands together. "He would like to see the whole mess swept under a rug."

"That doesn't sound like Griffin."

"Trust me, all politicians have an ego. Even the best of them. He likes his persona of no-drama. If I had to guess, I'd say this little incident scared him."

With a sly grin, Wolfe stood. "I hope he realizes not everyone likes him."

Clark nodded. "He's a realist, he does."

"As a favor to him, I'll finish the job."

"Thank you."

Just before Wolfe opened the door to leave, Clark's phone rang. He said, "Hang on, Michael. This call's from Joseph." He paused and said into the receiver, "Ryan Clark."

He was silent for a while. "Where in London?" More silence.

Wolfe stood next to the unopened door.

Pointing to the seat in front of his desk, Clarke motioned for Wolfe to sit again. "Okay, he's still here, I'll tell him." He ended the call and directed his attention to the retired CIA agent, who had not sat down. "Dimitri Petrov was spotted in London."

The retired Marine did not comment.

"Since you're going to Colorado, CIA wants McGill to go to London."

"Not sure that's a good idea."

"Why not?"

"He and Jonathan Chapman did not part on the best of terms."

"Chapman is the one who requested him."

"He's also the one who wanted him arrested and sent back to London some years ago." Wolfe paused. "I'm sure you're aware he was granted citizenship by Griffin right after that incident."

"Yes, I'm aware of that fact."

"I'm not going answer for Ian, have Chapman call him personally."

He turned and left the FBI director's office.

7,000 Feet Above the Central United States

"Why the bloody hell does he want me?" McGill's voice over the speakerphone in Wolfe's Baron B55 sounded thoroughly ticked off.

"Petrov's been located in London, so Chapman thought of you first."

"You go."

"Can't. Walker is in Colorado, and they want me there."

"Damnit, Michael, they're doing it to us again. We're both retired. A fact nobody seems to remember or care about. Hell, I'm also a US citizen."

"I reminded Director Clark about that. Here's the bottom line, Ian. The president's ego has been bruised because, all of a sudden, people are plotting against his presidency. And, guess what? Both of us owe him a favor."

McGill did not respond. Finally, he said, "Chapman needs to personally call me and grovel."

"I told them that. Although, I left the groveling part out."

"Good. When are you returning?"

"I'm over Ohio at the moment."

"Call me when you get back."

The call ended, and Wolfe dialed Nadia's cell phone. She answered almost immediately.

"Is everything, okay?"

"Yes."

"You never call me when you're flying."

"I normally don't have anything to say. However, you and I need to fly to Fort Collins, Colorado, tomorrow. See if Ben and Nova can stay with Alexia for a few days."

"He'll like that. Not sure about Nova."

"As long as she's with Ben, things will be fine. Besides, she's never been on a plane."

"Well, Michael, maybe it's time for her to experience flying."

"You want her to go with us, don't you?"

"Maybe."

He chuckled. "She would come in handy."

"See? I knew you'd approve."

Chapter Forty-Eight

COLORADO

The hunting cabin, owned by the estate of one Arman Alexander, received few visitors. At an altitude of 8,000 feet, it remained within the tree line and difficult to spot from low-flying planes or helicopters. This suited Morgan Walker perfectly. Built in the early sixties, the structure featured a few amenities the original owner found necessary. A large fireplace, a wood-burning cook stove, and an indoor toilet. Water, provided by a cistern, allowed for cold showers and a toilet flushing into a septic tank. Electricity was provided by solar panels added when Walker first started using the place.

As a place of solitude, the general cherished his time spent in the isolated location. A loner by nature, his career in the military suited his wanderlust.

During his stay, temperatures dipped into the upper thirties and low forties during the night. Walker spent most mornings splitting wood as fuel for the stove and fireplace. The physical exertion and solitude allowed him to reconstruct where his plans had gone astray. After several days of contemplating its failure, he concluded it had been perfect.

Having too many individuals with knowledge of his strategy probably resulted in its demise. Although, only he and Samantha Edgar knew the ultimate goal.

He stood on the front porch as the fading light of afternoon approached. Speaking to no one, he said, "Maybe it is time to find a new country. One that appreciates men with vision." He folded his arms as he listened to mountain sounds. The cry of a mountain lion off in the distance caused him to turn in the direction of the sound. "I agree, my friend. Predators need prey to pursue. In this country, too many have become sheep and are unworthy of the efforts of a true hunter." He turned and went inside.

Fort Collins, Colorado

Nadia Wolfe used her laptop to do a property search for Larimer County. Utilizing the owner's name function on the county property search website, she discovered where the hunting cabin owned by the estate of Arman Alexander was located.

Wolfe stood behind her as she worked. "I'm a little surprised Walker hasn't tried to hide who owns the property."

"Michael, someone would need to know the general is related to the Alexander name. If you didn't know, you wouldn't be able to do the search."

"How do we locate the property?"

"Using the property deed's legal description and the coordinates found on the county website, I'll do a search on Google Earth." After a few minutes, she found the location of the cabin. She zoomed in until the view was at a height of twenty meters. "It's hidden by trees, but you can barely see the front of the structure."

"Zoom in closer."

"It won't let me. In this location, there won't be a street view. No streets."

"Got it. Zoom out, I want to know how to get to it."

Nadia adjusted the view and then switched to map mode, which allowed her to create a step-by-step path to the cabin.

"I didn't know you could do something like that."

Turning her attention to her husband, Nadia smiled. "There's a lot you can do with the tools on the internet. You just have to know where to find them."

Tilting his head, he stared at the image on the screen. "So, technically, we can use this program to familiarize ourselves with the surrounding area and figure out a way to approach without being seen."

"More or less, in rural areas like where the cabin is, the view will be by satellite, with limited details."

He patted his wife on the shoulder. "That's a civilian satellite. Give me the longitude and latitude. Joseph will have access to a satellite image where we can count the leaves on the trees."

She wrote it on a piece of paper and handed it to him.

By the time they returned to the hotel room from dinner, Nadia's computer had received a link to multiple highly detailed images of the area surrounding Walker's cabin. Wolfe reviewed them. "We're set. But we'll need to do a little surveillance to see if he's there." He looked at Nova who lay in the middle of their hotel room, her head up, eyes closed, front paws crossed, and panting slightly. "You ready to help out tomorrow, girl?"

She opened her eyes and appeared to smile.

"Guess you are."

West of Fort Collins

Dressed in camo clothing picked up at a hunters' supply store in Fort Collins, Wolfe and Nadia parked their rented Jeep Wrangler several miles from the cabin owned by the family of General Walker. Nova, with her black-and-tan coat, blended into the landscape as well as the two humans.

Wolfe referred to the satellite pictures stored on a small tablet and guided the party to within several hundred yards of their destination. His training as a sniper aided the stealth of their approach.

The cabin itself sat next to a clearing. However, the bulk of the building remained hidden from prying eyes above by the forest canopy. After studying his surroundings for a few minutes, Wolfe whispered, "It appears abandoned."

Nadia nodded but remained quiet.

Turning to Nova, Wolfe said, "Alert."

The dog's ears perked, and she settled into a crouch, her head swiveling.

"Now what, Michael?"

The retired Marine took a prone position and said, "We watch."

The former Mossad agent followed her husband's lead and lay down next to him. The three settled in for a possible long wait. After an hour, Nadia asked, "Is this what being a sniper is about, Michael?"

He whispered, "Yes," not taking his eyes off the cabin.

As time marched on, the sun arrived at its zenith and

then slowly moved toward the west. Nothing in this part of the forest moved.

Checking the sky, Wolfe finally said, "Time to go." He had started to rise when Nova lowered her head and emitted a soft growl deep in her throat. Returning to his previous position, he said, "Something is up." Once again using his binoculars, he studied the area surrounding the structure.

They watched as a man approached the cabin from the west. He carried a tote bag and entered the small house. Wolfe said, "It's Walker. Let's go."

Slowly, the three moved away and retraced their steps back to the Jeep. Keeping his silence until they were back in the vehicle, he said, "Okay, we've established he's here."

Nadia smiled. "I take it you have a plan."

"None, whatsoever. Our task was to locate him." He sat behind the wheel and stared ahead. Taking a quick glance at his watch, he started the Jeep. Halfway down the mountain, he retrieved his cell phone from his cargo pants pocket. He thumbed in a number and waited.

The call was answered on the fourth ring. "What did you find, Michael?"

"He's at the cabin."

"You saw him?"

"I believe I just said that."

"Is he alone?"

"Unknown, we only saw him."

"Can you subdue him and bring him in?"

"Joseph, my instructions were to find him. We've found him."

There was silence on the phone call for a few moments. "Things have escalated since you left Washington."

"How so?"

358

"Samantha Edgar."

"Let me guess. She slipped out from under the watchful eyes of the FBI?"

"Yesterday morning. She was at a Days Inn near Quantico under twenty-four-hour guard. Somehow, she slipped out of a second-floor room in the middle of the night. No one knows how. You can imagine the agency's embarrassment. The president is furious."

"Why wasn't she in a detention center, Joseph?"

"Optics. Keeping her at a motel kept the news media from being suspicious."

"Sounds like Nadia and I need to wash our hands of this and go home."

"Sorry, Michael. As Homeland Security Agents, you have the authority to arrest Walker and bring him in."

"Joseph, need I remind you, our status as agents of Homeland Security is for hiding our real identity."

"Well, as far as the president is concerned, you two have the status to do so. Arrest him, Michael, and bring him in. Since you know where he is, do it quickly and quietly."

"And take him where?"

"Once you have him in custody, the FBI will take over. Communicate through me. I'll coordinate everything through Clark. The fewer individuals who know, the better."

"This whole situation gets stranger by the hour."

"I can't argue with you."

"We'll get back to you."

"Looking forward to it."

The call ended and Wolfe turned to Nadia. "We're Homeland Security agents again. Did you bring your ID?"

"I always have it when we leave the property."

"As do I." He concentrated on the mountain road

heading back to Fort Collins. "They want us to arrest Walker."

She chuckled. "And do what with him?"

"The FBI will collect him."

"Why don't they arrest him?"

"As Joseph said, they are trying to keep this out of the media."

"In other words, we don't exist."

"That's how I see it. I guess we go back early tomorrow morning and grab him before sunrise."

Chapter Forty-Nine

LONDON

A black Jaguar XF pulled up to the passenger departure zone at Heathrow International. Blackout windows obscured the passenger in the back seat. The driver, a man whose biceps stretched the fabric of his suit coat, wore sunglasses and an uninterested expression.

Ian McGill stepped off the curb, opened the rear passenger door, and slipped into the car. He tossed his duffle bag on the floor and shut the door. Immediately, the car pulled away and headed toward the airport exit.

Turning to the man sitting beside him, McGill said, "I want you to remember, I'm a US citizen."

Jonathan Chapman nodded and studied the former SAS soldier. "I'm aware of your status, Sergeant Major, and I want to thank you for coming. It's been a long time, Ian."

"Yes, sir. I apologize if you feel I've been disloyal, but I moved to the US because I have no family left here in the UK. In America, I have a beautiful piece of land with a warm house and a wife who I love and adore. I didn't have that here."

With a smile, Chapman looked ahead. "Disloyal would not be my word of choice. I have missed your wise counsel, old boy. Something I have found hard to replace in these troubled times."

The retired SAS sergeant smiled. "I understand Dimitri Petrov was spotted here in London."

"Two nights ago. One of our sources spotted him in a particular unfriendly pub in Chelsea. It's been confirmed he frequents the place. He always sits at the bar and confers with the same two individuals."

"What kind of mischief has he been up to?"

"Can't prove anything, but we suspect he's been involved in the disappearance of three MI5 agents."

"Three?"

"Yes."

"Why don't you pick him up?"

"Because, every time someone tries to follow him, he vanishes into the crowd. It's almost like he has a keen radar for detecting our people."

"You want me to tail him?"

"No, we want you to bring him in."

McGill chuckled. "And why do you think I can do that if no one has been able to so far?"

"Has he ever seen you?"

"Not to my knowledge."

"See, you're perfect for the job."

"What if he won't go quietly?"

Chapman glanced at the sergeant major. "Use your imagination."

"And then what?"

"You'll be on a plane for the States within the hour."

"No repercussions?"

"None whatsoever. Only His Majesty's gratitude and congratulations."

"Where's the pub?"

Sitting by himself at a corner table, McGill sipped on a Guiness as he observed the room. After spending the three previous evenings watching for Petrov in this particular pub, he suspected Chapman's intel about the ex-Stasi policeman might have been mistaken.

He threw a ten-pound note on the table and prepared to stand when he saw his target enter the pub. Settling back in his chair, he observed the man via a reflection in a mirror behind the bar.

Petrov ordered something from the bartender and then turned to the man he sat next to. At this distance, hearing the conversation would be an impossibility. But the body language told him they were talking in hushed tones. Each man leaned toward the other when they spoke.

With this revelation, McGill stood and sauntered out into the night. He took up station in a dark alcove across from the tavern.

Two hours later, Petrov exited the building. He paused as he lit a cigarette. After looking both ways, he turned and headed toward the River Thames four blocks from their location.

The East German used several tricks to ward off someone following, but McGill had seen them before. Eventually, the sergeant major observed his target enter what appeared to be an apartment building. He waited until a light appeared in a window on the third floor. Satisfied with his night's work, he made note of the address and the surroundings. Ten minutes later, he headed back to his car parked a block from the tavern.

As soon as he returned to his hotel room, he called Chapman. The retired SAS major said, "Did you find him?"

"Aye. He's staying in an apartment house within spitting distance of the River Thames."

"Do you know which apartment?"

"Third floor, fourth window on the southwest side, nearest the street."

"You're sure."

"Aye."

The call went silent for a few moments. "Ian, do you want to be in on the raid?"

"Nah. I'll wait outside and see if he gives you boys the slip."

"Be back at the apartment at 3:00 a.m. I'll let MI5 know you are there."

"Aye."

When McGill arrived at the apartment building, he was greeted by an old SAS friend. "I was told you would be here, Ian. How are you involved?"

The two men shook hands. "I followed him here. Didn't know you were with MI5, Bobby."

"Had to do something exciting. What about you?"

"Moved to the States to help a friend, fell in love, and retired."

"Yet, here you are."

"Yes, here I am. Apparently, I have a hard time saying no to an old major I served under." He looked at the apartment and asked, "Where are you with surveillance?"

"We've slipped a camera under the front door and took a picture. Is this the man you followed?" The MI5 agent offered a small tablet with a picture on the screen.

"Aye, that's him. His name is Dimitri Petrov. Nasty bloke. I chased him around the States earlier this year."

Glancing at his watch, Bob said, "We're going to breach the front door in fifteen minutes."

"I'll stay right here."

"Chicken?"

"No. I've had my share of things that go boom. I'll be content here."

McGill's friend laughed and patted him on the shoulder. "Suit yourself. See you after the fireworks."

Standing in a dark alcove across from the apartment building, the retired sergeant major watched the window he knew to be Petrov's. He saw a flash and then heard a muffled roar. More flashes of light and gunfire broke the stillness of early morning.

Training took over, and McGill dashed toward the front door of the apartment building. Flinging it open, boiling smoke billowed down the stairwell and hall. Screams from the wounded reminded the sergeant major of his days in the Middle East during the height of the Second Gulf War.

Taking the stairs two at a time, he arrived on the third floor to see men bleeding heavily from gaping wounds. He searched for anyone who still seemed alive. He found one; it was his friend, Bobby.

"McGill…"

"Don't talk, Bob. I'll try to stop the bleeding."

"The door. The door was booby trapped. He knew someone was coming. How?"

"Stay with me, Bob."

The man stared at McGill, but the light in his eyes faded, and he grew still.

Later in the Day

"Seven dead." Chapman paced behind his desk. McGill sitting in the chair in front watched but remained still. The MI6 director stopped pacing. "Any sign of Petrov?"

"No, the apartment appeared abandoned."

"What's your assessment?"

"You won't like what I'm going to say."

"I might not, but I respect your opinion."

"MI5 has a leak."

"I would have to agree. Any idea where he might have gone?"

"No, but I know someone I can ask."

"Who?"

"His buddy at the pub. I'm heading over there after you and I finish here."

"Keep me informed."

The clock above the bar proclaimed the time to be twelve minutes past nine. McGill, sitting at the same table in the back of the room, watched the man he intended to question enter the bar. He sat at the same barstool as he had the previous night. The spot occupied by Petrov remained empty.

McGill rose and sauntered over to the bar and sat next to the newcomer. He said to the barman, "Guiness." With a nod, the attendant moved down the bar to fill a glass. Glancing at his neighbor, he noticed the man had what appeared to be scotch, neat. He drained it in one gulp and waved the glass just as the bartender sat the Guiness down.

The man sitting next to McGill said, "Another house scotch."

The barman grabbed the empty glass and headed toward a shelf of whiskey.

McGill took a swig of his Guiness. "Now, this is the nectar of the gods."

"Too bitter for me."

"Aye, but ya get used to it."

The man drinking scotch stared at McGill for a while. "I've never seen you here."

"Been sitting at a table. Saw a vacant seat, so I chose to sit here."

"The chap who normally sits there won't be back."

"Huh. Fortunate for me. Did he say why?"

The bartender placed the new drink in front of the scotch drinker. Picking it up, the man shook his head. "No. He was a strange one. Had a German accent and disliked London. My guess is he went back to Germany."

"Well, good luck to him."

The two men sat in silence for several minutes. Finally, the scotch drinker said, "He said something a little odd the last time I saw him."

"Oh?"

"Yeah, something about he'd be leaving with a bang. It sounded odd at the time. Like I said, he was a strange one."

"Sounds like it."

———————

McGill left the pub a little before ten without learning anything else about Petrov. After walking out the front of the pub, he noticed movement across the street. In the blackness of an alcove, he saw the glow of a cigarette as someone inhaled. Turning toward his parked rental, he slowed his pace and occasionally wobbled, just a bit, to mimic the walk of an inebriated patron.

He kept tabs on the person's whereabouts using their reflection in car windows parked along the street. Whoever it was, crossed to McGill's side of the street and quickened their step. The retired SAS sergeant major stopped and leaned against a van. In the reflection, he saw the man narrowing the gap between them. He also saw a dark-colored blackjack in the man's hand, and he wore a dark balaclava.

As the attacker drew near, he raised his hand with the weapon and began to swing when McGill twirled around and planted a fist in the man's stomach. At the same time, he raised his left hand to stop the downswing of the weapon while his right elbow crashed into the assailant's jaw.

The man dropped to the sidewalk like a puppet with its strings cut. Reaching down, McGill ripped the balaclava off his head. Dimitri Petrov's unconscious face could be seen in the streetlights. The retired SAS sergeant major rolled the body over and he secured the man's hands with his belt.

Taking his cell phone out, he made a call to Chapman. The call was answered on the second ring. McGill said, "Guess who I just ran into."

Chapter Fifty

3:55 a.m.

Utilizing hands-free night-vision goggles purchased at a sporting goods mega store in Fort Collins, Wolfe and Nadia navigated the wooded land south of General Walker's cabin. With the dim light from a waning quarter moon, Nova kept herself between them.

When they were a hundred yards from the small structure, Wolfe signaled Nadia to move toward the left side. He patted his left leg, the dog's signal to stay with him.

The cabin remained dark. The stillness of the night broken only by creatures of the forest. Clouds played hide-and-seek with the moon as Wolfe grew nearer. He heard a squelch in his earpiece as Nadia announced she was in position to provide backup, should he need it.

Placing his left palm in front of Nova, she remained next to Wolfe's left leg. His right hand held an IWI Mini-Uzi given to him by Josef Rubin on his last trip to Israel. The compact gun handled better in confined spaces and

369

exerted more lethal force than a pistol. He prepared to advance farther toward the cabin door when Nova's head abruptly turned in the direction of Nadia. The dog immitted a soft whine, and Wolfe said, "Go."

After leaving Wolfe and Nova, Nadia made her way to the west side of the cabin. Using the satellite pictures, they had determined a convenient spot for her to provide backup. A small clump of white birch trees, twenty yards from the structure, provided cover and good visibility of the rear, side, and front. When she felt comfortable with her position, she keyed her microphone once to tell Wolfe she was in position. Even knowing where he was, she did not have visibility of her husband.

A twig snapped behind her, and she spun to see what appeared to be a large caliber pistol five feet from her position.

"Well, well, if isn't Nadia Picard."

She recognized the voice. "Samantha Edgar. What are you doing here?"

"I suppose I could ask you the same thing. But I know what you're doing. Sneaking up on the general." Edgar paused and clicked off the safety. "If you're here, that means your meddlesome husband is as well."

Nadia kept her attention on the woman.

Lifting a cell phone to her lips, she said, "We have company."

"Who is it?"

"The Picard woman."

"Kill her."

Through the green-hue image, Nadia saw Samantha

smile as she inserted her finger in the trigger guard. A flash of dark and lighter hues pushed the gun away just as Edgar's finger finished putting pressure on the trigger. The gunshot broke the morning silence as the bullet shattered a window on the cabin's west side.

Nova growled as she clamped down hard on Edgar's forearm. Nadia heard two snaps as the dog's powerful jaws broke both the ulna and radius bones in the woman's arm. Her screams of pain echoed in the broken early morning quiet of the forest.

Still wearing her NVGs, Nadia scooped up the Springfield Armory 1911 .45 ACP and pointed it at the struggling ex-CIA agent. Nadia said, "Release."

Nova released Samantha and went to Nadia's side.

"Get up, Sam."

"That dog almost killed me."

"No, if she had wanted to kill you, you'd be dead. Now, stand up."

"That dog is dangerous. It needs to be put down."

"Actually, she is very gentle, except when someone points a gun at her family."

Wolfe appeared behind Samantha. "Where's Walker?"

"I have no idea."

Looking at Nova, the retired Marine said, "Seek."

The dog turned and ran toward the cabin.

The ex-CIA woman said, "I'm bleeding here. Some help."

Wolfe grabbed her shoulder and pushed her to a kneeling position. "Tough shit. You can bleed out as far as I'm concerned. Where's Walker?"

"Who?"

Wolfe pointed the Uzi at the woman. "Are you sure you want to play that game?"

"I have no idea what you're talking about."

Early dawn lightened the sky in the east enough that Wolfe did not need his NVGs. He flipped them up and knelt beside Edgar. Staring her in the eye, he said, "If Nova had not stopped you, Nadia would probably be dead. That would have pissed me off, and you would also be dead. Now, my patience is running thin, and I don't have time to argue with you any longer. One more time, where is Walker?"

She stared at Wolfe but did not reply. He whistled once. Ten seconds later, Nova stood by his left leg.

Edgar stiffened. "What's the dog going to do?"

"Eat you. If you move." He touched the German shepherd's head, and she looked up, her brown eyes inquisitive. Wolfe said, "Guard."

"What about my arm? It's broken."

"You started this. Now you have to pay the price. Remember I told you not to move. Be sure you don't." He turned to Nadia who, at the moment, tried desperately to hide her grin. "Let's check out the cabin."

Ten minutes later, after searching the empty cabin, Wolfe turned to Nadia. "He's gone. It appears Samantha's been here for a while."

"I would agree, Michael." She started opening drawers in the small kitchen area. "Uh, oh. Guess what I just found." She pointed to two cell phones. "Those are Tracfones. Prepaid with no contract."

"Makes sense. Can you tell anything about them?"

She picked one up, punched numbers, and studied the screen. "Last call was to a Washington, DC phone eighteen hours ago." She studied the phone. "Alexia could tell us whose number it is."

Wolfe offered his wife his satellite phone. "Be my guest."

"Are we on Mountain Time here?"

"Yes." He glanced at his watch. "It's almost seven at home."

She made the call. "Hi, Alexia. Can you check a phone number for us?" Silence. "Thanks." After reciting the number, she said, "I'll wait." Five minutes later, she said, "Again, thanks, Alexia. Sorry to bother you so early." The call ended. She said, "It's a number at the George Bush Center for Intelligence in Langley, Virginia. It belongs to the CIA."

Wolfe grinned. "Of course it does."

Southwest Missouri

The FBI took custody of Samantha Edgar at the airport in Fort Collins. Wolfe, Nadia, and Nova flew back to their property and arrived in the late afternoon. Both were tired, but Nadia took the Jeep and drove to Stockton to pick up Ben. Wolfe stayed behind to make phone calls. He climbed the stairs in the hangar to his second-floor office. After checking the security system, he made his first call.

"Joseph, we've identified a phone number called by Walker's at least five times in the past week. He did it from a burner phone."

"Whose number, is it?"

"I'm pretty sure this information is way above my clearance."

Joseph did not respond.

Wolfe continued. "As the director of the CIA."

"Acting director."

"As the acting director of the CIA, you won't like my answer."

"I'll have to live with it. Again, whose number, is it?"

"It is a cell phone owned by the CIA."

"Damn." Joseph sighed and said, "Give me the number."

Wolfe recited it. "Walker bugged out about twelve hours before we did our early morning raid on the cabin. However, Samantha Edgar was there. We turned her over to the FBI."

"Where's Walker?"

"Don't know. But my guess is the person he called would." He waited a moment. "What's going on, Joseph? How many individuals are involved with this conspiracy?"

"That's a question I need answered. Let me get back to you."

A chime on his security system showed the location of a possible intruder. Normally, it meant a four-legged trespasser, but he needed to check it out just the same. Initiating the camera indicated by the signal, he saw nothing at first. The camera fifteen feet above the ground showed shadows due to the lateness of the hour. He switched it to low-light mode and saw the intruder. A man dressed in forest camo stood next to a tree. He held a high-powered rifle.

He grabbed his cell phone and dialed Nadia. When she answered he said, "Where are you?"

"I just got to Alexia's, why?"

"Have a cup of coffee and don't come home just yet. I'll call you back."

"Michael, what's going on?"

"We have a guest." He ended the call and whistled for Nova. The dog trotted into his office and sat next to him. Scratching her head, he said, "Our work for the day isn't done yet, girl."

The equipment he kept in his second-floor office was far superior to the civilian-grade equipment they purchased in Fort Collins. He gathered the NVGs, forest camo clothing, comm link, and his Barrett .50 caliber sniper rifle while he followed the intruder's progress. After checking which cameras were tripped, he could tell the man had gained access on the northwest corner of the property. Between the hangar's location and where Wolfe knew the man to be, a half a mile of thick Ozark woods existed.

Residing in this particular half mile would be numerous trip wires and military-grade night cameras sensitive to movement. When the retired Marine finished donning his wardrobe, he would be invisible once he entered the tree line.

Ten minutes later, he and Nova entered the eastern wooded area and moved toward where he suspected the intruder would appear. He listened for sounds of someone disturbing leaves and twigs. He heard nothing. Nova neither heard nor sensed anything because she lay in her normal position, not her alert pose.

After waiting ten minutes, without hearing what he expected, a thought occurred to him. "Shit." He backed out of the tree line and made a dash toward the door leading to his second-floor command center. At the bottom of the stairs, he made the hand signal for Nova to stay. She hesitated but remained where she was and watched him climb.

When he got to the top of the stairs, he froze. General Morgan Walker stood inside his conference room with a Glock 21 pointed at the retired Marine's chest.

"Nice setup, Wolfe. I've heard about it, but didn't think it would be this elaborate."

Wolfe said nothing. He leaned against the doorframe with his left arm hidden.

"Where's the family?"

"Not here."

"I can see that. Your Jeep is missing. Where are they?"

"Do you really expect me to tell you?"

"Not really. Thought I would try. You know, you've cost me a lot of money, personnel, and planning time."

Wolfe shrugged.

"It's gonna cost you."

Making a gesture with his left hand, Wolfe signaled for Nova to advance up the stairs. When he felt her at his heels, he looked at Walker. "The FBI has you on their most wanted list. Edgar is now their guest in Colorado, and your contact at the CIA has been compromised."

The general's face grew crimson and he raised the Glock.

Ducking behind the wall, he yelled, "Contain."

Nova sprang through the door and, before Walker could adjust his aim down, she clamped her jaws hard on his gun arm. The Glock rattled to the floor and Wolfe dove for it.

Chapter Fifty-One

SOUTHWEST MISSOURI

Christian County Sheriff Blake Perry took Wolfe aside and asked, "What happened, Michael?"

"You want the official story or the truth?"

With a chuckle, Perry continued. "Tell me the truth and then I can listen to the official story."

Wolfe pointed to the young man coordinating FBI agents. "You and I have nothing to do with the official story. That man will handle the details." He smiled. "The victim was a director at the National Security Agency who was running a—"

"Stop right there, I'll defer to the official story. Did you kill him?"

Taking a deep breath, Wolfe nodded. "He surprised me in my office. I fell for the oldest trick in the universe. A fake intruder in the northwest section of my land. By the time I figured it out, he had already made his way to my second-floor office. When I got there, he wanted to know where Nadia and Ben were. Thank gawd they were in Stockton at the time.

"Anyway, I taunted him, and he pulled the Glock on me. Nova rushed in, broke his arm, and he dropped the gun."

"That's when you grabbed it and shot him, right?"

"No, that's when he pulled a smaller caliber pistol from an ankle holster and fired a shot at Nova. That's when I shot him."

"So, you were protecting your dog?"

Wolfe flashed a small smile. "No, I was ending the life of a terrorist. Long story, Blake. But yes, I was fighting for Nova. She's saved Nadia's life, and now mine. She's part of the family."

"Okay, I can work with that." Blake turned and wandered toward the gaggle of reporters and the spokesman for the FBI.

While watching the sideshow, Wolfe's cell phone vibrated. After checking the caller ID, he answered, "Wolfe."

"I understand Walker paid you a visit."

"He did."

"And?"

"Let's put it this way, Joseph. He won't be causing you or the president any more trouble."

"Did you, do it?"

"He shot at Nova and me."

"Where?"

"He was in my second-floor conference room above the hangar."

"Okay, you're covered under the castle doctrine." He paused. "The phone number belonged to an analyst in the North America division. She was reporting to Walker as part of her job and apparently oblivious to the overall plot."

"What kind of hold did he have over these women, Joseph?"

"All I can tell you is Samantha confessed to having an affair with him. She's being transferred to Quantico this afternoon."

"I hope this was the end of it."

"Me, too. The president is very thankful for your help."

"Remind him, Nadia and I are retired."

Joseph laughed. "I'll remind him."

The phone call ended, and Wolfe reached down to scratch Nova's head. "You earned your keep this week, girl."

The dog just panted and appeared to smile.

―――――――

By the time Nadia and Ben returned, only a few county sheriff's cars remained. Wolfe met her and their son at the back door, and they embraced. Ben giggled as Nova licked his face, and the two ran off to his room.

"Is it over, Michael?"

"I certainly hope so."

"Has anyone determined what the general was trying to do?"

"If they have, they've not enlightened me."

She returned to the deck, folded her arms, and stared up at the stars overhead. He stood behind her, his arms around her waist. She said, "Are we ever going to be safe here, Michael?"

"Yes."

"How can you be so sure?"

He rested his chin on the top of her head. "I'm not ready to give up on this place yet, Nadia. It feels like home now."

"Yes, to me as well."

"I think we'll be fine if certain people would stop assuming we want to help."

"Stop raising your hand every time someone asks for volunteers." She placed her hands on his. They stayed like that for several minutes. "Alexia asked me if I wanted to work for her. She's been impressed with how much I've learned on the computer." She turned in his arms and looked up at him. "What do you think?"

"Sounds like a heck of an opportunity. Maybe you can learn how to hide us from satellites."

She gave him a puzzled look.

"You remember when you first got here, Alexia's business partner was able to hide my land in Howel County from satellites."

With a faint smile, she said, "I do, now that you mention it."

"So, I say, take advantage of this opportunity and learn as much as you can."

Embracing her husband, she placed her head on his chest. "I think I will."

Epilogue

WHITE HOUSE

A Month Later

Joseph escorted Wolfe, Nadia, and Nova into the oval office. As soon as the door shut behind them, the newly confirmed CIA director smiled.

"The president will be here shortly. He's heard so much about Nadia and Nova, he's looking forward to meeting both of you."

Nova stood next to Wolfe's left leg. He gave her a hand signal to stay. She sat and panted.

Nadia said, "This is my first time to visit the White House. It's smaller than it looks on TV."

The director smiled. "The magic of electronic media." He paused and asked, "Would either of you like coffee?"

Both Wolfe and Nadia shook their heads.

At that moment, President Roy Griffin entered the room from the hall where his private office resided. He turned to his chief of staff and said, "Hold my calls. I'll let you know when I'm available again."

"Yes, sir." The man returned to the hall and closed the door behind him.

Griffin walked up to Nadia and offered his hand. "Mrs. Wolfe, I am honored to meet you."

Nadia's cheeks grew crimson as she shook his hand. "Sir, the honor is mine."

POTUS turned to Michael. "Thanks to both of you, Michael. This country is in your debt, once again."

With a slight smile, Wolfe said, "Our pleasure, sir."

"Please, let's sit." Griffin moved to the wood rocker, made famous by John F. Kennedy, and sat. Wolfe and Nadia sat on the sofa facing him. Directing his attention to the German shepherd, the president said, "This must be Nova."

At the mention of her name, the dog tilted her head. She looked at Griffin and then at Wolfe. He touched her head. "It's okay, girl. Friend."

Nova appeared to display a smile, lay down, and crossed her paws.

"She likes you, sir."

After admiring the canine, the president turned his attention to his guests. "Joseph told me you can give me an update on the Walker affair."

"I'm sure the CIA can provide more details, sir."

"Yes, but I wanted to hear it from you, Michael. You and your wife were the ones with the most at risk. I want your perspective."

Glancing at Nadia, Wolfe returned his attention to the president. "Well, sir, per your agreement with Uri Ben-David, Ian McGill and myself were successful back in May. You know the details of our brief journey to the mountains of Azerbaijan. Unfortunately, the Iranians discovered why the helicopter crashed. This caused a cascade of events. When the list was first circulated by the Iranians, there were only ten names on it. Those were individuals they felt might have been responsible for the crash."

Griffin frowned. "This is news."

"Yes, sir. General Morgan Walker became aware of the list through his division of the NSA. This occurred at the time Dwight King's health started to decline. With King's attention diverted, Walker learned about the list and usurped it for his own purposes. Samantha Edgar, who at the time was having an affair with the general, helped him devise a plan to undermine your presidency. She also had a plan to introduce him to the public as a better candidate for the office."

"Huh. So, there was a real list?"

"Yes, sir. From notes found in Walker's mountain cabin, we found the original list. Ian's and my name were not on it. The general is the one who added Nadia's and my name plus a few others." He paused, waiting for the president to ask a question. When none came, Wolfe continued. "I never understood why Samantha Edgar gave the information to William Fischer. She refuses to discuss the matter.

"We can only speculate, but Fischer must have known the information would be explosive if leaked. He hid the flash drive in a safe deposit box and mailed Joseph an envelope with the key and instructions on how to retrieve it. I flew to Washington and did so.

"This was about the time Senator Hendricks was drawn into the plot by Walker. They knew Emma Elliot would be an individual they could manipulate once she was director of the CIA. What they did not know was she had her own agenda. A major mistake on their part."

POTUS took a deep breath. "And I assisted at this stage."

Wolfe gave the president a grim smile. "I'm not sure that

was a bad thing, sir. Elliot unintentionally drew attention to the plot. From that point forward, the success of the conspiracy depended on zero attention. That didn't happen. The other mistake made by Walker was letting his ego get in his way. He recruited too many individuals with knowledge of what was going on. This almost single-handedly became his downfall."

Griffin rocked the chair with slow back and forth movements, but he did not say a word.

Wolfe continued. "If you had not nominated Elliot to the office of directorship, the plot might have been overlooked and secretly executed. We would be having a totally different discussion."

Joseph spoke for the first time since Wolfe started his narrative. "Sir, the bottom line is all of Walker's conspirators have been uncovered and are in custody."

"What about this Petrov character?"

Wolfe smiled. "With the help of Ian McGill, MI6 took him into custody in London about a month ago. Ian was put on a plane and returned to the US that night."

"What happened to Petrov?"

Wolfe shrugged.

"So, he's no longer a threat?"

"Jonathan Chapman would be the one to answer that question, sir."

The president remained silent for a few moments as he contemplated the situation. Finally, he smiled. "What can I do for you two? This country owes you a debt of gratitude. But I would rather the public not know the details."

Nadia said, "The only thing we would ask, sir, is to be left alone."

Griffin pursed his lips. "I understand and will do my best to adhere to your wishes. But…"

Wolfe landed the Baron and parked it in the hangar a little after noon the next day. Nova scampered out to find a tree. Before getting out, Nadia turned to her husband. "Do you think we can stay retired this time?"

"I certainly hope so. But with politicians, you never know."

"I noticed. We didn't exactly get a commitment from him to abide by our wishes either, did we?"

"No, we didn't."

The cell phone in his back pocket vibrated. He retrieved it and studied the Caller ID. Accepting the call, he said, "Wolfe." After listening for a few minutes, he rolled his eyes. "Jerry, does the president not understand the word retired?" He listened for a few more minutes. As he did, he looked at his wife. She crossed her arms and frowned.

Taking a deep breath, he said into the phone. "When did this happen?"

Also by J.C. Fields

vinci-books.com/seankruger1

A murder with no witnesses. A suspect with no identity. A truth worth killing for.

FBI Special Agent Sean Kruger is hunting a ghost. The suspect in a high-profile Wall Street murder doesn't exist, and every witness account is suspiciously identical. As Kruger digs deeper, he realizes he's not the only one searching—someone else wants the truth buried for good.

Turn the page for a free preview…

The Fugitive's Trail: Chapter One

After descending from the thirty-fourth floor, the elevator doors opened revealing an expansive deserted lobby. Glass and steel comprised the front wall from floor to the top of the atrium four stories above. Crystal chandeliers hung from the ceiling, adding a note of elegance to the otherwise industrial look of the lobby. A firm hand on the man's back pushed him out of the elevator toward the building's entrance.

Two security guards escorted the man. Both were big and muscular, biceps stretching the material of their dark gray suits. One was slightly taller and on the right of the man. The other guard was shorter, to his left and slightly in front. The only other occupant of the lobby, besides the three men walking toward the front door, was at the security desk. He was a tall young black man dressed in a dark blue blazer, white shirt, and tie. He nodded at the guards as they escorted the guest toward the front door.

The man being escorted could see through the front glass a black Suburban waiting at the curb—the same vehicle he had been pushed into earlier in the morning. As the guard in front reached to open one of the building's front doors, he was turned slightly toward the guest, exposing his weapon.

While the guard's attention was trained on opening the door, the guest's left hand extracted the Glock from the belt holster on the man's right hip. At the same time he was reaching for the gun, his right leg lifted. With as much force as he could, he kicked at the leg of the taller guard behind him. His shoe slammed into the kneecap of the man's left leg, which bent in the wrong direction and the guard collapsed screaming in pain.

His left hand, which now held the Glock, rose and the trigger was pulled twice. The shorter guard was forced back against the adjacent glass door and collapsed. The now unescorted man rushed through the door in front of him, turned to his right, and ran.

Before the guard at the front desk could get out of his chair, the entire incident was over. The man had disappeared into the crowd on the street.

The lobby guard hurried over to the two men on the floor, saw a pool of blood spreading under the shorter guard. The taller guard was writhing on the floor, trying to straighten his now ruined left leg. Hurrying back to his desk, he picked up a phone and dialed 911.

———

The driver of the black Suburban sat stunned as he watched the man rush out of the building, turn right, and disappear into the midday crowd. He slammed the Suburban into park, opened the door, and rushed into the building. As soon as he was through the front doors, he stopped.

His first sight was the carnage of the dead man slumped against the glass and the shattered leg of the other. At the same time, his cell phone rang. Glancing at the caller ID, he sighed. The pending conversation would not be pleasant.

Staring out the window of his thirty-fourth floor office, Abel Plymel realized he had made a hasty decision, a decision made in anger. He needed the man alive.

Turning back to his desk, Plymel picked up his cordless phone and dialed the cell phone of one of his security guards. It went unanswered, totally unacceptable. He paid them to answer their phones twenty-four seven.

He dialed the cell phone of the second guard, no answer. Finally he called his driver, who answered on the fourth ring. His eyes grew wide as he listened then suddenly threw the handset at his office door.

The Fugitive's Trail: Chapter Two

KANSAS CITY, MO

Standing in the front room of the now empty house, it seemed alien to him. Not the place where he'd raised his son. Looking around the room, he smiled, opened the front door, and stepped out. He twisted the knob to make sure it was locked, closed it, and walked to his new car parked in the driveway, a Ford Mustang. Sitting in the driver's seat, he stared at the house for several minutes before making a call on his cell phone. It was answered on the second ring. He said, "Sandra, this is Sean Kruger."

"Sean, I was just about to call you. Did the cleaning service do a nice job?"

"Yes, they did. They left about ten minutes ago. Thank you for recommending them. Please let the Carsons know I'm out of the house a day early."

"They'll be thrilled. Have I told you how much they love the house?"

"Several times, Sandra."

"And the neighborhood, their little girl is already planning sleepovers—"

"Sorry, Sandra, I don't have a lot of time. I just wanted to tell you my keys are on the breakfast bar in the kitchen."

Sandra was quiet for a second and then said, "I'll give the Carsons a call and let them know."

"Thank you for all your help these past few months. I wish I could talk longer, but I'm late for an appointment."

"You're more than welcome. Why don't you call me after you settle into your new condo. We can have dinner." She paused for half a second. "My treat."

Hesitating for a few seconds, he finally said, "I'll do that." Although he knew he never would. He ended the call and smiled. Sandra O'Dell was a nice person and a very good real estate agent. But, if he had not cut her off, she would still be chattering about sleepovers. As for the dinner, the thought of listening to her for several hours made him shiver.

He sat in the car for a few seconds, then opened the door and stood up to look at the house one last time. It had been his home for seventeen years. A lot of good memories were here: his parents moving in to help raise his then one-year-old son, the joy of watching them interact with their grandson on a daily basis, watching a little boy turn into a bright and talented young man. There were also sad memories.

Finally, after staring at the house for several minutes, he sat back down in the car, started the engine, backed out of the driveway, and accelerated the Mustang toward his new home. It was the first day of a new chapter in his life.

The condo was a newly renovated two-bedroom unit on the west side of the Kansas City Plaza. The extra bedroom would serve as his office and a place for his son Brian to sleep when home from college. One of the reasons he had chosen this particular unit was the open living space. The living, kitchen, and dining area were all one room separated only by a breakfast bar in the kitchen. But the main reason he liked the place was the balcony. It had a clear view of the Plaza, which was spectacular at night.

Fifteen minutes later, the Mustang was parked in his designated parking slot. It was approaching dusk and the shadows from adjacent buildings were growing long. He sat quietly in the car and thought about the hectic and emotional four months since his mother's death. The doctors had told Kruger it was a heart attack, but he disagreed. He had a Ph.D. in psychology and knew the mind was far more complicated than most people imagined. His father and mother had been married for sixty years, marrying right after high school. Something died inside his mother when his father passed away two years ago. She would put on a happy face and say nothing was wrong. But Kruger could tell she was hurting. Finally, after Brian moved away for college, she quietly passed away one night in her sleep.

Even as a non-practicing Catholic, Kruger believed in a hereafter. He was comforted with the concept of his mother and father together again. But occasionally doubt crept into his faith. As one of the FBI's premiere profilers, he had seen the darkest recesses of the human psyche. And sometimes he wondered how a benevolent God would allow such terrors to occur. But that was for religious philosophers to debate, not him.

As he opened the car door, he heard a woman scream, "Let go of me, you bastard."

His first reaction was to draw his service pistol, a Glock 19, and run in the direction of the voice. As he rounded the northwest corner of the building, he saw two muscular, tattooed young men: one white and the other black. The black guy was holding a woman by the arms as the white guy dug through her purse. Kruger was fifteen yards away when he stopped. Taking a Weaver stance, he yelled, "FBI, on the ground *now*."

The black guy was startled and released the woman, who quickly ran toward Kruger. The white guy turned around, stared at Kruger, and said, "Shiiiittttt, you ain't no FBI. Show me a badge, mutafukr."

Kruger yelled again, "*On the ground now!*"

The black guy looked at Kruger and then at his partner. He appeared to be choosing whether to get on the ground or run. The white guy threw the purse on the ground. Reached behind his back and pulled out a snub-nosed revolver. As the guy raised the revolver in his direction, Kruger didn't hesitate and fired the Glock twice. Both shots hit their target. The white guy dropped the revolver and grabbed his chest. Two circles of red appeared high on his chest and shoulder. He dropped to his knees and then fell back. The black guy bolted in the opposite direction as fast as he could. Kruger quickly moved to the fallen gun and kicked it aside, still pointing his Glock at the man on the ground.

He looked back at the woman, saw she was okay, and reached for his cell phone. He punched in 911 as he trained the Glock on the prone assailant. He said to the operator, "My name is Sean Kruger; I'm a special agent with the FBI. I have shots fired and a man down. I need an ambulance and a squad car." He was asked for the address, which he gave and ended the call.

The white kid stared up at him with wide eyes. The blood loss was moderate. Kruger did not offer assistance and kept the Glock pointed at the man. Within five minutes, a patrol car arrived and one of the two officers told Kruger to drop his weapon and stand aside. Kruger complied, laying the Glock on the ground. He put his hands above his head and backed up ten steps. One patrolman checked the wounded man, and the other officer cuffed Kruger and led him to their squad car.

Within ten minutes, five patrol cars and two ambulances occupied the parking lot of Kruger's new condo. He watched from the back seat of the patrol car as the wounded man was placed on a gurney and loaded into one of the ambulances. As it sped away, a Kansas City police sergeant opened the squad car's back door and leaned in.

"You want to tell me how you got involved."

Kruger stared at the police officer and said, "The lady was in trouble, I helped her out."

"You live around here?"

"Yes, second floor, apartment A."

The sergeant continued to stare at Kruger. "Lady lives on the second floor also and she's never seen you before."

"Because I just moved in today, *sergeant*." Kruger spat out the police officer's title with as much sarcasm as he could muster. "Are you going to take these cuffs off?"

"Not yet, just cool your heels." The sergeant shut the door and walked away.

Sitting back in the seat with his hands cuffed behind him was difficult and uncomfortable, but he managed. Dusk had turned to night and the area was bathed in the artificial glow of street lamps, police car headlights and the rotating blues and reds of their emergency light bars. Finally after another fifteen minutes elapsed, a man in a suit opened the door.

"You Kruger?"

Nodding, "Yes, who are you?"

"Detective McAdams. Get out."

Swinging his legs out of the squad car, Kruger leaned forward and stood. McAdams reached around and unlocked the cuffs. "Sorry about the cuffs, Agent Kruger. Your story checks out."

Kruger rubbed his wrists, trying to get the feeling back. He said, "May I talk to the victim?"

The detective shrugged and nodded his head in her direction. "Suit yourself, you're free to go."

As he was walking toward the woman, she rushed to him, hugged him, and said, "Thank you. I'm not sure what would have happened if you hadn't come along."

Surprised by her embrace, he limply returned the hug and said, "Glad you weren't hurt. My name's Sean Kruger."

The woman backed away, smiled, and said, "I'm Stephanie. I really don't know how to thank you, Sean. I've never been in a situation like this."

"Well, to be honest with you, it's a first for me too."

Stephanie smiled and said, "One of the officers asked me if you lived around here. I've never seen you before. Do you?"

Nodding, Kruger said, "I bought 2A and just moved in today."

She stared at him for a few seconds and said, "I moved into 2B a week ago, but I've been out of town on business. I had just gotten home from the airport when those two grabbed me. Hope this isn't a common occurrence around here."

Shaking his head, he said, "This can happen anywhere. It's safe—at least that's what I was told."

She smiled. "Good, I like the area. And with a good-looking FBI agent living next door, I feel even more secure."

Kruger returned the smile. It had been a long time since

he had enjoyed a conversation with a woman. The conversation felt out of place in this situation, but he didn't care. He immediately liked her. She was a petite woman in her late thirties or early forties, several years younger than he was. She was strikingly beautiful, with naturally curly brown hair she wore touching her shoulders. Her pale blue eyes sparkled in the streetlights of the parking lot, and her smile was infectious. Realizing he was staring, he said, "I'm glad you feel safer." He chuckled. "Hell of a way to meet your new neighbor."

She brushed the hair off her forehead, tucked her newly returned purse under her arm, looked up at him and smiled. She said, "It will be a great story to tell our grandchildren." She walked over to the police sergeant, thanked him, and headed toward the building's rear entrance door.

Kruger watched as she opened the door, walked through it, and disappeared into the building. Not really sure how to take her last comment, he decided it was going to be fun trying to find out.

Stephanie Harris climbed the one flight of stairs to her condo. She was intrigued by this man who had just prevented something very unpleasant from happening. The ability to assess individuals quickly had allowed her to rise to the level of senior vice president of sales at a large greeting card corporation. Her assessment of Sean Kruger was very positive. Maybe it was an infatuation with the white knight coming to her rescue, or a high school–type crush, she didn't know. Her experience tonight should have left her shaking and concerned about the safety of her new residence. But it didn't. Knowing he was next door gave her comfort. The decision was made; she wanted to get to know this tall, good-looking FBI agent.

She unlocked her front door, walked to her bedroom and threw her purse on the bed. Exhausted from her business trip and the parking lot incident, she changed into jeans and a baggy sweatshirt. After checking her messages on the phone, she had an idea. Since he wasn't wearing a ring on his left hand, she assumed he wasn't married. But she wanted to find out for sure. She grabbed her apartment keys and walked to his front door.

Kruger was unlocking his door when Stephanie walked up to him and said, "Hi, I didn't properly introduce myself when we met in the parking lot earlier. Too many distractions, I guess."

He smiled and said, "You could say that."

She offered her hand and said, "Stephanie Harris, Mr. Kruger."

Shaking her hand, he said, "My dad was Mr. Kruger. I'm Sean. It's nice to meet you, Stephanie Harris."

"I really appreciated what you did in the parking lot. Do you think that young man will be okay?"

He nodded. "Probably. One of the patrol officers told me before I came up, both the white guy and his partner were well known to the local cops. In fact, they already had the black guy in custody. Both were out on parole. I imagine this little incident will change that status."

"Good. But, I would really like to thank you properly. Can I buy you dinner tomorrow night at a place of your choosing?"

He shook his head. "No, I'm afraid that won't work."

"Oh… I'm sorry, I mean…" She paused for a few moments, looking disappointed, "I didn't realize you were married."

Kruger laughed. "No, I'm not married, that's not what I meant. I'm a little old-fashioned. I'd love to have dinner with you tomorrow night. But you can't pay for it. I will. Since you've lived here a week longer than I have, you get to pick the restaurant."

Smiling, she said. "Houston's. It's my favorite place. Knock on my door at seven."

The Fugitive's Trail: Chapter Three

NEW YORK CITY

NYPD Police Detective Preston Alvarez was approaching his mid-forties and had over twenty years in the department. During those twenty years, his blue-gray eyes had seen a lot. This morning he saw barely controlled chaos as he pulled up to the crime scene. At least ten patrol cars sat parked around the office building. Their light bars were rotating and reflecting off the building's glass façade.

An EMT vehicle was just pulling away from the scene, its light flashing and siren screaming. He pulled in behind a patrol car and put his unmarked detective car in park. Pushing his rimless glasses up to the bridge of his nose, he stepped out and stared up at the building, forty stories of glass reflecting the midmorning sun. He ducked under the crime-scene tape, gave his badge number to a patrolman with a clipboard, and walked through the unblocked side of the glass front entrance.

A crime scene tech was taking pictures of a body on the floor to his right, just inside the front entrance. A patrolman stood next to him, watching. Alvarez said, "Any witnesses?"

The patrolman nodded and pointed to a black man dressed in a dark blue blazer standing next to the large reception desk. The desk was situated in front of a bank of elevators. The witness was talking to another patrol officer with three stripes on his sleeve. Alvarez walked over to the two men, showed his badge, and said, "I'm Detective Alvarez. What's the story here, Sergeant?"

The sergeant turned to Alvarez and said, "This is David Leonard. He mans the security booth for the building. He was here when the incident occurred." The sergeant turned to Leonard. "Tell him what you just told me."

Leonard stared at the sergeant and then at Alvarez, his eyes wide. "Man, the guy moved like lightning. One second he's walking between these two big guys and the next, the big guys are on the ground and he's running out of the building."

"Whoa, slow down," said Alvarez. "Who did what to whom?"

"Well, see, the two big guys, they work for P&G Global on the thirty-fourth floor. They brought this guy in thirty minutes before all this happened. That's when, see, they pushed him out of the elevator and walked toward the front door. The shorter guy—I don't know his name, but I see him and the taller guy all the time with Mr. Plymel. See, the smaller guy was in front; the taller guy behind. Anyway, see, the guy in the middle is looking scared, man, real scared. Just as they're going out the front door, the guy in the middle does this karate thing, and man, just like that"—Leonard snapped his fingers—"the guy kicks the guy in back in the knee. He grabs the gun off the hip of the guy in front and shoots him. He did all of that in one fluid motion, man—one fluid motion. Man, he was fast." He paused and shook his head. "I never seen anything like it. It looked more like a movie stunt, but it was real. He then pushed the front door open and ran that way." Leonard pointed to the right side of the building.

Alvarez said, "So they brought him in thirty minutes before all this started. Is that what you're telling me?"

Leonard nodded. "Yeah, man, thirty minutes. I checked my computer log. I'm supposed to keep track of who comes and goes."

Alvarez wrote in a small notebook and said, "Do you know why he was brought here?"

Leonard shook his head. "Nah, I don't ask questions man, I just watch the lobby."

Alvarez nodded. "Okay, Mr. Leonard, don't go anywhere. I'm going to the thirty-fourth floor and see what they say." He pointed at the sergeant and said, "Would you come with me?"

The scene on the thirty-fourth floor was the same as the lobby: police officers talking to various individuals, and crime-scene investigators taking pictures. As soon as Alvarez walked out of the elevator, a man several inches shorter and in a very expensive suit walked up to him.

"Are you in charge of this investigation?" the man asked.

Alvarez stared at the man. "Who are you?"

The shorter man snorted. "I'm Abel Plymel, CEO of P&G Global. Have you caught the man responsible for this mess?"

Alvarez shook his head. "Not at the moment. We're trying to find out what happened."

Plymel's face reddened. "Isn't it obvious? A man stormed in here and started threatening my employees. My security guards subdued him and escorted him out of the building. Now one of them is dead and the other severely injured. What are you doing about it?"

Alvarez frowned. "He stormed in here?"

"That's what I just said. Are you deaf?"

Ignoring the last comment, Alvarez turned to the sergeant standing next to him. "Go back down and see if you can find any more witnesses. I'll stay here and try to straighten out the conflicting stories."

The sergeant nodded and headed back to the elevator.

Plymel continued to glare at Alvarez.

Alvarez said, "When you say 'stormed in,' what do you mean? We have a witness that said he was escorted by two men into the building."

Plymel turned and looked at a taller man standing a few feet away and then looked back at Alvarez. Alvarez watched as the taller man turned, walked to a hallway, and quickly vanished out of sight. Plymel said, "Just that. The elevator opened and this crazed man steps out and starts threatening our associates. He was very belligerent and knocked a vase of flowers off the receptionist's desk. Then he started yelling. When we confronted him, he threatened everyone with bodily harm."

Alvarez nodded and wrote in his notebook. "Who saw the man?"

"I and several staff members tried to reason with him. He wouldn't settle down. That's when our two security guards forced him back into the elevator."

Nodding again, Alvarez said, "Okay, I'll need to talk to each of the individuals who were involved. Is there an office I can use?"

Several hours later, Alvarez stepped off the elevator. He looked around and saw David Leonard and walked over to him. "Mr. Leonard, tell me again, what time did you see the suspect escorted into the elevator?"

Leonard looked down at his desk and was silent for a few moments, then said, "I didn't see him enter the building. I must of missed him."

Alvarez frowned, stared at the black man, flipped a few pages on his notebook, and said, "Two hours ago, you told me you saw the suspect escorted into the building by two men. The same men he later killed and wounded."

"I must of misspoken. I didn't see that."

Alvarez leaned over so he could whisper. "Are you fucking with me, Mr. Leonard?"

The man looked away, shook his head, and said, "No, I didn't see him come in the building. Honest, I didn't."

Alvarez straightened up, shook his head, and walked out through the front door of the building.

An older man, who had been standing several feet from the lobby reception booth, watched as the detective walked out of the building. He took a cell phone from the inside breast pocket of his suit coat and dialed a number. It was answered on the second ring. He said, "Yes, this is Alton Crigler. Would you tell the director I need to speak to him." He paused and listened, then said, "I understand. Tell him it is of the utmost urgency." Another pause. "Yes, he has my number. Thank you."

Grab your copy…
vinci-books.com/seankruger1

About the Author

J.C. Fields is a multi-award-winning and Amazon best-selling author. Many of his fourteen published novels have been awarded numerous gold, silver and bronze medals in the Reader's Favorite International Book Awards contest.

Over the past several years, many of his numerous short stories have been featured on the YouTube Podcast Fear From the Heartland, a part of the Chilling Tales for Dark Night network.

After a decade as an independent author, he signed a publishing contract with Vinci Books. Vinci Books is a world-class publisher created to offer independent authors the best of self-published and traditional publishing.

His passion for helping new authors reach their dream of publishing is reflected in his activity with numerous area writing groups and serving on the boards for the Between the Pages Writers Conference and the Ozarks Creative Writers Conference.

He lives with his wife, Connie, in Southwest Missouri.

Acknowledgments

With the publication of this book, the fourth installment of the Michael Wolfe Saga, I celebrate ten years as a published author. The journey, over the past decade, has included the most enjoyable years of my life, with the exception of the year I married my wife and the years our sons were born. Those years were wonderful on a different level.

This period also saw my growth as a husband, father and writer. I do not dread Monday mornings anymore; I embrace them as the start of a new week.

A lot has changed during this time, namely the team who assist me in getting my novels published. I am indebted to the following individuals.

Sharon, Shirley, Conetta, Michael and Lori, my critique group, continue to assist with correcting mistakes I make in first drafts.

For her continued counsel and support, Sharon Kizziah-Holmes was the first person to encourage my writing and continues in that role today.

My editing team, Kate, Nanette, Shirley and Bonnie, you four have the arduous task of making sure my books maintain continuity and possess fewer grammatical missteps.

To the team at Vinci Books, thank you for your support and confidence in my writing. Your concept of being a world-class publisher created to offer authors the best of independent and traditional publishing has been a perfect match for my journey as a writer.

Paul J. McSorley continues to turn my novels into audiobooks with great success. I look forward to many more years as partners.

And last, but not least, my wife, Connie. Thank you for taking this lifetime journey with me. I feel so blessed to have you along for the ride.